UNSEEN

EVIL LURKS AMONG US

JEFFREY JAMES HIGGINS

Black Rose Writing | Texas

ISBN: 978-1-68433-823-8 (Paperback); 978-1-68433-869-6 (Hardcover)
PUBLISHED BY BLACK ROSE WRITING
www.blackrosewriting.com

Printed in the United States of America
Suggested Retail Price (SRP) $21.95 (Paperback); $26.95 (Hardcover)

Unseen is printed in Baskerville

*As a planet-friendly publisher, Black Rose Writing does its best to eliminate
unnecessary waste to reduce paper usage and energy costs, while never
compromising the reading experience. As a result, the final word count vs. page count
may not meet common expectations.

For Cynthia Farahat Higgins,
a fearless warrior dedicated to fighting evil in all its
forms.

ACKNOWLEDGEMENTS

Foremost, I would like to thank my wife, Cynthia Farahat Higgins, for her loving support and academic insights. Being married to one of the world's leading experts on the Muslim Brotherhood and Islamic terrorism was my secret weapon in writing this crime thriller. Cynthia is a hero in the battle against radical Islam. I could not have written this novel without her.

Thanks to the late Richard Marek for editing *Unseen.* It was an honor to have my work reviewed by the editor of such classics as *The Silence of the Lambs* and *The Bourne Identity.* May he rest in peace.

I appreciate the time and effort my beta readers invested in critiquing *Unseen.* Their valuable insights and suggestions helped make this a better book. Thanks to James Higgins, Nadya Higgins, Dr. John Hunt, Stephen Cone, Richard Maloof, Quent Cordair, Jonathan Brooks, Mathew Stiglitz, Susan Stiglitz, and Cynthia Higgins.

International Thriller Writers has supported me in many ways, and I am indebted to them. Thanks to the talented writers in the Royal Writers Secret Society for their constructive criticism. Sisters in Crime has also been a valuable resource for knowledge and friendship.

My author portrait was taken by Rowland Scherman, an award-winning photographer who has captured icons of American culture. View his work at www.rowlandscherman.com.

Once again, thanks to Reagan Rothe and everyone at Black Rose Writing for publishing my novel.

UNSEEN

EVIL LURKS
AMONG US

"The truth is not for all men, but only for those who seek it."
—*Ayn Rand*

CHAPTER ONE

Evil was everywhere. It arrived with a smile, an extended hand, a sultry look. It came masked in beauty, cloaked in temptation. The more seductive the package, the more dangerous what lay hidden within. Evil was everywhere—deadly, unseen.

Austin had seen much violence and death during two decades spent hunting the devil, and he recognized darkness when he saw it. He understood the zealotry, the predation. An image of Vanessa flashed in his mind and a lump formed in his throat.

He raised an Amstel Light to his lips as the murmur of patrons filled the dusky Ritz-Carlton bar in Georgetown, a wealthy neighborhood in Northwest Washington, DC. He took a long swig and used his peripheral vision to observe Sam Baker at the next table, careful not to look directly at him. At six-three and two hundred pounds, Austin had difficulty remaining inconspicuous—even more so after losing all his hair to alopecia—but appearing to belong was as important as his surveillance technique. Attitude meant everything.

I'll do it soon.

Austin had been watching Baker for weeks, and he knew the man's every gesture, until he could almost read his thoughts. Baker smiled, with eyes soft and welcoming, putting on the charismatic mask he wore when speaking with narcissists, parasites, and manipulators. Baker nodded and leaned forward in his red leather chair, maintaining eye contact with the man opposite him.

Across the dark mahogany table from Baker, Senator Dale Hansen blathered about a bill he had pushed through Congress—just another one of his stories floating on a sea of pontification and self-aggrandizement. He probably intended to bedazzle Baker with his effectiveness, but he spoke a little too fast, and hunger showed behind his eyes, like a lion salivating after wounded prey.

Austin wished he had come to kill the senator.

Senator Hansen stopped to sip a 2005 Chateau Margaux, and Baker glanced at his Rolex Submariner, one of the many possessions he used to advertise his membership in the gentility of the West. For months, Austin had researched Baker—born Samir Muhammad al-Bakri—a Qatari financier who had millions in personal assets and enjoyed unlimited access to the world's financial centers. Baker loved to own things, things other people did not have, things they would never have.

"I will reshape this country, given enough time and support," Senator Hansen said. Beneath his sliver mane of hair, he grinned with perfect teeth, an expression he used to make his constituents feel like they were the most important people on earth. His look said, "I'm listening," and it was pure bullshit.

"Very impressive," Baker said, dipping his head in exaggerated acknowledgment of the senator's accomplishments. It was obviously a gesture designed to feed the senator's ego and soothe his inherent insecurity, flaws the politician had overcome with ruthlessness and ambition.

Senator Hansen leaned forward and nodded, mirroring Baker's movements. "This is only the beginning. Together, we can achieve anything."

Baker smiled, and Austin realized Baker had the senator psychologically under his control. Baker may have been unknown to the public, but he held the actual power—money and influence—things Senator Hansen coveted.

Austin's eyes drifted over the bar's redbrick walls, exposed metal, and floor-to-ceiling windows—industrial and elegant. The room smelled of wood polish, alcohol, and power. Beyond glittering bottles of small-batch bourbons and through thick glass windows, a seventy-foot smokestack towered over the hotel. The relic from the building's origin as an incinerator plant had become a landmark on Georgetown's waterfront. From garbage to elegance, from waste to wealth. Austin smirked at the irony.

"We haven't discussed the reason I requested this meeting," Senator Hansen said.

"I'm well aware of your plans," Baker said. "You'll have my full support."

Senator Hansen expelled a long breath and his body relaxed, as if his tension had melted away. "Thank you, Sam. Thank you very much."

"That's what friends do. Now, I need something from you." Baker slid a manila folder across the table.

The muscles in Senator Hansen's jaw twitched as he took it. "Of course. I'll review this tonight."

Baker bowed his head in thanks.

Austin did not know the contents of the folder, but he knew Senator Hansen wanted Baker's money, and he knew what Baker needed in return. The al-Azhar Islamic Cultural Center development project meant everything to Baker. Once completed, it would become a bridgehead against the United States—Baker's key to victory.

Austin could not let him succeed.

Austin had heard enough, and he wanted to make his move before Baker ended the meeting. He stood, dropped a twenty-dollar bill on the table, and walked toward the exit, forcing himself to look away from their table as he passed.

He stopped at the far side of the room, away from the sounds of the bar, and slipped an earbud into place. He stuck his hand into his trouser pocket, wrapped his fingers around his cell phone and pressed send.

Baker's phone rang, and he looked at it. He would not recognize the incoming number, but a late-night call could be important. Baker excused himself from the table and adjusted his belt over his growing paunch as he walked to the far end of the bar. He raised the phone to his ear.

Can I go through with this?

"Hello," Baker's voice came over the line.

Austin swallowed.

"Hello?" Baker said again.

"This is Officer Philip Augustus with the DC Metro Police," Austin said. "Is this Mr. Baker?"

Across the room, Baker's body stiffened. "Speaking. What's this about, officer?"

"Sorry to bother you, sir," Austin said. "We caught a man breaking into your car and he claims you gave him permission to use it. We assume he's lying, but we need you to confirm you don't know him and inspect the car."

Austin could have just followed Baker out of the bar, but he wanted to make sure the man left alone. He also wanted to speak with Baker— needed this to be personal.

"I'm in an important meeting," Baker said. "Do you require my presence?"

"Yes, sir, it should only take a minute to confirm the damage is new. Can you meet us in the garage?"

"I'll be there soon." Baker hung up.

Baker would be distraught at the thought of damage to his brand-new Mercedes Benz, which had cost him over two hundred thousand dollars and served as his inner sanctum amid Washington's gridlock. Austin turned away to conceal his smile.

Baker returned to the table, and Austin could not hear what he was saying, but the senator looked down and his bottom lip hung low—a petulant child deprived of dessert. Senators loathed adapting to other people's schedules.

Austin smiled again.

The Canal Square parking garage was only two blocks away, a five-minute walk if he hurried. Austin dashed through the Ritz-Carlton's lobby and out into the oppressive humidity. The air clawed at his clothing and warmed his skin. Was Baker immune to Washington's damp heat after living most of his life in the Middle East? Austin glistened with sweat, and it was still only the middle of May.

He turned right and walked past nineteenth-century Federalist row houses, their uneven bricks covered with thick layers of paint—almond, apricot, robin's egg. He turned left on Thirty-First Street NW and followed an old stone wall through the historic neighborhood. Weekend revelers hung close to the taverns on M Street NW, one block beyond the garage, and behind him in restaurants along the Potomac River waterfront. He hustled up the deserted street as the witching hour approached.

Austin walked onto a flat bridge over the C&O Canal, a waterway that bisected Georgetown from east to west. Through the darkness, the remains of antique levees and locks jutted out of the mud. The preserved canal looked much had as it had when early inhabitants of Georgetown used barges to transport freight along the river. He glanced over the railing into the shallow, muddy waters below, and his nostrils tingled with the earthy odor of decay.

He crossed the bridge into the shadow of the Canal Square parking garage, and the clip-clopping of his shoes echoed into the night. On the far side, he stepped off the sidewalk onto a dark path paralleling the canal. He scanned the area, then slipped into the umbra of a soaring hickory tree.

With a single fluid and practiced motion, he brushed back the flap of his jacket and drew his Beretta. He held the handgun against his leg and waited. His mind wandered to Vanessa's red, full lips, her silky, black hair cascading over her shoulders. Her kindness, her innocence. Her death. His chest ached.

This is for you, Vanessa.

A minute later, Baker's heavy footfalls broke the silence and the doughy man waddled across the bridge.

Austin's hands shook, and his heart tried to beat out of his chest. He steeled himself.

"And they cried with a loud voice," Austin recited under his breath, "saying, how long, oh Lord, holy and true, dost thou not judge and avenge our blood on them that dwell on the earth?"

Baker walked off the bridge beneath the warm glow of a streetlamp and headed to the parking garage.

I can do this. Be strong.

Austin glanced up and down the street a final time, then stepped out of the shadows. He towered over Baker.

"Good evening, Mr. al-Bakri," Austin said, his voice deep and feral.

Baker recoiled, mid-stride, and swiveled to look at him. "Pardon me?"

Austin lifted the Beretta and centered the front sight on Baker's nose. Baker raised his hands, like a basketball player trying to block a shot.

Austin pulled the trigger, slow and steady, careful not to jerk the weapon. Flame exploded out of the muzzle, and the gun kicked in his hand. A .22LR bullet exited the gun at 1,280 feet per second and slammed into Baker's forehead, snapping his head back like a punch. A plume of blood and brain matter clouded the air behind him as the bullet passed through his skull.

The gunshot reverberated off the brick walls and faded as it moved down the street. Behind an ephemeral puff of smoke, Baker's mouth fell open, and his eyes became unfocused, like a computer screen shutting down. He wobbled for a moment, as if unsure what to do, then his knees buckled and he pitched forward, his body collapsing upon itself.

Austin reached out and pushed Baker, aiming him toward the embankment, but the man was too heavy—a dying farm animal—and his body fell hard on the path. It made no matter. Austin would stick to his plan.

Baker lay facedown with his upper body on the path and his legs stretched out on the sidewalk. The back of his head appeared wet and uneven, where the bullet had removed a large piece of skull. Blood flowed out of him as if poured from a carafe. His legs twitched.

Austin stepped back to avoid the pooling liquid and watched the life leave Baker's body. Blood snaked toward the canal's edge, rolling over the dirt like lava. Austin lowered his gun to his side.

What have I done?

His pulse raced, and a chill tingled his spine. He was a murderer now—one of *them*—a criminal who violated the most sacrosanct law of God and man. Thou shall not kill. He flashed back to his father, who had beaten him with a belt and screamed, "God punishes all sinners."

The earth seemed to spin, and Austin put his hand on the streetlamp to steady himself. He had crossed a threshold, and he could never return. He shivered, despite the humid night. Austin scanned the street, then used his sleeve to rub his fingerprints off the metal pole.

Nearby, the voices of a man and woman broke the silence, getting louder, closer. People coming to witness his sin.

Austin turned to flee but tripped on a root and fell. Pain shot from his ankle to his knee, like an electric shock, and he grimaced. He staggered to his feet and tried to put weight on his foot. The pain came in intense, pulsing waves—an angry sea. His ankle warmed, already swelling.

Excited voices drew near, and panic seized him. He needed to escape. The stakes were his freedom, his mission, his life. He ground his teeth and limped along the northern bank of the canal.

He disappeared into the darkness.

CHAPTER TWO

Malachi Wolf knew a gunshot when he heard it.

In the seven years Malachi had been a DC Metropolitan Police officer, he had heard gunfire far too often. Adrenaline surged through his veins and fired his senses like a slap in the face.

He stopped with his hand on the door handle of Kelly's Irish Pub and stared across M Street NW. A taxi trolled past four inebriated women as they stumbled down the sidewalk in front of a closed ice cream shop. No one reacted to the sound of the shot.

Malachi pulled his gold detective's badge out of his pocket and clipped it on his belt as he jogged across the street. He swept his sport coat back and gripped his Glock-19—a compact, nine-millimeter, semi-automatic handgun—but he did not break leather. The shot had come from the direction of the river, so he dashed to Thirty-First Street NW and turned south.

"*Aidez-moi . . . mon Dieu*," a woman screamed.

Malachi snapped his holster open with his thumb, drew his gun, and ran down the street. A young man held a pregnant woman in his arms, and they backed off the sidewalk, their eyes riveted to something near the canal. Malachi slowed as he neared them.

They turned and gawked at his gun, wide-eyed, afraid.

"Detective Wolf, Metro Police," he said. "What happened?"

"There," the man said, in a heavy French accent. "We hear the auto backfire, and we see this." He pointed at the path along the northern side of the C&O Canal.

Malachi approached the bridge and stopped. A man lay prone on the dirt path, his wingtip shoes splayed out at unnatural angles and blood pooling beneath him. Malachi leapt in front of the woman, putting himself between her and the pathway.

"Get against the building," he said.

He shielded them with his body and shuffled them behind cover.

"Who did this?" Malachi asked.

"*Je ne sais pas qui a fait ça*," the woman said, and sobbed.

"We see nothing," the man said. He pulled the woman's face into his chest.

"Wait here," Malachi said. "Understand?"

"*Oui.*"

Malachi leaned against the brick building and peeked around the corner. The path appeared deserted. He rolled away from the wall with his gun extended and moved forward. He knelt beside the man, who had a gaping hole in the back of his head. White brain matter oozed out, and Malachi recoiled. He collected himself and slipped two fingers over the man's carotid artery, confirming what he already knew. The man was dead.

Malachi had not seen or heard a car on the street, which meant the killer was close. Malachi's eyes flashed to the canal, then back to the dead man.

The victim's head pointed down the path and blood ran toward the canal's edge. The dirt walkway was ten feet above the canal and blanketed in darkness below a thick canopy of trees. To his right, Taylor's Seafood appeared closed, and a solitary light bled out of its dining room. A handful of windows glowed in a five-story residential building on the opposite side of the canal.

The dark pathway provided a perfect escape route.

He stood at the edge of the path and knew with absolute clarity that the next action he took could have lifelong consequences. This decision mattered. As a new homicide detective, he wanted to protect the crime scene, but his instincts as a street cop drove him to chase the killer. He wished he had his radio with him. He kept his eyes on the path and pulled out his phone with his free hand.

"9-1-1, what's your emergency?" the operator asked.

"This is Detective Malachi Wolf, badge thirty-three, sixty-six. I need assistance. I have shots fired at Thirty-First Street NW and the C&O Canal. One victim down and unresponsive. Suspect may have fled west through the canal. Have patrol set up a perimeter and send a unit to hold the scene."

"Copy. I'll roll EMS."

"Advise Lieutenant Collins in the Homicide Branch that I'm here and tell responding units there's an armed detective in plainclothes on the scene. I'm going into the canal."

His heart pounded like timpani in Beethoven's Fifth Symphony. He drew a Surefire tactical light from his pocket and flashed the beam down the path, which stretched west out of the city. Fifty feet away, trees leaned toward the canal and dense foliage blocked his view.

The shooter had to be down there.

Pursuing killers had been the only thing Malachi cared about since the incident, seven years ago, when he had abandoned his PhD in economics and become a cop. This could become his first homicide case—his first test—a chance to validate the choices he had made. An image of his ex-wife, Alison, and his twin daughters flashed in his mind.

He clenched his jaw and plunged into the shadows.

Malachi extended his arms and rested his Glock against the flashlight in his left hand. He swept the beam back and forth as he moved. A muddy footprint marked the earth where the killer had likely been standing when he took the shot.

Pebbles crunched under Malachi's shoes as he moved along the edge of the path. Heavy vegetation grew out of the canal, and ivy climbed a stone wall on his right. The killer could wait in ambush, but according to the theory of loss aversion, the shooter should be far more concerned about getting caught than waiting for the thrill of murdering his pursuer.

He paused and listened. Bugs droned around him. A siren wailed in the distance.

He walked heel-to-toe, giving himself a stable shooting platform. He focused on the trees in the distance, alert for movement, then he scanned the thick vegetation around him. His light illuminated another muddy footprint, similar to the first. He strained to see farther down the path and kept moving. Sweat rolled down his forehead, and he blinked it out of his eyes.

Something splashed in the canal.

He jerked his head toward the sound and crouched to make himself a smaller target. Another splash farther west. He leaned over the edge and fixed his gaze on the water. A third splash. He shined his light, and a large frog slipped below the surface of the brown water.

He smirked, glad no one had seen him startled.

Malachi hurried along the path and found a footprint in the soft ground. Then another. It was midnight, but still simmering, and the heat enveloped him like a sauna, warming his skin beneath his shirt. The thick air left an organic, earthy taste in his mouth. Overhead, cicadas chirped in the trees, protesting his intrusion. Sirens blared louder, closer.

The path narrowed under Wisconsin Avenue and an arched bridge rose above him, constructed with heavy slabs of gray stone and topped with a wrought-iron fence. He ducked to avoid banging his head and walked under the bridge into darkness. His light revealed graffiti on the wall and a used condom on the path.

Something thudded in the distance. He shined his light down the canal. Two shots rang out, and bullets ricocheted off the stone arch with a loud whine.

Malachi dove onto his stomach, landing hard in the dirt. His elbows stung from the impact. Another round struck the bridge, showering him with dust. He pressed against the ground, willing himself to be smaller, invisible. The gunshots resounded off the stone. A fourth shot kicked up dirt inches away.

He was dead if he stayed there.

Malachi rolled to his left toward the canal, but misjudged the distance, and his momentum carried him over the edge. He flailed for a handhold, but his fingertips slipped across the rounded lip of the path.

He fell.

His arms and legs flapped in the air, and his body rotated, disorienting him. His flashlight flew out of his hand and plunged the canal into darkness. He landed on his side in six inches of mucky water, and the impact knocked the air from his lungs.

Malachi lifted his face out of the water and gasped. His lungs burned. He took shallow breaths and clutched his ribs with his left hand. His body throbbed. He had lost his flashlight in the mud or water, but he still held his Glock. Malachi lowered his hands to push himself onto his knees and submerged his gun in the water. He yanked it out and cursed. He crawled toward the edge of the canal and leaned against the stone wall, gulping air.

Malachi raised his gun over his head and scanned the top of the wall, which was silhouetted against the night sky. He was soaking wet and sore, and fear clutched him as he waited for the shooter to show himself.

A police car raced down Wisconsin Avenue, the siren resonating under the bridge as if Malachi was inside a metal drum. If the killer was coming, Malachi would have seen him by now. Maybe the police car had scared the shooter away.

Or maybe he waited in the darkness above.

Malachi kept his gun trained on the edge of the path. His breath returned, and despite the pain, nothing seemed broken. He sloshed through the muck to a ragged line in the wall and holstered his gun. Water ran out of the barrel and down his leg.

He grabbed the stone where it had cracked and separated from the wall, dug his shoe tips into the crevice, and hoisted himself. The jagged rock cut into his fingers and his shoes slipped on the damp surface as he climbed. Ten feet in the air, he poked his head over the edge and peered down the path. The tunnel was pitch dark, as black as a tomb. He looked west, where he had seen the muzzle flashes.

Nothing.

He dug his elbows into the dirt and pulled himself over the top and onto the path. His knees scraped the rock, and he winced. He stayed low and crawled away from the edge. When no one fired at him, he stood, drew his gun, and leaned against the side of the bridge. He pulled his phone out to dial 9-1-1, but the shattered screen sliced his finger and water dripped from the headphone port.

He was on his own.

Malachi's pulse thumped in his temples, a clear sign of his waning athletic conditioning. He had abandoned his daily runs after that fateful day in Boston. It no longer brought him joy, but he had also stopped for another reason—something he needed to keep secret.

The smart move would be to return to the crime scene and wait for backup, but he was furious and in pain. The man had tried to kill him. His growing rage warmed his face, and he shook his head to clear his thoughts.

He raised his gun and moved along the canal—hunting his prey.

After twenty yards, the wall opened on his right. He leaned into the entryway, gun first. Concrete stairs with iron railings led up to brass doors at the entrance to the Georgetown Parking Garage. He turned and squinted down the canal where it grew fuzzy in the darkness.

Where is he?

People tended to turn toward their dominant side, and eighty-five percent of the population was right-handed. He played a hunch and climbed the stairs to a brick patio in front of the garage entrance. Off to his right, a flight of stairs led to street level. A muddy footprint dripped down the second step.

He jogged up the stairs to Wisconsin Avenue. Blue lights flashed in the distance on Thirty-First Street NW near the body. He walked into the street and scanned the dark and deserted shops.

The killer was gone.

CHAPTER THREE

Austin fled down Wisconsin Avenue and crossed the street in front of the Georgetown Montessori School to avoid exterior cameras at the Thai Embassy—an escape route he had planned weeks before. He hunched behind parked cars as he moved. A patrol unit prowled down Water Street NW at the bottom of the hill, and its spotlight flashed across the park toward the Potomac River.

The police car turned up the avenue, and Austin flung himself to the ground. He crammed his body between the curb and a parked Honda. The patrol car rolled by without stopping. He got up and hurried down the hill, staying low and using cars for concealment. His injured ankle ached but functioned.

His mind raced, on the verge of panic. Who was that in the canal? It must have been a cop. No one else would have chased him into that dark canal—only cops did that, and Austin had almost been forced to kill him. The best-laid plans fell apart so fast. He would remember that lesson next time.

Austin stopped at the United Bank and peeked around the corner. Water Street NW looked clear, and he scuffled across it into Georgetown Waterfront Park. He moved with purpose, feeling exposed, and lumbered to a retaining wall on the northern bank of the river. Sweat rolled off his bald head. He knelt and scanned the park.

No one pursued.

He breathed more easily and followed the riverbank toward a cluster of waterfront restaurants. The sounds of laughter came from outdoor tables at Tony and Joe's Seafood restaurant. He stopped beside a thicket of trees.

He still held his Beretta Model-70S, a compact, semi-automatic handgun, perfect for assassinations and once the issued firearm of the Israeli Mossad. The 40-grain, hollow-point rounds penetrated bone and expanded on impact, tearing through soft tissue and organs. Small bullets often bounced around inside a body, but he had fired so close to Baker that the bullet had passed through his head.

Police sirens clamored through Georgetown's streets. Austin looked around and confirmed he was alone. Tourists had learned to avoid Washington's parks at night.

He grabbed the top of a chicken-wire fence, installed to keep people away from the river, and pulled it toward him. A rat scurried through the underbrush. He climbed over the fence and tumbled into the thick vegetation. His ankle objected, and he bit his lip to keep from crying out.

He pushed through the heavy growth and made his way to the water. He held onto a branch at the river's edge, leaned over the surface, and grasped the hull of his sea kayak.

Whirring rotors grew louder, closer. He peeked through the trees as a helicopter's searchlight cut between buildings and moved along the canal. The din of sirens filled the air. His plan had him farther away by now.

He removed a watertight pouch from the cockpit and placed his Beretta inside, then pulled a cell phone and GPS tracking unit out of his pockets and dropped them in. Austin had affixed the GPS to Baker's Mercedes two weeks before and had tracked its movements every day, anticipating Baker's appearance at the Ritz-Carlton.

He lowered the bag into his kayak, balanced both hands on the cockpit coaming, and eased himself inside. He laid his paddle across the cockpit and pushed off from shore. The boat wobbled, and he lifted the paddle for balance, like a tightrope walker.

Austin snorted at the pseudonym he had used with Baker, "Officer Philip Augustus." Had Baker recognized its significance? The thought evaporated, and he pictured the pink mist spraying in the air.

Austin had killed before, in self-defense, but this was murder, an unforgivable crime in the eyes of God. He had become a sinner, now and forever. He shook his head and willed his thoughts away. There would be time for soul-searching later.

Too much time.

"But the fearful, and unbelieving, and the abominable, and murderers, and whoremongers, and sorcerers, and idolaters, and all liars, shall have their part in the lake which burneth with fire and brimstone: which is the second death."

He dug his paddle into the water and propelled the kayak forward. Trees along the shore veiled his movements, and the kayak's dark color made it almost invisible at night. Almost.

His life depended on his remaining undetected for the next few minutes. The adrenaline in his system metabolized, and fear flickered in his chest. He submerged the paddle into the river again, pulling with one hand and pushing with the other, his strokes perfected by years of practice. Cool water swirled around the paddle blades and his kayak skimmed across the surface. He pointed his bow toward the Virginia shore.

Halfway across the Potomac, Austin swiveled and looked back at Georgetown. A dozen red and blue police lights reflected off the brick buildings. The helicopter's spotlight flashed farther to the west. As he had expected, the search focused inward, not toward the water. He let out a deep breath and resumed paddling.

His kayak faded into the night.

CHAPTER FOUR

A cacophony of sirens echoed off Georgetown's buildings, and the sound of the air unit's beating rotors bounced off the ground. Malachi holstered his gun and held out his badge for an approaching police car on Wisconsin Avenue. The marked unit pulled up beside him and the officer in the passenger seat lowered his window.

"You Detective Wolf?" he asked.

"Yeah. That prick shot at me in the canal. I think he came out here."

"You're all wet."

"Maybe you should be the detective."

"You hit?"

"Just put it out on the air for me."

The officer frowned, and Malachi regretted his tone.

The officer keyed his radio and broadcast the suspect had fired at an officer. Dispatch repeated the call, and the officer hung the microphone on the dashboard.

"Is the perimeter set?" Malachi asked.

"Every available unit is here. Nothing yet."

Malachi nodded. He had had his chance and had blown it. Now it would be up to patrol.

"Do me a favor. Drive me back to the crime scene, then secure this stairwell until I can get an evidence tech to preserve a boot print on the stairs."

"Hop in."

■   ■   ■

Police blocked Thirty-First Street NW at both ends, and yellow police tape flapped in the wind between orange cones. Malachi climbed out, conscious he was covered with mud and smelled like a pond. He flashed his badge and credentials at the officer guarding the scene.

"Detective Wolf, homicide."

The officer wrinkled his nose, squinted at his credentials, and compared the photo to his face. "Sorry, detective. I didn't recognize you."

"I'm new to homicide."

The officer handed him a clipboard, and Malachi signed the login sheet, a written record of everyone who accessed the crime scene. They needed an accurate list to preempt potential defense claims that another suspect, not emergency personnel, had left DNA, fingerprints, or other evidence. Malachi may never make an arrest, but he needed to follow procedure if he ever hoped to get a conviction.

"We've got one victim with a GSW to the head," the officer said, referring to a gunshot wound. "He's DRT," the officer said, and smirked. DRT was short for "Dead Right There." Cop humor could be dark.

"Where's the couple who heard the shot?" Malachi asked.

The officer nodded across the street. "Over there. French tourists on vacation."

The pregnant woman had stopped crying, but her shoulders hung, and her face wrinkled like she could start again at any moment. A patrol car screeched to a stop behind them and a sergeant jumped out, barking orders into his radio.

"Hey, Sarge. Detective Wolf, homicide." Malachi showed him his identification.

The sergeant gawked at his muddy clothing. "What d'ya need?"

"Push out the crime scene a little more and send a couple officers onto the path to make sure no one walks through. Hold the witnesses until we can talk to them."

"You got it, Detective."

Malachi had been to a dozen murder scenes while he had been assigned to patrol, but he had never been in charge. Now, after having sacrificed so much to become a detective, he needed to perform well. He tried to remember everything he had learned in homicide school and hoped the sergeant would not notice his inexperience.

"Any sign of the shooter?" Malachi asked.

"He's in the wind."

Malachi walked to the scene, careful not to step on evidence. The victim appeared to be his late fifties or early sixties and well dressed—a contrast to the gangbangers and drug dealers Malachi had seen when he patrolled the impoverished neighborhoods of Southeast Washington.

The victim's suit, watch, and shoes all looked expensive, which meant this would be a high-profile investigation. A gang-related killing was easy for people to dismiss as the savagery of a fringe culture, which would never affect them, but the murder of a tourist or wealthy businessman meant no one was safe. Murders like this made headlines and drew political pressure.

"Sweet Jesus, Mac," Detective Thomas Jones said, walking up behind him. "Tell me that wasn't you."

Jones was black, sixty-two years old, and wore a trimmed beard over his double chin. He smiled and flashed a gold-capped tooth. As a detective-one, Jones had been Malachi's senior partner since Malachi joined the Criminal Investigations Division three months before.

"Hey, Jonesy. I trailed the perp down there and he took a few shots at me. I had to dive over the side."

"Pop off any rounds?"

"Never saw him. It was dark as hell." Malachi dropped his eyes to his shoes, ashamed he had not returned fire. It had happened so fast, and he had been too exposed on the path.

"Next time, wait for backup. You supposed to catch bad guys, not bullets."

"I know I—"

"You can take the boy out of patrol, but you can't take the patrol out of the boy."

Malachi's cheeks burned. His education and intellect had contributed to his meteoric rise through the department, and he had reached homicide faster than any detective before him, engendering both awe and envy. Despite that, he still felt like an impostor, and he relied on Jones to show him the ropes before his career plummeted back to earth.

"Any chance we can take this one?" Malachi asked.

"This be a unique way to catch your first body, that for sure. Hill and Rodriguez are next up in the rotation, but I think I can get the lieutenant to give it to us."

"Yeah?" Malachi wanted this one.

"Least she could do after you almost got yourself shot. Besides, you need to break your cherry. What we got?"

"White male, approximately sixty years of age. Single gunshot to the head. No witnesses."

Jones noticed the French couple. "Who they?"

"Tourists. Heard the shot but saw nothing."

"Welcome to DC," Jones said.

The woman buried her face in her husband's chest, and he wrapped his arms around her.

Vacations, where memories are made.

"I found footprints between the body and a stairwell off Wisconsin," Malachi said. " How do you want to handle this?"

"You here first, you work the scene."

"Got it."

Jones handed him latex gloves. "I'll chat up the wits."

Jones had mentored him in the fine art of homicide investigation since Malachi arrived in the unit. The mandatory retirement age was sixty-four, and as Jones prepared to close out his career, he seemed to want Malachi to carry on his legacy. How would Malachi manage after Jones retired?

Malachi focused on the scene. His superpower had always been his ability to understand variables and use reason to predict outcomes.

He squatted and leaned over the corpse. The man lay facedown in the dirt, with his head canted to the right, and an expression of shock and horror frozen on his face—a billboard of his last emotion. The human expression unsettled Malachi, as if he were viewing the shadow of an extinguished life.

He lowered his face to the body. A torn flap of skin hung off the victim's forehead near the entry wound. The hole appeared to be the size of a twenty-two or twenty-five caliber, nothing bigger than a thirty-eight.

He scanned the ground for a brass casing but saw nothing on the pathway or sidewalk. No casing could mean the killer had used a revolver, a conscious choice to limit evidence, or the shooter could have picked up his casing, an indication of a calculated mind. The casing could also be stuck in the boot tread of a responding officer or submerged in the canal.

The back of the victim's head splayed open where the bullet had exited. It was the trademark of a hollow point bullet or a plus-P round, which used a rod to pull the bullet open like an umbrella. The bullet had expanded on impact, bored a wide cavity through the victim's brain and pancaked against the back of his skull, taking three inches of bone with it. White, gooey brain matter, pebbled with bone fragments, coated the ground.

An image of his father's face flashed in Malachi's mind. His skin had been so pale as Boston Police officers tried in vain to breathe life into his dying body. The man who raised him, the man he had tried to emulate— ripped from Malachi's life forever by radical Islamists. Death had followed Malachi from that moment forward, like a car tailgating too close, or footsteps behind him in a darkened parking garage, growing louder, closer. Malachi's eyes burned and he blinked away the memory.

He wiped his forehead and focused on the job at hand.

A wallet bulged out of the victim's back pocket. Malachi pulled on gloves and lifted it out, careful not to smudge any fingerprints. In the front compartment he found an international driving license with the name, "Samir al-Bakri," and a residential address in Doha, Qatar. An employee identification card from North Star Development used the same picture, but with the name, "Sam Baker."

Malachi stood and examined the crime scene, trying to imagine how the murder had happened. Based on the position of brain matter and body, Baker had been facing the path when shot. He probably would not have gone down the muddy path wearing thousand-dollar shoes, which meant he had walked up or down Thirty-First Street NW then pivoted to confront his attacker.

Malachi's first thought was robbery, but a Rolex remained attached to the victim's wrist, and he had hundreds of dollars in his wallet. Social psychology posited trying to infer motive from a scene could be dangerous, because once he favored a particular theory, he would be more susceptible to confirmation bias. He needed to keep an open mind and let the evidence guide him.

This location, shrouded in darkness and away from Georgetown's traffic, had given the killer a natural escape route. There had been little chance anyone else would have been walking along the canal late at night. It appeared the shooter had been lurking in the shadows, yet robbery was not evident. Something about the scene did not feel right.

It looked like an ambush.

A security camera hung from the side of the building ten feet from the body. Black paint frosted the lens and droplets of dried paint hung off the bottom. He knelt and inspected a shoe impression in the mud below it. The ridges cut deep, probably left by a size thirteen or fourteen boot. The footprint could have been left by one of the police officers who walked through the scene—something he would check from the crime scene log—but the impression lay close to the wall and likely belonged to the killer. When tech arrived, he would have them photograph the footprints and preserve them in plaster.

Residential, commercial, and retail buildings lined both sides of the street but he did not see other cameras. The buildings had all been closed when Baker died, except for a condominium complex across the canal, and most of its windows remained dark. They would have to knock on every door along the perpetrator's escape route to determine if anyone had seen anything. Sometimes solving a case involved a bit of luck.

The murderer had struck in the heart of Georgetown, escaped the police perimeter, and vanished like a ghost. A deep sense of foreboding fell over Malachi, for reasons he could not articulate.

CHAPTER FIVE

Malachi flushed with embarrassment. He had been fortunate to be nearby when Baker was shot, but he had let the killer slip away. His opportunity to catch a villain and become a hero had vanished, and now he would be known as the new homicide detective who had let a murderer escape. Not how he had envisioned his first homicide case.

At six o'clock in the morning, he sat at his desk, a gray block of steel only a soulless government procurement officer would purchase. Jones had asked him to query the department's databases, because Jones lacked tech savvy, something Malachi knew to be true after watching him struggle with a smartphone. Malachi pecked at the keyboard with one hand and drank a Starbucks dark roast with the other. He prioritized caffeine over efficiency. Investigation was the affliction, long hours the symptom, and coffee the cure.

He glanced at his phone, longing for Alison. He wanted to call, but he knew she did not want to hear from him. Not now. Not ever.

The first twenty-four hours were the most critical in a homicide investigation. Malachi and Jones had spent the night mining the crime scene for evidence, and Malachi had only run home to scrub off the pungent canal water and change his clothes before coming into the office. The Homicide Branch occupied a three-story brick building at the corner of M Street SW and First Street SW, four blocks from his condo.

Malachi had fallen behind. The meeting was about to begin, and detectives assembled in the conference room behind him. Jones would brief everyone, but he could not start until Malachi built a deeper profile of Baker.

Malachi Googled the names Sam Baker and Samir al-Bakri and scanned dozens of news articles. He found pictures of Baker with Washington's elite—power brokers, members of Congress, and agency heads. Before his murder, Baker had been the CEO of North Star Development, a firm that supported real estate projects in the United States and abroad. Through North Star, Baker had backed many political candidates and social causes. Malachi grimaced. Baker had possessed money and influence, which meant his murder would draw significant attention.

North Star had financed the al-Azhar Islamic Cultural Center, a five-hundred-million-dollar construction project, just across the river in Fairfax County, Virginia. A photograph above a recent article showed a smiling Baker standing beside Amir al-Kadi, president of the American Islamic Shura, and Muhammad Baseem, director of the Council for American-Muslim Peace.

Detectives filed into the conference room, and he caught a few questioning looks as they walked past his desk.

Malachi felt like an outsider, as if he did not quite belong. He had been a doctoral candidate in economics until his father was killed, and he dropped everything to enter law enforcement. He saw himself as an academic among men of action. His world had revolved around ideas, not violence, and he had never fantasized about carrying a badge and gun. His conversion from civilian to cop, his immersion in blue, had happened overnight, like having an epiphany . . . or a stroke.

Time was short, so he bookmarked the open-source articles to read later. He closed the browser and ran a wants and warrants check and a criminal history on Baker, both of which came up negative. He checked Baker's name and date of birth in the registry of motor vehicles and found his driver's license and two vehicle registrations. There were no records before 2006. Had that been when Baker moved to the United States?

Next, he ran Baker in the MPD internal database, but only found three parking tickets, two for a 2018 Mercedes Maybach and one for a 2015 Land Rover HSE. Patrol had found the Rover in one of Baker's two underground parking spots at his residence in the Capitol Condominiums, but the Mercedes remained missing, and Malachi had issued a lookout for it.

Someone tapped on Malachi's shoulder, and he jumped.

Jones stood behind him holding two steaming cups of coffee. His shoulders slumped forward and his head hung low. He wore the exhaustion of a sleepless night like a heavy pack. He handed Malachi another Starbucks dark roast. The aroma smelled black and strong. Malachi gulped down the last of his coffee and started the new one. He drank coffee like most people drank water.

"What up?" Jones asked.

"Looks like Sam Baker, born 'Samir al-Bakri,' immigrated from Qatar. I'll request his records from Homeland Security."

"Hmmm."

"Baker was big money, a financier who worked with politicians on a national scale."

"Shi-it," Jones said. He dragged the word out in two long syllables, as if the slower the word rolled off his tongue, the more meaning it carried.

"Yep, it's a red ball."

There would be pressure from Chief Ellen Ransom to close this one fast. Letting a power broker's murder go unsolved would tarnish the department and cause problems when it came time for the mayor to ask the City Council for next year's funding. A higher calling drove Malachi, but he could not ignore the politics.

"I'll give the LT a heads up and ask her to assign us some help on this one," Jones said. "Let's brief the boys."

"I need a minute," Malachi said.

"Don't keep Big Momma waiting."

Calling Baker a "financier" had focused Malachi's thinking. He scrolled through his email contacts and sent a request for information to an analyst he knew at FinCEN, the Financial Crimes Enforcement Network in the US Department of the Treasury. He asked her to find bank accounts affiliated with Baker and any Suspicious Activity Reports involving large deposits, withdrawals, or transfers. The law required banks to report transactions over ten thousand dollars.

Malachi logged in to LexisNexis, a large database of public records, and typed in Baker's information. The search returned dozens of potential hits, and he downloaded the data for an exact match. He scrolled through a long list of addresses, telephone numbers, registered vehicles, and other public records. Baker had listed his Capitol Condominiums address starting in 2016, and before that, he had lived on Seventh Street NW. Everything prior to 2006 was in Doha, Qatar.

Malachi yawned, his body heavy with fatigue, then his world turned colorless in a flash and everything appeared in black and white. He scrunched his eyes shut and rubbed them with the heels of his hands.

Not now. This can't be happening again. Please . . .

He opened his eyes and the color blindness passed, but nothing looked as vivid as it had a minute before.

Be strong, focus.

He returned his attention to his screen. Baker had three aliases listed: Samir Muhammad al-Bakri, Mohammad al-Bakri, and Samir Mohammed Bakri. It appeared he had changed his name to Sam Baker in 2006, and Malachi made a note to search for a name change filing to determine if Baker had done so legally or just Americanized it on his own.

LexisNexis listed three variations of Baker's social security number, all off by one digit, which could be typographical errors or signs of deceit. The number began with a 579, which meant the government had issued it in Washington, DC. Malachi opened his email and sent an immigration search request to his contact at the Department of Homeland Security. Immigration would have an A-File on Baker containing data from the time he applied for a visa until they granted him permanent residency or citizenship—a treasure trove of personal information.

"Best be joining us, Wolf," Lieutenant Lashonda Collins said.

Collins, a heavyset, matronly black woman in her mid-fifties, had risen through a sea of testosterone to supervise their homicide squad. She exuded a calmness that only came from inner strength, and Malachi trusted her to watch their backs as they battled inside the bureaucratic coliseum.

"Be right there, LT. I'm wrapping this up."

She pinched her face as if she had just bitten into a lemon and disappeared into the conference room.

Malachi's neck warmed. Since his father's death, Malachi's temper had taken on a life of its own, and the slightest provocation stoked the always-burning coals like a strong wind. His inability to control his emotions scared him, but his fury also felt familiar, comforting.

The Middle East connection could be relevant, so Malachi emailed Detective Brian Pinker and asked him to file an official request for information with the Federal Bureau of Investigation to determine if they had anything on Baker. The Metropolitan Police Department worked with the FBI when elected officials became involved in crimes. Unfortunately, the FBI seemed to think the MPD worked for them. To facilitate interagency cooperation, MPD had assigned a liaison to the FBI, and that man was Pinker.

Contacting Pinker was the official procedure for querying the Feds, but Malachi had worked with Special Agent James Winter at the Drug Enforcement Administration's Special Operations Division, a law enforcement and intelligence fusion center. Winter could get Malachi what he needed without the red tape, so he emailed him and asked for any mention of Baker in the intelligence and federal law enforcement communities. Nothing suggested Baker was a player in that world, but if he had an affiliation with criminal or terrorist groups, Winter would find it.

"Detective Wolf, I'll make it plain," Collins said, glaring at him from the doorway. "I gave you this case because you were first on the scene and because Jonesy said you were ready. Don't make me regret it."

"Sorry. Coming."

Malachi had joined the department to become a homicide detective and find some tangible measure of justice. He had thought of little else since graduating from the academy. He had given up everything to make it, both in his personal and professional lives, and he could not screw up.

He walked into the conference room, plopped down beside Jones, and handed over his notes. Four detectives—two sets of partners assigned to back them up—sat around the coffee-stained conference table.

Collins cleared her throat at the head of the table. "The deceased is a fifty-eight-year-old Qatari national. He—"

The door swung open and Assistant Chief Barney Nuse entered, sucking the oxygen out of the room. Nuse was a bureaucrat's bureaucrat—everything Malachi detested about government wrapped in an expensive suit and bad comb-over. He valued rules over success, process over mission. Nuse ran the Investigative Services Bureau, which controlled the Criminal Investigations Division and Homicide Branch, and he reported directly to Chief Ellen Ransom.

"Don't let me interrupt," Nuse said. "I'm only here to let you know that the chief has taken a personal interest in the outcome of this case."

Malachi assumed Nuse had been the kid who raised his hand in class and reminded the teacher to assign homework before a holiday weekend. The student who followed the rules, but missed the point of the lessons, and never made friends. Now he commanded their division.

"Chief," Collins said, and turned back to address them. "The victim is Sam Baker, age fifty-eight. Citizen of Qatar. Lived downtown at Capitol Condominiums. Patrol's holding down his apartment until the warrant's signed. This is the first homicide in Georgetown in a long minute and it's gonna get some flash, so I need all hands. Jones, give us a quick rundown of the crime scene."

Jones stood and tugged his belt up, but it hit his belly and slid back down. He always looked ruffled, as if he had just rolled out of bed, but his mind was sharp, and he saw everything—a black Sherlock Holmes.

"One shot to the melon, through and through. No bullet or casing. Crime scene is searching, but I'm not optimistic. We have shoe imprints pointing down the canal, size thirteen, either from a hiking boot or a military-style combat boot. Two French tourists discovered the body but didn't eyeball the shooter. No video, no wits. Our victim, Mr. Baker, A.K.A. 'Samir al-Bakri,' was a financier. Big money."

Jones opened a file and ran through a long list of fibers, fingerprints, and other evidence collected at the scene. He read Malachi's notes on North Star and Baker's background, then he sat down.

"Thanks, Jonesy," Collins said. "Maybe we'll catch a break and recover DNA. Ask the M.E. to hurry the autopsy. Wolf, finish Baker's background, identify next of kin, and follow up at the scene. We need physical evidence. Look for cameras that may have captured our doer."

"Roger, LT," Malachi said. "I saw a camera near the scene, but someone had vandalized it."

Collins turned to Detectives Johnson and Brown. Both men were in their fifties, and Malachi had never seen them apart. They seemed competent enough, but not the type to volunteer for anything. "You two hit the neighborhood. Bang on every door. Someone saw something."

Neighborhood surveys rarely paid off, but police solved most crimes with bread-and-butter policing by asking questions, collecting evidence, following every lead. Johnson and Brown seemed unhappy.

Collins checked her notes, then addressed Detectives Lance Hill and Rodrigo Rodriguez across the table. "Hill, you and Rodriguez knock out the warrants for Baker's apartment and cars. Paper his telephones and social media. When you're done, help with the canvass."

"That's a full day shot," Hill said. He glared at Malachi. "Thanks, College."

Hill was capable, but abrasive. He seemed to take all of Malachi's offers to help as threats to his competence, and he never missed an opportunity to comment on Malachi's education—something Hill did not have.

"We've got nothing," Malachi said. "We need a witness."

"You could have saved us the trouble if you shot that asshole instead of going for a swim," Hill said.

Malachi's ears burned and the muscles in his neck tightened. Outrage grew inside him, as if he was filling with helium. He needed to let it out or burst.

"Fuck you," Malachi said.

"There a problem here?" Collins asked.

"No, Ma'am," Hill said.

Malachi glared at him. "Sorry, LT."

Rodriguez, Hill's partner, averted his eyes, as if the confrontation had embarrassed him. Rodriguez was the newest member of the squad and the only detective more junior than Malachi. His initials, R.R., led to the nickname, "Train." Rodriguez was a hard charger who seemed driven to put bad guys behind bars. Malachi had liked him immediately.

"Anything else?" Collins asked the group.

"Did Wolf find anything at the bottom of the canal?" Hill asked, smirking.

Johnson and Brown forced muffled laughs.

"That's enough, son," Collins said, narrowing her eyes.

"Hey, College," Hill said. "If you didn't see the shooter flee, why did you abandon the scene and run into the canal?"

"Economics," Malachi said

"Excuse me?"

"I knew the killer would use the canal," Malachi said, "because that incurred the lowest cost for the highest gain. Based on the available data, it was the killer's most effective and efficient choice. It's called rational choice theory in economics. Simple."

Hill's face turned red.

"That's all I've got," Collins said. "Find our perp and let's put him in the jug. God don't like ugly." She adjourned the meeting.

Rodriguez grabbed Malachi's arm as he walked past. "Hill's a prick."

"Don't worry about it," Malachi said.

"At least you don't have to deal with him every day. Anyway, I'm glad you didn't get popped last night. New blood gotta stick together. Let me know if you need help."

"If you want to help, find a witness."

CHAPTER SIX

God watched him. Every immoral act, every lie, every crime—he saw them all—and Austin had committed the ultimate sin. God would judge him.

Austin bolted upright in bed. His pulse raced, and a cold sweat dampened his body. He flicked on the light and climbed out of bed. Flames of pain radiated up his leg. He grabbed his swollen ankle and held it until the pain dwindled to a dull throb, then he limped to the window.

Sophie, his cream-colored cocker spaniel, lay at the foot of the bed and followed him with her eyes.

"I'm fucked," Austin said.

Sophie raised her head and cocked it.

What have I done?

He had killed a man and not in self-defense. Murder. He had made a conscious decision to sin, planned the crime, and ended Baker's life. If the authorities caught him, he would spend his life in jail. Worse, he would face God's justice.

"And I used the name of a legend as an alias," he said. "What a joke. I should have chosen Lucifer."

Sophie stretched her back and yawned.

No, he was not evil. He was fighting for goodness, fighting for Vanessa. He gazed out the rain-splattered glass at the Vietnamese restaurant across the boulevard, its neon sign glowing in the damp night. He had chosen to live in Northern Virginia because of its proximity to DC, a reasonable commute for both work and play.

Vanessa had liked it.

He stared into the rain, but only saw her. He remembered the first time he had seen her. She had glanced back over her shoulder and her onyx hair had fallen over her shoulders. The sunlight had illuminated her brilliant smile, her sparkling eyes, her ivory skin. Their eyes had locked, imprinting the moment on his memory for eternity. She had been one of only three women staying at the Special Forces base in Eastern Afghanistan. Twenty-six, stunning, and brave, she had been the center of attention and could have picked any young, rock-hard soldier, but she had chosen him. She was the only woman he had ever loved.

He limped back to his bed and rummaged through a drawer in his end table until his fingers wrapped around a white plastic container. He pulled it free and shook it.

Almost empty.

The faded label showed the Oxycontin had expired. Two years ago, he had taken the drugs for back pain but stopped when the familiar feelings had returned. It had taken every ounce of his willpower to quit before things turned ugly. But now, a strained tendon was a legitimate injury, and he needed pain medication.

"A doctor would prescribe it for me, for Christ's sake."

Sophie looked at him and blinked.

"I know what you're thinking, but I'm not taking these to escape. I need to function at work. I'm dead-ass serious. These are mission essential."

Sophie snorted.

"What do you know? I saw you drink out of the toilet yesterday."

Austin twisted off the cap and tapped a pill into his hand. His mouth dried at the touch of the soft, powdery tablet. He curled his tongue to salivate, popped the Oxycontin into his mouth, and swallowed with a practiced motion.

"There, it's done. I'll get back on the wagon in a few days."

Sophie rested her head on the floor and continued to watch him.

Austin had killed before, but war was not murder. He had seen many lifeless bodies over his career—in Afghanistan, on the streets of Southeast DC . . . Vanessa. But Baker had been different. Austin's foul deed.

He shambled across the room, opened his dresser drawer, and withdrew a silver necklace with a lapis pendant. Vanessa had purchased the blue gem in Kabul and worn it almost every day. He had removed it from her belongings after she died, days after his hair had begun to fall out.

I should stop killing.

He could quit, but if he did, evil would win. Real wickedness. They would not stop until they destroyed everything he loved—unless someone annihilated them first.

God had to see the virtue in his quest. He would continue, even if it meant damnation.

He hobbled into the bathroom, poured a glass of water, and gulped it down. His heart rate slowed, and he relaxed. He could not afford panic. Not now. Not with stakes this high.

It was a chess game.

Killing Baker had been his initial salvo against the enemy, and despite his planning, the police had almost caught him. He had thought the street was clear, but a couple had come upon the body within seconds, and he had twisted his ankle, like an amateur. His training and experience had made him cocky, but this was different. He was not trying to catch a criminal. He was becoming one. Austin needed to start over and study his new avocation.

He looked at Sophie, and she wagged her tail.

"What went wrong, girl?"

Sophie plodded across the carpet and looked up at him.

"They were on me so damn fast. The gunshot alerted a woman, and that cop came out of nowhere."

Sophie cocked her head.

"You're right. I'll have to be stealthier next time. I'll get a silencer."

Sophie's tail thumped against the floor.

"I need to think like a predator."

CHAPTER SEVEN

Dawn shimmered off the Potomac River with a million points of light. Malachi settled into a chair on the balcony of his two-bedroom condo, which overlooked Southwest Washington's waterfront, and he watched a small fishing vessel motor past. To find a motive, he needed to learn more about Baker, so he opened his MacBook Air, clicked on a browser, and typed "Samir al-Bakri."

Research came effortlessly to Malachi and was far more comfortable and familiar than other aspects of police work. Before the Boston Marathon bombing had turned his life upside down and launched him into his new career, the academic world had been all he had ever known. Insecurity gnawed away deep inside him and drove him to accomplish something before everyone realized he was not a cop, not one of them.

The doorbell rang, and Malachi went to the door. Jones stood in the hallway holding two coffees.

"So much for my high-security building," Malachi said.

"Your concierge recognized me," Jones said, and handed Malachi a coffee. "Even if he didn't, my badge works like a master key."

"What's up? You miss me already?"

"I'm heading in and thought you may want a lift," Jones said.

"I planned on doing a little research first, away from the distractions."

"We gonna need something. Neighborhood survey didn't pan out, and the bullet and casing are still M.I.A."

"I located Baker's wife in Qatar," Malachi said. "I asked the State Department to help with the death notification."

He led Jones onto the deck.

"Damn, son. You got a view here. How's a detective-two making seventy grand a year afford this trendy hood?"

"I bought into the waterfront renovation early, using my inheritance from Dad."

Jones softened. "You look like shit."

"Didn't sleep much," Malachi said. "First case . . . you know, I've wanted this for a long time."

"You ain't taking this homicide personal, are you?"

Malachi stared at the water. "I'm doing my job."

"I mean because of your pops," Jones said. "Because of what happened."

Malachi had always planned to follow in his father's footsteps as an economics professor at the University of Chicago. His father had taught him to trust economics as the only objective way to analyze life—a science that made sense out of chaos. His father had come from the "Austrian school," advocating for laissez-faire capitalism and minimal governmental intervention, and he had subscribed to the free-market ideas of Ludwig Von Mises, F.A. Hayek, and Milton Friedman. Malachi had chosen the same path and entered a PhD program in economics at Harvard University. He had been near the end of his fourth year of study, when his world turned upside down.

"I couldn't focus on esoteric concepts once I understood what kind of evil lives in the world," Malachi said.

"Can't change human nature," Jones said.

"Maybe not, but I can fight back. Terrorism robbed me of my father."

"Sam Baker is not your father," Jones said.

"I know that."

Two days after Islamic zealots had murdered Malachi's father in the Boston Marathon bombing, police killed one and arrested the other, leaving Malachi without a chance for vengeance, without an outlet for his rage. Malachi left Harvard and applied to police departments all over the country before he landed at MPD. Armed only with his economics degree and a desperate need to preserve life, he became a sheepdog, transforming himself from victim to protector.

"Nobody you arrest will bring him back."

"If we had only run a little faster, or a little slower . . ."

"Ain't your fault your pops died."

Another boat motored up the river and Malachi stared into its foamy wake.

"We didn't always see eye to eye. We argued. The things I said to him . . . the things I'll never be able to say—"

"I never even met my daddy," Jones said. "Your pops knew you loved him. Remember the good shit. The rest of it . . . well, it don't do any good to think about it."

"Fuck."

"Time, son. Give it time. Trust me, I know what I'm talking about."

Malachi nodded.

Jones stood. "I'll catch you at the office, but don't be late. LT's hot to close this one."

Malachi watched Jones leave, and when the door shut, the silence overwhelmed him. The absence of his wife and children echoed off the walls.

His ex-wife, Alison Bancroft, had also been a graduate student at Harvard, though she had studied sociology, not economics. They had planned to finish school, marry, and move to Washington, DC, where she would work for a think tank and he would find a teaching position. Then Malachi's father died, and everything changed. Life had a way of throwing curve balls, or in this case, fastballs aimed at his head.

His father's sudden death had instilled in Malachi the need to live for the moment, and he had married Alison one month after the funeral. Driven by a new calling, Malachi had joined MPD and moved to DC. Alison dropped out and joined him, then she gave birth to their twins.

For a while, life had been good, but it had not taken long to discover Alison did not share his passion for justice. She needed an academic, not a cop, and on their third wedding anniversary, she left him, taking their four-year-old girls and his heart. That had been three years ago. Three years of emotional purgatory. Three years alone, while his children grew up in Virginia without him.

Malachi paid child support and saw his girls at least once a week, but at night, he watched endless Seinfeld reruns to block out his dark thoughts. He satisfied his jealousy by cyber-stalking Alison online and trying to decode her life from her Facebook and Twitter posts. This lonely prison had become his life, and he clung to his job for meaning. Failing at work would mean psychological death. It would finish him.

The Baker murder was his first test.

Malachi's fingers tingled, and he looked down at his hands as if they belonged to someone else. Fatigue tugged at his limbs.

It was getting worse. His symptoms had progressed faster than expected. No one knew about his ailment but concealing his episodes had grown more difficult. He needed to achieve as much as he could, while he remained physically able to be a cop.

The clock was ticking.

■   ■   ■

At nine o'clock, Malachi walked to the Homicide Branch to continue his research. The office hummed with activity, and he tried to ignore the noise. He lifted a baseball off his desk and rolled it in his hand, engaging the right side of his brain. The baseball had been signed by retired Red Sox pitcher Mike Timlin, and he kept it on his desk as a whimsical oasis in a desert of bureaucratic gray.

Jones sat across from him talking on the telephone. He hung up as Malachi sat down.

"State Department talked to Baker's wifey in Doha."

"She coming?" Malachi asked.

"Nope. She wants the body sent back."

"I was hoping she'd shed some light on this. Baker didn't have any family here. I went through the evidence inventory from his condo, and it doesn't look like he had a girlfriend . . . or a boyfriend. I guess we can rule out a family squabble."

"Maybe."

They had searched Baker's residence in Capitol Condominiums, a spacious unit half-a-mile north of the National Mall, with a view of the

Washington Monument. The manager had confirmed Baker lived alone and traveled often.

Malachi tossed the baseball, the weight familiar, comforting.

"Baker was Muslim and bigotry against Islam is on the rise," Malachi said. "Could this have been an act of Islamophobia?"

"Seems more like a hit," Jones said.

"Train served a grand jury subpoena on Baker's financial accounts. Baker had business dealings all over the world, and millions of dollars moving around, but nothing jumped out at me."

"Someone wanted to smoke him, so who benefits? If it's not about pussy, it's the cheddar."

"Baker's net worth was eighty million, and everything goes to his family," Malachi said. "He had serious connections. How about a political motive?"

"Jones, Wolf, my office," Collins shouted across the squad room.

Jones grimaced. "We need to find something fast."

The pressure on their department had been immediate. It seemed Baker had known every elected official in Washington, and they swamped Chief Ransom with calls demanding resolution. It never occurred to politicians that homicides were not solved the same way legislation was passed, but to a hammer, everything looked like a nail.

Malachi followed him into the lieutenant's office.

"What up, Lieu?" Jones asked, pulling out a chair.

Collins chewed on a lollipop, something she had started to help quit smoking. "Don't bother sitting. I just took a call from Nuse. John Wesley, Senator Hansen's chief of staff, claims the senator met Baker at the Ritz-Carlton on Friday night, just before the murder. The senator wants to give a statement, but he's worried about the press. Nuse agreed to have you conduct the interview in the senator's office."

That came as a surprise to Malachi. They did not conduct interviews on witnesses' terms, but Nuse was a climber and an asshole—an incompetent bureaucrat who could not investigate himself out of a paper bag—and he probably saw an advantage in sucking up to the senator.

"That may make the senator the last person to see Baker alive," Malachi said. "Let's see if he can help us with motive."

Collins leaned forward on her elbows and leveled her eyes at him. "I'll lay it down for you. There are rumors Senator Hansen may run for president, and he doesn't need any adverse publicity. The last thing I want to do is piss in his oatmeal. He's expecting you in his office in two hours. Get a statement and keep the senator's role in this quiet . . . for now."

"This gets better and better," Jones said.

Chapter Eight

In Washington, people viewed everyone and everything through a political lens, and Senator Dale Hansen's interview would not be immune. A three-term Democratic powerhouse from Virginia, the senator was from a family that had lived in Richmond for two hundred years, and his ancestors included a former governor and three federal judges. He came from money and did not seem shy about using his position to make more of it. Like many members of Congress, he had doubled his net worth since taking office.

Corruption thrived in DC.

Jones and Malachi waited in overstuffed leather chairs in Senator Hansen's anteroom in the Russell Senate Office Building. A receptionist and a legislative assistant, both young women, sat behind desks across from them. Malachi and Jones had arrived on time, but the senator kept them waiting while he met with someone, likely a donor or influence peddler, which told them where they ranked on the senator's list of priorities.

The assistant—all blond curls, blue eyes, and curves—caught Malachi's eye and smiled. Most of the staff on the Hill seemed young, the offspring of donors and cronies, and she looked like a recent college graduate. Did she find him attractive or was she just excited to meet homicide detectives? Either way, her attention boosted his ego. He had not dated in a long time.

Maybe it's time to change that.

The door to the senator's inner sanctum opened and a fat man, equal parts perspiration and anxiety, hurried out of the office. A moment later, a man with salt-and-pepper hair and a sprayed-on tan approached them and smiled. He wore a gray suit, Italian shoes, and a Hermes tie.

"Good morning, detectives. I'm John Wesley, the senator's chief of staff. Thank you for coming. His schedule is packed today."

"I hope this murder hasn't inconvenienced him," Malachi said.

Alarm flashed across Wesley's face, and he glanced at the legislative assistant.

Jones looked sideways at Malachi. "We understand the senator is a busy man."

Wesley nodded and led them into an office with wood paneling and a high ceiling. Senator Hansen emerged from behind his desk to greet them, and Malachi recognized him as a regular guest on CNN. Wesley introduced them, and they shook hands.

"Welcome," Senator Hansen said. "It's very nice to meet you."

He smiled with the whitest teeth Malachi had seen in a long time and grasped Malachi's hand in both of his, as if they were long-lost relatives. Politicians possessed the ability to make you feel special, like you were the only person in the world who mattered. It was all cajolery and Malachi reminded himself not to fall for it.

Wesley led them to a sofa and chairs nestled around a coffee table covered with photographs and mementos. Malachi and Jones sat on the sofa opposite them. As the senior detective, Jones would take the lead and ask questions while Malachi took notes.

"We don't want to waste your time, so let's get to it," Jones said. "You saw Sam Baker on the night he was killed in—"

"Before we begin," Wesley interrupted. "I want to make sure we're keeping this conversation confidential."

"This a murder investigation, Mr. Wesley," Jones said. "Our interview notes go into the file, but we understand the senator's concerns. We can put a lid on it, keep it out of the public eye."

"The senator wants to cooperate," Wesley said, "which is why he volunteered to come forward, but any association with murder could have serious political repercussions for him."

"We straight. Nobody will leak from our end, but it could come out at trial."

"*If* you find the killer," Wesley said. His face shriveled into a sneer, not a challenge, but cold, as if he doubted their ability.

Maybe he understood the situation better than they did.

"That's why we're here," Jones said.

"Very good," Senator Hansen said. "Chief Ransom promised me you will handle this with discretion, and I trust her judgment."

It had not taken him long to drop the chief's name, and his intent seemed clear. Their careers rested in his hands, and any leaks would come back to bite them.

"When and where did you meet with Sam Baker?" Jones asked.

Malachi pulled out his notepad and scribbled notes. He would keep them short, because everything he wrote became discoverable, and any inconsistencies would be scrutinized by defense counsel if the case ever went to trial. But he also had to document enough to memorialize the senator's statements. It was a balancing act. What Hansen told them could lead to a suspect or it could turn out the senator was involved. Either way, they needed to lock him into a statement.

"I had a drink with Sam at the Ritz-Carlton on Friday evening," the senator said. "I read that he was killed near there, so I assume it happened not long after he left me. God . . . Sam. I can't believe he's dead. What a tragedy. A real loss."

He sounded sincere, but successful politicians survived by manipulating perceptions, and he could probably conjure any persona he needed on command.

"How did you know Mr. Baker?" Jones asked.

"I believe I first met Sam two years ago at a fundraiser. His company, North Star Development, made a sizable donation to my reelection campaign."

"How sizable?"

"I don't remember the exact amount."

"We can get you the campaign records," Wesley said.

Jones nodded. "Why did Baker support your campaign?"

"He liked my politics," Senator Hansen said. "You'd have to ask him about his motivation . . . but that's impossible now."

"You mentioned you *first* met Mr. Baker at a fundraiser," Jones said. "How many times did you meet him, in total?"

"Only a handful, but we also spoke over the telephone."

"About what?"

Jones used open-ended questions to force the senator to do most of the talking. They rolled off his tongue with ease, nonthreatening, like an old friend chatting on the porch after dinner. Malachi had a lot to learn.

"Oh, I don't know," Senator Hansen said. "Let's see, he often talked about hosting events for the Democratic Party. He offered support."

"In exchange for?"

"There was no exchange, Detective Jones," Wesley said. "That would be illegal." His beady eyes fired with suspicion, like a father interrogating his daughter's prom date.

"I didn't say it was criminal," Jones said, chuckling. "But why so much face time? Baker could have mailed you a check."

Senator Hansen adjusted himself in his chair and the leather creaked beneath him. He did not appear comfortable talking about his donors.

"Political support is more complicated than that," he said. "Often donors want to confirm my positions on certain issues. Sam seemed very concerned about the rise of Islamophobia."

"And on the night of the murder, what did Mr. Baker want to confirm?" Jones asked.

Senator Hansen leaned back and crossed his legs. Much had been written about body language, but there were so many variables involved it was not a reliable science. Malachi had learned to spot clusters of potentially deceptive behavior, but he never jumped to conclusions.

"Sam asked me to support an Islamic cultural center in Alexandria," Senator Hansen said. "It was an excellent proposal, and I plan to help in any way I can. Virginia has a long history of slavery and discrimination, and I saw the center as an opportunity to protect my Muslim constituents. Inclusion, diversity, and equality are my goals, and don't forget, Islam is a religion of peace."

"The al-Azhar Islamic Cultural Center?" Malachi asked.

Senator Hansen's eyes darted to Malachi, then to Wesley. "Yes, that's correct."

"Baker was a financier," Jones said. "Do you know where his money came from?"

"North Star is an international company, headquartered in Doha, so it's possible the money came from Qatar. It's not my business to know how a private company funds its projects, and if anything untoward occurred, I wasn't aware of it. Sam asked me to support the project and I intend to do so."

Jones paused for a moment and watched the senator, his forty years of experience collecting, analyzing. He reminded Malachi of a hawk circling a field.

Wesley checked his watch.

"Where did Mr. Baker go after he left the Ritz?" Jones asked.

The senator raised his finger in the air. "I'm not sure, but now that I think about it, Sam received a telephone call moments before our meeting ended."

Malachi perked up at the mention of a telephone call. Rodriguez had subpoenaed the toll data on Baker's telephone, which showed an incoming call minutes before the murder. They had requested an emergency subscriber check, something AT&T allowed under exigent circumstances, but the call had come from a prepaid phone. A burner. Anonymous.

"Who called him?" Jones asked.

"I don't know, but Sam said it was urgent and left."

Jones spent another fifteen minutes questioning Senator Hansen about other meetings, Baker's mood, his habits, his family. It was a fishing expedition and Hansen did not bite.

Wesley kept his eyes on his watch, as if awaiting his own execution. He tried to end the interview several times, but Jones ignored him, and Senator Hansen played along.

"I'm afraid that light on the clock means I have a vote on the floor," Senator Hansen said, stopping the interview.

"Thanks for your cooperation," Jones said. "We may need to talk again."

"I don't think there is anything else the Senator can tell you," Wesley said. "If you have any further questions, call me and I'll pass them along."

"That's not how it works," Malachi said.

Wesley stared down his nose at him, as if Malachi had an infectious disease.

"I'll make myself available if you need anything," Senator Hansen said. "This is all so sad, so very, very sad."

The senator's transition from helpful to mournful looked seamless, and Malachi marveled at how he could switch between emotions. No wonder he had won in a landslide.

The senator escorted them to the door, flashed his patented smile, and patted Malachi on the back. Jones and Malachi thanked him, then walked through reception and out into the hall.

"I think we're being played," Malachi said, "but I don't know how."

"Bamboozled? Maybe."

The senator had been the last person to see Baker before the murder and he was a person of interest in their investigation, at least until they could clear him, so they drove to the Ritz-Carlton and interviewed the bartender. He confirmed Hansen's alibi. The bartender had recognized the senator and knew Baker as a regular customer. He remembered the senator had continued to drink and return calls long after Baker departed.

Senator Hansen did not kill Baker, but he could have ordered the murder. Had their meeting been a way to set Baker up? Malachi had a natural distrust of politicians. He was a registered Democrat, like most Washington residents, but he was apolitical, except where fiscal policies relied on economic myths. He had not yet formed an opinion about the senator.

Malachi scratched Senator Hansen off their suspect list. A list with no other names.

CHAPTER NINE

The Baker murder remained a mystery, but Malachi took a few hours off, refusing to miss the birthday party for his twins, Riley and Samantha. He had sacrificed enough for his job.

Malachi walked into his kitchen to finish the French roast remaining in his coffee maker and poured the thick, dark liquid into a mug with "World's Greatest Dad" printed on the side. Alison had bought it for him as a gift from his daughters. His girls had bounced up and down with excitement when he had unwrapped the mug, and that image of them, full of anticipation and love, had etched itself into his mind. The mug reminded him of the loving family he once had and the excruciating loneliness of his new life.

His stomach clenched.

Alison's affair remained the worst of it. He had missed so many signs—her sudden obsession with her appearance, her unexplained absences. She had grown more distant, colder while his job consumed him, until she had finally sought comfort in the arms of another man. After he found out, he had walked around in daze, his shoulders hunched and his feet dragging, hiding the giant hole where Alison had cut his heart out of his chest. He should have hated her for it, but down deep, he knew he bore some of the responsibility.

Malachi finished his coffee, grabbed two gift-wrapped boxes, and headed into Virginia. He loved his girls more than anything on earth, and while he doubted Alison would ever return to him, he held onto the fantasy of being a family again. He would do whatever he could to get them back.

Malachi arrived at Alison's house in Old Town Alexandria, a historical neighborhood across the Potomac River, just eight miles from his condo. She lived in a nineteenth-century brick townhouse off the city's bustling King Street in a home which had probably cost more than a million dollars, money her wealthy parents must have provided. A plaque beside the front door read "Bancroft," Alison's maiden name. The sign looked new.

Did that mean anything?

Alison had enrolled in American University to finish her PhD in social policy, and now they both lived in the DC area as planned, only not together. Malachi never would have predicted he would become a detective and divorced with two children before he turned thirty.

Whose life is this?

The day remained hazy and humid, and kept everything out of focus. The heat sapped his energy and made him want to lie down in the shade and close his eyes—the kind of southern weather that had inspired mint juleps, sweet tea, and afternoon naps.

Alison answered the door wearing a white sundress. Her long black hair flowed over her shoulders. She tensed when she saw him, as though his arrival surprised her, but she forced a smile and invited him inside.

"The girls will be happy you made it," Alison said.

The girls.

"I wouldn't miss it."

He was glad to get off the front porch. Holding two pink-bowed birthday gifts outside the house where his family lived apart from him felt excruciatingly sad. Malachi's body grew sluggish, as if his spirit had turned off the lights and gone to bed.

"Girls, your father's here." Alison shouted.

Riley and Samantha came running down the hallway and jumped on him, almost knocking the presents out of his hands. They had fair skin and dark black hair, just like their mother, except their bright blue eyes radiated excitement and hope instead of anger and bitterness. His anguish melted away under the heat of their love.

"Daddy, Daddy," they screamed.

"Look at you. Seven years old and almost grown up."

He set down the boxes, pulled his daughters into a bear hug, and lifted them off the floor.

Riley curled her bottom lip. "We miss you. You didn't come to the park with us."

His throat tightened. "I'd be here every day if I could, sweetheart."

Malachi glared at Alison. She had caused their sadness and destroyed his family, but he would not let it ruin their daughters' childhood. He would have a loving relationship with them, no matter what.

Samantha chewed on her finger. "What did you bring us?"

"Open them and find out."

They pounced on the presents and squealed as they unwrapped their stuffed teddy bears.

"I love you, Daddy!" Samantha said.

"Thank you, thank you, thank you," Riley said.

"There are books inside too," he said. He always gave them books because he believed reading sparked intelligence, curiosity, and wonder.

Someone knocked on the door, and Alison opened it. Jones stood on the stoop holding a giant Raggedy Anne doll.

"Uncle Jonesy," Riley screamed.

"Hello, Munchkins." Jones bent down and kissed the girls.

Jones had known the twins for less than a year, but they had taken an immediate liking to the big man.

Alison smiled as Riley and Samantha played with their teddy bears. Malachi hungered for his family. Maybe it was the idea of Alison he still loved—the Alison from their wedding, the Alison in the delivery room, the Alison who cared for his children. She did not want him anymore, but his family lived so close, just out of his reach. Hope lingered.

"Try these, Miss Alison," Jones said and handed her a paper bag.

She unfurled it and peeked inside. "What are these?"

"Genuine chili half-smokes."

Alison's brow furrowed.

Malachi leaned over and examined the contents of the bag. "I'm stumped too."

"It's obvious you two ain't from Chocolate City. Half-smokes are a DC tradition. Smoked pork and beef sausages covered with chili sauce, onions, and mustard. From Ben's Chili Bowl on U Street. You heard of that, right?"

"Sounds familiar," Malachi said.

"Mac, you got a long way to go before you can call yourself a Washingtonian. You too, Miss Alison."

They all walked into the microscopic backyard where four of Alison's fellow students drank margaritas beside a smoking barbecue. Malachi and Jones introduced themselves then dug into the cooler and cracked open diet cokes. Malachi wanted a beer, but they had to return to the office after the party. If they failed to develop a lead soon, the chance of solving Baker's murder would drop exponentially. Malachi should not have come to the party, but he did not want to be one of those cops who always prioritized work before family. Even a brief visit made a difference to his girls. And to him.

"Thanks for coming," Malachi said. "My girls love you."

"Makes me wish I was a pops. If the good Lord hadn't taken my Gloria from me, I think we would've had children. Maybe I should adopt you, Mac."

"You would have made a wonderful father," Malachi said.

Jones nodded. "Any progress with your research?"

"Nothing helpful."

"You'll find something."

As a seasoned cop, Jones bled blue. Police work seemed to be his only passion, other than jazz, and he treated the department like family. They had only been partners for a few months, but Malachi considered Jones his mentor and not just because he knew how to build a prosecutable case. Jones had consoled him during his darker moments.

Malachi glanced around the patio for Alison but did not see her. Her colleagues stood in a circle, an impenetrable clique of female academics. His eyes drifted to the women's waists and ankles, looking for the telltale bulge of concealed weapons. He did it without thought, a behavior ingrained during his years patrolling the streets.

"We can head out soon," Malachi said.

"We've got time. I wouldn't miss your baby girls' party."

"Thanks, I—"

"Excuse me, everyone," Alison said from the doorway. "I'd like you all to meet Chad."

A tall, chiseled man stood beside Alison with his arm around her. He had curly blond hair and a bright smile, and Malachi wanted to knock it off his face. When had Alison started dating?

"Hey, Chad," one of Alison's friends said. "I've heard so much about you."

Alison looked at Malachi. "Chad's a doctoral student at American."

She had ambushed him. Malachi's blood boiled.

Alison introduced Chad to her friends then led him to Malachi. Chad stuck out his hand, and Malachi suppressed the urge to punch him.

Malachi grabbed Chad's hand and shook it, squeezing a little too hard and holding on a little too long. He could not stop himself. He wanted to rip Chad's arm off and beat him to death with it. He stared hard into his eyes until the smile slid off Chad's face. That stupid fucking smile that said, "You lost her, and I have her."

Alison's body tensed, and she bit her lower lip. She leaned forward on her toes, like a referee in a boxing match, ready to jump in and break them up.

"Nice to finally meet you," Chad said. He tried to pull his hand away.

"What's nice about it, Chad?"

Chad frowned.

"You enjoy wrecking my family?" Malachi asked. "Is that it?"

"I, uh . . ."

"Tell me what's nice about meeting me."

"Come on, Brother," Jones said. He laid his hand on Malachi's arm. "We need to bounce."

Malachi released Chad's hand and faced Alison. "Thanks for having me over. Very considerate of you."

He hugged her, and her body stiffened at his touch. How could he still love her?

Malachi walked into the house with everyone's eyes burning a hole in his back.

Jones followed him into the kitchen. "You dropped a turd in that punch bowl."

Malachi opened his mouth to respond but stopped when his girls entered the room. He scooped them into his arms.

"Happy birthday, my angels. Uncle Jonesy and I have to get back to work."

"Stay, Daddy," Samantha said, more an order than a request.

Riley frowned.

"Your pops and I have to catch a thug," Jones said.

"We miss you," Riley said.

"I'll come back next weekend," Malachi said. "I promise."

They left and Malachi headed across the front lawn to his car, his anger weighing him down like an anchor. He wanted to go back inside and knock Chad unconscious.

Alison had divorced Malachi, and he had no right to be angry. He had experienced his share of one-night stands—emotionless encounters that could not hurt him—but he had never dared extend beyond the limits of physical relationships. His mother had abandoned him when he was eight years old, then Alison had done the same thing, and he could not risk it happening again. Malachi lived within the green zone of his heart.

Jones stopped him. "Listen up, Mac. Getting up in that boy's grill was a bad idea. You smack him, and you'll get suspended. Put your anger into your work."

"I know, I know. That was immature. I don't know where it came from."

"It came from you being a man."

"I just miss her. That's my family. I—"

"I understand."

"Shit," Malachi said, and slumped against his car.

Jones put his hand on Malachi's shoulder. "I feel you, but you have to get yourself under control. Whenever I see that look in your eyes, I know what's coming."

"I've always had a bad temper, but it's getting worse. I'll restrain it."

"Now you talking right. Come on, let's hit the office."

"I'd still like to knock the smile off that smug prick's face."

"True dat."

Malachi drove back alone, his knuckles white on the wheel as he crossed the Fourteenth Street Bridge. The Potomac smelled pungent, like algae blooms, dead fish, and fresh earth. It reminded him of the yard behind his brownstone in Boston after a rain, when the soil turned to mud.

His eyes drifted to the water below. People crossed the Potomac every day without noticing it, as if it hid in plain sight. The Nation's River was a living monument, a witness to good and evil, to national independence and slavery. Flowing hundreds of miles from the Appalachian Mountains to the Chesapeake Bay, it separated DC from Virginia, and supplied Washington with both its drinking water and identity. The brown, turbid water drifted through the bustling city—dark, dangerous, and unseen.

CHAPTER TEN

Austin fidgeted in his seat in the last row of the lecture hall inside the Franklin Cultural Center at Washington Colonial University. Professor Riccardo Bellini paced on stage, delivering a diatribe to the packed room about Israel's treatment of the Palestinians.

"He's hot," a young student sitting beside Austin whispered.

Her girlfriend giggled.

At forty-three years old, Bellini retained the physique of a professional athlete. His dark hair and Roman nose—classic Italian features—made him popular with his female students.

"Israel's illegal occupation of Palestine and the continued growth of settlements is the most egregious war crime in history, and the world is letting it happen," Bellini said. "Every day, some Palestinian mother's son is murdered. Every day another home is destroyed. The Palestinians have been subjugated by an evil Israeli regime, which oppresses them and keeps them in poverty."

Austin opened his satchel and pulled out a folder containing several of Bellini's speeches. He had downloaded and printed them in the university's library to avoid leaving an electronic trail. He flipped through the reports, half listening to Bellini.

"Israel was illegally formed on land that historically and rightfully belongs to the Palestinians. I can only assume racism against people of color was what motivated that historic land grab . . ."

Austin scanned a paper Bellini had written, titled "The Gaza Massacre," which claimed the Israeli military had used overwhelming force against civilian populations in both Operation Cast Lead, in 2008, and Operation Pillar of Defense, in 2012. Bellini made only a cursory mention of the violence perpetrated by Hamas and Palestinian insurgents before both Israeli actions. The facts Bellini had omitted revealed his position more than what he had written.

"The Palestinians have had their fertile land stolen and their rights to mine the earth taken away by Israeli invaders," Bellini said, his voice rising. "Israel has no right to exist. It's an illegal government formed through coercion and murder."

Austin dropped his hand into his pocket and rolled Vanessa's pendant in his fingertips. It had been over one year since an Afghan National Army soldier murdered her and three others inside a forward operating base in Afghanistan's Zabul Province. He should have joined her on that intelligence-gathering trip, but he had needed to debrief sources in Jalalabad. Maybe if he had gone, he could have saved her. If only . . .

His temples throbbed. He needed more Oxycontin, and he needed it soon.

"An occupied civilian population, especially one living in forced poverty, is incapable of engaging in effective resistance. No moral equivalence exists between sporadic attacks by rock-throwing demonstrators and the systemic genocide perpetrated by the Israeli government. The Israeli military's war crimes are well documented."

Bellini strode to the edge of the stage. "Palestinian violence is morally justified. Resistance to tyranny is a necessary good. As for the rest of us, I say Boycott, Divestment, Sanctions. That's how the peace-loving world will stop Israel's genocide."

Anti-Semitic bullshit.

Austin rubbed his eyes. The glue holding his fake beard and eyelashes tugged at his irritated skin. His disguise had cost him over nine hundred dollars and had taken hours to apply, but his anonymity was worth it. He scratched his chin, and his headache worsened.

He slid Bellini's speeches back into his satchel. Austin had spent a career searching for clues, and his analysis came with practiced effort. Bellini was one of them. No doubt. He needed to be removed.

Austin stared at Bellini and smiled.

I chose you.

CHAPTER ELEVEN

Malachi and Jones stood inside a cavernous electronics store in a dying strip mall in Greenbelt, Maryland, and flashed their credentials for Elmer Smith. The pudgy loss prevention officer wore his flashlight, keys, and employee ID on his belt as if he thought he was Batman. His eyes lit up when Jones identified them as homicide detectives, and Malachi pegged Elmer as a cop wannabe.

Patrol had located Baker's Mercedes inside the Canal Square Parking garage, and based on Senator Hansen's comments, Malachi believed the killer had used a burner phone to lure Baker to his death. AT&T did not have a subscriber for the phone, but it had been purchased at this store.

"Murder po-lice?" Elmer asked, emphasizing the first syllable.

"That's right. MPD," Jones said.

"Wow," Elmer said. "That's what I want to do. I'm here getting law enforcement experience."

Nailed that one.

"We need your help to solve a murder," Malachi said, stroking Elmer's ego.

Elmer radiated excitement. "My help?"

"Our killer bought a disposable phone here on April 20. If you captured video of the purchase, you may solve this for us. Want to join our team and help us out?"

"You betcha. Cops gotta support each other. Come with me."

Malachi and Jones followed Elmer past pallets of inventory and through a warehouse that reeked of cardboard. They entered a cluttered, gloomy office, and Elmer slid behind a desk. A Washington Nationals bobblehead jiggled beside the computer.

AT&T had confirmed the only call made on the disposable phone had been to Baker, and that call had hit a cell tower in Georgetown. Train had obtained a warrant and pinged the phone hoping to pinpoint its location but did not get a return, which meant the phone was off. Malachi doubted the killer would use the telephone again, because it had fulfilled its purpose when a bullet passed through Baker's brain.

Cameras existed everywhere, a fact both helpful and disconcerting, so the killer may have been caught on video. Malachi handed Elmer AT&T's response, which listed the phone's number and the International Mobil Equipment Identity number of the chip inside it.

"I'll ask Wendell to pull the inventory receipts," Elmer said. "He's my manager. He can confirm when the product came in and when we sold it. If it passed through here recently, I'll have video."

Elmer made a call, and Malachi and Jones shot each other looks while Elmer tried to explain what they needed. Elmer waited while the manager looked up the information, then hung up.

"We sold that phone on April 20, at 2:31 p.m., but Wendell told me not to give you anything without a warrant." Elmer looked crestfallen.

"I understand, Elmer," Malachi said. "He's the boss."

"Yessir."

"We can get a warrant, but that would take all day and if there's nothing on your tape, we'll have wasted valuable time," Malachi said. "One day is an eternity in a homicide case, as I'm sure you know. If there's evidence on your video, I'll ask a judge for a warrant, but we need to know if it's there."

"Well, I don't think—"

"We're hoping for some professional courtesy on this one," Malachi said. "You know, from one cop to another."

Elmer beamed. "Don't tell Wendell I'm doing this and promise me you'll get a warrant."

"We straight," Jones said.

Elmer logged into an old IBM desktop computer, with a monitor the size of a microwave oven. His half-eaten lunch sat on the desk, and the room stank like day-old hot dogs. Elmer scrolled through folders on his computer looking for video recordings from April 20. Malachi moved behind him and watched over his shoulder.

"We keep the recordings until the end of the month then I delete them," Elmer said.

"So, April's recordings are gone?" Malachi asked.

"Uh, sometimes I don't get around to deleting them for a while."

On the screen Malachi saw computer files going back to February.

"Here it is," Elmer said.

Jones winked at Malachi and grinned.

Sometimes they solved cases because they were lucky, but good fortune lay at the intersection of hard work and opportunity. They ran down every lead, and if the killer had made a mistake, they would catch it. They made their own luck.

The folder contained twenty-four files from April 20, each a recording from one of six cameras. Elmer opened a file and scrolled to 2:21 p.m., ten minutes before the purchase.

"This camera covers the last two rows of shelves where the prepaid phones are displayed," Elmer said.

Jones sidled up beside Malachi, and they watched customers clad in sweatpants and spandex stroll up and down the aisle—the world's most boring television show. At 2:26 p.m., a white male, about six-foot-three, stopped at the display. He wore a white sun hat and large sunglasses and sported a bushy beard.

"Now there's a real *bama*," Jones said.

Elmer and Malachi both turned and stared at him.

"Bama?" Malachi asked

"Keep forgetting that you're not from DC," Jones said. "He's a bama. He dresses like shit. That beard gotta be fake."

The man selected a mobile phone and appeared to read the box, then he stuck it under his arm and walked out of view.

"Let me switch to the registers," Elmer said.

Elmer opened another file and fast-forwarded to 2:29 p.m. After a few seconds, the man appeared at the register. He counted out cash, instead of using a credit card. He took his receipt and phone and walked toward the exit.

"Do you have exterior cameras?" Malachi asked.

"Yes, but only the inside cameras record."

"Catch him leaving?" Jones asked.

Elmer switched the feed to another camera, and they watched the man walk toward the exit. The man paused in front of the automatic doors and looked up.

"That son-a-bitch is looking into the camera," Jones said.

"He knew we would come for the video," Malachi said. "He's looking at us."

Jones shook his head. "Dis'n us."

"Good job, Elmer," Malachi said. "I'll get you that warrant. You may have helped us solve this murder."

Elmer's face lit up.

"Mac, see if tech can work some magic on that video quality," Jones said.

"Will do, and I'll send it to my contact at DEA and have him run it through facial recognition software. Maybe we'll get a hit in a federal database."

Malachi leaned in and examined the man's face more closely. Malachi could not be certain, but he could swear the man was smiling.

CHAPTER TWELVE

Malachi leaned back in his desk chair and listened to a vending machine hum in the hallway inside the now-vacant Homicide Branch. Baker's murder had been premeditated, and Malachi needed a working theory about how and why it happened. The *how* seemed clear. The killer had worn a disguise, purchased a burner, lured Baker to his death, and then escaped through the canal. The killer had probably painted the security camera near the murder scene, even though it had not been recording.

But Malachi could not figure out *why* someone had killed Baker. Money, power, and betrayal had been the classic motives for murder since man first climbed out of trees and started killing with rocks. Rodriguez had subpoenaed a dozen financial institutions, hoping to find irregularities with Baker's accounts, but Baker's millions remained untouched and nothing seemed amiss. Malachi had spoken to Baker's financial manager in Qatar, but he had shed no light on motive.

Malachi opened an email from DEA Special Agent James Winter, who had responded to his request to run Baker through the Special Operations Division's databases. Winter indicated he had found something and asked Malachi to call. Malachi dialed the phone.

"I ran al-Bakri through DEA's internal Firebird system," Winter said. "He's listed as the CEO of North Star Development, which was named in two DEA money-laundering investigations that targeted transnational drug trafficking organizations. The traffickers funneled drug proceeds to Hezbollah and Hamas. They—"

"Baker's company sent money to Hezbollah and Hamas?" Malachi asked.

"Don't get excited. North Star received eighty thousand dollars from an account connected to the Lebanese Canadian Bank in Beirut. That bank was shuttered for laundering drug money for Hezbollah. In the other case, North Star received twenty-two thousand from an account linked to suspicious charitable donations to Hamas."

"Was anyone at North Star indicted?"

"No allegations of criminal conduct, only peripheral connections to bank accounts that appeared dirty," Winter said. "North Star's transactions may have been legitimate."

"Think it's worth tracking down?"

"I pulled the cases in DEA's electronic file room, and it looks like all smoke and no fire."

"Sounds like a dead end."

"I also ran al-Bakri and North Star in our fusion center databases and got a hit on an FBI investigation. The case agent is Special Agent Horn in the Washington Field Office."

"Any idea what the FBI case is about?"

"I didn't want to ask our FBI liaison without checking with you first."

"Don't bother. I'll go through MPD," Malachi said.

Malachi thanked him and ended the call. He returned to his computer and emailed Detective Pinker and asked for any information the FBI had on Baker. Malachi did not mention what Agent Winter had found, because he wanted to see if Pinker came up with it on his own. Like many government employees, Pinker did the absolute minimum and could never be fired—another clog in the bureaucratic pipeline.

Malachi read an email response from the FinCEN analyst he had queried. She said there were hundreds of overseas financial transactions involving North Star, but no evidence of wrongdoing. North Star had a long history dealing with shadowy financial institutions, but so did many other businesses. Baker may have committed crimes, but there were no pending charges against either him or North Star.

Malachi's cell phone buzzed, and Alison's number displayed on the screen. His heart jumped.

"Hey, I'm glad you called," he said.

"That was quite a performance at the party."

Malachi knew he had acted like an ass, but she had ambushed him with her new boyfriend, and plunged a knife into Malachi's back.

"You could've warned me he would be there."

"Malachi, it's been years. You must have assumed I was dating."

She had moved on and he had not . . . *could* not.

"I'm at work," he said. "What do you need?"

"So, you won't apologize for—"

"Are you kidding me?"

"You embarrassed me in front of my friends. You—"

"My wife is fucking some other guy and I'm supposed to apologize."

"Ex-wife," she said.

"I have to get back to work."

"Wait. I'm presenting a paper a week from today, and I need you to pick the girls up from school."

His pulse pounded in his neck. "Fine. I'll take the girls whenever I can get them."

"Thank you—"

He hung up without saying goodbye. His shoulders sagged, as if his arms had become too heavy for his body. He wanted to blame Alison for his behavior, but he could not. She had built a new life, while he held onto a memory, onto something which no longer existed.

Malachi returned to his computer and plowed through dozens of articles about Baker, who had financed construction projects all over the world and donated handsomely to Islamic charities and political campaigns. The press portrayed Baker in a positive light, especially the financial newspapers.

Malachi arched his back and rubbed his strained and bloodshot eyes.

He opened a negative op-ed piece, which insinuated Baker had undercut construction bids by influencing politicians to help North Star win contracts. Another article noted Baker donated to Islamic charities involved in questionable activities overseas and funded mosque construction across the country. Malachi read a recent article by Dr. Zahra Mansour, a fellow at a think tank for Middle East affairs, who accused Baker of supporting radical Islam. In a similar vein, several conservative websites called Baker an Islamist who enabled terrorism.

Could Islamophobia be a motive?

Baker had asked Senator Hansen to support the new mosque project in Alexandria. The al-Azhar Islamic Cultural Center was a five-hundred-million-dollar project to build the largest mosque in the United States. Advertised as more than a prayer site, it would serve as a cultural center and spread the virtues of Islam. It would also offer education and guidance for the victims of religious discrimination, lobby for additional protections for Muslims, and provide legal defense funding. The project had the usual detractors, including several intolerant Christian and Hindi associations and a smattering of alt-right and white supremacist groups.

Following religious bigotry as a motive, Malachi Googled the al-Azhar Islamic Cultural Center. He found a dozen news stories about a demonstration against its construction, all of which were rehashed versions of a Washington Herald news story. He pulled the original story, which had run six months ago.

ALEXANDRIA, Va. — Approximately 80 people gathered last night to protest the planned construction of the al-Azhar Islamic Cultural Center in Alexandria City, which is scheduled for completion late next year. According to the American Islamic Shura, the building will serve as a mosque for Muslims in Northern Virginia and as a cultural center to promote religious tolerance across the county. Protesters carrying Confederate flags cheered as speakers claimed the mosque did not belong in a Christian country. The New National Order, a self-proclaimed white nationalist organization advocating racial separation, organized the protest...

The demonstration had not drawn many protesters, but any rally of racists was likely to get some coverage, and Malachi wondered if the press empowered evil by giving it unwarranted attention. He searched for the New National Order and found dozens of news stories.

The New National Order's website looked amateurish, festooned with iron crosses, propagandistic slogans, and hate. It looked like Hitler's Facebook page. Dylan Miller led the organization and his quote, "Blood and soil make America strong," ran across the website's banner. It sickened Malachi, who was Jewish and had lost relatives in the Holocaust. They had been murdered because people like Dylan Miller believed in racial superiority.

If nothing else panned out, Malachi would interview Miller.

In another Washington Herald article, the president of Atlantic Real Estate Development, David Ellison, accused Baker of cheating his company out of one hundred million dollars by influencing the Alexandria City Council and stealing the development rights for the land where the mosque was planned. One hundred million sounded like motive, but it was a gigantic leap from losing a contract to murder.

Malachi picked up the telephone and called Detective Matt Ryan in MPD's Homeland Security Bureau, a unit that collected intelligence on local terrorist organizations, gangs, and hate groups. If the New National Order was a local threat, Ryan would know. Two years ago, when Malachi investigated crimes against persons, Ryan had worked with him on a string of aggravated batteries. Members of Mara Salvatrucha, known as MS-13, had slashed the faces of innocent victims as part of a gang initiation. Ryan was a curmudgeon, but his insights into the gang had helped Malachi identify and arrest the suspects.

Ryan picked up after the first ring.

"Sorry to bother you so late," Malachi said. "I have a quick question."

"It's never quick with you, Wolf."

"This time it is."

"I heard you caught one over there."

"That's why I'm calling. I'm looking for motive and my vic ran into the New National Order. Ever heard of them?"

"Those dickheads? They're a small group of white nationalists down in Virginia. They are regulars at white power rallies, but I haven't connected them to anything serious yet. They're mostly losers living in their mother's basements and looking for something to make them feel special."

"No connections to violence?"

"Most of these guys like to fight and have minor rap sheets, but no murders."

"What about their leader, Dylan Miller?"

"I'm sure I have a picture of him. Hold on, I'm still at my desk. Let me check."

Malachi listened to Ryan clicking on his keyboard. Bigotry could be a motive, but one usually secondary to money, revenge, or whatever. Criminals found it easier to hurt someone they considered sub-human.

"I sent it to you," Ryan said. "Holler if you need anything else."

Malachi thanked him and hung up. He opened his email and downloaded a surveillance photograph showing a dozen young men, all dressed in black, marching beside a Nazi flag on the National Mall. Ryan had circled a tall man leading the pack in red ink. Malachi zoomed in, and Dylan Miller's face stared back at him with beady, black eyes.

Eyes filled with hate.

CHAPTER THIRTEEN

Austin showered, dressed, and walked into his bedroom. Sophie watched him from the doorway. He popped two Oxycodone into his mouth and washed them down with a slug of beer. The pills had not reached his stomach, but knowing they would soon carry him away was enough to lighten his mood.

He opened a bureau drawer and removed Vanessa's pendant. He carried it with him every day and sensed her presence. To the world he was a ruthless killer, a monster—but would Vanessa approve?

What am I becoming?

Sophie plodded into the room, her mouth dripping with water. She looked at him.

"Stop judging me," Austin said, "Don't make me regret rescuing you. The pound would take you back."

Sophie snorted.

"Just kidding, girl," he said. He scratched behind her ears.

He grabbed his Beretta off his nightstand. From the back of the drawer, he dug out a suppressor which he had purchased at a Virginia gun shop. Luckily, he lived in one of forty-two states that permitted silencers. Austin could always explain his purchase as an attempt to protect his hearing during target shooting, a viable excuse he hoped he would never need to use. He had also paid cash at a gun show for a threaded gun barrel.

Austin screwed the long black tube onto the threaded barrel. It added seven inches to the length of the firearm but would reduce the decibel level of a discharge. He carried the Beretta into his living room, where his satchel lay open on the table. He inserted the firearm into internal straps, making sure the barrel lined up with a small hole in the leather, then swung the bag over his shoulder and headed out.

Sophie whimpered as he shut the door.

.   .   .

An hour later, Austin leaned against a tree on Madison Lawn at Washington Colonial University and watched students hustle to their summer-session classes. The Modern Middle East Studies School lay beyond the courtyard, and somewhere inside, Professor Riccardo Bellini prepared for his last class of the afternoon.

Austin stared at Bellini's third-floor office window and checked his watch. He powered on his new phone, dialed Bellini's office number from memory, and pressed send.

Bellini answered on the second ring.

"Professor Bellini?"

"Yes?"

"This is Professor Leinhardt from the engineering college," Austin said. "I've detained a student with a book bag full of stolen tests. We're standing behind Adams Hall." Austin bit his lip wondering if he had pushed too far with this pseudonym—a surname likely familiar to the professor.

Riccardo groaned. "A student? One of mine?"

"I'm afraid so. Can you come down and confirm these belong to you?"

"I have a lecture about to start. I can only spare a few minutes of my time."

"Thank you, professor. A few minutes are all I need."

Austin watched Professor Bellini exit the building and hustle across the brick courtyard. Bellini nodded at two female students, who smiled back at him. He turned and leered at their bodies as they passed. The girls looked like undergraduates, only nineteen or twenty years old.

What a scumbag.

Austin adjusted his satchel on his shoulder and hurried past Locke Hall, which had been named after the seventeenth-century philosopher and now housed the university's administrative offices. The massive gray-brick building could have been plucked out of downtown Vienna, and it contributed to the campus' charm.

Austin jogged across the street to Adams Hall. Bellini had a reputation as a stickler for punctuality, and since it was the first day back after the Memorial Day weekend, he would not relish being late to his lecture. Austin glanced over his shoulder and confirmed the Professor was headed his way.

"For he is the minister of God to thee for good. But if thou do that which is evil, be afraid; for he beareth not the sword in vain; for he is the minister of God, a revenger to execute wrath upon him that doeth evil."

Austin walked behind the building and stopped with his back against the wall. He slipped his hand inside his satchel, found the Beretta's grip, and pointed his trigger finger down the slide. He assumed an athletic stance and waited.

Ten seconds later, Bellini rounded the corner.

Austin stepped in front of him and Bellini canted his body to allow him to pass. Their shoulders bumped, and Austin swung his satchel against Bellini's rib cage. He pulled the trigger three times.

Clack, clack, clack.

The odor of smoldering leather tickled his nostrils.

"Watch yourself," Bellini shouted.

Austin glanced around to make sure they were alone, then he lifted his finger off the trigger. He wanted to flee, but he had to confirm the professor was dead. The image of Baker's bloody, lifeless body had haunted his sleep for days and when he closed his eyes, he could see the hole in Baker's forehead, as if he stood in front of him. It had imprinted on his vision like a screensaver, always present. He needed to be sure.

He stopped and turned to witness his deed.

Bellini held his side and looked down at his ribs. Blood expanded across his white dress shirt and dripped over his fingers. He looked up and locked eyes with Austin before he bent at the waist and vomited.

Bellini seemed to lose his balance and spun around, reaching out and grabbing at the air. He fell hard on the ground, still holding his side with one hand. The red stain on his shirt darkened. He coughed, and blood dribbled down his chin. His arms flailed for a moment then stopped. He lay crumpled on the ground, motionless. His arms were splayed out as if Austin had crucified him. Blood bubbled through his shirt and stained the ground. It was done.

"The blood will wash away your sins and purify you."

The sight of the Bellini's body did not nauseate Austin. This kill had been easier. He looked at the corpse, and a flash of terror jolted him—an irrational fear the body would open its eyes and come for him.

The silencer had quieted the shot, and Austin doubted anyone had heard. The parking lot remained empty, and classes had begun, so it would be some time before anyone discovered the body. But he could not rely on that.

He had to get to the water.

Austin walked away, careful to keep a normal pace. He wanted to run but that would draw attention. He traveled south along the sidewalk, passing two students in front of the Hamilton Library, and entered Foundry Branch Valley Park. He picked his way through the woods to his kayak, which he had stashed near the Key Bridge Boathouse. Austin stripped down to his swimsuit, pulled a bag from the cockpit, and stuffed his clothes inside. He dragged his kayak into the water, climbed in, and pushed off. Within minutes, he became one of a dozen boaters enjoying the river on a warm summer day.

A moment of dread rolled through him like a wave. Would God punish him?

He recalled YouTube videos of Bellini defending Islamists. The professor had covered for evil men, lied about their intentions, denied their horrific deeds. He had spread their vile ideology and enabled them. He had deserved to die.

God will reward me.

The assassination had been easier than expected but he could not get cocky. Overconfidence led to sloppiness, and it would only take one mistake to end his life. He thought about Vanessa and smiled. She had been so young, so good, so pure. What his life could have been.

Austin dug his paddle into the river and headed for the Virginia shore. He had much left to do.

CHAPTER FOURTEEN

"We got us another body," Jones said and hung up the phone.

Malachi stopped reading the evidence inventory displayed on his computer screen.

"Where?"

"Professor at Washington Colonial University. Dropped in a parking lot in broad daylight. District Two detectives called it in."

It had been eleven days since Baker's murder. Eleven days since Malachi and Jones had caught the case. Eleven days and they were not even close to solving it.

"What are you thinking?" Malachi asked.

"Two upstanding citizens of Ye Olde Georgetown cut down. Something's in the air."

"Who's on deck?"

"Hill and Rodriguez. It'll be good for Train to get hands on."

"Yeah."

"Let's back them up," Jones said, "and make sure Train gets a good start."

"Give me ten minutes to finish this case review."

"Don't take too long," Jones said.

Malachi reached for his keyboard and his hand burned as if he had shoved it into a fire. "Shit," he said, and held his hand against his chest.

"What happened?" Jones asked.

"Uh . . . nothing. I'm fine."

"You don't sound fine."

"I spilled coffee on my hand. It startled me that's all."

"That so?" Jones stared over his computer screen, his eyes penetrating, scrutinizing.

"Really, Jonesy. I'm okay."

Jones watched him, seeming unconvinced.

"Go ahead," Malachi said. "I'll be along soon."

"Catch you there, Mac." He walked out.

The skin on Malachi's arm burned from his fingers to his elbow. He inspected it and saw nothing wrong. It was neurogenic pain, as real and torturous as if he held his arm in an oven, but this was an affliction created by his mind. The myelin sheath coating his nerves had degenerated, causing symptoms as bizarre as they were unpredictable. They came like a mugger in the night—violent, aggressive, without warning.

He remembered the first attack as if it had happened yesterday.

A few weeks after his father's funeral, he had been walking down Commonwealth Avenue when his vision blurred. He had rubbed his eyes, but the world grew fuzzier. He took a taxi to the emergency room, where nurses initiated an emergency protocol, worried he had suffered an ischemic or hemorrhagic stroke. An ER doctor put him through a battery of cognitive testing and blood work, then sent him for a brain MRI.

While Malachi waited for the doctor to return, the vision returned to his right eye and the blurriness improved. He chewed on his lip waiting for the diagnosis.

The doctor looked serious when he returned to his bedside.

"Did I have a stroke?"

"The good news is there's no sign of blockage or hemorrhage."

"Thank God," Malachi said.

"But I'm concerned about something else."

Malachi cringed. "What?"

"Two small lesions on your brain, just above your brain stem. They—"

"Tumors?"

"Not growths. Abnormalities. The radiologist wouldn't classify them, so I'm referring you to our staff neurologist."

"What does this mean?" Malachi asked.

"I can't give you a diagnosis, because many things can cause lesions, but this is not an emergency."

"And my temporary loss of sight?"

"The lesions are in the distal, posterior area of your brain, and may be causing your vision problems."

"Are lesions caused by disease or something genetic?"

"You should consult with neurology to figure out what's going on."

Malachi shivered at the memory. Over the following months he had undergone additional testing and many neurological appointments. It had not taken long to receive his diagnosis.

Multiple Sclerosis.

The disease affected his brain, spinal cord, and optic nerves by causing his own immune system to erode the protective fat around his nerves. Scar tissue had built up, causing the lesions the doctor had seen on Malachi's MRI. The lesions interfered with his brain's ability to communicate with the rest of his body, creating fatigue and a plethora of other symptoms.

Fortunately, Malachi suffered from relapsing-remitting MS, the least destructive of the disease's three classifications. His symptoms came and went, brought on by stress, hot weather, a flu, or anything that interfered with his immune system. He had no warning the disease would strike, and once or twice a year, he had to treat his worst attacks with IV steroids to reduce the inflammation.

Malachi could live his whole life like this, or his disease could progress to secondary progressive MS and worsening symptoms. If that happened, he would have to leave the police department. But until that day, he would accomplish as much as possible.

A timer wound down on his career.

The burning in his arm subsided as mysteriously as it had come, and Malachi flexed his hand. He finished reviewing the evidence and shut off his computer. He knew he should drive out to Washington Colonial University and help Rodriguez the same way Jones had helped him. Focusing on something other than Baker would help clear his head,

Georgetown did not have many murders. Malachi had analyzed the data, like any good economist. For many years, Washington, DC reported one of the highest murder rates in the country, with an average of 380 murders per year, in a city with a population of 600,000. Homicide rates had dropped all over the country in the twenty-first century, and Washington's body count had declined to 167 per year. But even that statistic was deceptive, because the vast majority of murders took place in the Southeastern quadrant of the city, a poor area with a majority black population. Northwest DC had little violent crime, and if it had been its own city, it would have been one of the safest in the country. Georgetown only suffered one or two murders per year, but now there had been two in eleven days.

Malachi grabbed his keys and headed for his car.

CHAPTER FIFTEEN

Yellow police tape surrounded Adams Hall at Washington Colonial University and blocked dozens of curious students from trampling the crime scene. The crowd clotted into groups of three and four underclassmen, their faces etched with worry. They exchanged hushed words as red and blue emergency lights reflected off the gothic stone buildings. Malachi scanned them looking for anything unusual—an angry stare, a smile, some window into the mind of a criminal.

He saw only fear and concern.

Washington Colonial University was one of the oldest universities in the country and enrolled over eleven thousand students and employed almost five hundred faculty. The main campus covered seventy-five acres in Georgetown, not including foreign campuses in Qatar and Saudi Arabia. The university spent thirty million in research every year and boasted an impressive list of distinguished alumni, including three former presidents.

Malachi flashed his identification to a university police officer and ducked under the tape. The body lay on the northern side of the parking lot, covered with a white sheet. The professor's right hand stuck out from underneath, exposing his tweed jacket sleeve. He had dressed himself that morning like he had done every day, with no idea that it would be his last. Malachi had not known the man, but he allowed himself a moment of sympathy before he closed the door on his emotions. Malachi could not empathize with victims, because emotions clouded his judgment and prevented him from doing his job.

Rodriguez and Hill stood a few feet away from the body.

"Work with the kindergarten cops to locate a witness," Hill told Rodriguez.

Rodriguez seemed tight, anxious. He nodded at Malachi.

Hill smirked at Malachi but kept talking. "Someone saw something. It's the middle of the day on an active campus, for fuck's sake. One of these pampered assholes saw our shooter."

"Officer Barnard said nobody has come forward yet," Rodriguez said, gesturing toward a heavyset university officer standing twenty feet away.

Hill's face turned red. "Well, it must be true if a fat fucking campus cop said so. They don't even carry guns. Go find out for yourself."

"What's the status?" Malachi asked.

"Professor Bellini was shot multiple times around nine o'clock this morning," Hill said. "No suspects and no murder weapon. Jones and the LT are talking to the university president."

"We're certain there isn't an active shooter on campus?" Malachi asked.

"Colonial activated their Emergency Response Team, and they're trying to herd students back into their dorms. They're supposed to be in lockdown."

"What do you need?"

"Seeing as how I spent two days canvassing the waterfront for your dead Arab, how about giving Train a hand dealing with these shit-magnet school security guards?"

"No problem."

Rodriguez exhaled, and a smile flittered across his face. Hill could be a tough partner to work with, worse for a new detective.

"One of these snowflakes must have seen the doer," Hill said. "Somewhere on a campus there's a coddled little man child with information, but he's hiding in his safe place and sucking his thumb. The world is a dangerous place, sweetheart."

"Come on, Train," Malachi said. "Let's talk to Colonial's finest and figure out the best way to canvass their students."

Malachi and Rodriguez walked past a group of university officers, and Malachi hoped they had not overheard Hill's comments.

"Find me a fucking witness, newbies," Hill shouted after them.

.   .   .

Thirty minutes later, Malachi and Rodriguez sat inside the Washington Colonial University Police Services Bureau, listening to Captain Arnold Schmidt fret.

"This doesn't happen here. I've been with Colonial for twenty-two years and no professor has been killed. Nothing like this. We don't allow guns on campus."

To Malachi, he sounded more like the victim than the officer in charge of protecting students and teachers. Malachi took the lead hoping to show Rodriguez how to finesse an interview and get the campus police working for them, not against them.

"I'm sure you've done everything possible," Malachi said, absolving the captain.

In 2001, a Colonial student had poisoned another student in a love triangle, but that had happened off-campus, and Malachi had never heard of a murder on school grounds. As special police officers, Washington Colonial University cops exercised full arrest powers on campus, but they only carried pepper spray, and they deferred violent felony investigations to MPD.

"We did everything. This wasn't our fault," Schmidt said. He sounded worried he might lose his job.

"Let's focus on finding the killer," Malachi said. "We need to speak with every student who was near the quad this morning."

"The administration will never allow that. Families pay big money to send their children to a safe environment. If you talk to students about murder, you'll frighten them."

"It's safe to say the murder is no longer a secret."

"Talking to students is a no-go. We need to protect them from this business."

"One of your students could be the murderer," Malachi said. "At a minimum, we need to interview the professor's students. As for the rest, can the university send out a notice asking anyone who was on the quad to call us?"

"Probably," Schmidt said, stroking his chin.

"We can publish a tip number for students to call in."

"I'll ask the provost," Schmidt said.

Schmidt called the provost and had a terse conversation. He hung up and turned to them.

"You can search Professor Bellini's office, but we need a receipt for anything you take. The provost will issue a statement with your tip number, and he agreed to ask the president about letting you speak to Bellini's students and colleagues, but you need to have a member of the administration present during interviews."

Malachi and Rodriguez thanked him and left.

Outside, Malachi pulled Rodriguez to the side. "If we knew a student or teacher was a witness or suspect, we wouldn't have to dance around their protocols, but we need the cops on our team."

"Makes sense."

"For now, we'll play ball and do the interviews here, but bring witnesses or persons of interest to our office. Let the university police think they're equal partners, and they won't get in our way. Most college cops worry they're perceived as security guards, so stroke their egos, but keep them at a distance."

"I'll get the list of Professor Bellini's students from the Paine Foreign Service College," Rodriguez said.

"Wait, what?"

"I'll get the student list from—"

"What did Professor Bellini teach?" Malachi asked.

"He taught graduate students in the Modern Middle East Studies School. Something about Islam and geo-politics in the Middle East."

Adrenaline hit Malachi's bloodstream. They had two murders in Georgetown, and both victims had been connected to the Middle East. It meant nothing by itself, but it seemed too coincidental. Murder was a statistical outlier, beyond the boundaries of normal human behavior, and commonalities between murders had to mean something.

"Interesting," Malachi said.

"Think it's relevant?"

"Get the list of faculty and students and let's start on the interviews as soon as the president signs off. We need to talk to witnesses while events are fresh. Memories distort over time, and an emotional suspect may slip up."

"Uh-huh," Rodriguez said.

Malachi realized he had been condescending. He was new to homicide too, but he had extensive experience solving violent crimes, and he did not want any mistakes.

"Sorry, Train. I'm sure you know that. A more reliable witness is video. I noticed two exterior cameras on Adams Hall. Has Hill pulled the video?"

"He asked for it, but I doubt it will help."

"Why do you say that?" Malachi asked.

"These students are still kids. Somebody vandalized the school and spray painted over the cameras in the parking lot."

"Holy shit."

.　　.　　.

Professor Bellini's office occupied a corner on the top floor of the Franklin Cultural Center. He had littered his desk with stacks of papers and books, creating an academic wilderness. Rodriguez sifted through papers looking for something obvious, but they would take everything back to their office and analyze it after they got a search warrant.

Malachi walked along the wall looking at framed photographs and certificates. A diploma for Bellini's master's degree at George Washington University hung beside a doctorate from Washington Colonial. In a photograph below that, Malachi recognized Professor Bellini standing with Amir al-Kadi, president of the American Islamic Shura. Baker had known al-Kadi too. Another connection.

Malachi's phone buzzed.

Alison.

His heart leapt, and he picked up.

"I want to confirm you're picking up the girls this afternoon," Alison said.

"Shit." His stomach knotted. "We caught another homicide. I can't make it."

"Dammit, Malachi. This is why we didn't work."

He recoiled. He was blowing his shot at getting her back, if he ever had one. "I'm at a crime scene, and I can't leave."

"I should have expected this."

"I'm sorry. Listen, I can't talk now, but I'll call you tonight. I want to talk to the girls."

"That's not a good idea. They're mad at you."

"Mad?"

"For leaving their birthday party, for not being around enough. Basically, for being you."

Ouch.

Malachi rubbed the bridge of his nose. "How will you get them home?"

"I'll ask Chad to pick them up."

"I don't want a strange man picking up my kids."

"It's fine. They call him Uncle Chad. Thanks again for the help."

"I'm sorry—"

She hung up.

Malachi's chest ached. He remembered Alison's smile when he had taken a knee and proposed to her on the Boston Common. She had radiated joy, and they had spent the weekend in bed at the Four Seasons, making love, laughing, becoming one. Had her personality changed, or had her anger always been there, lying dormant? Malachi yearned for her to look at him the same way again. He needed his family back.

He slipped the phone into his pocket and stared at the photo of al-Kadi.

.   .   .

Sweat beaded on Malachi's skin inside the sweltering conference room he shared with Jones, Hill, Rodriguez, Johnson, and Brown. Collins stood at the end of the table sucking on a lollipop until she stained her lips and tongue cherry red. Hill finished summarizing the evidence collected from Bellini's murder and looked up from his notes.

Two murders in less than two weeks in Georgetown—one of the safest places on earth—seemed coincidence enough, but two victims associated with the Middle East, and two crime scenes with security cameras painted black confirmed it for Malachi. They were looking for the same suspect, but why had the killer targeted a Qatari financier and a Washington Colonial professor?

"We're agreed these homicides are connected?" Collins asked.

"That's our working theory," Jones said.

Hill scowled.

"Detective Hill?" Collins asked.

"Yeah, right," he said. "But it's only a theory . . . and a thin one."

"You have a better idea?" she asked.

"Not yet," Hill said. He glowered at Malachi.

Hill did not appear to like the thought of working with another team of detectives and Jones was senior to him—hell, Jones was senior to everyone—which meant Jones would lead the investigation. Sharing did not seem to be in Hill's wheelhouse.

"We need to find the connection between Baker and Bellini," Malachi said. "They both dealt with the Middle East and probably knew some of the same people, like Amir al-Kadi. I've done almost two weeks of digging into Baker's life, so it makes sense for me to do the background on Bellini too."

Rodriguez nodded as Malachi spoke, but Hill looked like he had stepped in dog shit.

"Objections?" Collins asked.

Everyone turned toward Hill.

"If College wants to sit in the office and research, I got no problem with that."

"Jones?" Collins asked.

"It's all good."

"Okay, each team focus on developing your own investigations in case these homicides aren't related," Collins said, "but I want you to keep each other in the loop. If anything of substance comes up, I expect an immediate update. We have hundreds of students to interview, so let's work together and identify a suspect."

If they were going to find the murderer, Malachi had to find the connection between Bellini and Baker, and he needed to do it fast. He had a bad feeling the killer was not finished.

CHAPTER SIXTEEN

Darkness had fallen over the city and the Homicide Branch's bullpen was long empty. Only the glow of Malachi's computer lit the room. Hill and Rodriguez had taken Brown and Johnson and returned to Washington Colonial where the university president had dedicated two classrooms for interviews. Malachi turned off the fluorescent overhead lights, because stark lights killed his creativity and inhibited his thoughts. Government offices diminished individuality with an aesthetic designed by the lowest bidder.

He ran comprehensive database checks on Professor Bellini and learned he had grown up in Berkeley, California, the youngest of three sons, born to hippies. He had completed his undergraduate studies in teaching at Berkeley and earned a Master of Arts in political science from George Washington University. He received his PhD from Washington Colonial and had taught political science there for the past eight years.

Bellini had received far less press coverage than Baker, but Malachi found a few of his published articles and recorded lectures online. He needed to discover what Bellini had in common with Baker. Baker was Qatari and had financed building projects related to Islam, and Bellini was a political science professor with expertise in Middle Eastern affairs, who taught an undergraduate course titled "Islam, the Middle East, and Peace." The provost had given Malachi remote access to Washington Colonial's library, and he opened Bellini's research papers and ran keyword searches for "Qatar," "Sam Baker," and "Samir Muhammad al-Bakri." The search returned zero results.

That would have been too easy.

After more than six hours of reading, Malachi understood Professor Bellini, whose politics had been very left wing and who had written and spoken about equality, social justice, and the evils of capitalism. In several articles, Bellini had justified Palestinian violence against Israelis, because of economic hardships in the region, and Malachi wondered what he would have thought about a financier like Baker, whose net worth exceeded one hundred million dollars. They were on opposite sides—the Marxist versus the entrepreneur.

Bellini had also written about bias against Muslims in America, and had hosted Amir al-Kadi, the president of the American Islamic Shura, to speak at Washington Colonial about the rise of religious bigotry. Al-Kadi was one of the most outspoken proponents of the al-Azhar Islamic Cultural Center and had appeared with Baker at the groundbreaking ceremony. Baker and Bellini were both vocal supporters of Islamic causes, so it was possible religious hatred had motivated the killer.

Malachi made a note to research threats against Muslims in the DC metropolitan area and returned to his Google search. On page eleven, he found an article praising Professor Bellini for his humanitarian efforts to support Muslim groups around the world. Baker had been involved with international groups too, including the Council for American-Muslim Peace.

Malachi clicked back to the search results. The summary text for the next website listed Bellini's name along with a dozen other professors. He opened the link and read an article by Dr. Zahra Mansour, a fellow at the Middle East Policy Institute.

Where had he seen that name before?

Malachi spun away from his desk and hefted the Baker Murder Book out of a drawer. The Murder Book was a daily log of their investigative activities, interviews, evidence, and notes. He flipped through the pages to the second day of their investigation and ran his finger through the notes he had taken when he researched Baker.

There it was—an online article listing Samir al-Bakri as a Muslim Brotherhood financier, by Dr. Zahra Mansour.

Malachi sipped his coffee, now room temperature, and reread the op-ed. Dr. Mansour had researched open-source articles and discovered

Baker had financed several mosques and Muslim advocacy groups—all connected to Muslim Brotherhood front groups. Using fake Facebook and Twitter accounts, Dr. Mansour had cyber-stalked Baker on social media and memorialized his statements supporting fundamental Islam.

Malachi felt a pang of embarrassment. Dr. Mansour had gone deeper than he had in his own investigation of Baker, and she had found connections—things he had failed to uncover.

In her article, Dr. Mansour said the Muslim Brotherhood founded almost every Sunni Islamic terrorist group in the world. Malachi had heard of the Brotherhood and knew they had been Egypt's ruling party, but he thought they represented moderate Islam. He made a note to research them more.

He printed the article and re-opened Dr. Mansour's piece about Professor Bellini. She had identified Bellini as one of many professors, from universities around the country, who shilled for Islamists. Dr. Mansour claimed Bellini spread propaganda by characterizing the Brotherhood as a moderate Islamic group. She said Bellini had advised US President William Follet to engage the Brotherhood in relations with Muslim communities both at home and abroad. Dr. Mansour called the Muslim Brotherhood a terrorist group which was attempting to infiltrate and subvert Western civilization.

Accusations linking both victims to an alleged terrorist group made Malachi rethink his theory.

Were Baker and Bellini killed by Islamic terrorists for not doing their bidding or because they knew too much? Had an Israeli assassin murdered them? Was the CIA involved? Maybe it was a red herring, but death and terrorism went hand in glove. At the bottom of the article, the author's biography stated Zahra Mansour received her doctorate in Middle East Studies from Cairo International University in Egypt and was now a senior fellow with the Middle East Policy Institute, in Washington, DC. She was also the author of several books on Islamic terrorism.

Malachi Googled the Middle East Policy Institute, a small think tank that published academic work from Middle Eastern scholars. The institute had advised several presidential administrations on national security issues and had helped craft foreign policy. The institute was located on D Street NW, a few blocks from the Capitol. Their website listed Dr. Mansour's email address, so he sent her an email and asked if she would answer some questions about her articles.

Malachi tapped the desk wondering what his next step should be.

A response to his email popped up on his screen and he opened it.

Detective Wolf, thank you for your email. I'd be happy to speak with you about the Brotherhood. How about meeting for coffee tomorrow morning? - Dr. Mansour.

Malachi sent her a meeting time and place. He decided not to mention the interview to Jones or anyone else until he had something tangible. Floating a conspiracy theory would tarnish his credibility, and besides, what harm could come from a meeting?

CHAPTER SEVENTEEN

Malachi's blood pressure rose as he battled Washington's traffic in Penn Quarter, a neighborhood sandwiched between the Capitol and White House. He pulled to the curb in a no-parking zone across from the National Archives on Seventh Street NW and threw his police placard and blue light on the dashboard. Being a cop carried some perks.

He entered Starbucks, and it took a few seconds for his eyes to adjust to the dark. When they did, he focused on a stunning woman standing before him. She appeared to be in her early thirties and wore a stylish skirt and a low-cut silk blouse. She had shoulder-length golden hair—more auburn than blond—and full red lips, which glistened like a candy apple. The woman took his breath away.

She noticed the badge on his belt. "Detective Wolf?"

"Dr. Mansour?"

She nodded and smiled.

He had expected a graying academic in flat shoes and horn-rimmed glasses. He shook her hand, and excitement rippled through his chest.

"Coffee?" he asked.

"Please."

They purchased venti dark-roast coffees and searched for a place to sit in the crowded shop.

"Let's go across the street to the Navy Memorial," Malachi said. "We can walk and talk."

Her chocolate-brown eyes exuded warmth, the opposite of Malachi's mother's cold, slate-blue eyes. Blue like ice.

"Do you usually interview people at tourist attractions?" she asked.

"Blending into crowds is less conspicuous than hiding in a corner somewhere. People are drawn to the attraction, not to the tourists, and it's difficult for someone to eavesdrop if we're moving around a noisy area. But to be frank, it makes my days more interesting."

"*Yalla.*"

"Excuse me?"

"Sorry, force of habit. *Yalla* means 'let's go' in Arabic."

"Okay, *yalla,*" Malachi said, and smiled.

They crossed Seventh Street NW to the Navy Memorial on Pennsylvania Avenue. Roman columns on the Residences at Market Square bracketed the north side of the memorial. Fountains rimmed the site, with brass reliefs and famous naval quotations carved into them, and a world map had been etched into the stone floor. A life-sized statue of a lone sailor in a pea coat stood watch beneath a flagpole designed to look like a ship's mast.

A dozen people walked through the memorial, but when Zahra captured Malachi with her deep brown eyes, they became the only two people in the world. He prided himself in his ability to talk to people—to persuade, entrap, motivate—but with her, his mouth parched. She was stunning.

"Sorry for the cryptic email," Malachi said. "I prefer to talk face-to-face."

"How can I help?" She maintained eye contact and seemed to absorb every sound and gesture. Most academics Malachi knew lacked social skills, but she radiated charisma and possessed emotional IQ.

"I'm investigating two homicides, and you've written about both victims."

Her eyes widened. "Oh, my."

"I'm looking for connections between my victims, and you wrote about their affiliation with the Muslim Brotherhood."

"I'm intrigued, Detective."

"Please, call me Mac."

"Mac? What's that short for?"

"Malachi, but no one calls me that anymore. It's too old and foreign."

Zahra flashed a beguiling smile. "What a shame. Malachi is beautiful, so antiquated and full of history. May I use it?"

He could not resist that look. "If you like."

They strolled around the perimeter of the memorial among the tourists, and Malachi caught snippets of conversations about their work, their lives, their opinions—all jumbled together into background static. No one could hear him, but he lowered his voice anyway. Homicide cases were sensitive, and the topic required a respectful tone, an acknowledgement that lives had ended unnaturally.

"Okay, Malachi, tell me. Who was murdered?"

"Samir Mohamed al-Bakri, also known as Sam Baker, and Professor Riccardo Bellini."

"Oh, dear. When?"

"Baker last week and Bellini three days ago," Malachi said. "I brought your articles with me if you'd like to see them."

"Samir al-Bakri is a Qatari financier who funneled Saudi money to the Brotherhood in America. Or *was* a financier, I should say. Professor Bellini was a Brotherhood apologist who gave credibility to their disinformation. I can't prove they bribed him, but whenever an academic is knowledgeable about Islam and repeats the Brotherhood's lies, they have to know what they're doing. The Brotherhood tried to bribe me after I immigrated to the US."

"You think they bought him?"

"Either an overt bribe from the Muslim Brotherhood or indirect payment through grants, a teaching position, or other career advancement proffered by proxies. Professor Bellini taught at Washington Colonial, and Saudi Arabia contributes millions of dollars to that university. Don't you think that influences Colonial's curriculum and whom they hire? Saudi Arabia also invests millions in well-known think tanks, like the Brookings Institution, organizations that advise our government on foreign policy."

She knew her stuff.

"That's why I'm talking to you. I've followed terrorism, but my expertise is crime, not politics. I thought the Muslim Brotherhood was a moderate group. Didn't President Follet support them when they took power in Egypt?"

"William Follet's regime backed the Brotherhood despite their stated plan to commit a genocide against Coptic Christians in Egypt. The Brotherhood has been infiltrating American institutions for decades and Follet's policies are proof that the Brotherhood's propaganda has taken hold."

Malachi sipped his coffee and examined a relief of Captain John Paul Jones onboard a ship during naval combat. It read, ". . . In Harm's Way."

A homeless man approached them, and Malachi canted his body to monitor him. Food stuck to the man's scraggly beard and his clothes looked soiled.

"Support the homeless for one dollar," the man said and held out his hand. He phrased it like he was collecting donations for all the city's poor and not just for himself.

Malachi shook his head, and the man wandered off, but Malachi watched him as he spoke.

"You're saying the Brotherhood used disinformation to convince our government they're a force for moderation in Islam, but in reality, they aren't?"

"Hassan al-Bana formed the Muslim Brotherhood as a Sunni Islamic terrorist organization in 1928, and it has been a terror group ever since. The Brotherhood formed al-Qaeda, Hamas, and almost every other jihadi terrorist group. For decades the Brotherhood has used its Secret Apparatus to wage jihad, while publicly calling for peaceful coexistence when speaking to westerner audiences."

"And the US government has fallen for it?"

"Almost entirely. The facts are common knowledge across the Middle East, but not in the West. The Muslim Brotherhood's goal is to destroy Western civilization and create an Islamic caliphate, a global government ruled by Sharia law."

Was that hyperbole?

"It's hard to believe," Malachi said.

"In 1991, the FBI conducted a search warrant at the residence of Ismael Elbarasse, the founder of the Dar al-Hijrah mosque, in Virginia. They seized eighty boxes of documents, including 'An Explanatory Memorandum,' which detailed the Muslim Brotherhood's strategy in

North America. The memo explicitly stated their goal of destroying the West through a process of settlement."

"How would they do that?"

"The memo outlined the Brotherhood's use of front groups, like The Muslim Students Association, the Islamic Circle of North America, and the Islamic Medical Association. In the Middle East, they engage in outright warfare, and they attack Europe through immigration and Islamic exclusionary zones, but those tactics are too extreme for the US, so they plan to destroy America through infiltration."

"If that's true, it's terrifying," Malachi said.

"It's true, and it has worked. The next step will implement Sharia compliance followed by general capitulation to Sharia law. That's their plan."

"Unbelievable."

"I know it sounds crazy. The Brotherhood openly talks about it in the Middle East, but the statements they put out in English say the opposite. Everything I'm telling you is corroborated by evidence. I'm sure you've heard about the Homeland Security whistleblower who alerted Congress that our counterterrorism efforts have been undermined by Islamist policies."

Malachi contemplated what she had said. Dr. Mansour was a respected, albeit controversial academic, and if what she claimed was verifiable, he would corroborate it.

Zahra's hips swayed when she walked, and his eyes drifted to her body. She stopped in front of a bronze relief of The Great White Fleet from 1907. It read, "Speak Softly and Carry a Big Stick."

"Would the Brotherhood kill Professor Bellini or al-Bakri?" Malachi asked.

"I have no earthly idea."

"How about a rival terrorist group or a splinter group?"

"The Muslim Brotherhood has no rival groups. They control or influence all of them."

"Would a counterterrorism agency have any reason to suspect my victims worked with the Brotherhood?"

"I'd like to think so, but I doubt it. The truth about the Brotherhood is not widely known in the US, and our intelligence services seem blissfully ignorant about jihadist infiltration."

"What about the Israelis?" Malachi asked.

"Certainly, but even people within the Israeli government have succumbed to Brotherhood disinformation."

If a terrorist organization wearing sheep's clothing had infiltrated the US, why had Malachi not heard about it? Instead, the media bombarded the public with stories about bigotry against Muslims. Was the media complicit in the Brotherhood's plan or were they ignorant?

"Let me ask you this. Is it possible the Brotherhood is just trying to counter Islamophobia?"

Zahra stopped and gave him a thin smile. She took a deep breath before she answered. "There's some bigotry against Muslims in America. Religious bigotry is nothing new—look at how Christians, Jews, and other minorities are persecuted across the Middle East—but the problem is not as big as they've led you to believe. Bigots commit three times as many hate crimes against Jews than against Muslims in the US. The FBI compiles crime statistics, so you can verify that. While the media has focused on Islamophobia, anti-Semitism has become culturally acceptable."

"I'm Jewish, and I didn't know the rates of discrimination were higher for Jews."

"Bigotry against Muslims is evil, but the Brotherhood invented the term 'Islamophobia' to play into Americans distaste for racism and bigotry. They use it to stifle debate. Point out fundamental Islam is antithetical to liberalism, and you're labeled a bigot. Discuss misogyny in the Middle East, and you're culturally insensitive. Talk about how Muslim countries treat religious minorities and you're a racist. That's how the Brotherhood preempts criticism of their fundamentalist, theocratic, political ideology. It's how they've kept their plan to destroy the West a secret."

"I had no idea."

They walked through the memorial, and the sun warmed Malachi's face. He noticed several male tourists watching Zahra. A woman smacked her husband, and the man blushed.

"Do you know the number one target of Islamic terrorism worldwide?" Zahra asked.

Malachi raised his eyebrows. He was out of his depth and opening his mouth would only prove it. "Tell me."

"Islamic terrorists target Muslims more than any other group. Speaking out against fundamentalism, Sharia law, and terrorism is not anti-Muslim. There are millions of moderate, peace-loving Muslims around the world and they need a voice. The Brotherhood does not speak for them. I'm a Muslim, Malachi, and they don't speak for me."

"That's not the narrative I've heard. I've had a personal interest in Islamic terrorism for some time, but I'm uninformed about the Brotherhood."

"Don't worry, most people have never heard what I'm telling you. I've been fighting for years to make people understand they're the victims of propaganda and disinformation. The facts are there for any rational, objective person to find, but changing people's epistemology is almost impossible."

She stopped to read a relief for Naval Special Warfare. It depicted US Navy Seals climbing out of the water onto a beach and read, "Failure is not an option."

The homeless guy approached them again. "Buy me a cup of coffee."

"Keep moving," Malachi said, and pulled his jacket open to expose his badge.

The man's eyes grew large, and he scurried away. He shot Malachi a murderous look from across the memorial.

"I had to leave Egypt because of threats I received from the Brotherhood," she said. "And other academics have slandered me since I arrived here. My life and career are at stake. Sometimes I wonder if reason is dead."

Malachi counted himself among those who had never heard about the Brotherhood's infiltration, and a pang of guilt shot through him.

"I need to understand this better to determine if it's relevant to my murders."

"I can't imagine how the Brotherhood would be involved in your investigations, but if they are, you need to educate yourself. They're dangerous. Visit my website and start with my articles. You can find

Amazon links to my books too, but don't take my word for it. Follow the footnotes and read the source material yourself. Never trust anyone's analysis."

"I'll do that. It seems I have a lot of catching up to do, Dr. Mansour."

She smiled, and a dimple formed on her cheek. Her eyes took on a sleepy, sensual quality. "Please, call me Zahra."

God, she was sexy.

"Thank you, Zahra."

Malachi took her business card, said goodbye, and watched her walk away.

It could be a bottomless rabbit hole, but radical Islam was the only connection between his victims, and he needed to see where it led. Besides, it meant he would have to speak to Zahra again.

CHAPTER EIGHTEEN

Austin drew hateful stares as he maneuvered through the crowd of women toward the stage. He wore a black tee shirt and jeans, innocuous attire, but masculine. The Women's Empowerment Rally had drawn close to ten thousand people—mostly female and mostly outraged.

Queen Latifah's voice blared out of massive speakers as they played her song, "U.N.I.T.Y." Austin stopped thirty feet from the stage. He wanted to see Linda Reynolds up close and look into her eyes.

The music lowered, and the event organizer returned to the stage.

"We're lucky to have her, so put your hands together and give a warm DC welcome to your champion and mine . . . Linda Reynolds."

The crowd roared and the woman beside Austin snapped her fingers in approval. Linda Reynolds strutted across the stage with a hijab draped over her head. She was not Muslim but had claimed she wore the headscarf as a sign of solidarity with women everywhere, a symbolic act of diversity and feminism. She had decried those who condemned the hijab as bigots, saying they did not understand it was a woman's choice, a sign of independence, a cultural celebration.

"Thank you all for coming out to support women's rights," Reynolds said, raising a clenched fist over her head.

The crowd cheered. A young white woman beside Austin caught his eye and sneered. He turned his attention to the stage, where Reynolds gripped the podium with both hands.

"I'm honored to look out on a sea of black, brown, and white faces all here to fight patriarchy. Men have repressed women since the beginning of time, but we're here today to stand together and say 'enough.'"

Austin looked at waves of dyed-pink hair, slogan-covered tee shirts, and unbridled anger. Did they understand the levels freedom and success women enjoyed in the United States, compared to the rest of the world or to any other time in history?

"Western civilization is racist and oppressive," Reynolds continued. "It's intolerant, and we have to tear it down."

The crowd applauded, and someone blew an air horn.

"For decades, Republicans in Congress and the White House have used the lies of individualism, capitalism, and nationalism to keep women down, keep white faces in power, suppress minorities . . ."

Austin's eyes wandered over the crowd and he registered more glares directed at him, but he no longer cared. The Oxycontin had begun to work its magic. He only had a few pills left, and he would have to visit another clinic soon. His foot still ached but had mostly healed, and he would have to pretend to limp to get a prescription. He had done his research and found two pharmacies suspected of being pill mills. He would go before DEA closed them.

"Capitalism is the root of all evil. It's a corrupt system that keeps people in poverty and allows the rich to get richer. And what does capitalism do for women? Women make eighty cents for every dollar a man earns. And who suffers the most? Ethnic minorities, religious minorities, women of color . . ."

Here it comes.

Austin floated on a bed of warm air. He could not feel his feet touching the ground. One strong breeze and he would sail up and over the stage, fly away on the wind. He would have to reduce his dose to function at work and start wearing sunglasses to hide his constricted pupils.

Austin watched Reynolds spout third-wave feminism, communism, and moral relativism. He tolerated most of it, but he knew what was coming next. Her support of Islamism was something he could not forgive.

On stage, Reynolds built to a crescendo. "I may not practice Islam, but I wear this hijab because bigots and white supremacists have targeted

Muslims across our country. Today, I am Muslim. You are Muslim. We are all Muslims."

The crowd cheered and Austin shook his head. Had they forgotten how women were treated in countries where Islam had been codified into law? Did they understand religious zealotry? Austin knew it too well. Religion claimed to instill moral codes, but people on the fringes used it to justify violence. He closed his eyes and heard his mother's screams.

Austin had grown up in the hamlet of Hemlock, in New York's Finger Lakes Region, surrounded by five hundred poor, uneducated, white residents. The region had become home to artists, hipsters, and atheists, but that was not the world Austin remembered. His life had been one of poverty and religious intolerance. His parents, Raymond and Margaret, had been Pentecostal Evangelicals, and Margaret—who claimed she had spoken in tongues as a child—held onto her religion like a safety blanket. Faith became the armature on which Austin built his life, but organized religion could also signify tyranny, obedience, and violence. A vengeful God punished those who could not measure up. "Weakness is a sin before God," his father would say after a night of trying to drink away his disappointment, frustration, and hatred. The beatings never seemed to end. Austin saw his father's face in his dreams. He could see him now.

The crowd cheered and brought Austin back to the present.

"Today we have members of the Council on American-Islamic Relations among us," Reynolds said. "Our criminal justice system has vilified CAIR, and the United Arab Emirates has designated them as a terrorist organization, but we will not let bigotry stop us. We also have the representatives from the American Islamic Shura and the Council of American-Muslim Peace with us. Stand with our oppressed brothers and sisters."

Austin weaved his way through the crowd toward Constitution Avenue. He drew nasty stares, and a young girl wearing a pink hat gave him the finger.

"Muslims in America have suffered under white male bigotry. The United States was founded in slavery and is rooted in genocide and oppression. It is the ultimate oppressor. Intersectionality urges all of us—gays, women, blacks, Muslims—to join forces against our common enemy. Rally together to combat white oppression, misogyny, and persecution in every form. Destroy the wickedness of the West."

The crowd cheered and hooted.

"Female empowerment!" Reynolds yelled. "Islam is peace! Unite against patriarchy! Down with Western racism! Down with capitalism! End toxic masculinity! Sisters, who is with me?"

The music resumed and Queen Latifah's voice echoed across the Mall again.

Austin stopped at the curb and looked back. "Mortify therefore your members which are upon the earth; fornication, uncleanness, inordinate affection, evil concupiscence, and covetousness, which is idolatry."

He had his next target.

CHAPTER NINETEEN

Dylan Miller was a bad person.

At nine o'clock at night, Malachi sat on his balcony with his MacBook Air in his lap, taking advantage of the mild weather before the worst of the summer's deep humidity hit. He sipped an Amstel Light and listened to the gentle clanging of halyards against sailboat masts in the Washington Marina. It sounded like a nautical symphony.

Baker had been murdered two weeks before, and the case grew cold. They needed to find a suspect soon. Miller had a criminal record and had served in the military, so he was no stranger to violence. Malachi read everything he could find about Miller and his merry band of racists—the New National Order—an organization built on white supremacy.

The group had less than one hundred members, which made it a mid-sized hate group. It had surprised Malachi to find how few of the 330 million people in the US identified as racists. The two-time election of a black president said volumes about how far the country had come since the days of slavery and Jim Crow. Fewer than one thousand hate groups operated in the United States, according to the Southern Poverty Law Center's website, and of those, seventy-two were Ku Klux Klan and one hundred were white nationalist groups. Twenty-one of those clustered around Washington, DC.

Miller founded the New National Order in December 2001, three months after al-Qaeda's attack on the United States. He listed his headquarters on South West Street, in Alexandria, Virginia, but when Malachi ran the address, it came back to a United Parcel Service store.

That meant Miller used a mailbox and probably ran the organization out of his house. Despite the group's amateurish nature, its membership included some violent members, making it possible that Miller or one of his minions had killed Baker.

The group's website read like a billboard for ignorance and intolerance. It proclaimed the superiority of the white race and called for segregation and the removal of "mud people" from the country. The site linked to other hate groups and reposted articles, which used pseudo-science to claim the superiority of Caucasians. The website alone proved the happenstance of race did not correlate with intelligence.

Malachi scrolled through the articles reading vapid arguments and a sense of disquiet settled into his bones. Thankfully, the New National Order was an anachronism and far removed from the opinions of mainstream America. Dylan Miller and his ilk were losers, no longer relevant in any serious way, but despite their lack of political power, they remained capable of violence.

Malachi read a post about the group's rally against the al-Azhar Islamic Cultural Center. It characterized the event as a fight against savagery and anti-Christian heresy. What did Miller know about Christianity? A photograph of Miller showed him behind a podium in front of a small crowd, all white, male, and young. Confederate flags and shaved heads speckled the crowd. Miller looked tall and thick, with pale skin, and brown hair combed over in Hitlerian style.

What an asshole.

Thunder rumbled in the distance. Malachi cooled himself with the crisp lager and stared out at the marina. Jones would pick him up at five o'clock in the morning to interview Miller. They had nothing tying Miller to either homicide, but his violent hate speech and his protest of North Star made him a person of interest.

Beyond the boats, the still water turned deep blue under a darkening metallic sky. Twilight was a magical time, when the moon was in full view, yet there was still light enough to see. The water smelled different when the air cooled in the evening, full of promise and adventure. Malachi remembered the excitement of childhood vacations on Cape Cod, running through the sand, camping on the beach, the hope of a first kiss.

He could smell the burning wood, the salty air. Memories were strange like that. Was he grasping at the past to find his identity?

He walked inside and paced across the living room in a dreamy state. He paused in front of his bookcase and looked at a first edition of Lord Byron's *She Walks in Beauty*. It was Alison's favorite poem, and he had recited it to her at their wedding. He still remembered the first stanza.

She walks in beauty, like the night
Of cloudless climes and starry skies;
And all that's best of dark and bright
Meet in her aspect and eyes:
Thus mellowed to that tender light
Which heaven to gaudy day denies.

Malachi had searched for months for a first edition of the poem and finally found one at a used bookseller in London. It had arrived three days before their third anniversary—the perfect gesture to show Alison how much he loved her. He had hidden the book in his office to surprise her, but he had ended up being the one surprised. He had returned home and discovered her note, which said their marriage was over and she had taken the children. That had been the worst day of his life, after his father's murder.

He pulled the book off the shelf and held it. The gift never given, a reminder of loss, a symbol of unreturned love. He should have sold it years ago, but if he did, the divorce would become real.

He returned the book to the shelf and went to bed.

Malachi closed his eyes and tried to fall asleep. In six hours, he would meet Dylan Miller, a man infected with hatred and racism. But was he capable of murder?

CHAPTER TWENTY

Malachi and Jones drove through Woodbridge, Virginia, an economically depressed community on the Potomac, twenty miles south of DC. Once a sleepy, wooded suburb of Washington, Woodbridge now had a crime rate almost fifty percent higher than the city. Malachi gazed out the car window at strip malls and urban blight, and could almost feel the hopelessness, the struggle, the underlying threat of violence.

They drove east on the Prince William Parkway and entered a wooded neighborhood dotted with apartment buildings, houses in disrepair, and twenty-year-old cars with faded paint. Malachi could estimate crime rates by the condition of parked cars because low income and crime were heavily correlated.

The population of Woodbridge was now forty-five percent non-white. Ironically, Dylan Miller, a white supremacist, lived in a neighborhood where he would soon be a minority. Malachi wondered if the changing demographics had influenced his racism or if rising crime rates had confirmed his ugly, tribalistic beliefs. Racism had deep roots in Virginia.

Two miles from Occoquan Bay, Jones pulled over on Fischer Avenue and parked. They exited the car and Jones limped to the sidewalk. He had been hobbling more in recent weeks. He was getting older and the thought of his impending retirement saddened Malachi.

"Second house on the right," Jones said.

Jones spoke without looking or gesturing, which would forecast their intentions. Malachi appreciated the little things Jones did—tradecraft that came from a career spent perfecting his profession. He was old but sharp as ever.

"How do you want to play it?" Malachi asked.

"Let's knock and see what happens. He a scrub. Long rap sheet, but nothing serious, and he's never been popped with a weapon."

"I'm sure he'll be happy to see us."

"He gonna love me," Jones said.

They walked toward the house and the heat from the concrete radiated up through Malachi's shoes. Jones hiked up his pants and adjusted the holster on his belt without removing his suit jacket. Malachi had his Glock snapped into a black leather holster on his hip and concealed under his jacket.

A white and black duo wearing jackets and ties in eighty-degree weather advertised them as cops, but it did not matter. This would be a direct interview, where they identified themselves and asked Miller to explain his whereabouts during Baker's and Bellini's murders.

Miller was only a person of interest and not a suspect, and since he would not be in custody, they did not have to read him the Miranda warning. Malachi assumed a white supremacist would not cooperate, but Miller could say something to incriminate himself. This would be their chance to feel him out, a check-the-box interview.

Weeds sprang through cracks in the sidewalk, and patches of uncut grass, brown and dying, covered the sloping front yard. The small, two-story house had been constructed with brick and faded-yellow vinyl siding. A dozen roof shingles were missing, and the rest appeared to be waiting for the next big wind to make their escape.

Malachi's watch struck six o'clock. They annoyed people when they arrived this early, but Malachi had not determined if Miller held a steady job, and they needed to catch him before he left. Many white supremacists worked on the fringes of society, struggling to turn their human capital into income, and Miller likely worked part-time in retail or as a laborer. Confronting Miller at this earlier hour would give them the advantage of surprise.

They trudged across the lawn to the stoop. Jones pulled open a rusted screen door and knocked. They stood on either side of the door, an old police tactic designed to avoid bullets fired through the threshold. No one had shot through a door at Malachi yet, but he acted out of muscle memory inculcated through years of training and experience.

Jones banged again, harder, louder. Malachi leaned off the stoop and peeked through a window.

No sign of movement behind the closed blinds.

Jones knocked a third time, and footsteps stomped down the stairs.

"Goddammit, I'm coming," a muffled voice shouted from inside.

Footfalls stopped behind the door, and Jones held his badge in front of the peephole.

Dylan Miller swung the door open. He wore a bathrobe, which may have been white once, but was not anymore and never would be again. He was about six-four and muscular—not gym muscles but the kind earned through hard physical labor— and his brown hair looked tousled, as if he had been asleep.

"Good morning Mr. Miller," Malachi said. "Detectives Jones and Wolf, MPD Homicide. May we come in and speak with you?"

Jones had decided Malachi should take the lead during the interview, since Miller was unlikely to cooperate with a black detective. If Miller gave them a hard time, Jones could use Miller's hatred against him like a cudgel. Miller would not enjoy having a black officer confront him.

"It's six o'clock in the fucking morning," Miller said.

"Yes sir," Malachi said. "We wanted to catch you before you left for work."

"Work? If y'all knew anything, you'd know I work nights."

"Doing what?"

"I only been asleep for an hour."

"This will only take a minute."

"Him too?" Miller said and nodded at Jones. It had not taken long for his racism to appear.

What a prick.

"Yes sir," Malachi said.

"What's going on?" Miller asked. "Y'all always come up in here blaming me for shit I didn't do."

"We're not here to accuse you of anything," Malachi said. "We're investigating a homicide, and we think you can help."

"I didn't do anything."

"Why don't you invite us inside before your neighbors get the wrong idea?"

Miller glanced up and down the sidewalk and wrinkled his forehead. "Make it fast. I've got to hit the sack."

They followed Miller into the living room, where a worn, olive-green couch lay opposite a flat-screen television, bracketed by a yellow bean bag chair and a faux-leather recliner. Miller flopped into his recliner and extended the footrest. His teeth looked brown and rotted, and he scratched his arm over his bathrobe—both signs of addiction. Opioids, like Fentanyl and Oxycodone, had ravished poor communities in Virginia. So had methamphetamine. What had Miller used to escape his bleak reality?

Malachi sat on the couch and Jones stood with his back to the wall, facing the stairwell. Malachi nodded at Jones to acknowledge Jones would watch his back while he spoke to Miller. Cops communicated in an unspoken language.

"How are you employed, Mr. Miller?" Malachi asked.

"Security. I manage twelve guards down at Willis Construction."

"How long have you worked there?"

"No one got killed at my job."

"The homicide occurred in the District of Columbia, and you didn't answer my question. How long have you been at Willis?"

"Three years. I didn't do shit in the city. I don't go there. It's too dark for me."

"Too dark?" Malachi asked.

"The nig—" He paused and turned to Jones. "No offense, but it's too dangerous for a guy like me."

Jones smirked. He had lived in the District during the riots in the seventies, and hearing racist comments was probably not new for him, but how long it had been since he had heard that kind of language come out of a white person's mouth? Miller believed the worth of a man resided in his race and not in his individual characteristics. Malachi got to the point to spare Jones too much of this.

"Can you tell us where you were on May 19, around midnight?"

"What day was that?"

"Two Saturdays ago."

"Who got killed?"

"Does that change where you were that night?"

"I'm off on Saturdays. I was here watching television."

Miller seemed a little foggy from lack of sleep and the early hour, but his eyes looked sharp and cunning showed behind them.

Baker's and Bellini's murders seemed well planned—elegant in their execution and simplicity—and Miller seemed capable of conceptualizing and carrying them out or instructing one of his brown shirts to do it. Hate groups attracted violent and dangerous people.

"Was anyone here with you?" Malachi asked.

"I work nights, so when I'm off, I can't sleep. I sat right here watching television. By myself."

"What were you watching?"

"I told you, the television."

"Which program?"

Miller stood up and gave Malachi a defiant look. "None of your Goddamned business."

Jones took a step toward him, and fear flashed in Miller's eyes. Miller routinely spewed racial hatred and had called blacks and Hispanics "dirt people," but now that he was face-to-face with a formidable black man, he seemed cowed. Bullies backed down when faced with strength and that was all these supremacists were, big bullies who believed their random race assignment made them special.

"Did you know Sam Baker?" Malachi asked, lowering his voice to calm Miller.

"No."

"What about Professor Riccardo Bellini?"

"No."

"Where were you during the morning hours, the day before yesterday?"

"Home sick."

"Can anyone confirm that?"

"I called in. Ask my boss."

"Are you familiar with Baker's business, North Star Development?"

Miller's face reddened. "I know those motherfuckers. Them Arabs want to put a mosque here. They're trying to push good Christian people out, but I did something about it. They done messed with the wrong people."

His anger sizzled below the surface, a symptom of his cheerless existence, and hearing the name North Star had triggered it. Miller probably considered Muslims more brown faces standing between him and his happiness.

"What did you do about it?"

"I got the boys together and we let them Arabs know they ain't welcome in Virginia."

"But that didn't stop them, did it? The mosque is under construction."

Miller looked like he was ready to explode. "At least we did something. No one else did shit while them sand niggers invaded our country. What did you do? Nothing. But we done it."

"Tell me how you stopped Baker," Malachi said, letting Miller's rage fill the room.

"I told you. I didn't kill nobody." The pitch of his voice rose as his stress tightened his vocal cords. People expressed emotions more through tone and body language than with words. Miller could have been grunting and gesturing and his defiance would have been just as obvious.

"But you wanted him dead and now he is."

"Fuck him and fuck you. I didn't kill that A-rab."

Miller was angry, but his tone sounded pleading, desperate, like a teenager accused of denting the family car. He stood with his hands on his hips, on the verge of being irrational. A twig about to snap.

A white flag with a black cross hung on the living room wall behind Miller. It depicted the ancient Celtic Cross, but a circle connected the four quadrants, turning it into a Sun Cross, the symbol of white supremacy. During his research Malachi had seen it used by the Ku Klux Klan, Neo-Nazis, and other white supremacist groups. Rallying around symbols was tribalism, but not inherently bad behavior. Fealty to a symbol representing a nation, cause, or religion was only wrong if the core ideology was evil, and in this case, white supremacy was a nasty belief system.

"You organized a rally to prevent Baker's company from building a mosque. You blogged about stopping North Star Development, and you asked your supporters to fight against a Muslim invasion. Now, Baker is dead, and you expect us to believe you had nothing to do with it?"

"I never met the man."

"How about Samir al-Bakri?"

"Sounds like another fucking towel head to me."

"Do you recognize the name?"

No answer. Miller paced back and forth with his hands out in front of him, fists balled. His anger had awakened him, and he seemed more lucid.

"If you didn't kill him, tell us who did."

"I'm done talking to you. I want you out of my house."

Decision time.

Malachi wanted to slam Miller to the floor, handcuff him, and throw him in a cell, but he needed evidence. They had nothing on Miller, other than his protest of North Star. His speeches had advocated resistance to Muslim immigration and the mosque construction, and he had been open about his racism, but he had never called for violence, so his speech remained legal and protected.

Malachi's jaw ached from clenching.

By law, they could hold Miller for twenty-four hours for questioning before charging him or even keep him for seventy-two hours if they could show proof of guilt to a judge. Failing to detain him would allow Miller the chance to flee but holding him without evidence was unlikely to illicit either a confession or cooperation. Miller had not asked for a lawyer yet, but if they arrested him, he would probably lawyer up.

Malachi eyed Jones who shrugged almost imperceptibly. This was Malachi's call.

"Okay, Mr. Miller," Malachi said. "We'll leave, but I want you to call if you think of anything that could help us."

Miller vibrated with rage.

If his performance was intended to make them leave, Malachi should have seen relief when he agreed to go, but Miller remained petulant. Malachi extended a business card and Miller stared at it.

"If you weren't involved with this and you're innocent, why won't you help us?" Malachi asked.

Miller snatched the card out of his hand. "Po-lice always hassling me, always accusing me of shit."

Malachi wanted to punch Miller into unconsciousness. The beast stirred inside him. He glared at Miller then followed Jones outside to the car.

"What do you think?" Malachi asked.

"I fix'n to open a can of whoop ass on that boy," Jones said.

"I know. He's disgusting, but he seemed truthful."

"Be careful. I've had people murder their own children and lie to my face. Sociopaths don't react like we do."

"Think Miller is our guy?"

"He's evil and he wouldn't hesitate to pop a cap in me. He thinks he's fighting a war, and if brown people ain't human, then killing them is moral. Miller and his people are dangerous."

"That's a deep insight," Malachi said.

"It doesn't mean he did our victims. Let's see if we can dig up evidence to link that punk-ass to them. We do that, we can slap bracelets on him."

"I wouldn't mind locking up that *bama*," Malachi said.

"Now, you're talking like a Washingtonian."

Miller was an asshole, but was he their killer? Had they made a mistake by not bringing him in for questioning? If Miller fled, Malachi may never find him again, but interviews were more art than science, and he did not believe Miller would give them what they needed. They would have to gather more evidence and try again.

Malachi hungered to solve the case. Maybe he needed to find justice for his father, or maybe he had to prove his worthiness for this job. Whatever drove him, Baker had powerful friends and a white supremacist suspect made for a volatile investigation. Malachi would catch Baker's killer, but he had to be careful not to let his career become a casualty.

Tick-tock.

CHAPTER TWENTY-ONE

Austin's heart jumped when Linda Reynolds exited the Westin Hotel at M and Twenty-Fourth Streets NW. He had located her hotel with a simple pretext call to the administrative offices of the Women's Empowerment Rally. She entered a taxi with three other women, and Austin followed them into Georgetown.

The taxi pulled to the curb, and Austin continued past it but watched his rearview mirror. The women exited and walked into La Seine, an elegant French restaurant set in an old brownstone.

The Oxycontin dried his mouth, sucking the liquid out of him like a parasite. He ran his tongue over his lips, floating on a narcotic cloud.

He glanced up and down the street. Heavy pedestrian traffic flowed by, mostly tourists shopping in Georgetown's high-priced stores. Unlike Baker and Bellini, this one would be risky, but Reynolds did not live in Washington, and this might be his only chance.

Austin made a U-turn, drove across Rock Creek, and parked on Twenty-Fifth Street NW in a two-hour spot. More than enough time. He checked his fake beard in the review mirror. The adhesive worked well but left marks on his face. He would have to deal with those later.

He lifted his satchel off the floor and unbuckled it, causing a black aerosol paint can to roll across the bottom. He confirmed Velcro straps secured his Beretta inside and kept its suppressor flush against the hole in the leather. He swallowed his urge to confirm a round was in the chamber and the eight-round magazine was full, having checked twice at home.

Austin exited the car, slung the satchel over his shoulder, and hurried down M Street NW.

He paused outside the windows to La Seine, and spotted Reynolds sitting with her group against the far wall. He grabbed his phone and dialed.

Reynolds looked at her phone and frowned, probably not recognizing the local number. She answered.

"Hello, this is Linda."

Austin needed to place the call for his plan to work but talking to her was unnecessary. He hung up, and a moment later, his phone vibrated— Reynolds calling back. He powered it off and entered the restaurant, careful not to leave fingerprints on the door handle.

The restaurant was all white linen and light oak—elegant but claustrophobic. Low ceilings and cramped rooms were the downside of housing a restaurant in a historic building. Utensils clinked against china plates as a dozen people dined. Austin's fake beard itched, and he forced himself not to scratch while the hostess checked her seating chart and led him to a small table near the windows.

Luring Reynolds outside would be difficult. She did not live in the city, and if he pretended there was a problem at her hotel, her friends may return with her. If he did not see an opportunity to get her alone, he would have to try at her hotel, but he wanted to avoid all the cameras and security if possible. He could travel to Los Angeles and take her at her house, but his plan required him to do it in Georgetown.

Reynolds picked up her purse, excused herself and stood up. Austin pretended to read the menu as she spoke to a waiter who pointed toward the rear of the restaurant. She moved down the long hallway and turned toward the restrooms.

Austin waited for three minutes, then pushed back his chair and followed. He entered the hallway and turned down a second corridor to the restrooms. An exit sign glowed over a metal door at the end of the hall. A red "occupied" sign showed above the handle to the first restroom door and the other room appeared empty. He leaned back into the main hall and confirmed he was alone.

This was dangerous, but worth the risk.

He would have to be silent. And quick. The hallway was cramped, so he unbuckled his satchel and drew his Beretta. He let it hang by his leg, the long suppressor extending beyond his knee.

The water ran in the bathroom.

He peeked into the hall again. Empty. If someone came, he would run for the exit.

The water stopped.

Don't let her scream.

The indicator switched to green and the door opened. Reynolds turned sideways to step around the door and exit the single-occupancy restroom. She saw him and flinched.

"Excuse me," she said and bladed her body to squeeze past him.

"I don't think I will excuse you."

His tone froze her, and she looked up. Her eyes challenged him, as if his very presence bothered her.

Hurry.

Austin raised his Beretta and pressed it against her forehead. She opened her mouth to scream, and he pulled the trigger. The gun bucked once in his hand with a metallic clack.

Her head jerked back, and brain matter splattered the restroom behind her. Her body crumpled onto the tiled floor.

Austin glanced down the empty hall. The distant murmur of voices and clatter of silverware came from the dining room. None of the guests seemed to have heard the shot, but someone would come to the bathroom, eventually.

Time to go.

He stepped into the threshold of the bathroom and took a last look. He flinched when he saw his reflection in the mirror. Even behind his fake beard and glasses, he could see his father's face in his own. The father who had beaten him, told him he was worthless, taught him to impose his will through violence.

He averted his eyes and stared at Reynolds. Her eyes were open, vacant, like windows into an empty room. Her hijab was wet with blood and stuck to a pipe under the sink. Her chest heaved with agonal breaths, the last gasps of a body unaware its brain had lost control. It would be over soon.

He did not worry about God's eternal vengeance. Not this time. This kill weighed less heavily on him than the Professor and far better than Baker. Was he becoming desensitized? Was that good or had something inside him died, something precious and irretrievable?

It did not matter. It had to be done. He had already lost the most important thing in his life—Vanessa. She had been the cornerstone of his life, and now she was gone. He had been adrift without her, but he had found a way forward.

He had anticipated feeling shame after killing a woman, because females were weaker, more empathetic, more nurturing. He remembered his mother's face, her smile, her warm embrace. She had been like that until his father died and something inside her changed. The memory of her brought back the only warmth he had experienced as a child until that too had been violently ripped away. He had thought killing a woman would be hard, but it had not been difficult. Not at all.

Reynolds engendered nothing but disgust in him. She was not his mother. She was the devil. He should run, but instead, he soaked in the image of her on the bathroom floor. Her smug smile had disappeared, replaced by a mask of pain. He had cleansed the earth of her. He warmed and felt something he had not experienced in years.

Happiness.

CHAPTER TWENTY-TWO

"All hands on deck," Collins shouted into the bullpen.

"What's up now?" Jones grumbled.

"Probably Nuse busting our balls," Malachi said.

"Or another student complained," Rodriguez said.

Hill was at the coroner's office and Detectives Johnson and Brown were interviewing students, so Malachi, Jones, and Rodriguez shuffled into the conference room. Collins hurried in behind them.

"Don't get comfortable," Collins said. "D-2 just called in a murder at La Seine on M. That's three murders since the nineteenth. That doesn't happen in Georgetown. We got a thug on tha gank."

"Gank?" Malachi whispered to Jones.

"Predator on the prowl," Jones said with a grin.

"Who has the lead?" Rodriguez asked.

"Jones, you take it, until we see if it's related," Collins said.

"On it, LT," Jones said.

"Wolf, anything linking the first two bodies yet?" Collins asked

"Both Baker and Bellini were associated with the Muslim Brotherhood. I don't know if it's relevant yet, but I'm digging into it."

"What the hell is the Muslim Brotherhood?" Collins asked.

"It's either an advocacy group for moderate Islam or a terrorist organization, depending on whom you ask."

"Figure it out fast. Get to La Seine and tell me what we've got. I need to inform the chief."

．　　．　　．

La Seine, a rustic French restaurant near the corner of M and Twenty-Eighth Street NW, lay in the heart of Georgetown's business district. Malachi entered the dining room behind Jones, and it took a moment for his eyes to adapt to the lighting. A large fireplace dominated the small dining area, and white linen draped over a handful of petite tables set with china and silver. Police tape blocked the hallway leading to the restrooms. A group of waiters and men in chef's uniforms huddled against the far wall, and a dozen patrons sat around a long table in an adjoining private function room. Two of them cried.

District Two Detective Mark Estes walked out of the room and guided Malachi, Jones, and Rodriguez out of earshot of the guests.

"Body is in the women's room," Estes said.

"Talk to me," Jones said.

"White female, forties, single GSW to the head. It's a fucking mess in there."

"Suspects?" Jones asked, without a trace of hope in his voice.

"One person heard the shot but thought someone had dropped a pan in the kitchen. No one saw anything unusual. The victim went to the bathroom and wasn't discovered until her friend checked on her."

"Where's the friend?" Jones asked.

"With the other patrons. The staff said a few diners fled before we arrived, but we held onto everyone else."

"Who was first on the scene?"

"Officer Burgess," Estes said. "He's a veteran. I have him out back securing the alley."

"Thanks, Estes," Jones said. "We got it from here. No one goes in or out until I say so."

"Copy that."

Jones faced them. "Rodriguez, have patrol stop anything suspicious in the area. It's been thirty minutes, but you never know. Then start the sign-in book and get the names of everyone who's been here."

"Will do."

"Wolf, you got the crime scene. Get the evidence techs rolling and see if our suspect left something. I'll jump on the interviews and identify our victim, try to get a suspect description. This place is small. Someone saw the suspect."

Malachi walked down the hall to the rear of the restaurant. Dark wooden beams framed stark white walls with black iron accoutrements, giving the restaurant an eighteenth-century atmosphere. The bathrooms were nestled near the end of a short hallway. The first door stood ajar, and blood pooled against the sill in the threshold.

Malachi donned rubber gloves and pushed the door open a few inches. It bumped against the victim's body. She lay on the floor, with her head canted against the base of the toilet.

The room smelled like iron, and he suppressed a gag. Significant blood spatter covered the mirror over the sink, and flecks of brain matter stuck to it. She must have been standing in the doorway facing out when the bullet or bullets struck her. He checked both sides of the door for a bullet hole, but the wood looked unblemished, meaning the door had been open when she was killed.

Malachi squatted beside the body and examined the hole in her forehead, which was reminiscent of Baker. Her clothing appeared expensive. She wore a large scarf around her neck, pulled halfway up the back of her head, probably a hijab.

He pictured her as a young girl, innocent, in need of protection and his chest tightened. He rubbed the bridge of his nose and detached himself from his empathy and sadness—a skill all cops had to learn.

What had the killer done after he shot her?

Malachi stood and walked down the hall. The kitchen lay to his left, and the exit door at the end. He pushed the steel door open and looked down a paved alley leading out to Twenty-Ninth Street NW. He jammed his pen in the doorframe to make sure it did not lock behind him and stepped into the alley.

He scanned the back of the building, and his eyes rested on a surveillance camera mounted above the door. He stood on his tiptoes and inspected it.

Black paint dripped from the lens.

．　　　．　　　．

Malachi met Jones on the sidewalk in front of the restaurant while he waited for tech to finish processing the scene. Jones looked haggard—his clothes disheveled, lines in his face, and bags under his eyes.

"I talked to the witnesses," Jones said. "Our victim is Linda Reynolds. One of her friends called her the strongest feminist voice of the decade. Nobody saw anything."

"I've heard of Reynolds. Her friend have any thoughts on who wanted to kill her?"

"Her assistant thought she was murdered for her activism. Reynolds has been threatened by dozens of white supremacists who hated her coalition of colors and her misandrist rhetoric."

"Did you ask them if they knew Dylan Miller?" Malachi asked.

"I did and no luck. Reynolds' assistant said the New National Order sounded familiar and they may have been one of the groups that threatened Reynolds. She's gonna bring us the file tomorrow."

"That's something. Could be a hate crime. I'll see if Reynolds filed any complaints with the FBI."

"Lady said they did, but confirm it later," Jones said. "We gonna have to talk with that Nazi puto again."

"Long shot."

"That pretty little hostess remembered a man at a back table. Came in after she seated the Reynolds party. Described him as tall and white with a full beard. Said his thick hair could have been a wig."

"Sounds like our phone suspect from the video."

"She said the guy split by the time the first patrol officers arrived, but half the customers fled when the screaming started, so that may not mean anything."

"The camera over the back door was spray painted black," Malachi said.

Hill and Rodriguez walked up behind them.

"That doesn't mean it's the same killer," Hill said. "Any idea how much graffiti is painted across this city, College?"

"No, but I can guess the probability," Malachi said. "Of all the graffiti, how much is on security cameras, and how many of those cameras are at unsolved crime scenes? Of those, how many were homicides? That one I know—just three."

Malachi's voice grew louder as he spoke, and his muscles tensed. Hill's constant criticism played on his insecurity about being a cop, made him feel like an outsider.

"I'm just saying—" Hill said.

"Don't just say something. I'll do the math for you if you need me to, but the chance that cameras were randomly painted at each of our homicides is something like a million to one."

"Yeah, well, if your killer was so careful when he shot Baker and Bellini, why would he off this broad inside a crowded restaurant?"

"Maybe he saw her go to the bathroom, aggregated the potential outcomes, and determined he was unlikely to get caught if he slipped out the back. It's called the expected utility hypothesis in economics."

Hill opened his mouth to speak but said nothing. He turned and stomped away.

"Sweet Jesus, Wolf," Jones said. "Take it easy."

Rodriguez grinned.

Malachi had to control his temper. It had become a problem after the marathon, and now he was inflicting his anger on cops.

Keep it together.

He turned to leave and stumbled. His feet tingled as if they were asleep, and his legs seemed sluggish, fuzzy. Humid weather triggered multiple sclerosis.

"You okay, Mac?" Jones asked.

"Yeah, fine."

Malachi entered the restaurant and watched the crime scene techs dusting the tables and chairs. They lifted hundreds of fingerprints, as expected in a public place. It would take organization, diligence, and time to identify all of them, and in the end, the killer's prints would probably not be among them.

He spoke with the hostess who said the bearded man had ordered a beer but had not paid. Malachi pulled all the charge records and reservations just in case.

They only needed the killer to make one mistake. One misstep or miscalculation and they would have him.

CHAPTER TWENTY-THREE

Malachi returned to his office at nine o'clock, his mind reeling with theories. He opened a research folder on his desk and reread the Muslim Brotherhood's *An Explanatory Memorandum,* which laid out the organization's strategy in North America. The FBI had entered the document as evidence in the Holy Land Foundation terrorism trial, the largest terrorism trial in US history. He flipped to a section he had highlighted and reread it.

"The process of settlement is a 'Civilization-Jihadist Process' with all the word means. The Ikwan (Muslim Brotherhood) *must understand that their work in America is a kind of grand jihad in eliminating and destroying the Western civilization from within and 'sabotaging' its miserable house by their hands and the hands of the believers so that it is eliminated and God's religion is made victorious over all religions."*

The FBI had seized the Brotherhood's strategic statement a few miles away from where Malachi read it. It explained the Muslim Brotherhood's North American strategy in their own words and refuted much of what Malachi had seen in the media. If his victims had been part of this, it must be related to their deaths.

He picked up the telephone and called Dr. Zahra Mansour.

"Dr. Mansour, this is Detective Wolf. Am I calling too late?"

"Hello, Malachi. It's not too late, I'm in bed catching up on some reading and please, call me Zahra."

Her voice sounded sultry, velvety, and her mention of being in bed felt personal, an intimate window into her life. Malachi imagined her auburn hair falling over her pillow.

"Sorry to bother you again so soon."

"I'm happy to help."

Malachi hesitated, not wanting to divulge anything sensitive about the most recent murder. The press had not connected the murders yet, but he had to see what Zahra knew. He stalled.

"What are you reading?"

"A book about the early battles of the US Navy. It's boring to most people, but I love nautical history. Stephen Decatur's victory over the Barbary Pirates created a lasting peace through strength. US history in the eighteenth and nineteenth centuries fascinates me."

Malachi loved early American history too. He decided to trust her.

"Do you know the name Linda Reynolds?"

"She's a third-wave feminist. I believe she spoke in Washington this week."

"Have you written about her?"

"No. Did something happen?"

Malachi deflated. "She was murdered. I'm trying to find some connection to the other victims."

"You asked if I'd written anything about her and I haven't, but I'm familiar with her work. Linda Reynolds is an apologist for fundamental Islam. She allied herself with some of the worst Islamist groups in the world. She frequented Palestinian rallies, supported Hamas, and used anti-Semitic language in defense of Islam."

"Is she associated with the Muslim Brotherhood?" Malachi asked.

"She doesn't have any formal connection, as far as I know, but she propagates their disinformation. Lenin referred to people like her as 'useful idiots.' The Brotherhood follows the old Soviet infiltration playbook and uses intelligentsia as puppets."

Another connection.

"I'm a little confused," Malachi said. "Why would an American feminist affiliate herself with Islamic groups? Aren't women mistreated across the Middle East?"

"You're right, it's a contradiction," Dr. Mansour laughed. "There's an odd alliance between gay activists, feminists, communists, and Islamists. It makes no sense if you understand how Islamists regard socialists, homosexuals, and women. Gay rights groups claim Islam is peace while gays are being thrown off rooftops in Iraq and Iran and jailed or killed all over the Middle East. Women have few rights in Islamic countries, and they're considered property under Islamic law, yet feminists like Linda Reynolds have joined forces with the same people who oppress them."

"Why?"

"Intersectionality. We live in an age when victimhood is considered a badge of honor. The theory of intersectionality claims all underrepresented groups lack societal power and need to join forces. But if Islamists ever impose Sharia law here, women, gays, and racial minorities will suffer a dystopian existence."

Malachi thought about that. Those alliances seemed irrational, yet Zahra's explanation made sense. All three victims had defended Islam, but how could that connect to motive?

"Are you saying that Islam is incompatible with minority rights?"

"Fundamental Islam is a supremacist ideology and antithetical to everything we cherish in the West. But that doesn't mean Islam can't change. We've seen reformations in Judaism, Christianity, and other religions. Islam just needs to reinterpret itself to become compatible with modernity."

"And the Brotherhood doesn't believe in a modern version of Islam?"

"They claim to be moderate, but they support a return to the seventh century. A significant number of Muslims around the world disagree with this fundamentalist interpretation, but dissenters are silenced."

"What percentage of Muslims are disenfranchised?"

"It's impossible to calculate. I was raised in a Muslim home, and I identify as Muslim, at least culturally. I celebrate the holidays and believe in God, but I don't follow Sharia law or the radical fundamentalism of the Wahhabi and Salafist movements. Call my version 'Muslim-lite,' a peaceful interpretation, which can coexist with other religions. Millions of Muslims agree with me, yet the Brotherhood's fundamentalism is backed by the US government."

Malachi was talking to the right person, but could she connect the dots for him?

"When we spoke before, you said President Follet supported the Brotherhood," Malachi said. "Both Professor Bellini and Reynolds were also on the political left. Is there a close association between the Brotherhood and the Left Wing?"

"The Left's embrace of identity politics has been exploited by the Brotherhood, but there are also many Republicans and conservatives who have fallen for the Brotherhood's disinformation. Stupidity is bipartisan."

Malachi laughed. "That's very true, and your explanation helps. I'm not keeping you, am I?"

"I'm enjoying talking to you."

"I took your suggestion and read up on the Brotherhood. People claim the Brotherhood in the US differs from the Egyptian parent organization. They say the group here is independent and moderate. They say—"

"That's the consensus, and it's absurd."

"Why?"

"Two reasons. First, the Brotherhood isn't officially in the United States. They're here, but they operate through front groups, such as the American Islamic Shura. Academics can't claim the Brotherhood's not here and that they're also a separate and more moderate branch."

"Do all AIS employees want to destroy the country?"

"Not everyone working for those organizations knows the bigger plan, but their leadership does. The Brotherhood has a long-term, generational strategy, and they're systematically implementing it. The Brotherhood's own documents admit they use front groups."

"By leadership, you mean people like Amir al-Kadi, Kareem Hilal, and Muhammad Baseem?"

"Definitely. Al-Kadi is the worst. He's evil."

"What's the second reason the Brotherhood in the US isn't moderate?"

"The Brotherhood's own bylaws say that every branch must adhere to the organization's core principles and one of those principles is Jihad. The Brotherhood's goals are well documented, and their leaders don't disguise them when they speak in Arabic. Any doubt about their intentions has been dispelled by the documents and recordings the FBI acquired. Apologists have to ignore the Brotherhood's own statements to claim they're moderate."

"Thank you, Dr. Mansour. May I call you again, after I've processed this?"

"You can call me *anytime*, and again, call me Zahra."

"Your husband doesn't mind?"

"I'm not with anyone, if that's what you're asking."

Malachi's stomach fluttered, and something stirred inside him. How could she do that with just the sound of her voice? He promised to call and hung up. He returned to his notes but could not stop thinking about her sharp mind . . . and those long legs.

The murderer had used burner telephones to call the first two victims, and Malachi had requested an emergency toll dump to see if Reynolds had received a similar call. Also, the description of the bearded patron at La Seine matched the man caught on video buying the first burner. The killer had used a gun every time, but ballistics had not come back on the slug pulled out of Bellini's body. Malachi hoped it would match the bullet from Reynolds, because there was nothing else to prove they were looking for a single suspect.

The killer had spray painted the camera in the alley behind La Seine, like at the other crime scenes, but the manager said the camera did not work and was only a prop to deter late-night burglaries. Malachi had noticed dangling wires, which made it obvious the camera was unconnected, so why had the killer spray painted it? It bothered him, and he did not have an answer.

Years ago, Malachi would have run to clear his head and help himself think—but not anymore. He could not run without thinking about his father.

He lifted the handset and dialed John Wesley, Senator Hansen's chief of staff.

"Detective Wolf, what can I do for you?" Wesley asked.

"I have three homicide victims, all connected to Islamic causes, and both Linda Reynolds and Sam Baker worked with Senator Hansen. I'd like to speak with the senator."

There was silence on the other end, and Malachi waited.

"Senator Hansen has no involvement with any of your cases." Wesley's tone had cooled. "The senator may have interacted with these people to serve the people of Virginia and the citizens of this great country, but he has nothing to do with their murders."

"I'm not saying he's involved, but he had recent contact with two of the victims and possibly all three. He may know how they're related."

"Listen carefully, Detective. Senator Hansen is not involved. He has cooperated and told you everything he knows. The Democratic Party has asked Senator Hansen to run for president and any further attempts to involve the senator in these crimes could damage his chances. It could hurt your career too. Do you understand what I'm saying?"

"I understand, but—"

"Good day, Detective."

Wesley hung up and Malachi stared at the phone. The hair on the back of his neck rose. That was not the behavior of an innocent man.

Chapter Twenty-Four

Malachi wanted to slap handcuffs on the vile bigot.

The New National Order had sent threatening emails to Linda Reynolds, which connected Dylan Miller to two of their homicide victims. At ten o'clock, Malachi and Jones planned to bring Miller in for questioning, hoping to pry an incriminating statement out of him. Miller may not have been involved but he had motive, opportunity, and a heart ravaged by hate.

Malachi had time before the interview, so he drove across the river to Alison's house and parked outside. She should be on her way to American University, leaving his girls home with their babysitter.

Riley and Samantha consumed his thoughts and pulled him across the river like a gravitational force. Before becoming a father, he had not understood how siring daughters would change his life, but there was something genetic, something ancient, that made him want to hold them, love them, protect them.

He resented Alison for not understanding his need to find justice for the dead. She did not need to be a psychiatrist to see the connection to his father's murder, but his career change had been more than an attempt to heal a psychological wound. When he had been sworn in as a police officer, he had become part of a thin blue line, a wall separating the innocent from the evil lurking in the darkness. What had started as a desire to seek justice had morphed into a duty, an obligation to use his intellect to protect the weak.

If his father had not been murdered, Malachi's life would have continued as planned and been stable and comfortable. Had he made the right decision? He pictured Alison lying beside him while his girls jumped on their bed. His throat tightened, and he choked back a sob.

What have I done with my life?

Samantha ran past a living room window. He felt exposed, more like a stalker than a father with a broken heart. If his girls caught him, he would be humiliated.

He threw the car into gear and drove away.

.   .   .

Jones parked on Fisher Avenue, out of sight of Dylan Miller's residence, and Malachi followed him to the door. Jones rapped on the metal screen, and they waited.

Something moved inside the living room. Malachi peered through the window. All the lights were off, despite the cloudy day, and a flickering television illuminated the interior. Why would Miller turn off lights, but keep the television on? He had to be inside.

A loud crack sounded from the rear of the house, like wood slapping together.

The back door.

Malachi jumped off the stoop, jogged to the side of the house, and peeked around the corner. Miller ran across the backyard toward the woods. He held a dark object in his right hand.

"He's running," Malachi yelled.

He bolted after Miller. His khakis tugged at his skin, and his heels pounded on the hard, dry earth. He pushed off the balls of his feet and lifted his knees up high. Sprinting electrified his muscles and comforted him, like the return of a long-lost friend. He had not run since that day in Boston, at least not for fun. The joy had gone from it.

A dense stand of timber—all white oaks, ironwood, and shortleaf pines—bordered Miller's property. Most foot chases only lasted a short time, and Malachi tried to shorten the gap before he lost sight of him.

Miller was younger than Malachi, but he ran with an uneven gait and his arms flailed, as if he inhabited someone else's body.

Malachi closed the distance.

Miller hit the woods at full speed, slapping pine branches away from his face, like a young girl in a playground fight. He clutched a small revolver, a thirty-two or thirty-eight caliber, holding it like a baseball with his fingers wrapped around the barrel.

Malachi slowed to draw his Glock and lost sight of him. Miller could easily turn and shoot, so Malachi stopped behind a large oak at the end of the yard and used it for cover. He glanced behind him as Jones rounded the corner of the house, huffing and puffing.

Malachi yanked his radio off his belt to warn Jones that Miller was armed, just as Jones called in their pursuit to dispatch.

When he finished, Malachi keyed the radio. "Dispatch, Homicide Twenty-Nine. Priority."

"Station is held for emergency traffic," the dispatcher said. "Go ahead Homicide Twenty-Nine."

"In foot pursuit behind 1599 Fisher Avenue. Advise Prince William County our suspect is armed with a handgun and wanted for questioning in a homicide."

"Ten-four. Copy suspect is armed."

Malachi clipped his radio back on his belt and rolled around the tree. Miller sounded like a bear crashing through the underbrush. The noise grew distant. Jones was too slow, so Malachi dove into the woods alone. Malachi looked over his sights as he moved through the dark woods.

Miller was at least thirty yards ahead and still running. Malachi jogged through a bed of pine needles and exposed roots, careful not to trip, then ran across a small clearing.

Somewhere behind the trees, Miller fell with a thump and swore.

Malachi picked up his pace and moved toward the sound.

Miller's red tee shirt flashed through the vegetation twenty-five yards away, as he stumbled into a clearing.

Malachi ducked behind an elm tree and leaned around the far side.

Miller limped through the brush, jerking his head around like a wounded animal. His hair looked disheveled, and he rubbed his knee as if he had injured it.

Malachi jogged after him with his gun up and closed the distance to ten yards. He slowed and walked heel-to-toe to minimize his sound. Smooth was fast. He kept his sights centered on Miller's back.

The ground sloped down a steep embankment and Miller had trouble keeping his balance.

Malachi leaned out from behind the rough bark of an oak tree and extended his arms in an isosceles shooting stance. He steadied his aim with his left hand.

"Drop the gun, Miller."

Miller spun around holding the gun.

Malachi gently took up the slack in the trigger and held his breath, ready to fire.

Miller tripped over a root and flailed his arms as he tried to catch his balance. The gun flew out of his hand. He toppled over backward, and his feet swung over his head as he tumbled down the embankment.

Malachi sprang from behind the tree and pursued him. Miller splashed into something as Malachi reached the point where he had last seen him. Malachi craned his neck and surveyed the embankment.

Miller stood in a small creek, up to his waist in brown water. He struggled to stand and fell back with a splash.

Malachi shuffled down the slope, trying not to slip. He reached the edge of the water and pointed his gun at Miller.

"Hands. Let me see your hands."

Miller shook the hair out of his eyes and looked at Malachi. Blood dripped down his forehead. He lifted his hands into the air and fell backwards into the water. He acted drunk.

Malachi kept his gun on him and pulled his radio. He slowed his breathing before talking.

"Dispatch, Homicide Twenty-Nine."

"Homicide Twenty-Nine, go."

"I have the suspect at gunpoint in the Marmusco Acres Creek, south of Fisher Avenue. Slow down responding units."

"Ten-four."

Miller raised his hands over his head and stumbled over the uneven creek bed toward shore.

Malachi stopped him when he was a few feet away. "Put your hands on the bank and crawl out."

"Help me out of the crick." Miller said, breathing hard.

"Do you have a weapon on you?"

"I didn't do noth'n."

Behind Malachi, Jones crashed through the brush. "Where you at, Wolf?"

"Down by the water."

Miller crawled out of the creek.

"Get on the ground," Malachi said.

Miller lowered himself onto his stomach.

Jones arrived at the top of the embankment and hurried down, his Oxford dress shoes slipping and sliding on the pine needles and loose earth. He made it to the bottom and covered Miller with his gun.

"Put your hands behind your back," Malachi said. "Look away from me."

Miller complied, and Malachi approached him from the side.

Jones sidestepped to keep a clear line of fire.

Two feet away from Miller, Malachi holstered and knelt on Miller's back. He pinned Miller's wrists against his back with his left hand. He unhooked his handcuffs from his belt, without taking his eyes off Miller.

Malachi held the chain between the handcuffs, forming a figure eight. He lifted Miller's left hand and slapped a handcuff against his wrist. The metal spun and locked. Malachi cuffed Miller's other hand and confirmed the handcuffs were snug. He retrieved his handcuff key and double-locked the cuffs to prevent them from tightening and cutting off Miller's circulation.

Malachi held the handcuffs to control them and patted Miller's sides, back, and legs with his other hand. Miller's clothes were cold and wet. Malachi did not find any weapons. He rolled Miller onto his left side and patted his front. He was clean.

"Sorry, Brother," Jones said. "I couldn't keep up. My knees ain't working like they used to."

"You made it, and that's all that matters," Malachi said. "Miller dropped the gun at the top of the slope." He jerked his head in that direction.

"I'll get it," Jones said, and hustled away.

A massive river birch hung over the creek like a canopy. Its rusty-cinnamon trunk had peeled, and its leaves cast shadows across the surface of the murky water.

"This is bullshit," Miller said. "Why are you doing this?"

"We came to talk. You chose to run."

Miller's pupils looked constricted, small pinpoints in white sclera, like distant balloons passing through the clouds. Every part of him seemed withdrawn, hidden from view.

"Didn't do shit. Po-lice always on me."

He spoke in short bursts, as if he was on something—probably meth. Paranoia could explain why he ran instead of just hiding in his house and not opening the door. Or maybe he had killed Baker and wanted to avoid arrest.

Jones returned with Miller's gun in his gloved hand. He smiled. "Caliber looks right. Let's see if ballistics can match this to our bodies. Let's head back to my ride and I'll ask Prince William County to get a search warrant for his house. We can question Miller at our office."

A police siren grew louder. Malachi watched Miller, who stared back at him with small, dark, soulless eyes—the eyes of a shark.

CHAPTER TWENTY-FIVE

A twinge of anger stabbed Austin's chest as he flicked on the television and turned to *This Week in the News*, hosted by Maya Shouman. She always led off her hour-long show, which aired five nights per week, with a segment covering the day's top stories. The second and longest segment highlighted her issue of the day, a narrative about how the American government or culture oppressed some group, followed by an interview with a newsmaker.

Austin could not remember the last time one of her guests had disagreed with her. Had anyone else noticed her guests always parroted the narrative from both the news stories she covered and her spotlighted issues? The news she failed to mention exposed her bias.

The murders in Georgetown had made national news, and Shouman breathlessly related them, as if the crimes expressed a greater problem in America. She used the murders to talk about a broader issue—Islamophobia.

Austin slumped onto the couch, half listening to her bullshit narrative. He alone knew the motive behind the murders, and it was not a fear of Muslims.

"Now, I'd like to welcome tonight's guest, Senator Feroz Abdullah, Democrat from Wisconsin," Shouman said. "He was the first Muslim-American to reach the Senate, and he has been a paladin for the downtrodden and oppressed."

Such objective journalism.

"Thank you, Maya," Senator Abdullah said. "It's a pleasure to be here with you."

"What's your take on the murders of three prominent defenders of Islam?" Shouman asked.

"Those murders were bigoted attacks against the religion of peace, which—"

"Clearly."

"That's right Maya, but what I find more troubling is a larger, insidious threat, which has resurfaced in this country."

"And what is that?"

"Racism. Hatred. Muslims are being targeted in record numbers, and these murders are proof of the intolerance in America's heart."

Austin had known his actions would be twisted into propaganda, but everything depended on his success. It was an acceptable unintended outcome.

"What can be done?" Shouman asked.

"First, I'm calling on Congress to enact greater religious protections for Muslims."

Shouman looked pleased and surprised, but she had to have known what he would say.

"Second, I'm calling on the FBI to investigate all three murders as hate crimes."

"Excellent," Shouman said.

Senator Abdullah's seamless recital of his agenda impressed Austin. The man understood how to manipulate an audience by triggering a sense of injustice and indignation. He allowed his audience to feel virtuous by agreeing with him. He acted like a psychological conductor and Austin pictured him waving a baton.

Austin's hands shook. He wanted to murder Shouman.

Before shooting Linda Reynolds, Austin had never dreamed himself capable of killing a woman, not after the abuse his mother had suffered at his father's hands. The violence had always come from some perceived transgression. Margaret had eaten too much at dinner—gluttony. Austin had mentioned a new bicycle he had seen at school—envy. Raymond had always justified violence as God's will, as if he had been chosen to deliver

God's punishment. But even as a child, Austin had known his father enjoyed hurting them.

What if sociopathy was genetic?

The week before his father's death, the beatings had intensified. Austin remembered Raymond stumbling home drunk, radiating malevolent energy and the sweet stench of cheap whisky. Raymond pointed at a red rose Margaret had sewn on her sweater, and said, "Vanity." He rained blows down on her, but she never cried, and her stoicism enraged him. He unbuckled his belt and whipped her until welts rose on her arms.

Austin had just turned thirteen, and as a man, it was his responsibility to defend his mother. He tackled his father, like his football coach had taught him, cracking Raymond's rib and knocking the wind out of him. Austin swung wildly, as his eyes filled with tears of shame.

Raymond recovered and knocked Austin unconscious. The rest of that night remained hazy, but Austin remembered blood gushing down his chin, his cracked tooth, and one other thing—the determined look on his mother's face while his father had beaten him.

Austin shook away the memory.

On television, Shouman wrapped up her show. "Please tune in tomorrow night for my on-air panel discussing bigotry in America. I will be joined by CAMP Director Muhammad Baseem, AIS President Amir al-Kadi, FMS President Kareem Hilal, and Senator Dale Hansen."

Austin broke out in a cool sweat. He paced across the living room and looked out at the neon lights along Arlington Boulevard. He ran his tongue over his broken front tooth, a blemish he refused to fix. He pictured his mother's expression.

Now I understand.

He snatched a medicine bottle off the table, popped two Oxycontin into his mouth, and swallowed them dry. He turned back to the television and fixated on Shouman's face.

"You're next."

CHAPTER TWENTY-SIX

Dylan Miller sat in lockup and refused to talk. He had asked for a lawyer, which was probably the most intelligent thing he had ever done. It always amazed Malachi when suspects talked, knowing they were under suspicion. Either they thought they could outsmart the cops, or they really were innocent. Miller's attorney needed time with his client, so Malachi and Jones had postponed the interview.

Miller had an old burglary conviction, which made him a convicted felon and prohibited from owning firearms. They could charge him for possessing the handgun, which carried a minimum mandatory two-year sentence. If Miller had ordered someone else to commit the murder, they could plea bargain the gun charge away in exchange for his testimony, but for now, they would let him sit and think.

Malachi leaned back and tapped his pen against his desk. If Miller had killed out of religious bigotry, the case would end with him, but if he had not been involved, they needed to find another suspect, and the only thing connecting the victims was fundamental Islam. Being a detective with a theory, but no hard proof, was like being an economist with a hypothesis and no experimental data. The tradecraft used by the killer in all three homicides showed planning and premeditation, though the murder of Reynolds seemed far riskier than the first two. Killing in a public restaurant did not fit the pattern, and Hill had called Malachi's single-shooter theory into question.

It seemed obvious the murders were related, but Malachi was aware of his susceptibility to selection bias, his predisposition to only see facts fitting his narrative. Once he assumed the murders were committed by the same person, all coincidental facts took on unwarranted weight. Maybe the connections to Islam were just that. Coincidence.

Malachi dialed Zahra.

"I need to learn more about the Muslim Brotherhood," he said. "Do you have time to meet me?"

"I'm taking a much needed personal day," Zahra said. "Don't you ever take days off?"

"Not when I'm on a serious case. We can do it another time."

She paused. "I plan to spend the afternoon on my sailboat. Want to join me?"

Malachi's heart raced. "I would love to spend the day sailing with you, but I'm working."

She giggled. "It's not a date. I can brief you on the boat for an hour or two and bring you right back."

For years, Malachi's social life had been more a quest to find sexual release than a search for another mate, but Zahra intrigued him on many levels. Beauty, bravery, and brilliance—a rare combination. Malachi did not understand enough about Islamic terrorism, and he needed a subject-matter expert to tutor him. At least he told himself he did.

"Tell me where and when."

.　　.　　.

Malachi met Zahra at the Safe Harbor Sailing Marina, near Ronald Reagan Washington National Airport, in Arlington, Virginia. She greeted him with a smile, and they walked across the wooden pier to her boat slip. She wore a sheer white cover-up over a skimpy black bikini, and he tried not to stare. Nothing scared away women faster than an ogling man.

"Have you sailed before?" she asked.

"A few times on Lake Michigan as a kid. In Boston, my college roommate sailed, so I took an introductory course and earned a US Sailing certification. We used to take nineteen-foot Flying Scots up the Charles River on weekends."

"Good enough. You can help me work the sails, First-Mate Malachi."

"Aye-aye, Captain."

"Yalla."

They boarded her sailboat, a thirty-one-foot Catalina 315, with a fiberglass hull, single mast, eleven-foot beam, and comfortable cabin. The appointments looked high-end, which meant she had probably paid six figures for it.

Malachi made small talk while she raised the mainsail and clipped a red jib to the forestay. She did not start the outboard motor. Instead, she pushed away from the dock and used the mainsail to guide them out of the marina. Sailing was a mixture of skill and talent, and navigating in and out of port was the most challenging part. Zahra's adroit handling of the craft impressed him.

They entered the channel and headed south down the Potomac River. Malachi estimated the wind at ten knots—about eleven miles an hour— perfect sailing weather. Zahra tacked across the channel, keeping the green buoys to starboard and red ones to port. They passed beneath the Woodrow Wilson Bridge, where grass broke the surface in the shallows outside the channel.

Zahra let the sails all the way out, and they ran with a northwest wind behind them. The Potomac widened and thick woods lined both shores as they moved away from the city. She sat beside him in the stern, with one hand on the wheel and her hair blowing in the wind. She smiled and butterflies fluttered in his stomach.

"Want to take the wheel?" she asked.

"You bet."

Malachi climbed over her, and as she slid down the bench to switch places, their legs brushed. The contact sent tingles through him, as if he was a teenager again, clumsy and unsure.

"I've got the helm," Malachi said.

"Keep us in the channel. We'll follow the river for forty-five minutes, then turn back. I'm sure you have work to do."

"Unfortunately."

She untied her cloth belt and lifted her cover-up over her head. Her bikini barely contained her breasts, and its Brazilian bottom revealed her athletic body. In Malachi's experience, academics holed up in libraries, hunched over ancient tomes—but she defied the stereotype. Judging by her tan, Zahra spent a fair amount of time outdoors.

Malachi felt overdressed wearing boat shoes, khakis, and an oxford shirt, so he pulled off his shirt and let the sun warm his chest. He worked out almost every day and knew his body looked lean and hard. He could see Zahra's eyes beneath her designer sunglasses as they roamed over his body.

"Your eyes are ice blue," she said.

"Like my mother's."

"They remind me of a wolf."

"I *am* a Wolf."

Zahra giggled.

Zahra awakened feelings in Malachi, primal and familiar, which he thought had long vanished. Alison and his girls had been the only people he loved since his father died, and he held them close, like rare and treasured possessions, but now, this gorgeous and erudite woman had his attention. The world came alive around her.

"I needed this," he said, his eyes lingering on her.

She smiled. "I hoped you'd call."

"I wanted to see you."

They sailed for half an hour, talking about sailing with the ease of two old friends. She spoke with a slight Arabic accent, transforming ordinary English words into something exotic.

"Your author bio said you're Egyptian."

"I grew up in Cairo. My ancestors have lived there for a thousand years. When my parents were young, Egypt was almost as liberal and free as the United States but that ended when the socialists took over. First the government came for our guns, then they came for the rest of our freedoms. As the Egyptian government became more totalitarian, it also became more Islamic—a one-two punch of socialism and theocracy."

"I didn't realize Egypt had been so free. I'm embarrassed to say I know little about your country other than what I learned about the Pharaohs in high school."

"Egypt used to be a vacation destination for Americans. The upper classes in Egypt were educated in both French and English schools, and students were taught to revere the West. In the 1950s, Cairo looked like Paris. Now it's a third-world dumpster." Zahra's voice trailed off, and she stared out at the water.

"That's a crime."

"Yes..."

"I'd like to see the pyramids someday."

"I wouldn't recommend any American visit now. The Islamists have ruined the country. It's not safe for anyone, unless you're a fundamentalist. It's even dangerous for Muslims. I told you more Muslims are killed in Islamic terrorist attacks than anyone else."

"Why is that?"

"Fundamentalists, both Sunni and Shia, believe in a strict, repressive form of Islam. Muslims who violate Sharia law or try to leave Islam are sentenced to death. Mullahs issue religious fatwas all the time. Sharia law is implemented by the state and enforced by police or through radical groups operating with the government's blessing."

"Your family suffered?"

"The socialists took my family's property, and then Islamists turned the country into an authoritarian, theocratic prison camp. My family lost everything. All Egyptians did. Living under Islamic theocracy is a waking nightmare."

"I'm a second-generation American, so it's hard to imagine living without basic freedoms."

"It felt like there was always something bad about to happen, as if everyone in Egypt awaited the apocalypse. It's worse for women. We're treated like second-class citizens all over the Middle East. Every time I walked down the sidewalk in Cairo, men tried to grope me."

"Is it really that awful?"

"Ten years ago, I took classes at Cairo International University. One day I parked at the university and when I opened my door, a man— another student—pushed me back inside the car and tried to rape me. I punched and kicked him, but he was relentless, ripping my clothes and grabbing me ... right in the parking lot."

"Didn't anyone see what was happening and try to help?"

Zahra's jaw clenched and her eyes hardened. "There were a dozen male students and teachers nearby. They saw, but no one did anything. That's real patriarchy."

"Unbelievable."

"It's commonplace. Women are raped in Egypt all the time, and it would have happened to me too, but I carried a kitchen knife in the car for protection. I'd have preferred a gun, but we weren't allowed to have them. I snatched the knife out of the center console and stabbed him in the neck. That worked."

"Thank God you were armed. What happened to him?"

"He ran away, with the knife sticking out of his neck and blood spurting everywhere. I thought I'd killed him. The police wanted to charge me, but my family had money and bribed them to drop the charges. Luckily, the man didn't die."

"Did the police arrest him for attempted rape?"

"Of course not. Living in a Muslim theocracy is hell for women. I was more careful after that. I hired a former French GIPN officer to give me self-defense lessons, so I would be more prepared. Fighting is more mental than physical, and I developed a combat mindset. I'm always ready to think my way out of trouble."

"Egyptian women must suffer from P.T.S.D."

"Sometimes I hear crying then realize it's just the water dripping, or I wake up at night to knocking that isn't there. But everyone has trauma, and I just have to move on. When terrible memories run like a loop in my mind, I recognize it and make it stop. I take control."

Malachi nodded and stared, transfixed by her.

"What is it?" she asked.

"You impress me, that's all."

"I hope that's not all."

They sailed down the center of the river, and Malachi stared at the water trying to imagine life without the rule of law. The basic safety and freedom he enjoyed was an anomaly in the world, and he was fortunate to have been born in the US.

"You mentioned you were Muslim," he said.

"My family's Muslim, but my parents weren't very religious—more culturally Muslim than anything else. We fasted on Ramadan, but my father only went to mosque for funerals, and we never talked about religion around the house."

"I can relate to that."

Malachi was neither devout nor convinced by the arguments made by any religion, but he recognized the societal benefits of institutions organized around moral codes. Religion had its place.

"The more I understood what the Islamists were doing to my country," Zahra said, "the more agnostic I became. When I watched the World Trade Center collapse on 9/11, I knew I needed to pick a side. That's when I came here. I could not let the Islamists ruin this country too."

"Are your parents still in Egypt?"

"They're in Cairo, and I worry about them every day. Whenever I call out the Muslim Brotherhood for terrorism, I worry my family will be arrested by the government or killed by a jihadist. Muslims who fight orthodoxy are considered the worst traitors, worse than Christians or Jews. You're Jewish, right?"

Malachi rarely talked about being Jewish. When he was young, it had made him feel different from the other Christian kids. He introduced himself as Mac because it sounded less ethnic. Jews were persecuted and discriminated against in the Middle East, so what did Zahra think about Judaism? Would his religion be a problem for her?

"I guess I'm Jewish the same way you're Muslim. My mother insisted we go to temple every week, but my father was an atheist. I had my bar mitzvah, but I never went to temple after I left home. I don't think about religion often."

Zahra smiled. "Some of my best friends in this country are Jews. I didn't know anyone who was openly Jewish in Egypt, but I always defended Israel, which was not a popular position in a country where everything's blamed on the Jews, even shark attacks in the Red Sea."

Malachi snorted.

The sun reflected off the water. They remained close to the city, but floated between wooded shores, as if transported into another time. Nature rejuvenated him.

"How did you become an expert on the Muslim Brotherhood?"

Zahra stared at the water then nodded to herself, as if she had come to a decision. "Three Brotherhood members raped and murdered my sister. It changed my life."

"I'm so sorry."

"It happened a long time ago."

Malachi put his hand on her shoulder, and when she turned to him, her eyes glistened.

"After that, I studied Islam on my own to understand the minds of the Islamists who had taken my sister from me and ruined my country."

"That's a healthy way to cope."

"It became an obsession. The more I read, the more dangerous they seemed. Their adherence to a strict interpretation of a seventh-century ideology is as anti-intellectual as it gets. I call it fundamental Islam, because it implements Sunni Islam as written in the Koran, Fiqh, Hadith, and Sirah."

"Hadith? Sirah?"

"Sunni Islam is more than a religion, it's a political ideology that instructs believers how to live. The Hadith is a collection of the Prophet Muhammad's words, and the Sirah is Muhammad's biography. Muslims use both as guides. The Fiqh is the scholarly and theological interpretation of the Koran, using both the Hadith and Sirah."

As she spoke about her field of study, she seemed to gather strength and become less emotional, more analytical, which was probably a defense mechanism against the horror of her sister's death.

"Is there broad acceptance on how to practice Islam?"

"It's codified into law. There are four schools of Islamic jurisprudence, and fatwas are official rulings on what's allowed and what's prohibited. Fundamentalist Sunni Islam made life in Egypt miserable, and my study led to a PhD and a career making policy recommendations."

"I have a lot to study."

Zahra took the helm and spun the wheel hard. The boom flew over their heads as the sail changed position and they came about. She pulled in the main sheet, heeling the boat to starboard, and they tacked back north along the eastern side of the channel. She handled the sails like an expert, reacting with muscle memory to the micro movements of the boat. The wind blew her hair across her face and she licked her lips to moisten them.

"I hate to talk business," Malachi said, "but, what do you make of these murders?"

"You tell me, Malachi."

He loved that she used his first name. Only his parents had called him that, and hearing Zahra use it warmed him.

"I don't know. Reynolds was the third murder victim in Georgetown with ties to the Middle East. You're the expert—how could Islam be connected to these deaths?"

"I'm an academic, which means I base my analysis on facts. I don't have enough information to guess why someone killed them, but they all supported the Muslim Brotherhood. Al-Bakri funded mosques and cultural centers and moved money to Muslim Brotherhood groups—like the American Islamic Shura. Professor Bellini indoctrinated a generation of students in the Brotherhood's disinformation, and claimed radical Islam was a religion like any other, instead of a fascistic ideology. Reynolds pushed a message of tolerance and inclusion, ignoring the bigotry, racism, and violence practiced by Islamists."

"If you had my job, where would you look for suspects?"

"Look for anyone trying to stop the spread of fundamental Islam. Look for someone willing to use extrajudicial methods. Someone willing to kill."

Malachi stared at the brown water. "And for someone with the skill to do it."

CHAPTER TWENTY-SEVEN

Malachi and Jones carried their coffees to a corner table inside the Ground Bean, a trendy cafe on the District Wharf. They sat with their backs to the wall, watching the crowd and the entrance. Malachi could never relax with his back to a door. Outside, the morning traffic inched down the street. The Homicide Branch would spring to life in an hour, which gave them time to discuss the murders alone.

"Four bucks for a cup of joe?" Jones asked. "You gotta be fucking with me. Why do you drink this froufrou shit?"

"Good coffee is like single-malt scotch or fine wine. Once you develop a refined taste, you can never go back." Malachi sipped his French roast, dark and velvety with nutty undertones. "It'll clear our minds."

"I'm gonna need more than this to get my head right," Jones said.

"Is Nuse up your ass?"

"Whole command staff's up there. I need a laxative."

"Anything look promising yet?" Malachi asked.

"Retirement."

"Don't even joke. Is Collins helping?"

"She's solid, running interference. If she had been my fullback in school, I would have set the rushing record and gone to the NFL. Only so much she can do, though. Nuse is sweating her."

"Who should we look at, other than Miller?" Malachi asked.

"Lot of people hate activists and rich folk. Reynolds didn't have gambling debts or financial trouble, and her home life was okay. I talked to her partner, and she seemed legit. Shi-it, it's possible Reynolds bumped into the wrong guy at the wrong time. Activist meets guy having a psychotic episode."

His face looked drawn, and dark circles had formed under his eyes. Malachi wished Jones' wife was still alive to care for him. Their whole squad had been assigned to support the homicides, but it was not enough. Jones had played this game for decades, but even he had not experienced this much political pressure. Their entire unit was under constant duress to solve the case by Nuse, who was compelled by Chief Ransom, who received daily calls from Mayor Donald Davis. The murders had turned into a glowing red ball.

"She wore a hijab," Malachi said.

"Don't start with that Islamic killer shit."

"Come on, Jonesy. Don't you see it? Three murders and the only thing linking them are their ties to Islam."

"Course I see it. We're probably looking at one killer here, but there ain't proof until we get ballistics back. You figure out how Islam turns into motive, then we'll find a suspect."

"Zahra, uh, Dr. Mansour said all three victims pushed a fundamentalist Islamic agenda."

"Zahra, huh? If I didn't know you better, I think you chasing more than a lead on this one. That beautiful lady is fresh. If she believed in extraterrestrials, you'd think ET done it."

"Give me a break," Malachi said, averting his eyes. Jones was right. He sought any opportunity to talk to Zahra.

"I seen that look before."

"She's impressive. She left her home in Egypt and came to a foreign land to confront evil. It's one thing for us to do it with guns on our hips and the government behind us, but she did it alone, with only her wits to protect her."

"Takes balls."

"We live in a land of privilege, luxury, and laws. It's hard for us to understand what it took for her to fight Islamists in Egypt. I can only hope I'd be as brave in the same situation. Seeing her do it makes me want to be with her."

Jones grinned. "It's more than her bravery, isn't it?"

Malachi took a sip of coffee. "I've always been an academic. Even as a kid I found comfort in books, but when I joined the department, I had to reinvent myself, be more extroverted. I had to apply my study of human behavior to reality, not just theory. Zahra's an academic, but she has charisma too. She's got it all."

"You smitten."

Malachi nodded. "It's hard to trust another woman and open up again."

"Because Alison left you?"

"Yeah."

"And your mom?"

"Probably."

"This lady's a different caliber," Jones said.

"She's all I think about. I hope it hasn't clouded my judgment."

"She's a smart woman, but Islamists? I thought we'd moved on to worrying about China and Russia."

"The Brotherhood's behind all Islamic terrorism, like a real-world version of Ian Fleming's SPECTRE. They're as secretive and deadly as the KGB during the Cold War, only worse, because deterrence doesn't work on them. They welcome martyrdom. At least the Russkis didn't want to die."

"I get why you're listening to her, but Islamists are all over DC. If our perp wanted to step-up and smoke one, he could find easier ways to do it."

Malachi stopped mid-sip. "Perhaps . . ."

"What?"

"It's what you said. These murders were well planned, but with every new homicide, the risk goes up. There must be a reason he needs to kill them now."

CHAPTER TWENTY-EIGHT

Austin leaned into the shadow of an old oak and watched Maya Shouman lock the front door of her house and jog down N Street NW through the heart of Georgetown. It was five o'clock on Saturday morning, and already the humidity stuck to him like a cobweb.

Shouman had been raised in the Palestinian territories, and he wondered if the heat reminded her of home, the same way the cold made him think of those snow-bound winters in Hemlock, New York. Maybe Shouman's twenty years of reporting from the Middle East had papered new memories over old, and she had reimagined her childhood as a cartoonish trope. Austin thought of his own life like that. The boy who had let his father beat him bore no resemblance to the man Austin had become.

Shouman wore a black running bra, partially covered by a red halter top, and black spandex shorts that hugged her shapely body. She seemed proud of her physique and worked hard to stay in shape, running every morning while most people slept.

The national media had always been a cutthroat business, and Austin knew if Shouman grew fat, some young reporter fresh out of journalism school would replace her on the air. The industry only tolerated beautiful talent, and there was always a new reporter, young and hungry, clawing his or her way to the top and willing to do whatever was necessary to get there. Austin had to hand it to her. Shouman had earned her position the hard way, working as a foreign correspondent for a wire service, then as a staff writer for the Washington Herald before her move to cable news. She thrived at the top, despite the competition.

Her work ethic was not the problem.

The streets were deserted at this time of day, which was probably why she rose so early. Having to stop and chat with doe-eyed fans was likely the last thing she wanted. Everyone needed time alone to think. And plan. She receded into the distance, and when she turned the corner, Austin lifted his bicycle off the ground and climbed on. A bicycle worked better than a car because it was silent, could go off-road, and could not be traced back to him.

He pedaled hard and raced south, letting his anger fuel him. He paralleled her and stopped behind a parked car on M Street NW. A minute later, she came into view as she crossed onto a dirt path. Pebbles crunched beneath her sneakers as she descended a steep bank into Rock Creek Park. The park ran north from Georgetown all the way into Maryland and was a frequent destination for picnickers, bicyclists, and joggers. If she followed her routine, she would turn around near the Washington National Zoo and come back the same way to complete her regular twelve-mile run.

He needed to hurry. He sped up Twenty-Eighth Street NW and locked his bicycle to a street sign on R Street NW. Austin grabbed his satchel, jogged into the woods, and descended a steep hill above the Rock Creek Trail. He fought his way through the brush covering the wooded bank and stopped thirty feet from the paved trail. The creek gurgled thirty feet below him, caressing rocks on its way to the Potomac and creating the most relaxing sound in the world. Austin took a deep breath and exhaled to slow his heart rate. He scanned the wooded embankment which obscured houses high on the ridge above him. He could have been in the wilderness, hundreds of miles from civilization, instead of in the nation's capital.

Austin burrowed into a thick mountain laurel shrub, which afforded him a view of the path in both directions. The glossy green leaves and pinkish flowers concealed him. His nostrils filled with the deep organic smell of soil and air supercharged with oxygen. He inhaled it deep into his lungs and checked his watch.

Soon.

A bicyclist rode down the path and Austin turned himself to stone. The human brain alerted to movement and recognizable forms, so he remained still, letting the branches conceal his human shape. The bicyclist passed without slowing.

Austin looked at his watch again. Shouman should have arrived already. Had she altered her route? His stomach tightened.

The sun rose, and the sky glowed blue, but the hill bathed the path in shadows. Shouman jogged into view, her athletic frame and swinging ponytail easily recognizable.

For someone who had spent so many years in the Middle East, it seemed sloppy to have such a predictable routine, but living in a wealthy and safe country distorted everyone's perspective. The world brimmed with evil, and Shouman was part of the appeasement machinery that allowed it to grow like a cancer.

He would demonstrate that she too was vulnerable.

He slid out of the shrub and stumbled, despite having rehearsed the maneuver in his mind. He dusted leaves and dirt off his sweatpants and confirmed no one else was coming. The park had been mostly deserted each of the past three Saturdays when he had stalked her, but bad luck and happenstance could thwart even the best-laid plans.

She slowed as she approached him. Sweat glistened off her skin. As a woman alone in the woods, she must sense danger. Robbery and rape were rare in Rock Creek Park, but they had happened. He checked his watch, pretending to appear disinterested in her. When he raised his head, she was fifteen yards away. He smiled to disarm her and slipped his hand into his bag.

Shouman stared straight ahead and did not make eye contact with him.

She was concerned.

He drew his Model-70S from his satchel and extended the silencer toward her like an accusatory finger.

She did a double take and slowed down. Her mouth hung open. He could see her mind racing, wondering if she should try to run past him or turn around, but it was too late. She was too close to do anything but attack.

Hitting a moving target proved difficult under the best circumstances, and Austin was not willing to chance a head shot. The silencer extended above his front sight, rendering it useless, so he pointed the barrel at her sternum and kept both eyes open.

He fired five times in rapid succession.

Her body jerked, as if she stumbled on uneven ground. She fell forward and landed face-first on the pavement. He stepped aside as she slid to a stop.

She rolled onto her back, and her chest heaved up and down with labored respirations. Blood soaked through her shirt.

He stood over her, and she lifted her head to look at him. She was older, but still beautiful, and revulsion at killing something so elegant clenched his bowels. He reminded himself that she was a monster who had facilitated the deaths of many people. So many Vanessas. The sickness in his stomach subsided.

She tried to get up, and her face wrinkled into a mask of pain.

This bitch had thought she was exempt from consequences. She sat on her throne in front of the camera and spewed her lies, immune from responsibility. Now justice had found her. He had found her. He watched her writhing body and her blood running across the pavement. He smiled.

"To me belongeth vengeance, and recompence; their foot shall slide in due time: for the day of their calamity is at hand, and the things that shall come upon them make haste."

Killing her was not a sin. It was a ritualistic immersion in blood. It washed evil away. He need not fear God, because he did the Lord's work.

Austin fired two more rounds into Shouman's chest, and her body jerked and quivered. He pointed the gun at her head, took aim, and double tapped two rounds into her forehead. His slide locked back—empty.

Her body went still. He filled with warmth.

"I am an angel of God."

His eyes darted up and down the path. Still alone. The pavement glistened with blood, like an oil slick. He needed to leave before he was discovered and forced to make a difficult decision about what to do with a witness. He slipped his gun into the bag and ran into the woods.

He climbed the steep embankment, and it took five minutes of all-out effort to reach the summit. His heart beat out of his chest from exertion. He brushed himself off, swung his satchel over his shoulder, and stepped out of the woods.

He unlocked his bicycle and rode to the waterfront, where he dismounted at the entrance to the Capitol Crescent Trail and walked to the Key Bridge Boat House. He unlocked his kayak, pulled it off an outdoor rack, and carried it to the water. Five minutes later, he paddled across the Potomac.

Austin paused in the middle of the river and watched people walking and jogging along a path at the water's edge. The sun climbed higher into the sky, and he let it warm his face. After a moment, he raised his paddle and continued toward the Virginia shore.

It was going to be a beautiful day.

CHAPTER TWENTY-NINE

Maya Shouman stared through Malachi with dead, unseeing eyes. Her ponytail had stiffened with dark, clotted blood, and her skin had paled, becoming almost translucent. Detectives Brown and Johnson had the lead, but Malachi was convinced this was his killer's work. It had only been five days since Linda Reynolds' murder.

A young bicyclist had discovered Shouman and dialed 9-1-1, then he had recognized her and posted a picture of her body on Facebook. The media had arrived minutes after the police. Patrol officers held a throng of reporters and camera crews at bay while crime techs processed the scene, but several enterprising cameramen had managed to climb through the woods, and pictures of Shouman trended online.

The crime scene had turned into a circus, but Malachi needed to see it with his own eyes. Shouman had been a prominent member of the media and the first victim killed in the early morning, but otherwise, she fit the profile. Shouman had advocated for the Muslim Brotherhood beneath a thin patina of journalistic objectivity. During her weekly show, she had perpetuated the narrative that Islamophobia swept the nation. Anti-Semitism had become far more prevalent, but she never mentioned it, which demonstrated her political agenda.

He moved out of earshot from the crime scene techs and dialed Zahra.

"Good morning, Malachi. I've been expecting your call."

"Sorry to call so early on a Saturday. You heard about it?"

"It is all over the networks. They used a picture taken from Facebook but blurred the face out. Is it really Maya Shouman?"

Down the path, the detectives rolled Shouman's body and searched beneath her. Her ponytail, now brown and encrusted, flopped onto the pavement like a dead fish. Blood spilled out of her open mouth and dripped off her lips.

"It's her. What do you think?"

"Makes sense."

"Because she's pro-Brotherhood?" Malachi asked.

"There's that. Shouman is one of many journalists who advocate, instead of report. She's more activist than journalist."

It seemed like media outlets were either to the political right or left these days. Declaring membership for one side or the other required adherence to dogma, even if it did not fit into traditional conservative or liberal ideologies.

"Most media is biased now, don't you think?" he asked.

"True, but the Brotherhood has adopted the Soviet model of infiltration and one plank of that strategy is controlling the narrative. The Brotherhood has been co-opting the media for decades and they've converted many journalists to their cause."

"You think Shouman worked for them?"

"I don't know if she spread their propaganda because she was trying to help them subvert the US from within, or if their lies fooled her and she acted in good conscience. I can only judge her by her behavior, and she routinely spread misinformation. She served as a tool for the Brotherhood, whether or not she was aware of it."

The detectives examined the blood spatter and moved through the crime scene to approximate where the killer had been standing. Johnson formed a gun with his finger and thumb while Brown moved to the spot where the first bullet had impacted Shouman. They acted out Shouman's last moments, like mimes from the underworld.

"You think Shouman's support for the Brotherhood's narrative placed a target on her back?" Malachi asked.

"Shouman was the most dangerous of all your victims, because she fought the culture war and reached millions of people. Her biased reporting carried the false credibility of objective journalism, which made it powerful and alluring."

"Could the killer have chosen her because the Brotherhood used her to spread its message?"

"That's possible, but what the Brotherhood is doing goes much deeper than that. They aren't just trying to spread lies—they want to control what the public sees. The Brotherhood has influenced curriculum in elementary and high schools across the country. They've subverted large swaths of the media and portrayed themselves as an oppressed minority."

"Victims, not attackers," Malachi said.

"In Europe, critics of Islam have been branded as extreme right-wing nationalists, and while that's sometimes true, the same criticism is used to attack anyone who voices problems within Islam. Calling pundits racists has been such an effective tactic that European speech laws have outlawed criticism of Islam as hate speech."

"But some of it's hate speech, right?"

"Define 'hate speech' for me."

"It's, uh . . ."

"You can't, because it is subjective," Zahra continued. "The people making the rules decide which facts and opinions can be expressed and which cannot. It's a tool of dictatorship."

Malachi watched the reporters craning to get a camera angle.

"I guess."

"For example, Islamists use a strategy called *Hijrah*, which they theologically define as warfare through immigration. They're exploiting immigration policy to subvert Western countries, but the tactic can't even be debated in Europe."

"Why haven't I heard about that?"

"Several respected scholars have suggested that open immigration from Islamic nations can be problematic, because immigrants who hold values antithetical to the West cannot assimilate in large numbers. I'm an immigrant and pro-immigration, but there are reasonable moral, political, and economic arguments for controlling it, and they have forbidden these discussions. Scholars who raise questions are being smeared as racists."

Accusations of racism were thrown around more than ever. A cold lump settled in his stomach.

"You're saying speech is being stifled here too?"

"It's starting. The strategy has been so effective in Europe that people are self-censoring what they say, which means the end of public discourse. The Brotherhood uses a similar strategy here and controlling the media is part of it. Shouman was at the leading edge of that effort, though she wasn't the only one."

"I've been trying to stop a killer," he said, "but what you're talking about is the slow destruction of America—destruction from within."

"It's bad, Malachi, and nobody's talking about it."

Malachi thanked her and hung up.

The killer had gained momentum and Malachi felt like a passenger in an out-of-control car. He wiped sweaty palms on his pants.

Johnson and Brown stood over Shouman while evidence techs bagged her hands to preserve any evidence under her fingernails. Television lights lit up the woods behind them. These homicides had hovered between local and national news since the first murder, but Shouman's death would push the story to the top of every broadcast.

Was that part of the killer's plan?

Collins skirted the path near the body and made her way to Malachi. She lumbered up to him, panting from the long trek through the park. Jones, Hill, and Rodriguez arrived behind her.

"I'm not surprised to see you here," Collins said.

"We have another prominent supporter of Islam dead in Georgetown," Malachi said.

"If these murders are related, you've got the wrong man in custody. Dylan Miller is still sitting in lockup."

"Shi-it," Jones said. "She's right, unless Miller ordered one of his peeps to do the deed."

"Oops," Hill said. He grinned.

"What are you going to do?" Collins asked.

"Cut Miller loose," Jones said. "His lawyer won't let him talk and we don't have enough to connect him to Baker's homicide. We can ask Virginia to charge him with the firearms violation and see if he wants to cooperate later."

Collins looked at Malachi. "Tell me your Brotherhood theory again."

"The Brotherhood is an international terrorist organization dedicated to subjugating the world to a fundamental form of Sunni Islam. They're the parent organization of almost every modern Islamic terrorist group. They fight open jihad in many places, but their strategy here is to infiltrate the government and the culture and destroy us from within. I know it sounds conspiratorial, and I was skeptical at first, but I've seen the evidence."

"Assuming that's true, how does it relate to our victims?" Collins asked.

"They were all fellow travelers pushing radical Islam."

"So, the killer thinks he's doing . . . what?"

"He could be trying to stop the spread of radical Islam or shine a light on the problem. I don't know."

"Goddamn it." Collins dug a lollipop out her pocket and stared off into the woods while she sucked it.

After a moment she faced Malachi. "Maybe the Muslim Brotherhood's a terrorist organization, and maybe our victims' ideologies are relevant, but the killer's motivation is secondary. We need to find him first."

"The Brotherhood's agenda needs to be exposed too."

"That's above your pay grade," Collins said. "Your job is to catch the killer. I'll ask Nuse to have the chief increase patrols in Georgetown. More cops on the street may slow our killer down."

"I doubt it," Malachi said. "He's motivated and smart."

Collins exhaled. "I have bodies leaking all over Georgetown. These cases have national attention, and the pressure will come down hard . . . on all of us. Find our killer and do it fast."

Malachi nodded. He hunted a killer, a serial killer, and uncovering a potential plot to destroy the country weighed him down. To solve these homicides, he needed to understand why his victims were killed, and that meant figuring out if an insidious terrorist organization was involved. And he had to do it soon. It was June 9, and there had been four murders in twenty-one days. Whatever drove the killer, he had increased his pace.

If Malachi failed, the streets of Georgetown would flow with blood.

CHAPTER THIRTY

Chief Ellen Ransom stormed out of Lieutenant Collins' office, followed by a retinue of underlings. She brushed past Malachi in the hallway, almost knocking the coffee out of his hand. He continued past Collins' office, where Nuse was yelling at her, and headed toward the bullpen.

Collins spotted him. "Wolf, find Jones and join the party."

"Yes, Ma'am."

Jones heard his name and looked up from his desk as he cradled his phone against his shoulder and jotted notes on a legal pad. Malachi pointed to Collins' office and Jones waved at him to go ahead.

"Have fun," Hill said, smirking.

Malachi knocked and entered the office. "Everything, okay, LT?"

Collins unwrapped a lollipop. "Where are we on these homicides?"

Nuse scowled and crossed his arms over his chest. More bureaucrat than cop, he had moved quickly up the ranks and had probably been awarded the top spot in the Investigative Services Division as a quid pro quo for some political favor. The bureau was the jewel of the 3,900-officer agency and leading it put him one step closer to becoming chief. Nuse had never been a detective, having moved from Patrol Services North to the Corporate Support Bureau, and onto the Professional Development Bureau. Malachi doubted Nuse could investigate his way out of a paper bag.

Jones walked in holding his notes in the air. "Just got off with the lab. Ballistics came back on Reynolds. We've got a match with the bullets pulled out of Bellini. They haven't compared them to Shouman yet, but we should have those by tomorrow. If it's a match, we're looking at one killer, for at least three of the four homicides."

"We assumed as much," Collins said, "but that doesn't explain why the victims were killed or who did it."

"All of them were connected to organized Islam, and that's where we'll find our motive," Malachi said.

"Why Islam?" Nuse asked.

"I think our suspect is driven by Islamophobia. Baker, Bellini, Reynolds, and Shouman all championed radical Islam in some fashion, and they all associated with Amir al-Kadi, the president of the American Islamic Shura."

"Just because these victims defended a religion doesn't mean they were killed for it," Nuse said.

"AIS is a front for the Muslim Brotherhood, which is a terrorist organization. The Brotherhood has infiltrated our government in an attempt to destroy the US through Jihad, and all our victims supported their efforts. We need to expose what's going on and—"

"Goddammit, Wolf," Nuse said. He leaned across the desk. "That's enough. It's not your job to uncover fantastical conspiracies. Your job is to solve homicides."

"I understand what my job is," Malachi said. His ears burned, and his hands shook. "Our suspect targeted influential people, enablers who promoted a fundamental version of Islam."

"Show me evidence for that outrageous claim."

"For starters, all four of our victims endorsed construction of the al-Azhar Islamic Cultural Center. I read about a strategy in Islam where they build mosques on the site of conquered churches to show the supremacy of Islam. They are constructing the cultural center across from an old Christian church."

"I don't want to hear this bullshit," Nuse yelled, stabbing his finger at Malachi. "It's bad enough that we may have a serial killer on the loose. If you try to link this to Islam, it'll take on a life of its own. The chief and the mayor will have my head . . . our heads, I mean."

"I thought you'd be more worried about catching the killer," Malachi said.

Nuse's face glowed red, and perspiration beaded on his forehead. "I don't want any more unsubstantiated theories. Do I need to pull you off this case?"

Collins stood up. "Chief, Wolf is a good cop and I need my entire team on this. If our victim's religious or political views are relevant, we'll report it. Until then, Wolf won't breathe a word of this outside this room."

Collins turned to Malachi. "You down with that?"

"Yes, Ma'am."

"You're both dismissed. Shut the door on your way out."

They left, and as Malachi closed the door, Collins stepped in front of Nuse with her hands on her hips. Muffled voices emanated from the office as he walked back to his desk. Hill and Rodriguez watched him over their computers.

"Nuse nominate you for an award?" Hill asked. He wore a smug smile.

"Fuck you," Malachi said. He set his coffee down and settled in behind his computer.

Collins' door opened, and Nuse stopped into the hallway. He glared at Malachi, opened his mouth like he wanted to say something, then stomped down the hall.

Malachi knew he could count on Collins to back him up.

"How was your meeting?" Hill asked Jones.

"Not good," Jones said.

"We're in trouble here, aren't we?" Rodriguez asked.

"If Wolf didn't keep shooting off his mouth," Hill said, "we could ride this out until the press coverage dies down."

Collins came into the bullpen and walked over to Malachi. "Not another word about Islam or terrorism. I'm not having it."

"You won't hear me mention it again," Malachi said, "but Islam is the link, and that's how we'll find our killer."

Collins hesitated. Had she had noticed his phraseology? He had promised she would not "hear him" mention terrorism.

"Maybe you're onto something, but nothing goes public," Collins said. "If you think these are hate crimes, I won't stop you from pulling that thread, but keep it on the down low until you have proof. You feel me, Wolf?"

"Yes, ma'am."

She stepped back and addressed the room. "The mayor's sweating the chief and the spotlight is on us. The chief promised to give us all the resources we need, so ask me if you want anything."

Jones shook his head. "We're coming up dry, LT."

"Find me a suspect and do it soon," Collins said.

"We're following every lead," Jones said. "We'll find the asshole killing these people . . . eventually."

"There's no prize for effort, Jonesy," Collins said. "Seriously, this one could hurt us."

CHAPTER THIRTY-ONE

Malachi researched Islam in America. Three and a half million Muslims lived in the US, which meant all four victims supported a political theology alien to ninety-nine percent of the population. America was becoming more atheistic every year, so many self-described Muslims could have casual relationships with Islam, just as Malachi had with Judaism. That made his victims further outliers, because they defended a fundamental version of Islam rooted in Sharia law—the extreme end of the religion.

Why had the FBI failed to uncover the Muslim Brotherhood's plot? Red flags were everywhere. Malachi had not heard from Detective Pinker about what the FBI had on Baker. Pinker was another bureaucrat obsessed with rules and regulations, as opposed to enforcing the law, and predictably, he had ignored his messages.

Malachi grabbed the phone and called him.

"Pinky, this is Wolf."

Malachi enjoyed teasing Pinker with his departmental nickname. Pinker had done nothing noteworthy as a street cop, and he had retreated to the safety of a desk job early in his career. Pinker showed no passion for confronting evil, just a desire to rule over his piddling kingdom. Malachi did not respect him and Pinker sensed it.

"What do you need?" Pinker asked.

"I'm working the Georgetown murders, and I asked you to check my victims against federal investigations."

"Did you run their criminal histories?"

Was Pinker being condescending or dense? "Gee, I didn't think of that, but since I have you on the phone, how about querying the FBI's databases?"

"If you ran a history on the subject of an active federal investigation, they'd get an alert and contact you."

Malachi did not want to tell him Agent Winter had already found Baker mentioned in FBI cases, because Winter had done him an unofficial favor. Besides, Malachi wanted Pinker to do his job.

"That's true if they created the alert and if they want to tell me about their investigation. I want you to run my case information against all FBI reporting. I'm interested in any connections to Islamic terrorism."

"I don't have unlimited access, but there are a few unclassified databases I can query. Send me the information again, and I'll get back to you next week."

"I need the classified reporting checked too, and I need it done now."

"I'll have to fill out classified request forms. It takes time."

"Chief Ransom left our office two hours ago, and she's monitoring the progress of this investigation. Would it help if I asked her to call the FBI for you?"

Malachi was bluffing. He would need Nuse to make a political call, and Nuse would lose his mind if he found out Malachi had contacted the FBI. Malachi pictured Pinker fretting in his cubicle. Having the chief call the FBI would reveal Pinker's incompetence—a bureaucrat's worst nightmare.

"No need for that," Pinker said. "Why didn't you say this was important? I'll look it up now."

Malachi gave him the names, address, and telephone numbers for all the victims, and Pinker sighed as his fingers clattered on the keyboard.

"Okay, I found Baker listed in an FBI investigation and Reynolds named in an intelligence report, but nothing on the other names. The FBI case agent is Special Agent Horn."

"Can you put me in touch with him?"

Pinker pounded his keyboard.

"Agent Horn has an overseas number listed, but the case is with Group Ten in the Washington Division. I'll have to track it down."

"Call me as soon as you have something," Malachi said, and hung up. Government bureaucracy muddled even the simplest tasks. Nothing seemed to work.

Malachi called the American Islamic Shura, and after being transferred several times, they connected him to the president, Amir al-Kadi.

"I'm investigating the four recent homicides in Georgetown," Malachi said.

"Such tragedies," al-Kadi said. "Islamophobia is blowing across this land like a Saharan wind."

"That's very poetic. Bigotry against Islam is a motive we're considering. What can you tell me about the victims?"

"The victims? Nothing, other than they were prominent members of our community and friends of Islam."

"But you knew all of them."

"Hardly. I had the pleasure of interacting with all of them at one time or another through my official duties, but I didn't know them beyond that."

Al-Kadi seemed eager to distance himself, which was odd. In Malachi's experience, a sudden death made people exaggerate their connections to the deceased, as if being closer to tragedy gave them some measure of importance or earned sympathy.

"You know nothing about them?"

"No."

"Enemies they may have had?"

"No."

"Any reason someone wanted to kill them?"

"No reason other than they were upstanding members of the Muslim community and intellectually honest. I think they were killed by a racist."

That was a good theory, but Malachi had decided not to charge the only racist connected to the victims. Malachi thanked him and disconnected.

Now what?

CHAPTER THIRTY-TWO

The pitted concrete and sharp edges of the J. Edgar Hoover Building cast shadows across Pennsylvania Avenue. The brutalist architecture projected the power and anonymity of the state, ugly and Orwellian, as if it had been designed by Stalin himself. The megalith loomed above a steady stream of bureaucrats flowing out of the building into the late afternoon heat. Malachi and Jones parked on Ninth Street NW, navigated between concrete barriers, and entered FBI Headquarters.

Special Agent Jane Evans was one of the FBI's two case agents on the investigations involving Baker and Reynolds. Malachi had asked Pinker to introduce him, but Pinker had hesitated, probably because he had been afraid Malachi would cut him out. Malachi had reminded Pinker that a killer was on the loose and any delay would be his fault, and Pinker had finally agreed to arrange the meeting.

Malachi and Jones showed their badges and credentials to an FBI police officer at the visitor's desk while another officer secured their firearms in a lockbox. He gave them numbered keys and escorted them into the lobby.

Pinker stood beside a petite brunette holding a thin manila folder. She looked young and fit, with hair that flowed over her shoulders and halfway down her back. An older man, wearing a glossy suit and a constipated expression, stood near her, talking on a cell phone.

The man hung up as Malachi and Jones approached, and Pinker introduced them to Supervisory Special Agent Del Shinwari. Special Agent Jane Evans introduced herself with an aggressive handshake, as if she was pretending to be one of the guys in their male-dominated profession. She led them into a small interview room off the lobby.

"Baker and Reynolds are mentioned in our reports," Evans said. "Detective Pinker has completed the inter-agency intelligence request forms, so I'm allowed to share a summary with you. I'm supposed to go through a formal process, but since these are homicides, I wanted to meet you right away."

"I appreciate you cutting through the red tape," Malachi said. "We have four unsolved cases and they're all related . . . somehow."

Pinker held up his hand. "Wolf, your victims were only named in reports, not listed as suspects. There's nothing here."

Evans narrowed her eyes at the formal tone Pinker used with Malachi. It was obvious they were not friends.

"We will run down every lead until something pans out," Malachi said. He turned to Evans. "What do you have?"

She scanned her file. "Linda Reynolds was mentioned in a counterintelligence operation. Those cases are classified, but I can tell you she was, um . . . in contact with a subject of another investigation. I pulled the report and without divulging anything classified, I can say she was present at a meeting with a Hamas operative."

"She met with a terrorist?"

"The meeting was public, and she was there with a couple dozen pro-Palestinian activists. There's no indication she knew she was meeting with a terrorism suspect."

"Interesting," Malachi said. "A Hamas terrorist who met with our victim could be a suspect in her death. Is he here in DC?"

"He left the country after meeting with members of Congress on Muslim Advocacy Day. Reynolds didn't arrange the meetings, and she was one of many activists invited to the gatherings."

"How did a terrorist get invited to Muslim Advocacy Day?"

Evans read the report. "He was a guest of Amir al-Kadi, president of the AIS."

Al-Kadi again. "I'd like to see that report."

"It's classified, but since Officer Pinker has clearance, I can let him review it tomorrow."

"Hmm . . ." Malachi scrunched his face. He could not rely on Pinker's judgment.

"We can try to get you a temporary clearance," Evans said, "but that takes time. The federal government has a huge backlog. If it makes you feel better, I don't think there's anything to this. The report named Reynolds along with twenty-three other activists, and there's no mention of her anywhere else in that investigation."

Evans seemed sincere, but Malachi still wanted to read the report, and he could not ask Collins to get it. If she heard he was running his theory down at the FBI, she would have a fit.

Someone knocked on the interview room door and it opened. A muscular bald man leaned into the room.

"Sorry, I didn't mean to interrupt," he said.

"No problem," Shinwari said. "We're reviewing files with MPD. Let me introduce you. Detectives Jones and Wolf, this is Special Agent Horn . . . Agent Evans' partner."

Malachi and Jones shook Horn's hand, and Horn's eyes lingered on Malachi.

What's his problem?

"Any of my cases?" Horn asked.

"Yeah," Evans said. "We're exploring links between homicide victims and two of our terrorism investigations."

"Go get those fuckers," Horn said. "They're everywhere."

"We haven't confirmed if they're related yet," Malachi said. "Your name was listed as the point of contact, but I thought they had you stationed overseas."

"Not anymore," Horn said. "HQ hasn't updated our database."

"MPD's bureaucracy is just as bad."

"Well, don't let me interrupt. I'll talk to Jane later." He nodded at Jones and Malachi and left.

"What else do you need?" Evans asked.

"What about Baker?"

"That's something I can give you more detail on. Baker's name came up several times in our investigation. That's the main reason I agreed to meet you. Our investigation was, um . . . closed down, but I always suspected Baker was involved in criminal activity. When I heard he'd been killed, I didn't shed any tears."

"What can you tell me?" Malachi asked.

"Last year, Agent Horn and I arrested an Afghan jihadi in the District. Ahmed Barakzai attended a mosque in Northeast DC, and our informant overheard him say he planned to fly to Syria to join ISIS. We put a wire on our snitch, and he met with Barakzai. Our surveillance team identified several other radical Muslims who met with him at the mosque. We grabbed Barakzai at Dulles as he was boarding a plane to Turkey, and the US Attorney charged him with providing material support to a terrorist organization."

"How was Barakzai related to Baker?" Malachi asked.

"The more we dug into Barakzai and his associates, the more they looked like, well . . . members of a terror cell. We didn't have enough evidence to charge anyone else, but we ran financial workups on all of them and discovered three of them, including Barakzai, worked for North Star Development."

"Baker's company."

"That's right. They all made small deposits consistent with their compensation for day labor, but we could not explain several larger deposits made to one of them, a Yemeni immigrant named Fekri Saeed. He received wire transfers that had been approved by Baker. It looked dirty as hell."

"Why wasn't Baker a suspect?" Malachi asked.

"Headquarters shut us down."

"Why?"

"Ah . . . the FBI had been getting a lot of pressure to stay out of the Muslim community. We were under the microscope, and when an assistant director learned our informant had met Ahmed in a mosque, he pulled the plug on our investigation."

"How could he close a terrorism investigation?"

"We were investigating material support by a low-level Afghan Islamist. Horn and I thought there was more to it, but we didn't have any proof and I think HQ feared bad publicity. They made us attend sensitivity training for implicit bias."

Malachi rolled his eyes. The interview room stank of disinfectant and body odor. The stark white walls gave him a headache.

"Your gut told you Baker financed the travel of extremists to Syria?" he asked.

"Or he funded them to do something else, but this wasn't the only case where headquarters tied our hands. It's not politically acceptable to investigate mosques or Muslims without explicit proof of wrongdoing."

"Do you have any idea who wanted to kill Baker?" Malachi asked.

"None," she said. Her body stiffened, and she turned to Pinker.

"So that's it, Detective," Pinker said. "Anything else?"

"Nothing right now," Malachi said. He looked at Evans. "Mind if I call you if anything comes up?"

Pinker frowned.

"Call anytime, and good luck," she said.

She handed Malachi her business card. He tried to take it, but Evans held on for a second too long and locked eyes with him. If he wanted to flatter himself, he would have thought she found him attractive, but he was not that lucky. She wanted to talk to him without her boss in the room. Malachi nodded to show he understood.

Pinker watched him. Had he noticed Evans' unspoken communication?

There was more to this story than Agent Evans was willing to talk about inside the headquarters of the FBI.

CHAPTER THIRTY-THREE

Special Agent Austin Horn stared out his office window, watching Wolf and Washington walk to their car. Had he made a mistake letting Wolf see him? He rubbed his sweaty palms on his trousers and licked his dry lips. Had Wolf noticed his nervousness?

Someone knocked on his cubicle and he stiffened.

"Yes?"

"Hey, Austin," Jane Evans said. "Sorry I didn't tell you about the meeting. It came up last minute, and I didn't think you'd be interested."

"No problem."

"Did you need me?" she asked.

"I found what I was looking for."

"You okay?" Jane asked. "You sound strange."

"My ankle's hurting again."

"Why don't you go home? Take the day."

Austin inhaled, composing himself. He forced a smile and turned to face her. She looked concerned. "I've taken enough sick days. I'll pop a few ibuprofen and be fine."

The Oxycodone made it hard to focus. His eyes drifted over her body. He loved the way her tight skirt accentuated her hips.

"What did you think of Detectives Wolf and Jones?"

Austin jolted, as if pulled from a dream. He met her eyes, and the corners of her mouth turned up, not much, but enough to show her amusement at his discomfort. She had caught him staring.

Austin cleared his throat. "They, uh, they have their work cut out for them."

"Do you think there's any connection between Wolf's homicides and our cases?" she asked.

"None I can see."

"But isn't it odd that two of his victims came up in our investigations?"

"Coincidence."

"Hmm . . ."

Austin turned his attention to papers on his desk. "Thanks for checking on me."

He felt her watching him and forced himself not to look up. When he finally did, she was gone.

Austin exhaled and spun his chair around to look out the window. A fine sheen of sweat had broken out on his forehead and his shirt had dampened. The police had made connections faster than expected. He did not know how or when, but they would identify him. He knew it with absolute certainty.

It was only a matter of time.

His cheek twitched and nausea rippled through his stomach until he thought he would vomit. Part of him wanted to run to his car and drive to the border, never to return. His instincts impelled him to flee, but he could not. Flight meant defeat, a life on the run, and worse—a failed mission.

My quest is righteous.

He pictured the face of his next target, and anger consumed him. The actions of his enemies were responsible for his behavior. They brought God's wrath upon themselves. They killed themselves. He pushed his negative thoughts from his mind, and his ego disappeared. He was a tool. A weapon. He had to stop them. The time for second-guessing was over.

The Angel of Death had taken control.

Austin grabbed a drop phone and dialed the only preprogrammed number in it.

"We have a problem."

CHAPTER THIRTY-FOUR

Malachi left his office for lunch, but instead of stopping at the waterfront for a sandwich, as was his usual practice, he drove downtown. This meeting would be his secret. He parked in a tow-away zone on Constitution Avenue, threw his police placard on the dashboard, and walked east along the National Mall. The white dome of the Capitol shimmered in the afternoon sun.

He crossed Constitution Avenue and climbed steep stone steps to the National Gallery of Art. Tall columns of pale-pink Tennessee marble bracketed the entrance, and he passed through heavy doors into the air-conditioned space. His eyes adjusted to the dark hall, and he gazed down a long corridor of polished limestone into rooms filled with Renaissance paintings and sculpture. Malachi never studied art, but he appreciated the timeless beauty of those works, and he visited the museum a few times each year to escape the endless sorrow he witnessed as a police officer. The treasures man had created reminded him goodness still existed.

Today, Malachi came for a different purpose.

He had called Special Agent Jane Evans and told her he wanted to ask a few more questions. He had suggested they meet at the museum, and she had agreed.

Malachi walked down the corridor, the impact of his shoes reverberating off the stone. A tingling sensation prickled his chest around his sternum. He stopped and grabbed his ribs.

Oh no, not now.

The muscles around his chest tightened, as if someone hugged him from behind, and Malachi placed a hand against the wall to steady himself. He tried to breathe, but the pressure intensified.

"Sir, are you okay?" a security guard asked, walking up to him.

"Fine . . . I'm fine," Malachi said, his voice soft and raspy.

Malachi's muscles spasmed and contracted, as if they were trying to crush him. He had difficulty taking a full breath.

"Are you having a heart attack?" the guard asked.

"No . . . no, I'm fine. It's not a heart attack. It's a muscular problem."

"Should I call an ambulance?"

"It'll go away by itself."

The guard looked skeptical. "Sir—"

"I just need a moment," Malachi said. "Thank you for your concern."

Malachi dug two Gabapentin capsules from his pocket and swallowed them without water. He smiled at the guard.

"There, all better," he said, trying to hide his discomfort.

The guard returned to his position, and Malachi hurried down the hall, taking small breaths to moderate his pain. He rounded the corner into the East Garden Court and leaned against the wall.

The crushing tightness, known as an "MS hug," was painful and scary to endure, the worst of his MS symptoms. His intercostal muscles constricted around his ribs, as if he wore a tight girdle. Difficulty breathing activated an internal alarm, and he tried not to panic.

Relax, it won't last.

Malachi had learned to live with pain, and he needed to fight through his MS to do his job. The Gabapentin acted as an anticonvulsant and alleviated neurological pain, but it took time to work. Time Malachi did not have.

He managed a deeper breath and scanned the garden. Roman Tuscan columns rose above a fountain surrounded by plants and trees. Visitors sipped coffees, chatted, and played on smartphones. Agent Evans waited near the fountain with her hair in a ponytail and her firearm bulging beneath her jacket. She watched him approach and gave a thin smile. Her eyes darted around the room, and she wrung her hands.

Malachi's symptoms lessened as strode across the rotunda.

"Detective Wolf," she said.

"Agent Evans." Malachi shook her hand. "Let me get to the point. I had the impression you wanted to tell me something else yesterday. Can you shed any more light on my murders?"

"I, uh, I shouldn't be meeting you without my supervisor or your liaison."

"I won't share anything you tell me with anyone at MPD. If you give me information, I'll investigate but keep your name out of it. This is just you and me talking."

She sank onto a bench behind her.

Malachi joined her and waited. Half a dozen visitors wandered around the grotto, but none within earshot.

"Yesterday I told you our case was closed after we connected our suspect to Baker," she said. "At first, I thought my bosses were nervous, because Baker was influential, but then they terminated another investigation. My squad handles Muslim extremists in the DC area, and we dealt mostly with al-Qaeda, but now our focus is ISIS."

Malachi nodded and kept quiet. A baby cried on the far side of the fountain. Someone near them drank French vanilla coffee, and the sweet odor made his stomach growl.

"After the Baker case, Austin and I—"

"Agent Horn?"

"That's right. We worked another tip about a facilitator who arranged travel to Syria for aspiring jihadists. We dug a little deeper and identified Qari Tawhidi, an activist with the American Islamic Shura. Are you familiar with them?"

"Baker knew the president, Amir al-Kadi," Malachi said.

"AIS was named as a front group for the Muslim Brotherhood in documents entered as evidence in the Holy Land Foundation trial. We submitted our intelligence reports and within days, we were told to drop the case unless we could charge Tawhidi."

"Did you?"

"We were swamped with other cases, and we hadn't generated sufficient evidence to prosecute, so we closed it. I would not have given it much thought, but the Baker investigation had also been killed, and Baker was affiliated with AIS."

"You thought Baker may be connected to the Tawhidi case?" Malachi asked.

"Both Tawhidi and Barakzai had done work for AIS. I asked my boss, Del, about the resistance, and he said the order came from our special agent in charge, who received his marching orders from headquarters. Two weeks later, headquarters forced my entire squad to sit through eight hours of mandatory Muslim sensitivity training."

She pinched her mouth and dropped her eyes to the floor, clearly uncomfortable speaking about internal FBI machinations.

"Do you think your case triggered the training requirement?"

"I'm not certain, but Horn and I weren't the only ones to have investigations suppressed. Other cases have been redirected or closed by the powers above. Austin was livid about it."

"I'll bet."

"Worse, we're under strict guidelines about investigating Muslim suspects. Years ago, we even had to bring representatives from Muslim advocacy groups with us when we journeyed into the Muslim community. I wouldn't mind, but often those advocates were associated with groups like CAIR."

"That's bad?"

She waited for a young couple to walk past before she spoke.

"American Muslims who oppose radicalism are targeted by fundamentalists, and we took members of a Brotherhood front group with us to interview them. It would be like bringing a member of the Gotti or Gambino families with us on interviews with the Italian community. We tried to establish cooperation and cultivate sources, but when we showed up for meetings, no one wanted to help."

"How does this relate to my victims?"

"Both Baker and Reynolds names came up in FBI reporting, but I didn't tell you everything." She leaned in closer. "You, ah, you have to promise to keep this between us, from one cop to another. I'm not sure why I trust you, but I do. Please don't make me regret it."

"You *can* trust me. I just want to close these cases. I think we're both here seeking the truth."

She exhaled, long and slow. "Maya Shouman's name came up in a classified case we worked on last year. I can't tell you about it, but she met with some nefarious characters. My boss told me not to mention it, because of the publicity around your cases. That made sense, but when we spoke, I decided it was too coincidental. What are the chances that three persons of interest in FBI terrorism cases all ended up dead in Georgetown?"

"Why do you think they were killed?"

"No idea, but I wanted to be frank with you. In my heart, I think they were all involved with terrorism on some level, even though I can't prove it. They were not good people."

"Why don't you investigate now?" Malachi asked.

"I think there's a problem inside the FBI. Austin thinks so too. Last year he got suspended for two weeks because he mouthed off about the interference. I told myself he was overreacting, that the bureau was pure, but now I think the FBI has been compromised. Other agents think so too."

"That's troubling."

"I hope my telling you helps."

"It confirms my victims' affiliation with radical Islam, but it doesn't bring me any closer to a suspect or motive. Is there anything else you can share?"

Agent Evans broke eye contact. "That's all. Good luck."

Malachi rubbed the back of his neck as he watched her walk away. She was still withholding something. There was more to this than he understood. What troubled him most was she had not just looked uncomfortable talking to him—she had looked scared.

CHAPTER THIRTY-FIVE

Malachi climbed into his car outside the museum and started the engine, then he shut it off. Dozens of pedestrians walked along the path ringing the National Mall. It was mid-June and soon, unbearably humid weather would envelop Washington—the unavoidable byproduct of building a city on a swamp.

He leaned back in his seat. Agent Evans' story disconcerted him. The FBI had the lead in domestic counterterrorism, yet several of her squad's investigations had been stopped when they implicated people affiliated with a Muslim Brotherhood front group. If what Zahra had told him was true, and he believed it was, it meant the Brotherhood could protect its membership from law enforcement scrutiny. How were they able to do that? How would it affect his homicide investigation?

The person with the most insight was Zahra, so he called her. He needed answers, but he would have used any excuse to talk to her.

She picked up on the second ring. "Hi, Malachi. How can I help?"

"What makes you think I need something and I'm not just calling to hear your voice?" He hoped that came out playful, because if she was not interested in him, he had sounded like an ass.

"That would be nice," she said. "I'd enjoy talking to you about something other than Islamists and murder."

Malachi smiled. That was the answer he wanted. "Maybe we can get together for a drink."

"I'd like that. I'm planning on taking my Catalina out again this weekend. Care to join me?"

His heart beat faster. "That sounds perfect. I'll bring a bottle of wine."

"Saturday, one o'clock, at the marina."

Adrenaline rejuvenated Malachi, but he still had questions only she could answer.

"I promise not to talk about murder this weekend, but . . . "

"I knew it," she said, and giggled.

He laughed too.

"I'm looking to put something I just learned into context, but it would be easier to do in person. I'm downtown near your office. Can I buy you a coffee?"

"You're in luck. I'm presenting a paper at the Institute later this afternoon, but I have time now. How about a quick lunch?"

His stomach fluttered, like a teenager with a crush.

Malachi picked her up and twenty minutes later, and they walked into Jaleo, a Spanish *tapas* restaurant on Seventh Street NW. Jaleo was one of the oldest restaurants in Penn Quarter, in the heart of downtown. It predated gentrification and had opened its doors when hookers roamed the sidewalks, long before condominiums sprang up like mushrooms. Penn Quarter had become the District's restaurant hub, a bustling neighborhood with ten thousand residents.

The hostess led them to a table by the windows overlooking E Street NW.

"I love this place," Zahra said.

"Thanks for coming."

"Anytime, Malachi."

His stomach fluttered.

She ordered a fresh salad with fruit and goat cheese, and squid with aioli. Malachi loved that she was athletic and thin, but not afraid to eat. He spent an inordinate amount of time thinking about his next meal, and he could not understand anyone who denied themselves that pleasure. Malachi ordered a plate with apple, salad, and Manchego cheese and a chicken sandwich served with piparras peppers. The plates were small, and she suggested they share, a familiar and intimate way to dine.

"What's your talk about this afternoon?" he asked.

"Historic connections between the Brotherhood and terrorism."

"Sounds interesting. I'd like to attend one of your events."

"They can be a little dry and academic, but the topics are fascinating, and they're the reason I immigrated here. I came to warn the West about the Brotherhood."

"And to have a better life?"

"If I find the right person." Zahra flashed her white teeth.

"I'm sure you have to prepare, so I'll make this quick," Malachi said. "Hypothetically, would it surprise you to learn that federal criminal investigations have been closed after they identified people working for Brotherhood front groups?"

"Not at all. The Brotherhood has been infiltrating the US government since at least the 1970s. They adopted the Soviet Union's model of infiltration, which was so effective the Soviets had spies throughout the government, including the deputy secretary of the Treasury Department. It's likely that Harry Hopkins, FDR's chief advisor—a man who lived in the White House—was a Soviet spy. Ironically, Senator Joe McCarthy became the poster child for intolerance because he held anti-communist hearings, but when the US Government released the Venona Papers in 1995, they proved McCarthy hadn't gone far enough. Communist infiltration was everywhere."

"The Venona Papers?"

"Venona were declassified intercepts between the Soviets and their spies in Washington, New York, and other American cities. The intercepts showed deep infiltration by large networks of communists and fellow travelers. Many Americans worked for Communist International, an organization directed by the Kremlin. They targeted education, government, and the media. US policy has been undermined since the 1930s."

Malachi shifted in his seat. Hearing this made him uncomfortable. It sounded like fodder for conspiracy nuts, except everything she had told him so far had been backed by facts.

"I'm embarrassed to say I'm unaware of the Soviet infiltration. Why haven't I heard about this?"

"The infiltration is the reason you didn't learn about it in school or hear about it in the media. The government never decoded most of the intercepts, so who knows how deep the infiltration went? If you're interested, several books address the topic and think tanks have hosted events addressing it. Read *The Venona Papers* or *Stalin's Secret Agents* to get an overview of the infiltration. You can even read some of the decoded messages yourself."

"I'll do that," he said, pulling out his notebook and jotting down the titles. "How did the Brotherhood come to emulate that infiltration model?"

"The Brotherhood was founded in Egypt in 1928, but the Communists had a relationship with Islamists even before the Bolshevik Revolution. In World War II, the Nazis worked with the Grand Mufti of Jerusalem and after the war, the Soviets continued their relationship and used Islamists as geopolitical pawns. Even the United States worked with jihadists in Afghanistan against the Russians. Obviously, that policy backfired."

"The enemy of my enemy . . ."

"It's a bad long-term strategy. The Brotherhood was an open terrorist organization in the early years, but crackdowns by the Egyptian government forced their military operations underground. The Brotherhood's Secret Apparatus stopped overt jihad in 1965 and franchised their terrorism under different banners."

"It sounds like something out of a Dan Brown thriller."

"Everything I'm telling you is true and verifiable. Even the Brotherhood's high-ranking defectors have admitted this, but the message doesn't seem to reach policy makers in America."

Malachi thought about Agent Evans's case being quashed after she linked jihadists to Baker. "You're suggesting the Brotherhood has infiltrated federal law enforcement?"

"A couple years ago, a Homeland Security employee blew the whistle. He said the White House had forced Homeland Security to purge their files of intelligence related to Islamists not involved in criminal cases. It was a devastating blow that blinded the agency, and similar obstruction has happened across the law enforcement, military, and intelligence communities."

"And that was the Brotherhood's influence?"

"Possibly."

"It's inconceivable."

"It's not just Homeland Security. The FBI has been forced to capitulate to Islamic interest groups. The Bureau prohibits investigations inside mosques, despite overwhelming evidence Islamists use them as command-and-control centers and sometimes, even as weapons depots for terrorists."

"That wouldn't happen for any other criminal organization. How high does the infiltration go?"

"That's the million-dollar question. In 2014, the administration intervened to stop the extradition of a top Hezbollah operative, because they thought it would interfere with their negotiations with Iran. Even the intelligence coming out of the Pentagon is tainted by think tanks infiltrated by Islamists. The Pentagon warned intelligence and law enforcement analysts not to use the term 'Jihad.'"

"Is it worse that this is happening or that no one is talking about it?" Malachi asked.

"We're experiencing end-stage infiltration," she said. "There's speculation that White House Chief Counsel David Burke has been co-opted, as have several of President Follet's advisors. The United States is in big trouble. This is the reason I moved here, and I need to stop it."

"That's depressing. I promise not to bring up work when we're on your boat this weekend. I want to get to know you better."

"Me too. It's difficult to meet quality people in a new country. Sometimes, I feel like a social recluse."

They finished lunch, and Malachi drove her back to the Institute. He pulled up in front of Zahra's office but instead of getting out, she swiveled in her seat, her face close to his.

"Thank you for lunch, Malachi," she said, her eyes wide and welcoming.

"I had fun. We have a lot in common . . . uh, I enjoyed talking to you," *I sound like an idiot.*

She giggled, and her face seemed closer. Had she leaned in?

Malachi stretched across the armrest and kissed her on the cheek. She smelled like lavender.

She kissed him back, and her lips brushed the edge of his mouth.

He moved his mouth over hers, and she parted her lips. He held the kiss for a moment. She tasted fresh, alive. She filled his senses and captivated his mind. She overwhelmed him. He pulled back and stared at her.

"Mmm," she said, and opened her eyes. They were brown, like coffee, with gold flecks.

"I, uh, I'm not usually this forward," he said.

She flashed a wide smile. "I don't meet many men, Malachi. Are you one of the good ones?"

"I hope so."

"I hope so too. See you Saturday."

Zahra slipped out of the car, and Malachi watched her walk into the Institute. His heart soared.

He put the car in gear and maneuvered through heavy traffic, replaying the kiss in his mind. He had never flirted with anyone associated with his work before, but this was different. She was not a cop, so an office romance would not be a problem, and she was an expert, not a witness or informant.

It took Malachi ten minutes before he could think about the case again. He would research the Venona Papers and the Secret Apparatus and devour whatever information he could find about Islamist interference in law enforcement investigations. Assuming everything Zahra told him was true, his killer could be a member of the military, intelligence, or law enforcement. He made a mental note to research disgruntled government employees.

Then he thought about the kiss some more.

CHAPTER THIRTY-SIX

At three o'clock in the morning, the silence on P Street NW created its own presence, the stillness of a tomb. Hundred-year-old trees hung over the residential street like a bedroom canopy. Austin leaned against a grizzled elm and dialed his phone. Someone picked up on the fifth ring.

"Hello?" a man answered, his voice strangled by the throaty timbre of sleep.

"Mr. Mohammad Sharif?" Austin asked.

"Yes."

"This is Officer Henry Curtmantle, DC police. I'm sorry to wake you, but we caught a suspect trying to break into your car." If a pretext worked, why change it?

"What?"

"We caught a car thief and you need to inspect the car so we can charge him. Please meet us outside. It should only take a few minutes."

"Who is this?"

"Officer Curtmantle, Sir. MPD. We're outside."

"Give me five minutes."

Austin pocketed his phone and scanned the beautiful brick homes around him, all dark and quiet.

He turned his attention to Sharif's residence, a three-story, nineteenth-century home with faded red brick and green shutters. The residence probably cost two million dollars but was attached to its Georgetown neighbors and did not have room for a garage or driveway, which required Sharif to park on the street with everyone else. The house stood on the top of a small rise, with a flight of steps leading to the street. Behind a curtain of leaves, lights illuminated the third-floor windows.

"And I will execute great vengeance upon them with furious rebukes; and they shall know that I am the Lord, when I shall lay my vengeance upon them."

Austin ducked behind the tree and waited.

Five minutes later, Sharif walked outside cinching a cotton robe around his ample belly. His plaid pajama bottoms hung over his slippers and dragged on the ground.

Austin's stomach tightened; then he felt something else, something new. Excitement.

Sharif descended the brick steps and paused halfway.

Austin remained still. His black jeans and navy-blue commando sweater blended into the shadows, camouflaging him.

Sharif continued down to the street. His car was parked twenty feet away, in front of his neighbor's minivan. He cast his eyes up and down the street and frowned.

Get ready.

Sharif walked to the driver's side of his Jaguar and bent to inspect the door. The glass remained intact, and there was no sign of forced entry. Sharif straightened and spun around as if someone was behind him.

Behind the tree, Austin sneered. He lowered his satchel to the ground and drew a buck knife from his waistband.

Sharif shrugged and walked back toward the house.

Now.

Austin bounded down the sidewalk in long strides. "Mr. Sharif," he said using his most authoritarian tone.

Sharif jumped and whirled around. He looked at Austin with confusion. Then his eyes settled on the knife.

"You can have anything you want," Sharif said.

"That's why I'm here. Vanessa never had a chance to get what she wanted, but I won't make the same mistake."

"Vanessa?"

Austin could not bear to hear Sharif utter her name. He tightened his grip on the knife—a primitive tool, the weapon of a savage.

"My wallet is in the house, you—"

Austin lunged and thrust the knife with a fluid motion.

Sharif raised his hands, but far too late, and the blade punched him in the gut. He staggered backward.

Austin grabbed Sharif's shoulder and plunged the blade deeper into his stomach. Warm liquid ran over his fingers.

Sharif scrunched his face into a mask of pain and grasped at the knife. He wrapped his fingers around the blade, now slick with blood.

Austin yanked the knife out with a slurping sound, and the blade sliced the soft flesh of Sharif's fingers to the bone.

Sharif recoiled, pulled his hands away, and gawked at the lacerations filling with blood. He looked at Austin and opened his mouth.

Austin thrust again and jammed the cold steel into Sharif's chest.

Sharif coughed, and blood bubbled over his lips. His body swayed as if he wanted to fall, but he hung on the knife like a wet coat on a hook.

Austin wrenched the knife out, scraping the blade against Muhammad's ribs.

Sharif fell to his knees clutching his chest and stomach. Intestines slid between his fingers, like uncooked sausage.

Austin hovered over him. Blood dripped off the blade onto the sidewalk.

Sharif shook his head, as if he had trouble catching a breath, then he coughed out a mouthful of thick blood. He opened his mouth and a gurgling sound emitted from his throat. He thudded face first onto the sidewalk. A crimson river oozed across the sidewalk and pooled against the curb. Sharif's chest expanded with a final breath, then stopped.

Austin surveyed the street. The homes stayed dark, with only a few bedroom lights visible farther down the street. No one had seen his victory.

Why had he not used his gun? He had only carried the knife as a backup, in case his gun misfired, and had never considered using it for the kill, not until he had crouched in the shadows and his thoughts had drifted to Vanessa. He pictured her pink lips, her perfect body, her smile. Tears welled up in his eyes and dripped onto his bloody knife.

He ground his teeth and squeezed the knife handle until his knuckles turned white. A snarl escaped his lips. He squatted over Sharif's body and sank the blade into the dead man's back. He pulled the knife out and stabbed him again and again. The steel blade clanked off ribs and made a sucking sound every time he withdrew it. He thrust the blade deep into Sharif until his knuckles slid into the viscid meat. He pounded the knife into Sharif over and over—the image of Vanessa's face before him. Tears ran down his cheeks.

His arm grew tired, and he pulled the knife out and stood over Sharif. His nostrils filled with the rancid odor of blood and feces. He clenched his fists and flexed his muscles. He had baptized Sharif in blood.

Austin had become a tool—an instrument of a vengeful and just God.

His rage evaporated, leaving him exhausted. He looked at the bloody pulp beneath him and gagged. He could not allow himself to vomit and leave more physical evidence. Austin swallowed the bile in his mouth. Blood soaked his clothes and stained his skin. He had lost control of his emotions and put himself at risk. He stuck the knife in his satchel and jogged around the corner.

Austin climbed into a used Toyota Corolla, which he had purchased weeks before with cash and hidden in a long-term parking lot in Virginia. He had stolen a plate off another Corolla and affixed it to his car. If a police officer discovered the stolen plate, Austin would face a hard decision, but he could not risk traffic cameras recording his own license plate. He would have preferred to make his escape by kayak, but Sharif's house lay too far from the river, and it was too risky to ride a bike this late at night. Everyone would be stopped once they discovered the body.

His impulsive attack on Sharif complicated his plan. He had never lost control before, so why now? Was it because Sharif was the most influential of all his victims?

His mood lightened; his guilt assuaged. He brimmed with righteousness. This murder was the best thing he had ever done, his crowning achievement. Next time, he would rein in his anger.

Austin drove across the Key Bridge, careful to stay under the speed limit, and headed home. He could see Vanessa looking down on him, smiling.

He smiled too.

CHAPTER THIRTY-SEVEN

The murder of Presidential Advisor Muhammad Sharif dominated the national news, and pundits, reporters, and other talking heads theorized about the motive behind his killing. The political Left theorized white supremacists had murdered Muhammad Sharif in a vile act of Islamophobia. The political Right posited the likely culprits were assassins from Iran or the Islamic State.

Theories were abundant but facts scarce.

Most murders were committed for mundane reasons—jealousy, infidelity, robbery—but Sharif had been a trusted presidential adviser, a Muslim, and the fifth person linked to Islam to be killed in Georgetown. Sharif had been stabbed, not shot, but his phone showed an incoming call just before his death, which fit the profile. Malachi's killer had struck again.

MPD investigated murders in DC, but when the victim was an elected official or presidential appointee, the MPD shared jurisdiction with Federal law enforcement agencies like the FBI, Secret Service, and State Department's Diplomatic Security Service. Sharif had worked for the last three presidents and was one of President Kenneth Follett's chief advisors, so the FBI intervened. The Homicide Branch became a beehive of federal activity, with FBI and MPD supervisors jockeying for control, but Malachi harbored no illusions about who would call the shots.

The FBI had parked mobile command vehicles outside Sharif's residence and in the parking lot behind the Homicide Branch. An FBI GS-15 acted as the liaison to MPD and passed regular updates to the White

House while an FBI assistant director oversaw a group of twenty special agents. Portable light stands littered the sidewalk outside Sharif's residence making it look like a movie set. Evidence technicians from the FBI's Washington Field Office and the Quantico Forensics lab searched like archeologists descended upon King Tut's Tomb.

The entire block had been cordoned off with yellow tape, and Sharif's body remained on the sidewalk. Dried blood stained the concrete barn red. Malachi would never get used to seeing victims of violent crime. The stillness of bodies taken before their time—the odors, loose skin, and flaccid muscles—the bloating and decay.

Malachi joined Jones, Rodriguez, and Hill.

"Welcome to the circus," Jones said.

"What does this mean for us?" Malachi asked. "Will the FBI push us out?"

"We keep doing our jobs and let the politics play out."

"That won't be easy with the FBI here."

A group of special agents behind them took notes as the assistant director gestured to the crime scene.

"The chief is fighting to keep MPD in charge," Jones said. "She ordered Collins to put her most senior detective on it, so as of one hour ago, I'm the lead."

"Better you than me," Hill said.

Jones grunted.

As the most senior person in the Homicide Branch, it made sense that Jones would have the case, but it meant Malachi had lost his partner on the Baker homicide. Sharif's murder was the ultimate red ball and would push everything else into the background. Police chiefs lost their jobs for mishandling investigations in the public eye, and Malachi knew Chief Ransom would spare no resources.

"You should call your Arab girlfriend about this," Hill said. "I'll bet she knew Sharif in Egypt."

"Make one more bigoted comment, and I'll knock you on your ignorant, lazy ass," Malachi said.

"Any time, College. I'm—"

"Not here, not now," Jones said. "The FBI's all over the place. Show a united front. Enough of this shit."

Malachi did not relish watching the FBI and MPD battle over jurisdiction, so he drove back to the office to research Sharif and cool off.

As a leading expert on Middle Eastern affairs, Muhammad Sharif had advised both Republicans and Democrats. Malachi did not know what advice Sharif had proffered to President Follet, but he had traveled to the Middle East with US delegations and the Administration's policies had his fingerprints all over them.

Malachi scanned dozens of news articles reporting Sharif's pleas for cooperation with the Muslim Brotherhood. When the Brotherhood had become the elected government in Egypt, Sharif had pushed for massive economic aid and the sale of thirty F-16s to then-President Mohamed Morsi. Sharif had called the Brotherhood "a moderate voice of Islam," which did not jibe with an organization that sought an Islamic Caliphate and targeted moderates and secular reformers.

Whenever a crisis hit the Middle East, Sharif had been there. Malachi viewed hundreds of photographs of Sharif and President Follet in the oval office, in cabinet meetings, at press conferences—always by the president's side, whispering in his ear. Malachi found several photos of Sharif with Senator Hansen, but they were group shots with other members of congress or cabinet members. Hansen's contact with multiple victims should elevate him to a person of interest, but as a public official, his connections made sense.

Was the killer trying to send a message with Sharif's murder? And if so, to whom?

.   .   .

Two hours later, Malachi poked his head into Collins' office. The stale odor of cigarette smoke lingered in the air.

"LT, can you spare five minutes for us?"

"Sure, I'm not doing anything today," she said.

Malachi and Jones walked in and sat down, and Jones gave Malachi a look that said this was Malachi's show.

"The first homicide was on May 19," Malachi said. "Followed by Professor Bellini on the May 29, Reynolds on June 4, Shouman on the ninth, and now Sharif on the thirteenth."

"Thanks, Wolf, I almost forgot we've got five bodies," she said. Her stress showed.

"My point is, the killings came ten, six, five, and four days apart. The killer has picked up his tempo."

"No kidding."

"Why have the killings accelerated?"

"Why don't you tell me?" Collins asked.

"It could be the blood lust of a serial killer who needs increasing levels of gratification, or he could be rushing before something happens."

"Before what happens?"

"I don't know."

"You're assuming the same perp killed Sharif," Collins said.

"We're all down with that," Jones said.

"I want to investigate all the murders as a single case," Malachi said. "The victims were all involved with the Muslim Brotherhood, but I don't know how that's relevant."

She lowered her reading glasses and looked over the top of the file at him. "You could be right, but I don't need Brotherhood theories. Not without proof. It'll be bad enough when people find out we've got a serial killer. We tell them there's a connection to terrorism and we'll have a panic."

"And if I'm right?" Malachi asked.

"Catch the killer first. You can find his motivation later. You remember what evidence is, right? I'm being real here. All you've got now is an unformed, unproven theory. Find me proof."

"It will not be easy now that the FBI has their hands in it, and worse if they've been infiltrated. I'll try to find the proof. I just hope I can do it before the killer strikes again."

"You best get going, before it's too late."

CHAPTER THIRTY-EIGHT

Jones hustled off the escalator at Union Station with his shirt untucked and his tie askew. Malachi handed him a coffee. Sweat beaded on Jones' forehead, but he took the hot cup and sipped it. Everyone around them moved with determination. The wheels of government never stopped.

"Sorry, I'm late," Jones said. "The FBI is as nervous as a virgin in a whorehouse. They have the lead, but they ain't making any progress, and they'll be happy to blame everything on us if things go south."

"That won't stop them from taking credit if we find the killer," Malachi said.

In law enforcement circles, the FBI was known for stepping on jurisdictional toes, refusing to cooperate, and holding press conferences to claim credit for the work of other agencies. It annoyed Malachi, but they did know how to promote themselves.

"One last time, for the record, this a bad idea," Jones said. They walked toward the Russell Senate Office Building.

"Wesley won't return my calls," Malachi said.

"That means he don't want to talk to you."

"Fuck him. We have five homicides and Hansen knew at least four of the victims. I don't know if he's involved, but he must have insight into how they're connected. He has to talk to us."

"He don't have to do shit, and we can't prove Islam had anything to do with this."

"We can't prove it *yet*."

"One call to the chief and we'll be handing out traffic tickets. I'm almost at retirement, so do me a favor, son, and go easy here."

Malachi pulled open the heavy door to Senator Hansen's office and Jones followed him into the anteroom, shuffling his feet like a child going to the dentist.

The young blond intern Malachi had seen during their last visit smiled at him. She wore a blouse with a plunging neckline that exposed the tops of her ample breasts.

"Good morning, Detective Wolf, right?" She rolled a finger in her hair and bit her lower lip.

"Good memory, Giselle."

She smiled and leaned forward.

Malachi had been attracted to her the last time they visited the senator's office, and she was every bit as beautiful as he remembered, but this time, he could only think about Zahra.

"We need to speak with the senator," he said. "I've left messages with Mr. Wesley, but he hasn't returned my calls."

Giselle's forehead wrinkled. "Let me check and see if the senator is available. Please have a seat."

Malachi sat down.

"You may remember me too," Jones said.

Giselle dialed her phone and did not react to Jones' sarcasm.

A minute later, Wesley exited the senator's office with a red face and pinched expression. He extended his hand with a practiced smile but gave Malachi an icy stare.

"Detectives," he said.

"We want to speak to the senator," Malachi said.

Wesley glared at Malachi, just long enough to be uncomfortable, and Malachi held his gaze, as if they were teenagers in a staring contest.

"The senator has no time for this."

"He knew all of our victims," Malachi said.

"Senator Hansen is a public figure, and he meets with thousands of people every year. He had minimal contact with your victims . . . professional contact only."

"The senator may have insights into the reason they were killed."

Wesley rested his hands on his hips and corrected his posture. He puffed out his chest, like a gorilla defending his territory. The language of violence was physical. Would he beat his chest?

"The senator had the unfortunate timing of being the last person to see Sam Baker alive. That's all it was—coincidence. He has given you a lengthy interview and told you everything he knows. We're about to make a big announcement and we cannot allow any public association with murder." The cordiality had left his voice.

"Let us decide that," Malachi said.

"Excuse me for a moment," Wesley said, and entered the senator's inner office.

Giselle grimaced. She had probably never seen anyone challenge Wesley. Senatorial offices were filled with smiles, promises, and backstabbing.

"What did I tell you, Mac?" Jones asked, shaking his head.

The door opened and Wesley walked out talking on his cell phone. "He's right here. Let me put you on with him," Wesley said. He wore a Cheshire smile as he handed the phone to Malachi.

Malachi knew who it was before he took it.

"Yes?"

"Listen to me, Detective Wolf," Nuse said. "You will hand the phone back to Mr. Wesley, apologize for bothering Senator Hansen, and walk out of that office."

"Thanks for your support, chief."

"Don't you dare get smart with me. If you bother the senator again, you're finished. Do you understand me, Wolf?"

"I understand you perfectly."

Malachi handed the phone to Wesley.

"Thank you for coming by," Wesley said, resuming his professional demeanor.

"We will solve these murders, Mr. Wesley, and I don't care who it hurts. I want you to know that. I'll never stop."

"I wouldn't expect anything less. Good luck, Detective."

"Let's go, Jonesy."

Jones glared at Wesley with a look forged on the mean streets of Southeast Washington, and Wesley took a half step back. Malachi opened the door and Jones followed him out.

They were halfway down the hall before Jones spoke. "Sweet Jesus. You know how to make friends. I lose my pension, I'm moving in with you."

Wesley was a political animal who saw their homicide investigation as a threat to Senator Hansen's career. Was that all he was protecting?

CHAPTER THIRTY-NINE

Austin sipped a Guinness Stout and licked the foam off his upper lip. The beer would mix well with his opioids. He sat at a café table on the Dubliner's patio and watched a parade of businesspeople, students, and tourists flow out of Union Station onto Columbus Circle.

His eyes lingered on his waitress's pale skin and light-brown hair, which hung below her shoulders. She flashed bright white teeth at customers, but her eyes held an old sadness. She tried to hide it, but it was there, unmistakable, powerful, a force living deep inside her. Austin tried not to stare, but there was something about her. Something familiar. Something troubling.

"Here you go," she said, clanking a plate of Irish poutine in front of him.

Austin inhaled the steam coming off the corned beef brisket and cheese curds, but what interested him were the French fries smothered in gravy.

"I grew up eating these," he said.

"You're Irish?"

"The dish is French Canadian. I grew up in upstate New York. We just called it 'poutine.' We ate it with Michigans."

"Michigans?"

"Hot dogs in casings, covered with meat sauce and chopped onions. Or with spiedies and hams with salt potatoes."

"How did you stay in such great shape eating like that?" she asked, her eyes drifting to his waist.

"Thanks."

She returned to the kitchen and the taste of poutine carried Austin back to New York. The waitress looked like Emily, the girl who had caused him so much trouble in high school. It had not been Emily's fault. She had been innocent, delicate, vulnerable.

Austin had just entered the ninth grade and walked the halls of Livonia Senior High School with students much older than himself, a big change from being the top grade in middle school. Even then, Austin had been big, as large as some seniors though not as physically developed.

Austin had never spoken to Emily, whose family had just moved to Hemlock, but she sat behind him in homeroom and was in all of his classes. She always seemed sad, afraid. Austin recognized the look, understood what it meant. He had suffered abuse too. He watched her during their classes, wanting to tell her he knew she had a knot in her stomach and an ache in her soul. He wanted to look her in the eye and tell her she was not alone, but he had not learned how to speak to girls, and he never said a word.

Austin took another sip of Guinness and watched the sidewalk. Everyone downtown walked fast, always in a rush. DC was slower than New York City, but faster paced than Hemlock. The constant motion made time blur, speed by until the days bled into weeks then months then years. Time passed faster now than when he was young, and life slipped by while he focused on his routine. That should be a lesson for him, but he did not know how to change. He could not stop to smell the roses and still accomplish his mission.

"May I get you another beer," the waitress asked.

Austin smiled. "I'm not supposed to drink when I have to return to work."

"Too bad. Anything else."

"Bring me another Guinness."

She raised her eyebrows. "You're sure?"

"The rules were made by people who don't know what I know. The rules weren't meant for me."

Her forehead wrinkled, and she left to retrieve his beer.

"The spitting image of Emily," he said to himself.

Emily had changed Austin's life. He could still remember her face when Chad and Vinny cornered her in the gym.

At the end of class, Mr. Ricci, the gym teacher, ran outside to break up a fight between two football players. The students retired to the locker rooms to change, except Emily, who had provided a mysterious note from home, and skipped class to sit on the bleachers and read a Judy Blume book. Austin took his time collecting dodgeballs, so he could watch her. She wore a thin cotton dress and cheap shoes, cloaked in the poverty of their blue-collar town, but she looked beautiful.

Two seniors, Chad and Vinny, exploded through the main doors laughing in a way that probably came at another student's expense. They stopped when they saw Emily, and Austin sensed trouble. Their sneakers echoed in the cavernous gym as they lumbered across the floor carrying thickness earned in the weight room. The stopped in front of Emily and she looked up, startled, yanked from the fictional safety of her book and back into the cruel world. Vinny said something and Chad laughed. She bit her lip and leaned away.

Austin bolted toward them and was ten feet away when Vinnie grabbed Emily's hair with one hand and her breast with the other. Chad laughed and put his hands on her too. Rage filled Austin, like it did when he heard his mother scream.

He tackled Vinny, punching him in the head as they skidded across the floor. Austin's knuckles grew slippery with blood, and Vinny's face turned to pulp.

Chad grabbed Austin from behind, but Austin connected with an elbow and Chad fell back. Austin did not possess the strength of the older kids, but he knew how to take pain—something his father had taught him.

He banged Vinny's head against the floor until Chad knocked him to the ground. Chad landed a punch on Austin's chin, but Austin rolled with it, twisted, and punched him between the eyes. Austin was much smaller but possessed with the need to protect. He would fight to the death.

Austin hit Chad over and over, and euphoria filled him until the world melted away and he could only see the target before him.

By the time Mr. Ricci pulled him into a bear hug, both Chad and Vinny lay unconscious. He only remembered flashes of the ambulance, the police, the expulsion. But he recalled Emily smiling at him and her eyes sparkling in a transient moment of victory they would always share. Fellow travelers.

It had all begun then.

"Here's your Guinness," the waitress said, setting it down on the table. "You're a bad boy."

"It's a matter of perspective," Austin said.

Her forehead wrinkled again. "Huh?"

"Rules are subjective and relative. Morality isn't."

She smiled. "I'm Ashley. I hope I see you here again."

"I'll always be here."

Austin watched her walk away then he finished his beer and left. Nothing mattered unless he won, and he had much left to accomplish.

CHAPTER FORTY

Zahra stood beside her sailboat wearing a Brazilian bikini, and Malachi could not take his eyes off her. He did not want to get caught ogling but her long legs, perfect tan, and revealing outfit were impossible to ignore.

"You made it," she said.

"Wouldn't miss it."

"Yalla."

They boarded, and she set the sails then steered them out of the marina. Malachi had told Zahra he needed to interview her, but in his heart, he knew that was a lie. He could not get her out of his mind. He desired her.

By the way she responded, she seemed to feel the same. At least he hoped she did. He had been alone for years, except for sloppy, drunken encounters fueled by whiskey and longing, which left him unsatisfied. Zahra was different. She was intellectual and accomplished, and she stirred something inside him that had been dormant for a long time.

"I don't want to talk shop today," Malachi said. "I came to see you and to get away from my investigation for a few hours, but I need to ask you one work-related question."

"I'm listening."

"What can you tell me about Muhammad Sharif?"

"Sharif's Egyptian, and I've followed his career for years. When Mohamed Morsi became Egypt's president, President Follet's administration supported him, despite Morsi's membership in the Muslim Brotherhood. While Follet's administration claimed the

Brotherhood was a force of moderation, Islamists infiltrated American government, media, and educational systems."

"Insidious."

"I'm impressed with how well they've implemented the Soviet model."

"And Sharif was involved?"

"Sharif advised two previous presidents, and Follett kept him on when he took the reins. Sharif has shaped decades of foreign policy and allowed Islamism to spread across the globe. He rose from an obscure policy expert to Follet's primary Middle East advisor."

"He fits my victim profile."

Malachi leaned over the gunwale and stared into the murky, opaque water. Would he be able to solve these murders before they destroyed his career? He body felt leaden, depleted, and he was not even close to identifying the killer.

"You look like you need a break," Zahra said. "Let me help you forget about work for a while."

A ten-knot wind blew behind them as they sailed south down the Potomac toward the Chesapeake Bay. Zahra's silky hair twirled in the wind. They sailed in silence, and he let the breeze carry away his stress.

"May I ask you a personal question, Malachi?"

"Of course."

She hesitated. "I don't want this to come out wrong, but you're not what I expected. You seem too intellectual to be a police officer. Is that an insulting thing to say?"

"It's a common misconception. Police officers come from a cross section of society. I was in a PhD program at Harvard before I joined the department."

Surprise registered in her eyes, and a sly smile crept across her face. "I want to hear the story behind that career change."

Malachi did not want to dampen the mood, but he wanted her to know everything about his life, everything about him. He needed to tell her.

"My father was killed in the Boston Marathon bombing. After that, I joined the police department. I know it sounds cliché, but I needed to do something."

"I'm so sorry, Malachi. I didn't know. You don't have to talk about it. You—"

"No, it's okay. I know I took a strange path. When I applied to the Metropolitan Police Department, I was required to pass a psychological evaluation. The tests and questions were transparent, asking about suicidal tendencies, if I enjoyed torturing small animals . . . that kind of thing. I tailored my responses to give them what they wanted."

"I'm sure you did."

"After the test, the psychologist asked me why a doctoral candidate chose law enforcement, and I said my father's death made me want to help other victims. She suggested economics may have been a way for me to create order out of the messiness of life, and when economics could not explain terrorism, I threw myself into criminology hoping it would be a more effective science."

"Makes sense."

"I've wondered if my career change was an overreaction driven by P.T.S.D. Did I join law enforcement to empower myself, and if so, was that wrong? Aren't men supposed to take action?"

"I think it was an understandable decision."

"I needed revenge, but police killed one bomber and put the other in jail, and my need for justice morphed into rage. I needed an outlet."

"Joining the police department was a noble act."

Malachi nodded and watched the waves.

His new career could be exciting and fulfilling, but his misgivings came in fleeting bouts of terror as he lay on the edge of sleep. His decision had cost him his family and guaranteed a life of financial mediocrity. He simultaneously loved and regretted his choice, but solving these murders would validate his decision.

"I never talk about this stuff with anyone," Malachi said.

"Everyone needs someone to understand their experience."

"Who do you have?"

"I'm close to my family in Egypt, but I'm living a different life here. I keep a professional distance from my colleagues. I'm always worried that mixing my personal and work lives will hurt my reputation and damage my credibility. It's harder for a woman."

"I'm glad you didn't keep your distance with me."

She blushed. "We don't work together . . . and there's something about you."

Zahra tightened the mainsail and secured the sheet to a cleat, then moved forward in the cockpit and lowered the jib. It billowed as the wind caressed its canvas folds. She kicked off her flip-flops and climbed on the deck, using a halyard for balance. She moved along the gunwale to the bow and expertly folded the sail.

Malachi's eyes lingered on her. The sun warmed his skin, and his stress evaporated.

Zahra lashed the jib with a line, returned to the helm, and maneuvered them close to the point on the western bank. With only the mainsail up, the boat slowed.

"We're looking for a small red buoy," she said.

Malachi eyeballed the brown water but saw only ripples. "I don't see anything."

"It's submerged. This is one of my favorite spots, and I don't want other people using my mooring. It's just below the surface, forty yards off the point."

"Why don't you anchor?" he asked.

"The river bottom is covered with fallen logs, muck, and debris. I've lost two anchors, so I gave up and set this mooring. It's a heavy anchor stuck on the bottom with a chain and buoy attached. There it is." She pointed ten yards off the starboard side.

Malachi still did not see it.

She turned the bow into the wind, luffing the mainsail and cutting their speed. A few seconds later, she spun the wheel hard to starboard.

"Take the helm and hold us steady," she said.

Malachi grabbed the wheel as she scampered forward, lay on her belly, and reached over the gunwale. She spread her legs for balance and arched her back as she stretched. He stared at her, electrified.

Zahra lunged over the side and came up with a bright red float at the end of a chain. She tied a line to it and threw it back into the river. The boat glided to a stop and rotated as the line tightened against the mooring.

She dropped the mainsail, and Malachi helped her lash it to the boom.

"Too easy," she said. She pushed a lock of hair behind her ear.

"You're beautiful," he blurted without thinking.

Her smile came from deep inside and was authentic, captivating . . . devilish. Zahra leaned in close, her face inches from his. "Thank you, Malachi."

His stomach fluttered.

Zahra had exhibited great courage by moving to a foreign land and speaking truth to power. Malachi had grown up with comfort and security, making it difficult for him to comprehend her strength. He wanted to help her, protect her. He felt like a better person around her. She cared about ideals larger than herself and understood his need to find justice, something Alison had never done. An image of Alison flashed in Malachi's mind, but her hold on him had vanished.

It was time to move on.

Malachi held Zahra's face in his hands and kissed her. She tasted like spearmint.

She hesitated then kissed him back, and his brain flooded with endorphins. He had missed the touch of another person, the intimacy of romantic love. He had been lonely, living with his pain, but now his world brightened and filled with hope.

She pulled back with her eyes closed, and her lips parted. She opened her eyes and smiled. It filled him and drove away his worry and doubt.

He pulled her onto his lap, and she draped her arms around his neck. He kissed her. She parted her lips and his tongue explored her. Her lavender perfume intoxicated him, as if he breathed her in.

Zahra ended the kiss. "I knew you wanted me."

"Since the first day I met you," he said.

Her eyes twinkled as if she knew something he did not, then she ran her nails through his hair.

Malachi slid his hand down the smooth, toned leg. He kissed her again, this time rougher, ravenous.

She bit his lower lip, playful and enticing, then shifted in his lap and brushed her breasts against his chest. She reached behind her back and pulled the drawstring of her bikini. Her top fell down, and she shrugged it to the deck.

Malachi glanced around, conscious they were outside. Another sailboat tacked across the river about seventy-five yards away, but the wooded shore appeared deserted.

"Afraid someone will see?" she asked.

"Just checking. You're breathtaking."

She climbed off his lap and offered her hand.

Malachi took it, lost in her deep brown eyes.

She led him forward, and his heart raced as if he had been running. Things were moving so fast. She opened the wooden hatch, and they climbed down the companionway into the cabin. She ushered him past the small galley and through the salon into the forward berth. She pushed open the door, and they entered a triangle-shaped stateroom wedged in the bow.

Malachi flicked the light on.

"Close the light," she said.

"Aye, aye." He shut it off.

Zahra guided Malachi onto the mattress, pushed him onto his back, and kissed him.

He caressed her body, and goosebumps rose on her soft skin beneath his fingertips. His thoughts grew hazy, and his heartbeat pounded in his ears.

She unbuckled his belt and hooked her fingers under his waistband. She looked at him with wide, hungry eyes, then pulled his khakis and boxers off. She stood at the foot of the bed and smiled.

Malachi propped himself up on his elbows and watched her. She pinched the bows on her bikini bottom, narrowed her eyes, and pulled the strings. Her bikini dropped to the floor. Malachi's eyes drifted down.

"Do you like my body?" she asked.

"You're gorgeous."

"I want you inside me."

"Come here, Dr. Mansour."

She giggled and climbed on top of him. They explored each other, awkward at first, then ravenous, passionate—magical. The sweet smell of summer lilac drifted into the cabin from shore. They made love, and the boat bobbed up and down in rhythm with their bodies.

Afterward, Zahra collapsed onto his chest, and sighed.

He stayed inside her, lazily stroking her thigh with his hand.

She cooed and lifted her face to his. "You were amazing."

Malachi gazed into her soft eyes and noticed tan flecks near her irises. He saw something else too—vulnerability. He kissed her again and pushed her hair away from her eyes. Her smile energized him. For the first time in years, he opened himself to something deeper. Something real.

"You're perfect," he said.

She smiled, then her eyes grew distant, and she turned away.

CHAPTER FORTY-ONE

Malachi finished a three-mile jog, his first pleasure run since the Boston Marathon. Something about Zahra freed him to try again, and the exercise melted away his stress and focused his mind. He had missed the clarity. He showered and dressed, then paused in his living room to watch Zahra on his balcony. Her courage, tenacity, and certainty made Malachi want to be part of something bigger, be a better person for her. His confidence rose around her. For seven years he had been on a mission to fight evil, but Zahra reminded him there was more to life. She made him happy, and he wanted to stay that way.

He stepped onto the balcony and handed her glass of Sauvignon blanc, and she smiled with wide, soft eyes. She had spent the day at her institute, while he chased leads in the Baker investigation. None of his efforts had panned out, and the anticipation of seeing her had driven him to distraction.

He dropped into the chair beside her and they watched the sky turn vivid shades of sienna and persimmon. It was his favorite time of day, and he filled with contentment. He had erected emotional barriers after Alison left him, but with Zahra, he had been reborn.

"It's beautiful," Zahra said.

Malachi fixed his gaze on her. "Yes, beautiful. I needed this."

"Tough day?"

"No progress. Our best suspect was a white supremacist tied to Baker, but we had him in custody when Shouman was killed, and I have nothing linking him to the murders."

"You're taking this personally."

"Hell, every case is personal. Every victim is a father or mother, a son or daughter."

"I have a feeling this case is special."

"Islamists killed my father."

Condensation beaded on his glass and a droplet of water ran over his knuckles. It was mid-June and the heat of the day clung to the earth. He knew he should not sit in the muggy air which could trigger his MS, but he wanted to live a normal life. He took another sip and watched two fishermen motor up the river in a Jon Boat.

"If it's not your Nazi, who else could it be?" she asked.

"He's a white supremacist, not a Nazi."

"Very sorry, I didn't mean to insult him." She laughed.

"I know more about white nationalists, separatists, and supremacists than I ever thought I would. They're all assholes."

"You think another hate group was involved?"

"The killer could be choosing victims because they support fundamental Islam, or because they facilitate Arab immigration, or million other reasons. Maybe he was ousted from the Brotherhood's ranks and wants revenge."

Something crawled under Malachi's skin, and he scratched his arm, but the sensation did not go away. An itch that could not be scratched—the strangest of his MS symptoms. He clawed at it.

Zahra placed her hand over his, probably interpreting his scratching as frustration. "It's okay if you don't want to talk about work."

"No, it helps. Without you, I may not have discovered the connection to radical Islam."

Malachi's phone vibrated, and Alison's name displayed on the screen. He wanted to ignore it but worried something could be wrong with his girls. He picked up.

"Chad left me," Alison said without preamble.

Elation flickered through Malachi, then Alison sniffled, and guilt replaced his happiness.

"I'm sorry. I know you cared for him. What happened?"

"He . . . he said he wasn't ready for an instant family. He—"

"Chad doesn't deserve you, and you're lucky you found out now before you ended up marrying him. You don't want another divorce. Our marriage gave you enough drama for one lifetime."

She laughed, making Malachi glad he could still cheer her up.

"Marriage to you wasn't all bad," she said. "What are you doing now? Do you want to come over?"

His pulse quickened. Alison had not invited him over in years, other than to see the girls. What did her invitation mean? Did she want him back in her life? Back with his children?

"I, uh, I have company right now."

"Oh . . . sorry to interrupt your date. I'll let you go."

Was Alison jealous? If his dating angered her, would she limit his access to the girls? He probably should not have said anything, but he refused to hide Zahra from Alison or from anyone else.

"Are you sure you're okay?" he asked.

"I think so . . . just a momentary lapse. Thanks for listening."

Malachi hung up and met Zahra's eyes. "Ex-wife."

"Are you close?" Her tone came out light and airy, but her body had stilled.

"We've kept it amicable for the girls. She just went through a bad breakup."

"I can leave if you need to talk to her."

"No, I'm where I want to be."

Zahra lay her head on his chest. The sun dipped beneath the horizon. "This has been a tough month for you, hasn't it?"

"My cases consume me. I feel this urgency, as if I'm the only one who can speak for the dead."

"You'll figure it out."

An idea floated at the edge of Malachi's consciousness, and he sat up trying to grasp it. If the victims all pushed radical Islam in the West, and if they supported the Muslim Brotherhood, maybe the killer wasn't Islamophobic—maybe he was trying to stop the Brotherhood itself.

"What is it?" Zahra asked.

"What if my victims weren't just fellow travelers? What if they were members of the Brotherhood's Secret Apparatus? Would killing a handful of Brotherhood operatives in Washington interfere with their plans to subvert the country?"

Zahra's eyes drifted down before she answered. "The Brotherhood is a massive, worldwide organization, and killing a few members wouldn't stop them, but their Secret Apparatus, the group waging violent jihad, is much smaller. The number of well-placed infiltrators is an even smaller subset." She nodded her head as though her thoughts were coming together.

"Would killing five people have an effect?"

"Yes, if the killer targeted the most influential infiltrators in the US. Look at your victims. Baker used foreign money to finance the al-Azhar Islamic Cultural Center. Professor Bellini's academic standing gave him an air of credibility to spread the Brotherhood's propaganda and indoctrinate our future leaders. Reynolds rallied activists in defense of fundamental Islam, and Shouman spread the propaganda and swayed public opinion. Sharif encouraged three presidents to support the Brotherhood."

Malachi turned in his seat, alert. It seemed so obvious. "They were all on the front lines of the propaganda war, winning hearts and minds."

"The Brotherhood designed its infiltration to destroy the United States from within. They've been more aggressive in Europe and in the Middle East, but the endgame is the same across the world. In Islam, they call this strategy *Amalia Jihadia Hadaria*."

"What does that mean?"

"Civilization Jihad Operation."

A chill flickered up his spine. If the killer was trying to stop the Brotherhood, not because they were Muslim or Arabic, but because they were trying to destroy the United States, then looking at Miller and his ilk was a mistake. Malachi needed to identify someone who knew what the Brotherhood was doing and had the skills to carry out the plan. Could it be someone in the CIA? Someone in law enforcement?

A thought hit him like a slap across the face. "I've been going about this all wrong," he said.

"Meaning?"

"I've been too reactive. I've been chasing this psycho all over Georgetown, always one step behind, when I should have been ahead of him."

Zahra smiled. "You know what he's trying to do now."

"He's going after infiltrators. I need to get inside his head. Who would I go after next? If I can think like him, I can predict who he'll target."

"In theory," Zahra said.

"Can you give me a list of the people you've identified inside the Secret Apparatus? I mean the most influential people, infiltrators who deny any affiliation with the Brotherhood."

Zahra thought for a moment. "I can put some names together, but I've identified them through analysis, so I don't have incontrovertible proof."

"We're quite a team," Malachi said.

She nuzzled her head against his shoulder. "Yes, we are."

"Are you blushing?"

"I'm thinking about our first time on the boat. Do you think I'm slutty?"

"No, I—"

"I don't make a habit of sleeping with men this fast, but something came over me. I hope you don't think less of me for giving myself to you too soon."

"I feel like I've known you forever."

"Me too, but I was afraid I moved too quickly."

"You're perfect," he said.

Zahra stood and took his hand. "Flattery will get you everywhere, Detective Wolf."

She led him into the bedroom, and Malachi's chest lightened, either from arousal or because he finally had a plan. Probably both. Everyone on Zahra's list would be a potential target. He could get ahead of the killer.

He could set a trap.

CHAPTER FORTY-TWO

Austin knew evil existed everywhere, but it was impotent without resources. Black and gray markets funded the Muslim Brotherhood and enabled them to spread like a virus. To slow the spread of the radical Islamic infection, Austin needed to hurt them where it counted—in the wallet.

Terrorist groups received financing from a myriad of illicit businesses, ranging from drug trafficking to the sex trade. Some Islamic charitable organizations funneled money to terrorist groups like Hamas and ISIS, and individual donors laundered money through financial institutions. Rogue States, like Iran and North Korea, funded terror groups from Hezbollah to the Taliban.

Tracking terrorist funding proved problematic when it involved countries vital to US interests, as evidenced by Saudi Arabia's involvement in the 9/11 attacks. Intelligence agencies across Europe and the Middle East agreed Qatar financed Islamic terrorism, yet the US engaged in a bilateral partnership with them. Qatar pretended to be a US ally, while secretly acting like an enemy.

If President Follet did not take action, Austin would.

Thanks to transparency laws, Austin had used public records to track money flowing into both the Al-Azhar Islamic Cultural Center and Senator Dale Hansen's presidential exploratory committee. Significant donations had come from Smith and Wadsworth, a lobbying firm with connections to Qatar. Even the company's leadership had maxed out their allowable individual contributions.

Austin had also used FBI databases to track Qatari money funneled through Smith and Wadsworth Executive Vice President David Hammond. Austin had contacted Hammond several weeks ago and identified himself as Frederick Barbarossa. He had asked Hammond to help his firm, Exploration Partners, win State Department approval for a billion-dollar oil exploration project in Kazakhstan. Hammond had seemed suspicious, but the promise of profit had kept him on Austin's hook.

Austin leaned back in bed, with Sophie on the floor beside him, and unlocked a new prepaid cell phone. He called Hammond's secretary, and after a minute on hold, Hammond picked up.

"We need to move forward with our project," Austin said. "I need to know if Smith and Wadsworth is onboard."

"I've discussed your proposal, and we're interested."

"I need more than interest. Will Smith and Wadsworth lobby for the pipeline?"

Hammond sighed. "This whole thing is highly irregular."

"I'm sure a billion-dollar project doesn't come across your transom every day," Austin said.

"I did a little research and found very little about Exploration Partners. It's an S-Corp out of Delaware with a simple website, but little else. I—"

"It's a new company, based in Delaware for tax purposes."

"I don't mean to insult you, Mr. Barbarossa, but it smells fishy."

Austin's cheek twitched. "I won't waste your time or mine. I represent significant foreign backers and they value their privacy. Surely you can appreciate that."

"Yes, but—"

"I can't confirm the names of our investors but perhaps you're familiar with Saudi Prince Abu Hassan?"

Hammond was silent, and Austin smiled. Prince Hassan dealt with many American companies and was considered a whale—a client with deep pockets.

"I'm aware of Prince Hassan, but due diligence requires—"

"We only need Smith and Wadsworth to massage the State Department into granting approval for the foreign contract. There's nothing illegal or untoward going on here. I'm sure my investors will be more than thankful for any help your firm can provide."

"Yes, of course."

"There's over one billion dollars at stake here, and to show our seriousness, I'm prepared to deliver a good-faith advance of five hundred thousand dollars, but I need your answer tonight."

Hammond exhaled. "I have a fiduciary obligation to my board," Hammond said. "I'll take the check and prepare the contract, but only with the understanding that I'll need more information before work begins."

"Understood. I just need things moving forward by next week. I'm on my way out of town, and I'd like to give you the check tonight. I'd prefer to be discreet, so meet me at the Dumbarton House, and I'll provide you with both the check and an information packet about the project."

"You can't come to my office?"

"Mr. Hammond, I'm giving you half a million dollars on good faith. Please extend me the courtesy of meeting outside your office. Six-fifteen on the bench in the garden outside the Dumbarton House."

"I don't like this cloak and dagger business. We should do this in your office instead of skulking through a garden like characters in a John le Carré novel."

"Thank you for understanding," Austin said, and hung up.

He was going to enjoy this.

CHAPTER FORTY-THREE

Malachi sat in his car at Continental University and waited for Professor Farouk Abdullah to head home for the day. Students hustled through the parking lot, and Malachi unclipped his seatbelt, in case he had to draw his Glock from a seated position. He shifted in his seat and stretched his back. Stakeouts brutalized his body and made him antsy.

Zahra had delivered a list of sixty-three names, as promised. The number shocked Malachi, and Zahra had claimed these were only people she was certain worked for the Secret Apparatus. Her full list of potential Brotherhood infiltrators topped three hundred. Thinking about it made him nauseous.

How long had this been going on?

Malachi had told Zahra he would contact the potential victims, starting at the beginning, but when he arrived at his office and reread the list, he changed his mind. If he contacted sixty-three people and told them he thought they worked for the Muslim Brotherhood and their lives were in danger, he would cause a public relations nightmare. Collins had told him to keep his theories about terrorism under wraps and accusing respected citizens of supporting a terrorist group would not be smart, even if he was trying to save them.

He narrowed the list to those working in the Washington metropolitan area, which reduced his potential targets to thirty-nine. The killer had only struck in Georgetown—which had bothered Malachi from the beginning—so he further culled the list to those who lived or worked there. Seven people matched his criteria, and of those Zahra had characterized two as minor players, so he scratched them off.

That left five potential victims: another Washington Colonial University professor, a lobbyist in a large K-Street firm, a Washington Herald reporter, a civil rights attorney, and Professor Abdullah, who taught at Continental University. Malachi would ask for their cooperation, hoping they would agree because their lives could be in danger. He was violating Collins' order, so he did not share his plan with Jones—for Jones' own protection.

What could possibly go wrong?

Professor Abdullah exited the side door of the political science building, and Malachi recognized him from the university's website. Professor Abdullah appeared to be in his late fifties with a receding hairline and trimmed beard. He wore a tweed jacket, glasses, and carried a leather attaché—classic professorial attire. Abdullah moved through the parking lot and Malachi intercepted him as he reached his car, which Malachi had identified through a Department of Motor Vehicles check. It would be that easy for the killer if he could access government databases.

"Professor Abdullah?" Malachi asked.

Abdullah jumped, and fear flashed across his face. "Yes?"

He knew he was in danger.

Malachi displayed his badge. "Detective Wolf, MPD Homicide. Do you have a moment?"

Abdullah glanced around the parking lot. "What's this about?"

"I'm working a homicide and there's a chance you're in danger. Will you join me for a cup of coffee?"

Abdullah followed Malachi to a Starbucks, and they sat at a table away from the counter. The coffee house smelled like hazelnut, and a handful of young people typed on laptops around them.

Malachi kept his voice low. "I'm investigating the recent murders in Georgetown. I'm sure you're aware of them."

"Yes."

"All the victims had some connection to the Muslim Brotherhood, and all worked or lived in Georgetown. I think the killer targeted them because of their ideology, and because they were part of the Brotherhood's Secret Apparatus."

"The Secret Apparatus dissolved decades ago."

"I have information that it still exists and is active here in the United States."

"That's very interesting, but what does this have to do with me?"

"You fit the victim profile, and there's a chance the killer will target you. It's just my theory, but I feel obligated to warn you, and I'd like your cooperation to trap whoever is doing this."

"Fit the profile? I have no connection to the Brotherhood."

"You've spoken in public about the dangers of Islamophobia, and you've characterized the Brotherhood as an agent of moderate Islam. Both statements parrot the Brotherhood's talking points."

Abdullah slammed his palm on the table. "How dare you accuse me of working for a foreign entity."

Three students at a nearby table looked over at them.

"I'm not accusing you of anything. I'm saying your behavior fits the profile of other victims. I'm here as a courtesy—to warn you."

Abdullah's face darkened. "That's absurd. I don't work for the Brotherhood. I've reached every one of my positions through intense research and academic rigor. I believe the Brotherhood is our best option to combat terrorism and foster peace in the Middle East. I assure you I'm not a mouthpiece for any outside organization. That's a slanderous accusation."

This is not going well.

"I'm sorry I offended you, but I'm trying to protect you. I want to set up security cameras at your residence and ask you to be more cautious traveling to and from the university. If you don't want my help, I can move on."

Abdullah stood up. "I don't need any security, and I'm not happy about this."

"Don't take offense, Professor. Here's my card. Call me if you see anything suspicious or if you change your mind about security."

"You may hear from me, but it won't be to ask for security."

"What does that mean?"

Abdullah snatched the card out of Malachi's hand and jammed it in his pocket. His face burned red, but he seemed more scared than angry. He stormed off.

Was he worried about the killer or because Malachi had discovered his connection to the Brotherhood?

Abdullah had been no help at all. If he was unwilling to cooperate, perhaps the Brotherhood would. They should be motivated to protect their own people, and Malachi still had AIS President Amir al-Kadi's number in his phone.

He dialed.

"I spoke to you two weeks ago about the Sam Baker homicide," Malachi said.

"I remember."

"Now I'm looking into four additional murders, and I need your help."

"And?"

Al-Kadi did not sound happy to hear from him. Malachi had been getting that reaction a lot.

"I think the killer targeted his victims because they supported the Brotherhood, and I was hoping you could tell me who would want to kill Brotherhood members?"

Silence.

"Mr. al-Kadi?"

"Why would you call me with this question?"

"Because AIS is affiliated with the Brotherhood."

"AIS is a nonprofit organization devoted to issues impacting Islam. It is not, nor has it ever been affiliated with the Muslim Brotherhood."

The sternness in his voice shocked Malachi. Malachi was trying to solve five murders and prevent the deaths of more Muslims. Between al-Kadi and Abdullah, he was fed up with the lack of cooperation.

"The FBI labeled several American Islamic organizations as front groups for the Brotherhood, including yours, and you have publicly supported the Brotherhood," Malachi said. "I'm seeking justice here, trying to save lives."

"Your suggestion that AIS is part of the Brotherhood is unsubstantiated. Your victims were not members of the Brotherhood, and they did not work for AIS. If you repeat these allegations, I'll be forced to take legal action."

"If you're not connected to the Brotherhood, how do you know if the victims worked for them?"

"You travel down a dangerous road, my friend. You should be careful."

"Is that a threat?"

"You sound like a smart man," al-Kadi said. "Take it any way you wish."

CHAPTER FORTY-FOUR

Malachi sat at his desk and reviewed the profiles of the four potential victims remaining on his list, certain the killer would target them. His meeting with Professor Abdullah had been awkward and confrontational. Would other potential victims have similar reactions?

Senator Hansen's image played over and over on the television mounted on the wall. Hansen had declared his candidacy for president, and he had become the media's shiny new toy. Malachi watched Hansen's smiling face and a wave of nausea passed through him. What would reporters do if they knew the senator had refused to answer his questions?

"Wolf, get in here," Collins shouted from her office.

Trouble.

Jones raised his eyebrows in an unspoken question, and Malachi looked away. Jones followed him into Collins' office.

"Sit," Collins said.

"You want me in on this, LT?" Jones asked.

"I need you to understand this too," Collins said. "Straight up. I'm gonna tell you what time it is, and I need you both to hear me."

Jones slid into the chair beside Malachi.

Two lollipop wrappers lay crumpled on Collins desk. Malachi clenched his jaw, knowing what was coming.

"This morning I received a call from FBI Supervisory Special Agent Del Shinwari," Collins said. "He called to remind me the FBI has the lead on the Sharif investigation, and he told me not to contact any suspects or witnesses without clearing it with him."

Del Shinwari had been born in Afghanistan. Was he Muslim? Malachi caught himself. Not all Muslims believed in fundamental Islam, and he needed to judge people by their individual behavior. Buying into religious stereotypes would make him no better than Dylan Miller or the Islamists.

"If the FBI's concerned we're ahead of them, they should start investigating, instead of trying to slow us down," Malachi said.

"The FBI is the least of your problems," Collins said. "I just got off the phone with Chief Ransom. Guess what she wanted."

"To congratulate us on our diligent and insightful work?"

"Knock that shit off. Her office received complaints from both Continental University and the American Islamic Shura. She asked why my detective accused a professor of being a terrorist and wanted to know how the murders were connected to the Muslim Brotherhood. I didn't know what to tell her, since there isn't any proof . . . none at all."

"That's not how it happened," Malachi said.

Jones leaned back and exhaled.

"That doesn't matter," Collins said. "I ordered you not to share your conspiracy theory outside this office and certainly not with civilians."

Malachi knew he was in hot water, but he would take the heat if it meant saving lives. The office seemed smaller than it had a minute ago.

"Our victims were all Brotherhood apologists and possibly card-carrying members," Malachi said. "The killer thinks he's protecting our country."

"A vigilante?" Jones asked.

Malachi could always count on Jones to get it.

"I don't care about an unsubstantiated theory," Collins said. "You ignored my order and I'm not having it. All eyes are on us and you know it."

"LT, I—"

"The chief won't tolerate bad press."

"Now that I understand the killer's motivation, I'm on the verge of breaking this," Malachi said. "I think we're looking for a spy, a soldier, or a cop, and I have a list of potential victims. I want to trap him. Give me a few surveillance teams and we can end this."

"I want to solve this as much as you, but you went behind my back," Collins said. "The chief also received a call from David Burke, the White House deputy counsel. He asked her why her people had harassed a Muslim professor. Apparently, al-Kadi contacted him too."

"David Burke's on my list of infiltrators," Malachi said.

"I won't even ask you how you got that information. This is out of my hands now. The chief gave me specific orders to cease and desist with that line of investigation."

"How did al-Kadi know I contacted the professor? That almost proves they're both working for the Brotherhood."

"That's not the crime you need to solve. I need—"

"We can't ignore the connections," Malachi said.

"We're not ignoring anything," Collins said, louder, angry. "The chief is heated, and she wanted you off the case. I told her you're too valuable to lose, but one more fuck up, and you could be bounced out of homicide."

"Shit."

Malachi's strategy had burned him faster than expected. He dropped his eyes to her desk and wondered what his next move should be.

"You best listen to what I'm saying," Collins said.

Malachi spoke without looking up. "I know talking about conspiracies makes me sound like a nut, but conspiracies exist, and if we're not identifying any, then we're missing them. Sometimes conspiracy theories are true, and we have to examine this, no matter how batshit crazy it sounds."

"I think Wolf's onto something," Jones said.

Collins looked from Malachi to Jones. "Between us, so do I, which is why I stood up for him. I also got the impression the chief doesn't enjoy being told what to do by City Hall or the White House."

She turned to Wolf. "I'll let you keep this vigilante thing as a working theory, but no more contact with potential victims. I mean it, Wolf. You step on your dick again, and you're gone."

CHAPTER FORTY-FIVE

Malachi shifted in the front seat of his Buick and craned his neck to catch the reflection of the parking garage in his side-view mirror. He waited for a dark blue 2018 BMW M5 belonging to David Hammond, a senior vice president for Smith and Wadsworth—one of the most influential lobbying firms in Washington, DC. Malachi had called Hammond's office on Seventeenth Street NW and pretended he wanted to meet with Hammond. He had learned Hammond would leave at six o'clock.

Hammond ranked high on Zahra's list.

Smith and Wadsworth lobbied for clients in a wide range of businesses, from accounting to the fossil fuel industry, and Hammond led their foreign policy division. According to a Washington Herald investigative piece, the firm represented businesses around the world, many of whom were affiliated with foreign governments. Lobbying firms often skirted the fine line between lobbying and acting as agents for foreign governments. More than twelve thousand lobbyists worked in Washington and thousands more remained unregistered. Hammond had big money backing him, and he wielded serious influence, at least in affairs relating to the Middle East. Hammond represented Saudi interests and had lobbied Congress during Muslim Advocacy Day. A Google image search revealed a photograph of Hammond standing next to Senator Hansen on the Capitol steps, with a caption reading, "Hammond lobbying for legislation to combat Islamophobia." Another article quoted Hammond supporting the al-Azhar Islamic Cultural Center.

Across K Street NW, a short iron fence protected a bronze statue of Admiral David Farragut in the center of Farragut Square. Malachi Googled him while he waited. Farragut, a Civil War hero, became famous for shouting, "Damn the torpedoes, full speed ahead," during the battle of Mobile Bay. Statues populated DC's parks, injecting a sense of history into its neighborhoods.

Malachi had told no one about this surveillance, and he had taken Collins' words to heart, but he remained certain the vigilante would target someone on his list. Malachi's job was to protect life and solve homicides, and if he lost his job for following his conscience, he could live with it, but he could not blindly follow orders and let a killer roam free. He planned to watch the five Secret Apparatus members on his list and try to determine who would be targeted first.

His watch read quarter to seven. Had he missed Hammond? Hammond's home lay on the western edge of Georgetown, in the Spring Valley neighborhood, an exclusive area dotted with large brick homes, wooded streets, and eighteenth-century streetlamps. Malachi would not be able to surveil Hammond's house for long before a neighbor called the police, and Malachi would suffer serious repercussions if Collins learned about his unauthorized surveillance.

The nose of a dark blue BMW poked out of the garage and stopped to let a group of pedestrians pass. Malachi squinted and matched the license plate number to the printout in his hand. The BMW pulled onto Seventeenth Street NW with Hammond behind the wheel.

Hammond turned right onto K Street NW and headed west. Malachi let several cars pass and then fell in behind him. The heavy traffic required Malachi to stay close. Hammond was probably heading home, so when they reached his neighborhood, Malachi would let him go. He could drive by later to confirm the BMW was parked at Hammond's house.

Hammond continued westbound in the left lane and took the underpass below Washington Circle. Malachi stayed in the right lane, three cars back. Hammond approached a freeway ramp—his fastest route home—but instead of getting on, he crossed over Rock Creek, and turned right onto Twenty-Ninth Street NW.

Where is he going?

Without cars between them to use as cover, Malachi let Hammond pull further away. If this had been an authorized surveillance and Malachi had other detectives helping, he would have paralleled Hammond on another street, but being alone left him no choice but to stay with him. Surveillance entailed constant risk-reward decisions—too close and get burned, too far and lose him.

Hammond continued north across M Street NW into a residential neighborhood, and Malachi stayed a block and a half behind. Hammond ascended Washington's alphabetic grid at a steady pace. He did not appear to be looking for a tail, but why would he? He slowed at Q Street NW and turned right without signaling.

Malachi gunned the engine to catch up. He stopped at the intersection and looked to his right. Hammond parked on the street. Malachi watched until a car pulled up behind him and beeped, then he turned right.

Hammond climbed out of his car and looked both ways for oncoming traffic. His eyes passed over Malachi's vehicle without recognition. Hammond jogged across the street and slipped through an iron gate in a long brick wall.

Malachi kept his head positioned forward but tracked Hammond with his eyes. Hammond jogged up a short flight of stone steps in front of a colonial, red-brick house. A sign beside the entrance read, "Dumbarton."

The Dumbarton House, a late eighteenth-century residence built in Federalist style, had been turned into a museum. Small museums sprang up in Washington like mushrooms, and Malachi had taken Riley and Samantha on a Dumbarton tour the previous year. His girls had been too young to appreciate the antiques or the history of the house, but they had loved walking through the manicured garden.

Malachi sighed. He had only planned to follow Hammond to get a good look at him, and Hammond's nighttime excursion came as a surprise. The museum must be closed. Was Hammond a patron? There was only one way to find out.

Malachi got aggressive.

He parked at the end of the block and exited his car. The heat took his breath away. The humidity had thickened, like a bathroom after a hot shower. Malachi hurried to the house, forcing himself not to run. Nothing drew attention quicker than a running man.

He climbed the steps and stopped in front of the two-story house. White columns framed the front door, which was blocked by a rope. He turned right on a red brick path and walked to the museum entrance. A closed sign hung on the door.

Where was Hammond?

Malachi rounded the corner, walked across a gray-slate patio, and peered into the backyard. A pebbled path and sculpted bushes surrounded an emerald-green lawn. A bronze fountain, shaped like a child with angel's wings, had turned green from oxidation. Hammond was not there.

Beyond a stone railing, stone steps led down to a second patio, one story below. On the far side, another flight of stairs led back up to a garden, but Malachi could not see through the thick bushes. Behind him, the Dumbarton House appeared dark and vacant. Humid air prickled his skin, threatening to trigger his MS.

Malachi descended the stairs to the lower patio. Brick walls rose on either side of him, and he used the balls of his feet to avoid making noise. He turned right and peeked through large windows into the Dumbarton's empty ballroom.

Thunder rumbled in the distance. Cumulous clouds crept eastward, changing shape like shifting continents in the sky. The misty air clung to his chest and back, sticking his shirt to him like the skin atop a bowl of old soup. It had not rained yet, but his clothing was soaked.

Malachi climbed the far flight of stairs to the garden and stopped a few feet from the top. He inched around an iron gate. Brick walls bordered the lush garden, creating an oasis in the city. Inside the walls, a path circled the lawn dominated by a sprawling maple tree. The perimeter of the garden came alive with plants—a pallet of reds, yellows, and oranges. Black-eyed Susans, hyssop, cheddar pinks, crested iris, rye, and dwarf sage ringed the garden. White butterflies skittered over fairy wings and the scent of chamomile and thyme tinged the warm air.

Hammond sat on a wooden bench, facing away from Malachi.

Malachi froze and held his breath. He retreated down the stairs and peeked over the top step.

What is he doing?

Hammond watched the far side of the garden, and Malachi followed his gaze. A man in a business suit climbed the stairs on the opposite side. He was tall, wore a full beard, and carried a leather satchel.

CHAPTER FORTY-SIX

Austin ascended the garden steps on the east side of the Dumbarton House. Hammond waited on the wooden bench, as directed. Austin trusted his own powers of persuasion, yet he had still surprised himself by his ability to lure a vice president from a powerhouse lobbying firm to this kind of meeting. Half a million dollars bought a lot of access, and Hammond seemed comfortable making shady deals. Greed, the same vice that led Hammond to fund terrorism, had become his Achilles heel.

Austin stepped onto the garden path, walking on narcotic-induced clouds. Pebbles crunched under his shoes, and Hammond looked up. Austin adjusted the leather satchel on his shoulder and Hammond's eyes locked on it, probably salivating over the check.

Austin carried a different kind of gift.

Hammond stood as Austin approached. Austin tried to soften his expression, but hiding his aggression came hard.

The smile slid off Hammond's face. Had he realized his mistake?

Austin wanted Hammond to experience terror—the same terror Vanessa and thousands of other victims had endured at the hands of the animals Hammond funded.

"Oh Lord God, to whom vengeance belongeth; Oh God, to whom vengeance belongeth, show thyself."

He reached into his satchel, pulled out his Beretta, and pointed it at Hammond.

Hammond's mouth dropped open, but he did not move, as if fear anchored him to the ground. He stood transfixed, his arms by his sides like a statue in the garden. He gawked at the handgun and his eyes riveted to the hollow end of the silencer.

"Police, drop the gun," someone shouted.

The voice had come from behind Hammond, who remained frozen. Austin peered over Hammond's shoulder toward the stairway leading up from the patio. Detective Wolf stood on the stairs with his head and gun poking over the top step.

"Drop the gun," Wolf yelled. "Do it now."

Austin's every sense heightened, and the world moved in slow motion. If he did not act, he would spend his life in a prison cell. Wolf stood twenty-five yards away, not an easy shot with a handgun, especially if Austin made himself a moving target—something he needed to do now.

Austin lowered his gun, knowing Wolf would not shoot without an immediate threat, and sidestepped to put Hammond into Wolf's line of fire. He turned and sprinted across the lawn.

"Stop, police," Wolf shouted.

Austin grit his teeth, awaiting the impact of bullets. He reached the steps and leapt into the air. He hurtled down the stairs and landed hard on the sidewalk. He stayed on his feet and broke left behind the brick wall.

Wolf never fired.

Where had his plan gone wrong? What brought Wolf to the garden? Were they onto him? Were his phones tapped? Was he being followed? Was he surrounded?

This could not be God's plan.

He dashed down Twenty-Ninth Street NW into a dead end. He could turn right into the alley behind an apartment complex or continue into an old cemetery. Without breaking stride, he bolted down a dirt path and into the cemetery. He headed toward the trees, forty yards away. He scanned the dense vegetation for police.

Behind him, Wolf shouted something at Hammond.

He had thirty seconds before Wolf exited the garden and reached the cemetery. He doubted he would reach the woods in time. He should have killed Wolf. He did not desire that, but now he might not have a choice. The mission came first.

He tightened his grip on the Beretta.

CHAPTER FORTY-SEVEN

Malachi bounded across the lawn toward the steps where the man had disappeared. Hammond stood wide-eyed and slack-jawed, as if paralyzed. As Malachi neared the stairs, he crouched and shuffled his feet to maintain a stable shooting platform. Malachi looked over the top step and leveled his gun in case the man tried to shoot around the gate.

Nothing.

He scampered down the steps, pressed against the wall, and leaned around the corner.

The man sprinted down a cemetery path and disappeared from sight.

The woods beyond the cemetery belonged to Rock Creek Park, and if the man reached them, he would escape. Malachi wanted to stop and call for backup, but if he hustled, he could catch him. Malachi raced down the street past a dilapidated sign for Mt. Zion Cemetery, an old Methodist burial ground for slaves and once part of the Underground Railroad. He hurried down the path, past decrepit picnic table and benches, all stained by time. Where had he gone?

Malachi slowed as he passed blanched stone monuments with rusted iron railings. Gravestones protruded from the earth at odd angles, their engraved names long faded. Thick oaks blotted out the sun, casting the cemetery into shadow. Uneven ground sloped down toward dense woods. Malachi held his Glock in a two-handed grip and pivoted side to side as he scanned the trees. He edged around a pile of thirty gravestones into the high grass.

The man had vanished.

Malachi lowered his gun and pulled out his cell phone. If he could get an airship and set a perimeter, he could try to corral the suspect in the park and then hunt him with a canine unit.

Behind him, an acorn popped on the ground. Malachi whirled around.

The man leaned out from behind the thick trunk of an oak tree and pointed his gun at Malachi's chest.

Malachi raised his gun.

"Don't do it, Wolf," the man shouted.

He knows my name.

Malachi stopped. The man stood behind cover, with only his head and gun exposed—an almost impossible shot for Malachi to make before the man pulled his trigger.

"Throw your gun on the lawn behind you," the man shouted.

His suspect had the drop on him, so Malachi lowered his gun, but held onto it. The department had trained him to never give up his weapon.

"Toss it toward the woods. I don't want to shoot you, but if you don't drop it, I will. Do it now, Detective Wolf."

The man's tone commanded obedience, and his use of Malachi's title seemed professional. He would shoot if Malachi failed to comply.

Malachi's stomach knotted.

Malachi eased his grip on his Glock and let gravity pull the barrel toward the ground. He dangled it with two fingers, as if he held a dead rat, then he tossed his gun behind him. It landed on the grass with a thud. If the man intended to kill him, he would shoot now.

"Get on the ground and lay on your stomach. Interlace your fingers behind your head."

Malachi had been taught the same commands. The man sounded like a police officer. If he wanted to kill Malachi, he would have done it already.

"I just want to escape, Detective," the man said, as if reading Malachi's mind.

Malachi knelt, but kept his eyes on the man, ready to dive for his gun if the man opened fire. Malachi lowered himself onto his stomach and put his hands behind his head.

A siren blared in the distance. Hammond must have called the police.

"Face away from me and don't move."

"Why are you doing this?" Malachi asked.

"Look away."

Malachi turned his head toward the woods, and the hair rose on the back of his neck. He strained to hear footsteps.

Was he going to shoot?

Ten seconds passed, and nothing happened. Malachi realized he had been holding his breath. He gasped and looked back at the tree.

The man was gone.

CHAPTER FORTY-EIGHT

Austin ran to his car, which was parked on Twenty-Seventh Street NW, near Kew Gardens. His hands shook as he fumbled with his car keys. He climbed inside, and on the third attempt, he inserted them into the ignition. The engine roared to life.

He pulled onto the empty street and slammed on his brakes.

A young girl on a bicycle swerved around his car in the middle of the street. He had nearly hit her.

"Shit."

She gave him the finger and continued pedaling.

A siren wailed in the distance. Sweat ran into his eyes. He needed to slow down and not make mistakes.

He swallowed his fear and sped past the girl. He turned left on P Street NW and drove onto the ramp leading to Rock Creek Parkway.

Had Wolf recognized him? Would agents from the Office of Professional Responsibility be waiting for him at home? Would they show up at his office and arrest him?

Austin merged into light traffic and traveled south on the parkway. The beating rotors of a helicopter vibrated overhead. He craned his neck to look through the windshield but did not see it.

Who would care for Sophie if he went to prison?

He could go on the lam and try to determine if an arrest warrant had been issued. Or he could risk everything and assume Wolf had not recognized him. Even if Wolf had identified him, could he prove anything? Austin had been careful, but criminals always made mistakes.

His car became another drop in the sea of traffic as he crossed the Memorial Bridge into Virginia. He was safe. For now.

His mission remained incomplete. He had to trust his process. He would stay home and wait, and if police did not come, he would go to work in the morning as if nothing had changed. A higher power watched over him, and he needed to be courageous. He needed to do it for Vanessa.

CHAPTER FORTY-NINE

Malachi exited Collins' office, deflated. Their murder suspect had been in his sights and he had let him escape again. Malachi had told Collins the whole story, because if they ever caught the killer, everything would come out in court, which meant his reports needed to be truthful and accurate.

He had come so close to catching the murderer. After the man fled, Malachi had dialed 9-1-1, and every available patrol unit had responded and set up a fifteen-block perimeter. An airship had arrived within minutes and flown low over the trees, yet somehow, the man escaped.

I'm incompetent. The words repeated on a loop in his mind, his doubt engraved on his soul.

Malachi and Jones had interviewed Hammond, who fit the victim profile. Hammond supported the Brotherhood and traded favors on Capitol Hill to increase the Brotherhood's realpolitik. Hammond had expressed gratitude to Malachi for saving his life, yet he still refused to cooperate and claimed his lobbying efforts were lawful. After the interview, Internal Affairs had been waiting for Malachi, and they had grilled him for hours. Apparently, they frowned upon unauthorized surveillances.

Malachi plopped down at his desk and ignored the eyes on him.

It had been pure luck Malachi had been present when the killer tried to murder Hammond. Even though Malachi had whittled Zahra's victim list to five potential victims, the odds were astronomical that Malachi would be present at the exact time of the attempted murder. That kind of luck only happened once in a lifetime, and Malachi had not capitalized on it.

Hill cleared his throat. "Hey, College. Help me out with some criminal justice theory. I thought you're supposed to hold the killer at gunpoint, not the other way around."

"You should take your act on the road," Malachi said. "Especially since police work doesn't seem to be working out for you."

"You're oh for two, College."

"Don't look so gloomy," Jones said. "You lucky to be alive."

"I don't feel lucky."

"Sounds like our suspect had tactical training. He would've got the drop on any of us."

"He must have moved around the trunk of the tree as I entered the cemetery. I focused on the woods and never saw him."

"Let me school you, young buck," Jones said, in the same tone Malachi's father had used. "You need to call for backup before you chase a suspect, especially one who's strapped."

"I know, I know." Jones was right, and Malachi's tactical failure was on display for all to see. Malachi's chin dropped to his chest.

"Don't fret, son. You saved Hammond's life, and the department will spin this as a victory. You're a hero."

"LT's pissed about the unauthorized surveillance."

"I ain't happy about that either. You can't go around acting a beast. You should have told me. Either you trust me, or you don't."

"I trust you," Malachi said. "I wanted to keep you out of it."

"Don't do me any favors."

Malachi drummed his fingers on the desk. "The more I learn about the Brotherhood, the more I understand why our suspect is doing this."

"He's a stone-cold killer."

"I'm not excusing murder," Malachi said.

"Sounds like you sympathize. Tell me you don't believe in vigilantism."

"I'd be lying if I said I hadn't fantasized about murdering my father's killers. I understand where it comes from."

"You can't be a cop and believe people can take justice into their own hands."

"It's an emotional response, not a rational one. I know extrajudicial killing is wrong but understanding the killer's motivation helped me get ahead of him."

The attempt on Hammond's life confirmed Malachi's theory, but questions gnawed at him. Why had the killings accelerated? Was their suspect on a deadline? Why did the killer only choose Georgetown? Did he live there?

Malachi sensed a presence behind him and looked up at Collins.

"You dodged a bullet on this one," she said.

"Literally."

"Nuse is livid about your surveillance, but public affairs just issued a press release," she said.

"And?"

"They painting you the hero for saving Hammond. Nuse's hands are tied."

"I'm not getting suspended?"

"We have to wait for IA's recommendation, but I can't see how they can do that now."

Malachi sighed and his body lightened. He had escaped punishment for now, but he had seen the look in Nuse's eyes. That bureaucrat would find a way to hurt him.

"Thanks, LT."

"Don't thank me. I'm still pissed you disobeyed me. You won't get away with that again."

She walked away, and Jones grinned.

Malachi returned to the file and reviewed the case, rereading every report, every lab analysis, losing himself in the research. He worked for hours until he finished the file. He sagged in his chair, and his eyelids drooped.

Jones slammed a half-empty bottle of Macallan single-malt scotch on the desk, and Malachi jerked his head up. He looked around the office. They were alone. He checked his watch—nine o'clock. He had worked for hours.

"Come on," Jones said.

"Not tonight, Jonesy."

"We need to celebrate."

"Celebrate what? I almost got myself killed, and I lost our suspect."

"We're celebrating the *almost.* Internal affairs will clear you, and your theory's right, which means it's only a matter of time until we nail this thug."

"If the LT catches me drinking in the office, I'm screwed."

Jones handed Malachi a paper cup, and they toasted.

"Clink," Jones said. "I'm glad you're okay, young blood."

"Thanks."

Malachi sipped the oaky scotch and rolled it over his tongue. It burned going down, then the flavor sweetened as the alcohol evaporated and activated different taste buds.

He closed his eyes and exhaled.

The image of the killer floated behind his eyes. The way the man had concealed himself and used cover showed tactical skill, and he had yelled commands like someone who carried a gun for a living. The way he had moved, the way he had planned the murders, the way he had spoken to Malachi—all of it seemed familiar.

The killer was a cop.

CHAPTER FIFTY

Electricity flashed through Malachi's arms and fired his nerve endings, causing him to flinch behind the wheel. His legs suddenly weighed five hundred pounds, and the brake pedal became encased in cotton. MS always created new and distracting symptoms, and this latest flare had wrung him out, physically and emotionally.

He parked outside Zahra's townhouse in the Capitol Hill neighborhood as the first raindrops spotted the street. He swallowed two Gabapentin and waited for the medicine to hit his system. Thick tears of rain splattered the windshield.

After being held at gunpoint, he only wanted to sleep and purge the incident from his mind, but Zahra had called, and when he told her what had happened, she insisted he come over.

Zahra lived in a two-story, Victorian townhouse on F Street NE, near Union Station. Once populated with crack houses, the area had gentrified as part of the developing H-Street corridor. Her narrow townhouse sported rose-colored brick, Romanesque eaves, and intricate detailing around the windows.

The door swung open as soon as Malachi knocked. Zahra threw her arms around him and nuzzled her face against his neck. She hugged him for a long time and when she looked up, her eyes glistened. She led him to the couch and poured him an Amstel Light.

"You could have been killed," she said.

"But I wasn't."

"We only just met," she said and laid her head on his chest.

Malachi held her and sipped his beer. They cuddled and his confidence returned. Her care enveloped him, recharged his soul.

"When I was in patrol, a robbery suspect shot at me," Malachi said. "I shot back and missed, but we caught the guy."

"You must have been terrified."

"Not really. Adrenaline dumped into my system, but I focused on tactics—staying behind cover, calling for backup, setting a perimeter—that kind of thing. Today was different. I let the killer get the jump on me."

"You think he beat you."

Malachi took another slug of stout. "Yes and no. Letting him get behind me was a big mistake, but violent encounters are dynamic, and I was rushing, intentionally endangering myself to catch him before he slipped away. I can live with that."

"Then what is it?"

"It made me question whether I'm really a cop. I mean, I almost have a PhD in economics from Harvard. Do I belong here? Do I have what it takes to carry a badge and gun? I spend a lot of time thinking about what justice means, for my father, for society. Should I be on the streets or working in a university? Am I playing cop or was I meant for this?"

Malachi had never spoken his doubts aloud to anyone, but there was something about Zahra. She could really see him. He wanted to let her inside.

"That you think about justice and are so critical of yourself is what makes you an outstanding police officer."

"You've been fighting Islamists for a long time. How do you stay committed?"

"I never wanted to do this. I wanted to marry and have a family, but Islamists made normal life impossible. I couldn't sit quietly, and watch them brutalize Coptic Christians, Jews, and other minorities. The men in Egypt wouldn't fight the fundamentalists, so I did."

"You're courageous. You—"

"I don't feel courageous. In Egypt I received death threats every night. I would lie in bed waiting for the calls. I knew it was only a matter of time until jihadists or the government's Night Visitors kicked down my door."

"Frightening."

"I was scared, but I couldn't show it. Any sign of weakness would have signed my death warrant. The only thing that kept me alive was my enemy's belief that I was protected by powerful people. I fostered that illusion. I still have nightmares almost every night. I still hear the telephone ringing when it isn't. I still hear banging on my door."

"I'm so sorry you went through that, but you're safe now."

They sat quietly, and Malachi sensed her staring at him.

"What are you thinking?" she asked.

"When my father flew to Boston for the marathon, he said something odd, and I can't get it out of my head."

"What's that?"

"He told me he was getting older and did not know when it would be the last time we saw each other."

"People think about their mortality when they age," Zahra said. "You don't think he had a premonition, do you?"

"Nothing like that, but I never considered it would really be the last time."

"You're doing all this for him."

Malachi nodded, but did not look at her.

"Try to meditate," she said. "Sit up straight, close your eyes and follow your breathing. Clear your mind and focus on the air going in and out of your lungs."

Malachi followed her instructions and the weight lifted off his shoulders. Then he pictured the killer standing behind the tree and his tension returned.

"It's hard to stop my thoughts," he said.

"It takes years. That's why they call it a meditation practice."

"It reminds me of my intense focus when I'm running. It's called 'being in the zone.' I'll try meditation. I need to do something."

Zahra kissed him on the neck and rested her hand on his thigh. His body responded to her touch. So much for his falling libido.

"I know how to take your mind off your cases," she said.

"I like where this is headed."

Zahra stood up and unbuttoned her blouse, then she took his hand and led him upstairs.

It had been a bad day, but things were trending up.

Chapter Fifty-One

Austin fidgeted on a wooden stool inside Hannigan's Irish Pub on Wilson Boulevard, a few blocks from his apartment. At eleven o'clock, the pub remained full of inebriated patrons. Austin placed his elbows on the bar and arched his back, trying to get comfortable, but the problem roiled his mind.

How did Wolf find me?

Beside him, a fat man wearing a faded Washington Nationals baseball cap laughed, and his body shook like gelatin. He bumped Austin's arm.

Austin frowned. He lifted a shot of Jameson Irish whiskey, swilled the syrupy liquid around, and smelled it. His mouth watered and he downed it.

He had made a mistake . . . somewhere. He was vulnerable.

Austin caught the bartender's attention and pointed at his empty glass.

The bartender, a burly man with short-cropped red hair and freckles, grabbed a bottle of Jameson and poured another shot.

Austin nodded, and when the bartender turned to another customer, he dug a tissue out of his pants and held it between his legs. He glanced around, unwrapped two oxycodone tablets from the soft folds, and stared at them.

He had injured his ankle weeks ago, but he still took the drug three times per day. Every day. When he had run out, he showed his ankle to a doctor, exaggerated the pain, and refilled his prescription. His ankle had healed and no longer merited narcotics, but he had visited three more doctors and tripled his stash of pills, paying with cash at different pharmacies. Despite all his efforts, he would run out soon.

Hammond was a righteous target, a dangerous man, and an important lobbyist. After Dumbarton, Hammond would be careful, retain bodyguards, become too difficult to kill.

I fucked up.

Worse, Detective Wolf closed in on him. It would end soon. He should have killed Wolf but doing so would have derailed his plan. He needed Wolf alive . . . for now.

He rolled the pills in his fingertips, wondering if he should conserve them and halve his dose. With alcohol, one could be enough.

Fuck it. He would probably be dead soon, anyway. He washed the tablets down with whiskey.

The fat man beside him laughed and slapped his friend on the back, bumping Austin again. The man's raucous horselaugh drew attention from patrons at several tables.

"You bumped me," Austin said.

The man glanced at him then turned back to his friend.

Warmth rose in Austin's neck and tinged his cheeks, as if the devil climbed toward his brain.

Relax.

The fat man guffawed and slapped his palm against the bar.

It's not worth it.

The man brushed Austin's arm again. He looked at Austin and smirked. He probably weighed two-fifty and muscle showed beneath his flab. He looked thick, like he had played football, but not recently. His brashness, lack of consideration, and body language screamed *bully.* Just like Chad and Vinny.

Not now. Not here.

The fat man bumped Austin a fourth time. He exhibited territorial behavior, like a dog pissing on a fire hydrant.

Austin slid his stool back and stood up.

"You keep bumping me, asshole," Austin said.

The man's shoulders tensed, and he faced Austin. He frowned and flexed his pectoral muscles, probably as an intimidation tactic. It was a classic pre-violence indicator he was psyching himself up for a fight.

"Got a problem, bud?" the man asked.

Austin hesitated. His ears burned.

"I've got a big fat problem . . . with a fucking tub of lard."

The man's eyes widened, then a smile crept across his face. He was probably used to pushing smaller men around.

"What did you say?" he asked.

Austin bladed his left hand and chopped the man's Adam's apple. Thyroid cartilage shifted with a crack.

The man opened his mouth and clutched his damaged larynx. His lips moved like a fish out of water. His face darkened.

The fight had ended before it really began, but heat flashed behind Austin's eyes. He grabbed a handful of the man's hair and slammed a right uppercut into his jaw. The fat man's head snapped back, and he fell backward knocking three patrons down like bowling pins.

The bartender rushed to the bar gate.

Austin hurried out the door. Behind him, patrons shouted, and a barstool crashed to the floor. He did not stop. Sudden violence created confusion, and people took time to process what had happened. He jogged to the end of the block, turned down a side street, and took a parallel route home.

Did I kill him?

Austin had not meant to use deadly force, just end the fight fast, but he had struck the man's cartilage flush. Usually people ducked or turned, but the fat man had stood still like a punching bag, seemingly unable to recognize the threat. If Austin had fractured his larynx, the man could die before an ambulance arrived. Another body.

Austin's first kill had come in Afghanistan.

His expulsion from high school had led him to a series of blue-collar jobs and a high school equivalency certificate, and joining the Marines had seemed like his only choice to escape Hemlock and a lifetime of crushed dreams. On his first deployment to the Helmand Province, an IED had rocked his vehicle and shredded the Humvee behind him. Shrapnel had incapacitated his M-60 gunner, and the Taliban had raked his convoy with small arms fire. Acting on instinct, Austin had bailed out of the vehicle, and fired his M-16 at muzzle flashes coming from a barren wadi.

He had emptied his magazine, reloaded, and kept firing until his sergeant ordered him to stop.

Three Marines had been killed by the IED, but Austin's quick action had taken the lives of four Taliban insurgents and prevented further deaths. He could still picture their pale skin and dead eyes, their *perahan tunban* clothing soaked with urine, feces, and blood. His first kills had not been murder, but now he had crossed a dangerous line.

Austin arrived at his apartment building as the distant sound of sirens grew louder. He seemed to be making a habit of drawing them wherever he went. He glanced up and down the block, but no one paid him any attention, and he entered the lobby. Perhaps he had not killed the fat man, only bruised him. He would have to check the news in the morning. And find a new place to drink.

CHAPTER FIFTY-TWO

"Jones, Wolf," Collins shouted.

Malachi and Jones entered her office, where Nuse leaned against the wall with his arms crossed. He caught Malachi's eye and grinned. Whatever this was, if it made Nuse happy, it had to be bad news for them.

"Sit down," Collins said. "You're not going to like this."

Malachi looked at Jones and raised his eyebrows. Every time they gained momentum some bureaucrat interfered.

Jones shrugged, and they both sat.

"What up?" Jones asked.

"We've got a problem—" Collins said.

"I'll tell you what's up," Nuse said. "I got a call from our chief counsel. An American Islamic Shura attorney representing Amir al-Kadi and David Hammond has officially warned us to cease all contact with them or AIS will sue for slander and harassment. It's not an idle threat either. They have pending lawsuits against law enforcement agencies around the country. What the hell were you doing?"

"Investigating a series of savage murders," Malachi said.

Nuse rested his hands on his hips. "I know where Hammond fits in after your fuck up the other night, but what does Mr. al-Kadi have to do with this?"

Malachi glanced at Collins, and she held up her hand to silence him.

"We connected al-Kadi to several of our victims," Collins said. "Wolf asked him about possible motives. The chief has already asked me to drop that line of inquiry."

"And what is 'that line of inquiry?'" Nuse asked, keeping his eyes on Wolf.

"The killer is targeting the Muslim Brotherhood," Malachi said, before Collins could respond. "All our victims sympathized with the Brotherhood's radical agenda, and they may have been undeclared operatives in its Secret Apparatus."

Collins close her eyes and rubbed her temples.

"Secret Apparatus?" Nuse asked. "Maybe the killer came down in a UFO. Seen any of those?"

"It's real," Malachi said.

"I'm not pleased . . . and neither is the White House. They called Chief Ransom this morning and told her not to ruffle any feathers, because the Muslim Brotherhood is helping them stop radicalism in the Middle East."

Malachi glared at Nuse. "The facts don't back that up. The Brotherhood is the puppet master behind all Islamic terrorism."

"The FBI doesn't agree with you," Nuse said.

"That's because they've been infiltrated."

"Al-Kadi called you an Islamophobe, and I don't think he's wrong. Tell me this, Wolf, do you think your Jewish faith has anything to do with your willingness to believe in a secret Islamic conspiracy?"

"My religion is irrelevant. Why is it acceptable to claim Judaism motivates me, but it's Islamophobic to discuss Islam and jihad?"

"It would explain your animus toward Islamic—"

"Don't bring up my religion again, unless you want a lawsuit."

"Jesus, I'm not listening to any more of this shit. If you keep treating upstanding citizens like suspects, I'll have the White House up my ass. Stop accusing people of belonging to secret cabals, or this will not end well for you."

Collins stood. "Chief, I hear you. Wolf's theory sounds like conspiratorial bullshit, and I didn't buy it either, at first, but all our victims supported the same agenda."

Malachi appreciated Collins trying to protect him, but enough was enough. "I'm doing my job and following the evidence."

"Evidence? Where's the evidence that any of the victims were members of the Muslim Brotherhood? Where's your evidence that some Secret Apparatus even exists?"

"We're interviewing people to get that evidence," Malachi said.

"Not anymore," Nuse said. "You're not doing another interview. Detective Jones will handle them."

"You're taking me off the case?"

"I wish I could, but the press thinks you're a hero and it would be too hard to explain. Officially, you're still investigating, but I don't want you leaving this office to talk to anyone."

"But—"

Nuse turned to Collins. "Is that clear, Lieutenant?"

"Yes, sir. You won't hear anything else from Wolf."

Nuse stormed out of the office.

Collins shot Malachi a sad smile and shook her head. His father had given him that same look.

"I'm sorry, Wolf," she said. "That's an order from the top. You've pissed off some powerful people."

"But—"

"I don't need to lay it down again, do I?"

"My theory is correct. I predicted the attempt on Hammond's life."

"I ain't saying you're wrong, but we need proof before we confront anybody. I don't have a choice here. You're grounded until things settle down. I need you to feel me on this."

"Fine."

Malachi trudged back to his desk, followed by Jones.

Hill snickered. "Tough week, College?"

Malachi ignored him. The red message light flashed on his desk phone. He dialed his mailbox and typed in his code.

"Detective Wolf, this is Agent Jane Evans. I, uh, I shouldn't say anything, but I wanted to warn you. My boss is pissed you didn't tell him about the Hammond surveillance, and he thinks you're trampling on our investigation. I don't know if this is coming from him or headquarters, but he is going to complain. I thought you should know. Be careful."

Malachi hung up and slumped back in his seat. The only way to catch the killer was to follow his theory, but he had made powerful enemies, and if he continued down this road, he would ruin his career.

What should he do?

CHAPTER FIFTY-THREE

The wind filled the mainsail, and Zahra pointed her boat into the channel. Malachi sat beside her and watched the river. He had called in sick to give himself a chance to think. Discovering the killer's motive had been a big step forward, but Nuse had benched him, leaving him tired and empty.

"There's a bottle of Sauvignon Blanc in the cooler," Zahra said.

"It's the middle of the day,"

"And?"

"I'll get the glasses."

"I think I know what will cheer you up," she said with a sly smile.

They had been out five times since their first date and despite his setbacks at work, she filled him with joy.

"Being with you relaxes me," Malachi said.

"I like it too, Malachi."

The way she said his name with that slight Arabic accent sounded sexy, and despite his frustration, she aroused him.

"I want to spend the afternoon sailing," he said, "but I need to figure out my next move."

"I'll help if I can."

"I'm effectively sidelined and can't question anyone else on your list. The powers that be don't want my theory to get out."

"You're in a tough position."

"I can't solve these murders under these restrictions. Worse, if the killer's correct and Brotherhood infiltrators are scheming to destroy our country, I won't be able to expose them. I'm up against AIS, my command staff, and the White House."

"What are your options?"

"I can follow their rules, slog away, and hope something breaks, or I can do this my way and investigate off the books."

"Would they fire you if they found out?"

"Count on it. Nuse is out to get me and Chief Ransom would sacrifice me in a heartbeat to save her career. If I get caught, I'm finished."

"You don't strike me as someone who can sit on the sidelines."

"I'm under a microscope, but I have to do what's right. I know it sounds corny, but I have to find justice."

"For your father?"

"Something like that."

She drummed her fingers on the wheel, stopped, and narrowed her eyes. "What if there's a third option?"

"I'm listening."

"What if you leaked your theory to the press?"

Malachi stared at his hands. "If I told a reporter the murderer was motivated to stop the Brotherhood, everyone would know I leaked it, and I'd get fired."

"What if you explained the ideological commonality between victims and let the newspaper put the pieces together themselves?"

"I suppose that would give me some cover. I could give an interview on background only, but I'd have to be careful."

He leaned over the gunwale and watched the water lapping against the hull. If his theory went public, it would be harder for Chief Ransom or the White House to suppress it. More importantly, the Brotherhood's plot would be revealed.

"At least I'd be doing something, and that's better than nothing."

"You're welcome to meet the reporter on my boat. If we sail down river, you'll have privacy."

"Thanks, but if anyone saw us on your boat, it would be tough to explain. I'll do it in a public place and come up with some excuse for being there."

"Be careful," she said. "People don't want this information to get out."

"I knew you'd help figure this out. Here, I brought you something."

Malachi pulled a wrapped box out of his knapsack and set it on the bench beside her. Her eyes widened, and he pictured her as a child, full of excitement and anticipation.

She checked their course, locked the wheel, and pulled off the wrapping paper. She folded it and set the box on top of the paper. Why did women save wrapping paper? He would have shredded it without thinking.

She opened the box and gasped as she lifted out an antique anchor.

"You mentioned your interest in nautical history, so I thought you'd appreciate it. It's a dingy anchor from the eighteenth century. It would look good hanging in your stateroom, but be careful, the flukes are sharp. I think people were less safety conscious back then."

"I love it, Malachi. It's beautiful."

"These last few weeks with you . . ." he trailed off, unsure if he should express his feelings.

"What?"

"I know we haven't known each other long, but I care about you. I—"

She smiled and put her arms around him. "Why don't you help me carry this into the cabin? Maybe I can take your mind off the Brotherhood."

CHAPTER FIFTY-FOUR

Malachi awoke in a panic. He sat up in his bed, shook himself awake, and reached for his MacBook Air. He booted up the laptop and opened the Washington Herald's website.

He had used a pay phone near the National Mall to call Dexter Hamill, a reporter he knew at the Herald. Hamill covered the metro crime beat and had written about the Georgetown murders. His articles often criticized police, but he showed both sides and seemed like a straight shooter.

Malachi had told Hamill that MPD ignored a plausible theory about the Georgetown murders, and promised to give him explosive information, but only on background and not for attribution. Hamill had agreed and interviewed Malachi on a bench behind Nationals Park. Malachi had explained the victim's connection to radical Islam and how he believed the killer wanted stop infiltration by the Brotherhood's Secret Apparatus. He had suggested Hamill contact the Middle East Policy Institute to get more information, knowing Hamill would be directed to Zahra. Hamill had seemed excited and had convinced Malachi to go on record as an unnamed source.

Malachi shuddered thinking about seeing the story in print.

The Herald's website loaded, and the story splashed across the front page, "Murder Victims Supported Muslim Brotherhood." Malachi could not swallow, and his skin grew clammy.

A rash of murders in Washington, DC's historic Georgetown neighborhood may be the work of a single killer. The victims, a professor, a journalist, a financier, an activist, and now a presidential advisor, were all connected by their defense of fundamental Islam and their support for the Muslim Brotherhood.

A source close to the investigation speculated that animus toward the Muslim Brotherhood may have been the murder's motivation and confirmed police believe the killer targeted victims based on their undeclared affiliation with that organization.

David Morton, a spokesman for the Metropolitan Police Department, would neither confirm nor deny the theory, saying details cannot be released during an active homicide investigation. Assistant Chief Barney Nuse said, "It's irresponsible to suggest a serial killer is loose in the District or Muslim Brotherhood members are being targeted."

The Muslim Brotherhood was founded in 1928 in Egypt as an organization seeking theocratic rule under Islam. Since its creation, the Brotherhood has become an international organization with branches in dozens of countries. It has been tied to terrorist groups around the world, including the Islamic State. It is disputed whether the Brotherhood operates inside the United States, or if they do, whether they follow the same agenda as the Egyptian organization.

President Follet's administration has embraced the Brotherhood in Egypt. Deceased Presidential Advisor Muhammad Sharif claimed the Brotherhood was the only moderate group the United States could engage to counter Islamic extremism. The Council on American-Islamic Relations, a group associated with the Brotherhood, has consulted with the FBI in the past.

Zahra Mansour, a senior fellow with the Middle East Policy Institute, disagreed with Sharif's assessment. "The Muslim Brotherhood was founded as a radical, terrorist organization seeking a worldwide Islamic caliphate, and they have utilized violence from the beginning. Brotherhood organizations around the world must adhere to bylaws which promote jihad. Any suggestion that the US-based organizations are different is plain wrong. Front groups like the American Islamic Shura (AIS) have a hidden agenda to destroy the West."

AIS President Amir al-Kadi said the murders disturbed him. "Islam is a religion of peace and if the victims were targeted because of their religion, then these are more examples of Islamophobia."

Kris Watkins, assistant to slain activist Linda Reynolds, called the Reynolds' murder "another extreme example of Western hatred and intolerance." Watkins called Reynolds "an advocate and protector of all minority groups," and said, "her murder shows how Islamophobia has been allowed to grow under a white, patriarchal society."

Why these five homicide victims were killed has not been determined, and no suspects have been identified, but the police continue to look at the connections between the victims and the Muslim Brotherhood.

Malachi's hands shook. It seemed obvious he was the unnamed source. The short story did not come to any conclusions, but Malachi's theory had entered the public domain and neither the White House nor his department would be pleased. Brotherhood front groups would spin his theory to their advantage by using it as an example of Islamophobia, but he doubted they wanted a public debate about fundamental Islam.

Malachi picked up the phone. He needed Zahra's opinion.

"Did you see it?" Malachi asked.

"They didn't put in my best quotes about the relationship between the Egyptian Brotherhood and their front groups here. I gave Hamill the Brotherhood's history and laid out their connections to terrorism."

"They have space limitations," Malachi said. "Hamill told me they wanted to publish this as breaking news, but it's only the first article and they'll dive deeper. I'm supposed to meet him tonight. Want to come?"

"I guess so. He interviewed me over the phone, and I'd prefer to speak to him in person."

"Going public put us on the Brotherhood's radar," Malachi said.

"I'm already on their radar, and I don't care. I don't take risks lightly, but these monsters have to be stopped."

"I'll pick you up at seven."

Malachi hung up, and his phone rang.

"You the source for that story?" Jones asked.

"I needed to do something."

"Goddammit, Mac. I wish you'd asked me first. You gonna get yourself fired."

"The threat's real."

"I been in this damn department for thirty-five years. You know how hard it was to be a black po-po in the eighties? Any idea what it took for me to make detective? I know about tough spots, but you don't bite the hand that feeds you."

"You're right, but it's done."

"You didn't ask for my advice before but listen to me now. The lieutenant wants you to call her. Don't admit you're the leak or they'll fire you on the spot and there ain't a damn thing you'll be able to do about it. But if you don't confess, they don't have shit."

"I stand by what I did."

"You stand by it, stand around it, stand on it if you want, but if you want to have a badge while you're dancing around, don't tell nobody you leaked that story."

Malachi called Collins.

"Hey LT."

"Did Jones holla at you?" she asked.

"I just hung up with him."

"Tell me you didn't leak to the Herald."

Malachi did not want to lie, but Jones was right. If he admitted he was the source, he would be taken off the case and fired. Leaking facts to the press was forbidden, at least by anyone outside the Chief Ransom's office. Collins may have called Jones first, because she wanted Malachi to lie.

"Okay, I didn't leak the story."

"That's what I needed to hear you say."

"I didn't leak it, but I'm glad it's out. My theory's right."

"That's not the issue."

"It's the only issue that matters."

"I spoke to Nuse and told him none of my people dropped a dime to the press. He didn't believe me, but he can't prove anything. If you did it, he better not find out. I can't protect you if he does."

CHAPTER FIFTY-FIVE

Austin read the story in the Washington Herald and smiled. His plan had begun to work. If the president and Congress did not designate the Muslim Brotherhood as a terrorist organization then he would expose Islamists as vicious animals and turn public opinion against them. By writing the story, Dexter Hamill had painted a target on his back and on Dr. Mansour's too. If Detective Wolf had leaked the information, then he would also be in the Brotherhood's crosshairs.

Austin wanted to see Hamill meet his sources, a foolish risk, but he needed to witness his plan taking shape. He used a pretext call to confirm Hamill was at work, and at four o'clock, Austin sat across the street watching cars exit the Herald's employee parking lot. Boring work, but he could take a few sick days before his boss started asking questions.

Two and a half hours later, Austin squinted through the evening glare, as Hamill drove a white Subaru out of the lot. Austin let him pass then fell in behind, keeping a van between them for cover. Traffic in Northeast DC remained heavy, and Austin stayed in the same lane to avoid getting too far behind. Hamill drove down New York Avenue into downtown DC then turned onto Massachusetts Avenue.

It did not take Austin long to notice the van he had hidden behind was also following Hamill. It did not pass when given the opportunity, and it slowed when Hamill did. Austin assumed the MPD was tracking Hamill to identify his source, and he considered breaking off surveillance, until noticed a red Lexus and a black BMW working in concert with the van.

They switched places after every turn, executing a standard three-car surveillance, but MPD cops did not use foreign cars.

Hamill arrived at the National Cathedral and pulled into the driveway. The sprawling property contained three children's schools, the Bishop's gardens, and other buildings—a decent place for a surreptitious rendezvous. The van, Lexus, and BMW all parked on Wisconsin Avenue outside the cathedral grounds.

Austin pulled up behind them and watched. Counter-surveillance should have spotted him, but they seemed focused on Hamill. What were they doing? He needed to be ready for anything. He opened his satchel and affixed his fake beard then donned a baseball hat and sunglasses. He exited the car, walked across the bright green grass, and sat on a bench in front of the cathedral.

Hamill walked into the visitor's entrance, followed by two men from the Lexus.

Austin carried his gun in a hip holster, but taking spontaneous action was ill advised. He would wait and see what happened.

A minute later, four men exited the van and walked toward the cathedral.

There would be trouble. Every instinct urged Austin to return to his car and drive away—save himself—but if they killed Hamill or his source, Austin's plan would unravel. His anger returned, and he dug his nails into his palm.

"Fuck."

He headed for the cathedral.

CHAPTER FIFTY-SIX

Incense permeated the cool interior of the National Cathedral. The 530-foot-long building was laid out from west to east in the shape of a cross, with the northern and southern transepts forming the crossbar. A tower rose 234 feet over the center of the cathedral and two smaller towers bracketed the western end.

Inside, sandstone columns rose high into the air, and their curved, elegant lines resembled wrinkled drapes. Flying buttresses and gothic arches laced the towering ceiling, like a spider web made of stone. Afternoon sunlight penetrated stained glass windows and cast a warm glow. Half a dozen tourists wandered around, their voices almost inaudible as their words disappeared into the cavernous space.

Malachi moved on autopilot, scanning the cathedral for threats.

He shifted in a leather-backed chair near the back of the nave and checked his watch. They were fifteen minutes early. Zahra sat beside him, biting her lower lip. She had already given Dexter Hamill an interview but talking to a reporter in person was more stressful. Most communication was nonverbal and a good reporter, like a good detective, could read an interviewee's mind.

The National Cathedral—officially the Cathedral Church of Saint Peter and Saint Paul in the City and Diocese of Washington—was the sixth largest in the world and sat on fifty-nine acres of land in Northwest Washington. The Protestant Episcopal Cathedral Foundation of the District of Columbia began construction in 1907 and it had taken eighty-three years and one hundred and fifty thousand tons of sand-colored Indiana limestone to build it.

"Tell me again why we're meeting here?" Zahra asked.

"This gives us more deniability than being caught with him in private," Malachi said.

"But people will see us."

"Sure, tourists. We'll find a quiet corner. Keep your eyes open, he should be here soon."

"I don't know what he looks like."

"He's middle-aged and balding. He'll be the guy looking at faces and not up at the stained glass like everyone else."

Tourists milled around the cathedral. Two walked down the nave toward the high alter, over five hundred feet away, and a dozen sauntered up parallel aisles on either side of massive stone piers. Many admired the colorful glass in the clerestory windows. Malachi watched to see if anyone appeared out of place, but they all wore the wide-eyed and open-mouthed expressions of tourists on vacation.

Malachi returned his attention to the entrance behind them, and almost on cue, Hamill walked into the cathedral. He had a receding hairline, round spectacles, and a soft belly which probably came from spending his days behind a keyboard. Hamill made eye contact with him.

Malachi touched Zahra's arm and motioned with his eyes. "Follow me."

He guided her into the aisle and their footsteps echoed off the marble floors. Hamill followed as they moved to the side of the nave and stopped in a small alcove. Light streaked through a sapphire-colored stained-glass window above them.

Hamill arrived thirty seconds later. "Thanks for meeting me."

"It's important," Malachi said, and introduced Zahra.

"I only gave you the tip of the iceberg," Zahra said.

"I want to be clear about the ground rules," Malachi said. "This is a dangerous game and how we communicate is critical." Malachi handed him a prepaid burner cell phone, a trick he had learned from the killer. "Only use this to call me. I've preprogrammed my burner number into it."

"This seems paranoid," Hamill said.

"Better to be safe," Malachi said. "We want to give you more background on the Brotherhood. Someone has to blow the lid off their plans, and it needs to come from a mainstream news source. Zahra—er—Dr. Mansour can give you all the proof you need."

"That's why I'm here. My editor's ready to follow up on the first article."

Over Hamill's shoulder, two muscular men with cheap suits and Middle Eastern features entered the cathedral. They focused on the tourists and never looked up. A hollowness spread through Malachi's stomach, and he pulled Zahra and Hamill behind a stone pier.

"I think you were followed," Malachi whispered.

"What do—?"

"Sh," Malachi said. "We need to slip out behind them. Zahra and I will go first. Give us thirty seconds before you leave, then call me on the burner from your car."

The two thugs moved toward the high altar, glancing into alcoves as they passed. Malachi guided Hamill and Zahra counterclockwise around the pier to stay out of their view.

Footsteps clattered near the entrance and four more men, with olive complexions, heavy beards, and determined expressions, entered the nave. Malachi had seen enough criminals in his career to know those bruisers were bad news. If they wanted to surveil Hamill, they would have sent one man inside, not six.

Malachi drew his Glock and pulled out his badge with his other hand.

"What are you doing?" Hamill asked.

"This isn't a surveillance. I think they want to hurt you."

"Who are they?" Zahra asked.

"I don't know," Malachi said.

"This is nuts . . . put the gun away," Hamill said, waving his hand like he was shooing a fly. "I'll leave now, and they won't see us together. Wait here and—"

"Keep quiet and stay behind the pier," Malachi said, too late to stop him.

Hamill scurried away, just out of Malachi's reach. Malachi peeked around the pier and watched Hamill walk toward the exit. He had to pass the men.

The four men closest to the door stopped and faced him. Hamill nodded a greeting and tried to pass, but they spread out and blocked his path. Hamill hesitated, unsure of what to do. The first goon drew a chrome revolver out of a shoulder holster, as if reaching for a pack of cigarettes. He pointed it at Hamill.

Malachi could not sit still and hide. He leaned around the pier and pointed his Glock at the man.

"Police, drop the gun," he yelled.

The man jerked his head toward Malachi then stepped to his right, putting Hamill between them. He raised his revolver and fired twice. The deafening sound of gunshots reverberated through the cathedral.

The bullets impacted the stone inches from Malachi, slapping it like a hammer. Bullet fragments and stone chips sprayed the air and ripped into his face. Malachi ducked behind the pier. His skin burned, and he could not open his eyes.

A woman screamed.

Malachi blinked to clear his vision. Another shot echoed through the cathedral, and something hit the stone floor with a thump. He squinted through dust and tears.

Zahra held her hands over her mouth, and her skin blanched.

Malachi positioned himself between Zahra and the pier. He squatted low and extended his Glock in front of him, keeping his finger on the trigger. He leaned around the column, so his head would not appear in the same place, then he popped out from behind the stone.

The four men all pointed guns in his direction, and Hamill lay on the floor, a pool of blood forming beneath his head. Adrenaline surged through Malachi's body, and everything slowed down as his senses heightened. He focused on his Glock's front sight and his vision narrowed, as if he was looking through a tunnel.

Malachi placed his sight over the chest of the man who had fired at him and aimed center-mass. He held his breath and squeezed his trigger three times in rapid succession. His hearing shut down, reducing the gunshots to distant pops. Everything moved in slow motion, and he achieved complete focus.

He did not pause to see if his shots hit their mark. He swung his sights onto the next man's torso and double tapped his trigger. He spun toward the third and fourth men as they dove to their right. He fired four times, and his rounds splintered a row of chairs behind them.

Both men he had shot lay on the ground. The first was on his back, not moving, his gun at his feet. The second leaned on his elbow and tried to get up. He still held a revolver.

Malachi took a breath, slid his front sight over the man's face, and fired a single shot. The thug's head jerked back, and a pink mist clouded the air behind him. The gun toppled out of his grip, and he collapsed backward.

Malachi swiveled back toward the other two hoodlums, as they popped up from behind chairs and opened fire. Bullets snapped in the air, moving at seventeen hundred feet per second. The rounds ricocheted off the stone behind him.

Malachi returned fire, popping off two rounds at each man. He rolled behind the pier and backed against Zahra to shield her with his body. She whimpered. A shot rang out from his left. The first men who had entered the cathedral moved toward them from the front of the cathedral.

He fired twice in their direction, and both men dove into the transept. The slide of his Glock locked back—empty. He drew his last magazine with his left hand, pushed the release with his thumb, and the empty magazine clattered on the floor. He slammed the new one into the gun and released the slide, chambering a round.

The men near the chairs fired again. The rounds smacked against the pier in front of Malachi and a cloud of limestone billowed in the air.

Malachi leaned out and fired back, then he pivoted and shot at the transept to keep the other goons' heads down. He pulled out his radio with his free hand.

"Dispatch, Homicide Twenty-Nine, Priority traffic."

"All units hold the channel. Go ahead Homicide Twenty-Nine."

"Ten thirty-three. Shots fired. Officer needs assistance at the National Cathedral. I have multiple armed suspects, and one civilian down. Roll backup and EMS."

"Copy Homicide Twenty-Nine. All units, ten thirty-three, National Cathedral. Shots fired."

Malachi grabbed Zahra and backed into a small alcove under a stained-glass window. He glanced at the closest exit doors. They were only thirty feet away, but they could not reach them without exposing themselves to the men behind the chairs. A round ricocheted off the wall behind them, and Malachi fired at the men in the transept. They ducked behind cover and out of his sight. Malachi and Zahra could not run, but if they stayed there, they would die.

They were trapped.

CHAPTER FIFTY-SEVEN

Austin moved through the northwest cloister until he reached the south tower perch. Gunfire had erupted the moment he entered the nave, and he had seen Hamill fall to the ground—dead.

Austin longed for his pills.

He looked across the cathedral where two groups of gunmen cornered Detective Wolf and Dr. Mansour. They outnumbered them, and Wolf and the doctor would not last long.

Austin bared his teeth and flexed his shoulders, his wrath boiling inside him. He let it control him.

He took cover behind a pier and drew his gun.

It would feel good to kill in defense of the innocent—a memory from his former self—a noble and righteous act. At least he hoped it would. He had become something else, and was no longer that man, but killing to protect others was God's will.

The Brotherhood were animals. This assassination attempt proved it, as if he needed any more evidence. Maybe now others would see the threat and notice the evil among them.

It was time.

He raised his Beretta.

CHAPTER FIFTY-EIGHT

Sweat ran down Malachi's face. The air smelled of gunpowder and rock dust. He pressed his back against Zahra, keeping her inside the alcove. They had nowhere to go. Two shooters stood between them and the exit and two more pinned them down from the transept. Eventually, one of their bullets would find its mark. If one group lay down covering fire while the others advanced, they would finish them. Malachi was down to his last magazine, and the police would not arrive in time to save them.

"We have to run for the exit," Malachi said, trying to keep his voice low, but his ears rang, and he could not hear himself.

"I . . . I can't move," Zahra said. "They'll kill us."

"If we stay here—we're dead."

One of the thugs in the transept fired, and a bullet skipped off the floor at Malachi's feet. The sound reverberated through the cathedral.

Malachi leaned out and fired twice at each man. They both dove out of sight. He turned and fired at the guys beyond the pier, and they ducked behind chairs. He could not tell if he had hit anyone.

Seven rounds left.

"On the count of three, run through those doors on our right. The main exit is off the hall. If we make it, get out and run down the steps. When you reach the ground, find cover. You go first, and I'll stay between you and the shooters."

"We won't make it."

"It's our only chance."

"Please . . . I can't."

"One . . . two—"

A barrage of gunfire erupted from the southern side of the nave. One of the men pitched forward and fell to the floor. He writhed in pain, clutching his chest as blood pumped out of him. He held his hands against the wound as if he was trying to stop water flowing from a faucet.

The gunmen in the transept fired at whoever had shot their compatriot. They were distracted. This was Malachi's chance.

"Now, move," he said.

"I'm afraid."

He grabbed Zahra's arm and pulled her toward the doors leading to the main hallway. He slammed the door open with his shoulder and glanced back into the nave. Across the aisle, a tall, bearded man fired at the thugs.

The man resembled the killer, and Malachi hesitated. Their eyes locked for an instant and Malachi saw something familiar, something he could not place, then the man resumed firing, and Malachi pushed through the doors into the north tower perch.

The cathedral exit lay before them.

Malachi stopped. Two gorillas in dark suits ran toward the cathedral with guns drawn.

"This way," he yelled.

He pulled Zahra to the right and ran down the northwest cloister. Two armed men burst into the building at the far end of the hallway and spotted them. Malachi hauled Zahra into an alcove. A bullet impacted above them, and limestone sprayed in the air.

Behind them, a wrought-iron gate blocked their access to a stone stairwell.

"In here," Malachi said.

He yanked on the handle, but the gate did not budge.

Locked.

The men shouted to each other in Arabic, and their voices drew closer.

Malachi and Zahra were trapped again.

"Dammit," Malachi said.

"Hold on," Zahra said. "Let me try."

She slipped her thin wrists through the bars and jostled the handle. The clasp clicked, and she yanked the gate open.

"Yalla."

Malachi took her hand and towed her through the opening into a narrow stairwell enclosed by fifteen-foot limestone walls. Light filtered in from a small window high on the wall and flickered off dust particles in the air. He slammed the gate shut behind them, as a round clanged off it, inches from his face.

"Upstairs. Now."

Zahra stumbled up the steps, her legs outpacing her coordination, and she braced herself against the walls as she moved.

"Slow is smooth, and smooth is fast," Malachi said, repeating a tactical adage.

"I'm trying."

The stairway curved counterclockwise, and they ascended, turning and turning, until they arrived at a metal door. He pushed past Zahra and forced the door open. They entered a balcony below a rose-colored, stained-glass window. A stone railing separated them from the nave and the cathedral floor fifty feet below.

The thug behind the seats pointed his gun toward the cathedral entrance far below them, but he did not shoot, and Malachi wondered if they had killed the mysterious shooter. The men in the transept moved down the aisle toward the cloister.

They were coming.

Malachi led Zahra across the open balcony, and the sound of her heels clacking on the marble floor echoed through the open space.

The goon below them looked up and his eyes met Malachi's. The man raised his gun and fired.

Malachi dove to the ground, wrenching Zahra down on top of him. Bullets ricocheted off the stone railing. Malachi crawled forward, staying low, and Zahra followed. They made it across the balcony, and he helped Zahra to her feet. Her face looked ashen, and she seemed to be in shock. He turned the handle on a door to their left. Locked. They entered another stairway, enclosed by red-brick walls, and climbed carpeted steps.

A door slammed below them. The men had made it to the balcony. Police sirens wailed in the distance.

"They're behind us," Malachi said. "Keep moving."

"Why are they chasing us?" Zahra asked. A sob escaped her lips.

"They want to kill us more than they want to escape."

"Islamists."

Malachi's thighs burned as they mounted the steep stairway, and he flashed back to running with his father. The familiar pain comforted him. At the next landing, he tried another door, but it was locked too. So was the next. They kept moving. He gasped for air and his pulse pounded in his ears.

Zahra stayed in front of him, driven by terror and the will to live.

The stairway ended at a door. If it was locked, they would have nowhere to go. Zahra grabbed the handle and pulled, and the door swung open. They stepped through the threshold into daylight.

Malachi followed her onto an open-air, stone walkway, which ringed the north tower. They were one hundred and fifty feet up, above the lead roof of the nave. He looked beyond the city and across the Potomac River into Virginia. He leaned over the railing and stared at the green lawn below. His stomach flipped and his head spun.

Not now . . . please.

He pushed himself against the stone wall and closed his eyes. Physical exertion brought on MS and vertigo was yet another symptom. The disease had progressed, and he needed treatment. He dug out two Gabapentin and swallowed them.

Zahra must have sensed his absence and turned back. "Malachi, are you hurt?"

"No, it's the height. It bothers me. Keep going."

He shut the door behind him, took a deep breath, and followed. Above their heads, grotesques and gargoyles kept watch over the city. A short stone railing was all that separated them from a deadly fall to the ground. After fifty feet, the walkway angled ninety degrees to the right following the square-shaped tower. They ducked under a gothic arch, moved through a short tunnel, and emerged on the walkway on the western side of the tower.

The exterior door slammed open behind them. The men were gaining. Malachi and Zahra jogged across the western walkway, ducked under another arch, and exited the tunnel on the northern side.

"Wait here," Malachi said.

He ran back through the tunnel and leaned out with his gun. When the men emerged from the tunnel on the far side, he would have a decent shot.

One of them poked his head around the corner.

Malachi cursed, wishing the triggerman had been less cautious. A thirty-foot head shot was difficult under perfect conditions, but Malachi's body heaved up and down with his labored breathing. He fired two rounds down the walkway but missed, and the man slipped out of sight. At least he had slowed them down. He hurried after Zahra.

Five rounds left.

Malachi and Zahra turned onto the eastern side of the tower, almost back to where they had started, and Malachi scanned the walkway for threats. They reached an open area over the lead roof, opposite the east tower at the other end of the cathedral. Malachi passed a humming generator and headed for a steel door. If they could not get through it, they would be forced to either climb onto the steep roof or shoot it out.

He tried the handle. It opened.

Malachi pulled Zahra into a room with gray pipes on the walls and construction materials stacked on the floor.

Nowhere to hide.

On the opposite side of the room, an open metal staircase rose four stories to the tower roof. They clambered up the steps, their footsteps echoing through the empty space. They passed cement beams where the next story began, but the floors had been removed for renovation, leaving the entire stairwell exposed.

The door burst open below, and footsteps clopped across on the cement floor. The men closed the gap.

Malachi leaned over the side. Two thugs aimed their handguns at him, and he ducked away from the railing. They fired. Bullets banged against the metal and buzzed through the air, like swarming bees.

"Run, Zahra."

He leaned over the railing and fired twice. Missed.

Three rounds.

The men separated and moved to opposite sides of the room, out of his view. Another round bounced off the stairs below him.

Malachi took the stairs, two at a time, catching Zahra as she reached the top.

She opened a door, and they climbed onto the roof of the north tower, 230 feet in the air. Tall pinnacles rose from the four corners of the roof, and in the center, a one-story brick structure covered the stairwell. The faces of angels carved into the stone stared down at them. The southern tower lay twenty feet away—too far to jump. They had nowhere to go but back. Or over the side.

The wail of sirens drifted up from below. The police had arrived but would never make it in time.

Malachi stuck his head back into the stairwell. The men climbed, their shoes banging against the stairs. He had less than a minute. He stepped out onto the landing and leaned over the railing to get a better angle. He caught brief flashes of the men as they ascended. He focused on the stairwell and avoided looking at the ground.

He had to do this.

He swung his leg over the railing, held on with one hand, and leaned out as far as he could. His head swam.

The men reached the landing two flights below. Their footsteps grew louder as they closed the distance.

Malachi aimed at the corner of the flight below him. Something flashed in front of his sight, and he pulled the trigger twice, firing fast.

A man shouted in Arabic, and his body tumbled over the railing. He bounced off the stairs and fell all the way to the bottom. He hit the concrete floor with a wet thump.

One round left.

Malachi pulled himself back into the stairs and swung his leg over the railing. The second shooter returned fire. A burning pain ran up Malachi's arm, and he fell back on the steps, landing hard on his side. He clenched his jaw and crawled through the doorway onto the roof.

"You're shot," Zahra said.

Blood oozed out of a long wound running down his right arm and soaked through his shirt. A bullet had grazed him and opened his skin like a zipper.

"I'm fine. Hurry."

He took Zahra's arm, and they ran around the structure. Their pursuer would have to come through the door which would give Malachi a shot, but he only had one round left, and one bullet rarely stopped an attacker. He would need to shoot him between the eyes.

Too risky.

He looked around, desperate, frantic. A wooden ladder rested against the base of the structure. The ladder was probably used for maintenance on the microwave and UHF antennas atop the lone structure. Did they have time?

He grabbed the ladder, wincing in pain. "Help me."

Zahra held the other end, and they leaned the ladder against the far side of the structure. She climbed up, and Malachi placed his foot on the bottom rung.

The stairwell door banged open.

Malachi climbed faster, trying to balance with the gun in his hand.

"He's coming," Zahra said.

Malachi scampered up the last three rungs and dove onto the roof beside her. He dropped his gun onto the pebbled surface and grabbed the ladder with both hands. He pulled it up after them, and pain shot through his arm like an electrical current. He lifted the end of the ladder and dragged it onto the roof as the man rounded the corner.

The brute saw him, raised his gun, and fired.

Rounds snapped through the air over their heads. Malachi rolled away from the edge toward the antennas in the center of the roof.

"Get down. He can't see us from there."

Zahra dropped onto her stomach next to him. Her chest expanded and contracted with deep breaths and her skin glistened with sweat. She buried her face in her hands and cried.

"It's okay. He can't get an angle to shoot us, and we have the only ladder."

"We're safe?"

"Yes. He would have to get to our level to see us and . . ."

The pinnacles.

Malachi's eyes darted from one pinnacle to the next.

The shooter grabbed the face of an angel on the southeast corner and pulled himself up. He maneuvered along the edge of the roof with his gun in one hand.

Malachi rolled onto his side, ignoring the pain in his arm, and regulated his breathing. He placed his front sight between the man's shoulder blades and steadied his aim.

The man hung from the angel by one hand. He turned and pointed his gun at them.

Malachi squeezed the trigger. His Glock jumped in his hand and the slide locked back—empty.

The man arched his back and dropped his handgun. He grabbed his chest with his free hand and lost his footing. His momentum swung him toward the edge, and his fingers slipped off the angel's head. He fell backward off the pinnacle. He bounced on the parapet, and his arms flailed in the air for a moment, as if he was trying to fly.

He disappeared over the edge and plummeted twenty-one stories to the ground.

CHAPTER FIFTY-NINE

Malachi slouched on a gurney inside a Mid-Atlantic Hospital ambulance parked in front of the National Cathedral. He held Zahra with his good arm. She had stopped crying, but her hands still shook.

In response to the mass-casualty event, ambulances from four hospitals had responded, and red and blue lights from two dozen fire and police cars reflected off the stone cathedral.

"How are you so calm?" Zahra asked.

"I'm always looking for bad guys, so when I'm fighting them, I relax. Confronting them is what I want . . . what I seek. Does that sound strange?"

Zahra looked down and nodded. "I get it."

"Don't think I'm crazy, but the violence relaxes me."

"That may be a little nuts."

Malachi laughed. "Seeing you in danger made it worse."

"You saved me."

An emergency medical technician climbed into the ambulance. He packed Malachi's bullet wound with gauze and bandaged it. The bullet channel looked shallow, and the wound had clotted, but Malachi worried about infection, and had agreed to go to the hospital for treatment. But first, he wanted to walk investigators through the scene.

He had counted ten assassins in the cathedral, men likely sent by the Brotherhood. He had killed four of them and their anonymous savior had shot two. The other four appeared to have escaped in the chaos, but police continued to search the grounds. It would have been helpful to catch a suspect alive, but Malachi did not regret killing any of those savages. They had tried to murder Zahra.

"I think the guy who saved us was the vigilante," Malachi said. "He wore the same beard in the cemetery."

"That doesn't make sense," Zahra said. "How did he know we were here?" Her eyes looked red and puffy.

"I don't know. He could have followed us to figure out how close I was to identifying him, or it's possible he wanted to stop Hamill. The question is, why did he intervene?"

Zahra nodded. She was quiet for a moment before she spoke. "Maybe he was there to protect Hamill, and he didn't kill you because he didn't want to murder a police officer. I'm grateful to him."

"That's possible, I guess." Malachi tried to make sense of it. "Whatever his motivation, I need to stop him."

Collins pulled into the parking lot and got out. She spoke to a patrol officer who pointed at their ambulance. She walked over, smoking a Marlboro Light. No more lollipops.

"They had us surrounded," Zahra said. "I wonder why they didn't wait for us to come out of the cathedral. It would have been easier for them to escape."

"I think they wanted to see who Hamill met. Clearly, all of us were on their list. Coming inside made sense if their goal was murder."

Zahra shivered.

Malachi hugged her, and they climbed out of the ambulance as Collins approached.

"You okay, Wolf?" Collins asked.

"I'll be fine. This is Dr. Mansour."

Collins shook Zahra's hand and turned back to him. "Lay it on me. The I.A. shoot team will be here soon."

Malachi briefed her on everything, including his decision to leak the story. He described Hamill's murder and how the man he believed was the vigilante had helped them escape. She shook her head when he told her how he had killed the assassin with his last bullet.

"You went old school. The Lord is looking down on you. The chance of escaping a ten-man hit team is almost zero. I wonder if you brought us closer to solving this or if you complicated things?"

"If we tie the shooters to the Brotherhood, it will confirm my theory," Malachi said.

Before Collins could reply, Nuse pushed through the police line. He strutted toward them with his fists balled, ready for a fight. His face glowed bright red.

"That's it, Wolf," he shouted from ten feet away. "You're through. I knew you were the leak, and now a reporter is dead. Look what you've done. This is a fucking goat rope. I'm not going down for this."

"I'm fine, Chief, thanks for asking. This is Dr. Zahra Mansour, a senior fellow at the Middle East Policy Institute."

That threw Nuse off his rhythm and he looked at Zahra, confused. "Ms. Mansour. I'm sorry Detective Wolf got you into this. I can assure you he won't endanger you again."

"It's *Doctor* Mansour, and Malachi saved my life. Maybe you should figure out why the Brotherhood tried to kill us instead of blaming him."

Collins stifled a laugh.

Nuse appeared unsure of himself for a moment. "I promise we will investigate this thoroughly. Now, would you excuse us for a few minutes? I need to speak to Lieutenant Collins and Detective Wolf about police business."

Zahra gripped the blanket around her shoulders, gave Nuse an icy stare, and walked to the front of the ambulance.

As soon as she was out of earshot, Nuse stuck his finger in Malachi's face. "You stepped on your dick this time. Do you deny meeting with that reporter?"

"I don't deny it."

"Then you're suspended until we can investigate how many rules you've broken. You're done."

Malachi stared daggers into Nuse's soul. He had enough. "Fuck you, Barney. Why don't you go fill out some forms and let the real cops catch the bad guys?"

Collins hung her head.

"That's it," Nuse said, sputtering. "Give me your gun and badge." His hands shook.

"Lieutenant Collins has my gun. I turned it over to her for the shooting investigation. You can take my badge and shove it up your ass—you petty, worthless bureaucrat."

Malachi tossed his credentials, and Nuse caught them against his chest. Nuse started to say something then stopped and stormed away.

"Don't say anything else until you talk to a union rep," Collins said. You can't run a game on this, not after stepping-to Nuse like that." She dropped her cigarette and rubbed it out with her shoe. "Let me see what I can do." She chased after Nuse.

Zahra came up beside Malachi and touched his arm. "You okay?"

"We're alive, so yeah, I'm okay."

Chasing a killer had been hard enough, but now Malachi had to worry about Nuse. Worse, the Brotherhood wanted to kill him, and they were dangerous. The clouds rolled in and twilight fell. The towers of the cathedral stood out against the darkening sky.

He needed to find the killer, and he wanted to stop the Brotherhood too. It was personal. But if he lost his job, he had given up his PhD and family for nothing. He would never find justice and never know if he was destined to be a cop. He would be adrift. Now that Nuse had suspended him, what options did he have?

Lightning flashed in the distance and the storm drew near.

CHAPTER SIXTY

Austin knew he neared the end of his life, one way or the other. Prison or death. He did not see a way out.

He had come face-to-face with Wolf three times, twice as the Angel of Death. He had been lucky to escape but that would not last. If he gambled his freedom long enough, he would eventually lose, but he had known the stakes before he started, and he only had one goal.

Complete the mission.

He reached into his drawer and removed his last bottle of hydrocodone. He could not purchase Oxycontin at the pill mill in southeast DC, because it had been closed, but hydrocodone was a strong analgesic and would do the trick if he took enough. And therein lay the problem. He had escalated from taking one Oxycontin pill as needed, to taking one every twelve hours. When the effects had diminished, he had increased to two tablets every twelve hours, then two every eight hours. The hydrocodone had worked, but he had needed more, and upped his dosage to six tablets per day. Then eight. Now ten.

He neared the toxicity level where he would overdose, yet the effects would continue to lessen with time. He had been here before, in high school. And keeping a medicine bottle in his desk at work was not smart. He had become sloppy, or careless, or both.

He knew how this would end.

He opened the bottle, shook two tablets into his hand, and swallowed them with cold coffee. He pushed his chair away from his desk and stared out the window, waiting for the hydrocodone to carry him away.

"Hey, there you are," Jane said.

Austin spun around, startled.

Jane stood in the opening to his cubicle. Her gray slacks clung to her legs, revealing her shape, and something stirred inside him.

"Where've you been?" she asked. "I've been looking for you."

"Wicked busy," he said.

"Did you hear?"

"Hear what?" He could still hear their bodies hitting the floor.

"Detective Wolf got into a shootout at the National Cathedral."

"He okay?"

"Yeah, but he left bodies up there."

The enemy grew stronger while bureaucracy diminished law enforcement's ability to fight back.

"Think it's related to the case?" he asked.

"Has to be."

"Thanks for letting me know."

"Maybe it has to do with—"

"Keep me informed if it impacts our investigations," Austin said. He turned his attention to an open folder on his desk.

"Will do."

He sensed her staring before she walked away.

Wolf had escaped unharmed. Saving Wolf and Dr. Mansour satisfied him, but not in the way he had thought it would. Three months ago, before his mission, saving two lives would have made him proud. They had needed protection, but his pleasure came from something else. Killing those men had exhilarated him to a level even his drugs could not achieve. He could tell himself the pleasure came from protecting the innocent, but the killing itself had intoxicated him.

Murder had become rapture.

Austin remembered his mother after the savage beatings Raymond had given them. She had puttered around the house for days, her face swollen and red. One night, Raymond came home drunk and staggered up to bed. Margaret followed him with a glass of water and something to eat, and Austin felt relieved his father was too incapacitated to abuse them. That night, Austin awakened to a metallic clank coming from their backyard. He wiped the sleep from his eyes, tiptoed to the window, and saw his mother digging in the garden with a hand shovel. She dropped a plastic bag into the hole, covered it with soil, and patted it down. She stared at the earth then looked back at the house—directly at Austin. He jumped back from the window, his heart pounding, not sure why he needed to hide.

In the morning, his father was dead.

His mother smiled as they carried Raymond's body away. The medical examiner called it a heart attack, death by natural causes, not unusual for a man in his fifties with a large belly, bad temper, and drinking problem. After Raymond's funeral, Austin dug up that plastic bag and discovered empty vials of calcium gluconate and potassium phosphate. At the library, he learned that high levels of calcium gluconate unbalanced electrolyte levels and could cause a heart failure when mixed with potassium phosphate.

His mother had killed his father. Austin never spoke about what he found, not with anyone.

Would God care that Austin enjoyed killing, even if the murders were moral acts? Austin had morphed into something else, mutated into a being that lived for death.

CHAPTER SIXTY-ONE

The ringing phone jolted Malachi awake, and he groped for it on his nightstand. The screen read 8:31 a.m., late for him to still be in bed.

Zahra and Malachi had stayed late at the police station giving interviews. After, they had driven to his place, but the adrenaline had kept them awake, and they had taken full advantage of being in bed and unable to sleep. Near-death experiences made Malachi crave sex, seek the touch of another, embrace life. Zahra had insisted on going home after they made love, saying she wanted to shower and sleep in her own bed. He knew she needed the comfort and familiarity of her own home after their traumatic experience, so he did not put up a fight. She had promised to take the day off to relax on her boat and then meet him for dinner.

Malachi saw Alison's number on the screen and accepted the call.

"Everything okay?" he asked, his voice deep and gravelly.

"No, everything's not okay."

"Is something wrong with the girls?"

"They're fine, no thanks to you. What do you think you're doing?"

Malachi slid his feet onto the floor and sat on the edge of the bed. What the hell was she talking about? Had she heard about the shooting?

"I'm fine. The incident shook me up, but I'm not hurt."

"Incident? What incident?"

"Nothing, ah, what are you calling about?"

"I'm calling to tell you to stop stalking us. I used to see you parked on the street watching our house, but I thought you had moved on. I know I have, and it's time you do the same."

Embarrassment stung his cheeks. Alison had caught him watching her house, and he hung his head in shame. "Listen, I'm sorry about that, but that was a long time ago."

"It was last night."

A jolt shot through him, activating his fight-or-flight response, and he stood up. "What are you talking about? I spent the night at the police station."

"I've seen you in front of our house every day this week. You've been using one of those shitty cars with the tinted windows from your department's auto pool."

"Hold on—"

"That pissed me off, but when you followed us to school this morning, I reached my limit. If the girls catch you following us, it'll confuse them."

Malachi had never followed Riley and Samantha to school. They attended a summer program at the Rockwell School in northern DC—one of the best private schools in the country—thanks to Alison's parents' generosity. He had not been there since parents' night six months ago.

His girls were in danger.

"That wasn't me."

"You have to stop."

"Alison, damn it, listen to me. I haven't been to your house in a long time, and I've never followed the girls. I wasn't there. I was involved in a shooting last night."

"Oh my God. Are you okay?"

"Tell me about the car you saw this morning."

"It's the same car you . . . I mean the same vehicle that's been outside our house. An old Chevrolet Suburban, black. It followed us to school and parked on the street when I left. I assumed it was you. I was so mad, I waited until I got home to call."

Malachi's blood ran cold, and he broke out in a sweat. Was the killer going after his family? Was the Brotherhood trying to intimidate him through his children?

"Listen to me," he said, trying to keep the fear out of his voice. "Call the school and tell them to keep the girls inside. Tell them someone is stalking your children and their father is coming to pick them up."

"You're scaring me."

Malachi paced as he spoke. "This is serious. Do it now. I'll call you when I have our girls."

He hung up, scooped his wrinkled jeans off the floor, and slid into them. He reached into his bureau drawer for his Glock and pulled out an empty holster. He had surrendered his gun.

"Damn it."

Malachi ran across the room and dug through bags in the rear of the closet. He pulled a snub-nosed, thirty-eight-caliber revolver out of a case—a personally owned gun he sometimes carried on his ankle as a backup. He scrounged around and found an old box of ammunition, then he loaded the revolver and jammed it into his jeans pocket.

It would take him thirty minutes to get to school during rush hour. He broke out in a sweat. His girls needed him. Malachi ran back across the room and pulled on a tee shirt. He grabbed his phone and called Jones.

"Hey, Mac," Jones said. "I was just about to call you. How are you and that fresh lady doing?"

Malachi's felt out of breath, as if he had been running. "Jonesy, I need your help."

"Whoa, what's up, my brother?"

"Alison called. Someone has been watching her house all week, and a Suburban followed her to school today."

"What you need?" Jones asked, all business.

Malachi felt lighter, knowing Jones had his back. "I'm heading to Rockwell now. Are you at the office already?"

"No, I'm in my ride about two blocks from the office. I'll swing by and pick you up."

"Thanks Jonesy. I'm probably overreacting, but it's better to be safe. Alison's asking the school to keep the girls inside."

"If the Suburban's still there, we can get a marked unit to stop it. Meet me outside in two minutes."

CHAPTER SIXTY-TWO

Malachi bounded down the stairs three at a time, too keyed up to wait for the elevator. He exited his building as Jones pulled up. Malachi jumped into the Impala, and Jones took off before he could slam the door.

"Thanks for doing this," Malachi said.

"Riley and Samantha are like my grandkids."

Jones cut the steering wheel hard and made a U-turn.

Malachi snatched the blue light off the floor and slapped it on the dashboard. This was not a police emergency, but his stomach quivered with fear.

"Who would stalk those beautiful kids?" Jones asked.

"The Muslim Brotherhood."

"Why?"

"That's what I need to find out," Malachi said.

Jones navigated secondary streets to avoid rush hour and made his way across town to Wisconsin Avenue. He headed north, weaving in and out of traffic. Drivers ignored their blue light, and Jones cursed under his breath. He activated his air horn, and people stopped texting or whatever else they were doing besides driving and moved out of his way.

"You don't drive like an old guy," Malachi said.

"Pay attention. Maybe you can learn a thing or two before I retire."

Malachi lifted the blue light off the dashboard as they approached Rockwell. The red-brick administrative building was set back from the road behind towering maple trees, and a circular driveway curved through the manicured front lawn. The classrooms, tennis courts, and playing fields lay beyond.

Jones slowed as they pulled into the driveway.

Malachi looked over his shoulder at the cars parked along both sides of Wisconsin Avenue, and he spotted a black Suburban with the dark profiles of men inside.

"There it is," Malachi said.

"Where?"

"Opposite the school in front of that pickup. At least two men inside."

"Got it."

The men swiveled their heads, tracking the Impala.

"They spotted us," Malachi said.

Jones continued around the driveway. "Shi-it. Why do they have to issue us these po-po cars?" Jones said. "We get burned on almost every surveillance."

The Suburban's brake lights flashed.

"They made us, and they're leaving," Malachi said.

"I'll call for patrol."

Rage boiled inside Malachi, and he clenched his fists. He had sworn an oath to protect the public, but this was a threat to his family, to his sweet, innocent children.

"The Suburban will be long gone by the time they arrive," Malachi said.

Jones grimaced. "We could follow them."

"If they see us behind them, we will end up in a high-speed pursuit, and we don't have criminal charges. Besides, that would mean leaving Riley and Samantha unguarded."

The Suburban backed up, trying to squeeze out of its tight parking space.

"What you want to do?" Jones asked.

"Stop them."

"Shi-it."

Jones punched the gas and accelerated through the turn. The Impala's back end slid and sprayed gravel onto the lawn. He countersteered and headed for the avenue.

Malachi looked past Jones out the side window. The Suburban pulled forward, edging out of the tight spot. It stopped and backed up again.

"Hurry," Malachi said.

Their tires squealed when they hit Wisconsin, and Jones cut a hard left and aimed for the front of the Suburban. The Suburban cleared the back bumper of the car in front of it and turned into the street. Jones stomped on his brakes and screeched to a halt, his engine a foot from the Suburban's grill. He blocked them.

"Shi-it, that was close."

The passenger door of the Suburban opened.

Malachi pushed his door upon and jumped out. He reached for his badge then remembered he no longer carried one. He fished his revolver out of his jeans pocket but kept it hidden behind the door.

"I'm suspended," Malachi said. "You need to handle this."

Jones flung his door open and stepped out holding his badge in the air. He rested his right hand on his holstered handgun.

"Police," Jones yelled. "Stay in your vehicle."

The passenger stopped and stared at him. He had an olive complexion and a thick black beard. The man was big. Really big.

"Get back in your vehicle," Jones said.

The man hesitated then climbed back inside. He did not close his door.

Malachi kept his eyes on both men, wishing he had his Glock. And the authority to use it. He adjusted his grip on his thirty-eight, sliding his hand to the top of the backstrap. The snub-nosed revolver's short barrel made it easy to carry but decreased its accuracy.

Jones leaned into the Impala and reached for radio microphone on the dashboard, but it was too far away. He slid into the driver's seat, unclipped the microphone, and held it to his mouth.

Malachi focused on the Suburban. The men spoke with someone in the backseat.

"Dispatch, Homicide Seven," Jones said.

"Go ahead Homicide Seven," the operator said, her voice hardly audible.

Jones leaned across the seat and turned the volume up.

The passenger exited the Suburban again.

"Back in your car," Malachi yelled.

The passenger looked at him, unconcerned.

"Dispatch, Homicide Seven," Jones said. "Send a marked unit to assist with a traffic stop at the Rockwell School, at Wisconsin and Fulton. Black Chevy Suburban, Maryland license one, Charlie, Victor, two, three, eight..."

The passenger walked toward their car. The driver opened his door too.

Malachi raised his revolver. "Police. Get back in your car. Now."

Jones grabbed the Impala's roof and pulled himself out. "I need you both to return to your vehicle."

Jones dropped the microphone and reached for his Glock. He brushed his jacket to the side and wrapped his fingers around the grip. He unsnapped the holster with his thumb and slid his gun out of his leather holster.

Malachi glanced at the driver. The man held a semi-automatic handgun.

"Gun," Malachi yelled. He pivoted toward the driver, keeping his isosceles stance, and applied pressure to his trigger.

The driver raised his gun.

Malachi squeezed his trigger and his vision narrowed. The revolver kicked in his hand. The shot sounded muffled.

The driver flinched, then pointed his gun at Malachi and fired. The car window shattered beside Malachi, spraying him with glass.

Malachi fired four more times until the hammer fell on an empty chamber.

The driver hunched over as if Malachi had punched him in the stomach, and his handgun clattered on the pavement. Behind him, the Suburban's rear doors swung open.

The passenger drew a gun from his waistband, fluid and fast, and pointed it at Jones. Flame shot out of the barrel, and the gunshot echoed off the school.

Jones fell back against the doorframe.

"Jonesy!" Malachi said.

The passenger swung his gun toward Malachi, and Malachi knelt, using the engine block for cover.

The passenger fired, and the round skipped off the roof near Malachi's head.

Malachi pulled a handful of loose rounds out of his pocket, and his hands shook as he fumbled to feed them into the empty chambers. Two bullets fell to the ground, but he ignored them and snapped the cylinder shut. He poked his head over the hood.

The passenger moved laterally to his right and crouched behind the rear end of a parked car. Malachi aimed at the top of his head, but the entrance to the school filled his backdrop, and he did not pull the trigger.

The passenger ducked out of view. He popped up behind the back window of the car and fired three times. The Impala's driver's side window exploded, and broken glass sprinkled the interior.

Malachi leaned to his left and saw Jones on one knee. Jones lowered his aim and fired twice through the other car's door. The passenger spun from the impact of the rounds. He fell out of sight.

"Homicide Seven, repeat the vehicle's description," the dispatcher's voice crackled.

Malachi turned back to the Suburban. Two heavyset thugs stood on either side, aiming handguns at him.

Malachi raised his revolver and the Impala's windshield exploded under a fuselage of bullets. Their bullets ricocheted off the car and splattered against the street sending bits of asphalt into the air. Malachi ducked and returned fire over his head.

"Homicide Seven, please respond."

Malachi crawled under the door and fired at the closest man's legs. The man jumped up and down holding his leg, then both men retreated to the Suburban.

Empty.

Malachi found his last two rounds on the street and fed them into his gun. He rotated the cylinder so they would cycle into the barrel next. He fired twice at the Suburban and both men disappeared from view. Malachi stuffed his empty revolver into his waistband.

"Homicide Seven, Dispatch."

Malachi crawled backward, scratching his knees and elbows on the rough pavement. He looked into the car.

Jones lay across the driver's seat. He opened his eyes and gasped for air. His gun was no longer in his hand.

"Where are you hit?" Malachi asked.

Jones reached for the transmitter, wrapped one finger around the cord, and pulled the microphone to his hand.

"Ten thirty-three. Shots fired. Officer down." His voice gurgled, as if he had water in his mouth. He spit and dark blood splattered the dashboard.

"Pass me your gun," Malachi said. "I'm out of—"

A metallic shattering crash filled the air, and the Impala's passenger door slammed into Malachi's head.

He awoke on his back on the street to the sound of screeching tires and the smell of burning rubber. He raised his head, and a wave of nausea rippled through him.

The Suburban rammed their Impala again, pushing it backward.

Malachi vomited.

"All units," the operator's voice came out of the radio. "Ten thirty-three. Officer down. Wisconsin and Fulton. Responding units identify."

Her voice sounded tiny, and her words made little sense to Malachi. His vision darkened, as if a cloud had blocked the sun, and he fought to stay awake. He had never been so tired. He closed his eyes to rest, just for a moment.

In the distance, police sirens filled the air.

CHAPTER SIXTY-THREE

Malachi lay on a gurney and tried to focus as two paramedics lifted him into an ambulance. His head pounded and he gagged, his mouth dry and vomitous. Police officers hurried back and forth across the street, their radios chirping with traffic.

"Take it easy," a paramedic said.

"What happened?"

"Looks like a concussion. We're taking you for assessment."

"Where's Jonesy?"

"Who?"

Malachi sat up and pain shot between his temples.

"Don't get up," the paramedic said.

Malachi slid his feet off the gurney. "I've got to find Jonesy."

"You need to sign a release if you're refusing treatment."

Malachi grabbed a vertical metal handle and climbed down to the street. His legs wobbled beneath him.

Patrol cars parked at odd angles with their doors open, blocking Wisconsin Avenue in front of the Rockwell School. Jones' Impala straddled the yellow lines, its hood crumpled, and headlights broken. Officers searched for evidence and interviewed bystanders. The passenger Jones had shot lay dead on the lawn, and the other suspects had vanished.

Malachi made his way toward a group of officers, and he peered into the Impala as he passed it. Blood puddled in the driver's seat and empty trauma dressings littered the ground. He did not see Jones. Panic rose in his throat, and he swallowed hard.

He jogged to the closest ambulance and looked inside. Empty. He ran to next one, also empty.

Malachi approached a sergeant he did not recognize. "Where's Jones? What's going on?"

"Who are you?"

"Detective Wolf, homicide."

"Officer involved shooting during a traffic stop. Looks bad."

"Where's Detective Jones?"

"Don't know him, but there's a homicide lieutenant over there."

A sizable crowd stood outside the school and Malachi scanned their faces. Collins stood on the lawn under a maple tree talking on her cell phone. He jogged over to her and froze when he saw the concern on her face.

"That's all I have so far, Chief," she said. "That's right. I'm heading to the hospital in a minute. Crime scene is en route."

"Where's Jones?" Malachi asked, bracing himself.

She pocketed her phone. "They took him to the emergency room at Mid-Atlantic Hospital. Why aren't you on your way to the hospital?"

"How bad is he? Did—"

"It's serious. Multiple GSWs to his upper body. He was unconscious in an ambulance when I arrived."

A sense of dread enveloped Malachi, weighing him down like a man inside a coat or armor. He could not feel his extremities. He rooted to the ground, lost inside him himself, unconnected to the world.

"I have to see him," he said.

"What the hell happened?

"Did they stop the Suburban?" Malachi asked.

"We put out an APB, but we haven't found it yet. Units are heading to the registered address. I assume the body over there came from the Suburban?"

"Where are my kids?" Malachi's voice sounded unnatural, higher than usual.

"Your kids?" she asked, wrinkling her forehead. "How are your children involved?"

"Alison saw a car following them this morning, and Jones and I came to check it out. I have to find my girls."

Malachi ran to the school.

"Wait, what?"

He heard Collins' question, but did not stop. A dozen members of the school faculty and staff stood in front of the administration building.

"Who's in charge? I'm looking for my children—Riley and Samantha Wolf."

"Oh, you're Mr. Wolf," a thin man with graying hair said. "I'm Assistant Principal Ben Chadwick. We received a call from your wife this morning. We have your children in my office."

Thank God.

Relief washed over Malachi. He exhaled and braced his hands against his knees. "I need to see them. I'm taking them home."

"Follow me."

Chadwick led Malachi to his office and opened the door. Riley and Samantha jumped up when they saw him and ran into his arms.

"Daddy, Daddy," they screamed.

Malachi wrapped his arms around them, barely feeling the pain in his lacerated arm. He choked back tears. They meant more to him than his own life.

He carried them outside, skirting the crime scene. He did not see Collins anywhere.

"Hey, Wolf," the sergeant he had with spoken earlier called out.

"Where'd the LT go?" Wolf asked.

"Mid-Atlantic Hospital. She told me to bring you there."

"My wife's coming to pick up the girls. She'll take me."

"Uh, I'm not supposed to leave your side. Lieutenant Collins needs your statement."

"Take us to the hospital."

They walked to a marked unit and Malachi put the girls in the back. He stepped away from the car and dialed Alison. "The girls are fine. They're with me."

"Oh my God, oh my God, oh my God," she said, before her voice caught, and she cried.

"They're fine, but something's happened. I need you to meet me at Mid-Atlantic Hospital. I'll give you the girls outside the emergency room."

"Hospital? Are they hurt?"

"No, it's Jones. Meet me as soon as you can."

CHAPTER SIXTY-FOUR

Malachi walked Riley and Samantha through the automatic doors of the Mid-Atlantic Hospital Emergency Room, and the antiseptic odor made him flash back to those horrible days after the Boston Marathon, to his pain and sorrow. Now Jones fought for his life, because Malachi had asked him for help. Guilt knotted the back of his throat.

Police officers huddled in small groups, talking in hushed tones. Collins stood in a corner with Hill and Rodriguez and a couple of captains who looked familiar. Hill made eye contact with Malachi and nodded.

Things must be dire if Hill is being friendly.

Collins saw him and walked over.

"How is he?" Malachi asked.

She bit her lower lip. "Not good."

"Who's sick, Daddy?" Riley asked.

"I'll talk to you in a few minutes, girls. Sit over there and let me talk to my boss."

He led them to seats in the corner near a television and returned to Collins.

"Tell me again what you and Jones were doing there."

Malachi's stomach twisted as he explained what Alison had told him and what had happened when they arrived at the school.

Collin's face pinched. "I wondered why Jonesy was making a traffic stop. I'll need you and Alison to talk to the district CAP detectives right away."

"She's on her way here now."

"Where did you get that revolver? I hope it's registered to—"

Collins stopped and turned toward a commotion at the front door.

Chief Ransom walked through the sliding doors followed by an entourage of brass. Nuse brought up the rear of the pack looking worried, and Malachi's anger toward him subsided. Tragedy prioritized events and bound people together. All officers faced danger and an injury to one felt like an injury to all.

Collins walked over and briefed the chief, and everyone in the group nodded as she spoke. At one point they all glanced at Malachi, and he assumed she had told them he had dragged Jones to the school.

The door to the emergency room opened, and a doctor with gray hair entered the waiting area. He scanned the room and made his way to Chief Ransom. Malachi joined them and caught the doctor in mid-sentence.

". . . multiple gunshot wounds to the upper abdomen and chest. One lung pierced and the right coronary artery nicked. He lost a massive amount of blood before he arrived. We did everything in our power, but we could not restart his heart. I'm very sorry. I know what a loss this is for you and for our city."

Collins covered her mouth and turned away.

Jones was dead.

Malachi wobbled on the linoleum floor and flopped into a chair. His eyes burned, and he could not swallow. He should have gone alone. Jonesy should be alive.

He can't be gone.

Tears filled his eyes, and he covered his face. His chest ached, and the world slid away beneath him.

Someone cleared his throat, and Malachi looked up through teary eyes at Nuse standing in front of him.

"I'm sorry for your loss," Nuse said. He extended his hand.

"Don't," Malachi said. "If you had listened to me, maybe this wouldn't have happened."

"Let's not play that game."

"This isn't a fucking game. I warned you about a terrorist conspiracy, but you covered it up, and now they're targeting my family and my partner's dead. Jones was like a father to me, and he's gone, thanks to you."

Collins stepped between them. "Now is not the time."

Malachi's grief and regret weakened him until he lost the energy to lift his hands. He wanted to close his eyes, stay there forever. But people counted on him, and he could not hide.

Malachi turned away from them. Alison hugged their girls against her legs. They had heard everything. Tears streamed down Alison's face.

Malachi wiped his eyes and walked over to them. He took Alison into his arms. The girls clutched her, scared and confused.

"What happened to Uncle Jonesy?" Samantha asked.

"I'll talk to you in the car, sweetheart," Malachi said, and turned his attention to Alison. "Detectives need to interview you. I'll go with you to the station."

"Oh, Malachi—"

"Not now."

He walked them outside to the sergeant's patrol car and Alison buckled the girls into the back seat.

"Why was that car following us?" Alison asked. "Were they trying to hurt the girls?"

"We'll talk when we're alone."

"Is this part of your case?" she asked, spitting out the words.

Malachi heard the anger in her voice—anger about his job, anger about his career decisions, anger over their failed marriage. Still, she had asked good questions. Did the Brotherhood want to stop him from investigating the murders or from uncovering something bigger?

"I think the Muslim Brotherhood sent those men," he said.

"You've investigated MS-13 and other criminals before. Don't they understand going after a cop is counterproductive? Even if they killed you, another police officer would take your place."

"They must think I'm a problem for them."

"Why you?" Alison asked, crying.

"I've been vocal about my vigilante theory. Maybe my being Jewish is a factor. I don't know."

Malachi's own answers did not satisfy him, and an idea hung just out of his reach. He grasped for it and the thought crystalized. Most of his information about the Brotherhood came from Zahra. If they wanted to kill him, was Zahra a target too? She had been quoted in the newspaper and had written numerous articles and policy papers attacking the Brotherhood. If they were willing to kill a cop, why not kill her?

What if Zahra had been the target at the cathedral?

Collins walked out of the hospital and joined them, but Malachi held his hand up to stop her. He pulled out his phone and called Zahra's office.

"Middle East Institute," a receptionist answered.

"Detective Wolf for Dr. Mansour."

"I'm sorry, Dr. Mansour is not in the office today. Would you like me to connect you to her voicemail?"

"Oh, my God," Malachi said, hanging up. "She's on her boat."

Collins raised her eyebrows. "And?"

"I have to go. Zahra could be in danger."

"You're hurt," Collins said. "You need to see a doctor."

Malachi turned to Alison. "I need your keys."

She looked at him with fierce eyes, then dug her keys out of her purse.

"Wait, the shoot team needs your firearm," Collins said, and put her palm out.

Malachi drew his revolver and placed it butt first into her hand.

"It's empty," he said.

"I'm sorry, Wolf."

"I have to go."

"You're injured and unarmed."

"I don't care. I have to find Zahra."

Malachi turned and jogged to Alison's car.

"Wolf, wait," Collins yelled after him.

Malachi did not stop.

CHAPTER SIXTY-FIVE

Zahra's Catalina silhouetted against the distant shore, and relief washed over Malachi. When she had failed to answer her phone, Malachi had paid a fisherman fifty dollars to take him to Fort Washington. He stood in the bow of an eighteen-foot Bayliner as it motored down the Potomac and waved to get Zahra's attention.

"Zahra," he yelled.

She swiveled behind the helm, and surprise spread across her face.

"Malachi? What are you doing here?"

He threw her a line and climbed onto the deck of the Catalina then pushed the Bayliner off and watched it motor back to the city.

"I had to find you."

"You're hurt," she said, touching his scalp.

"I'm fine."

"What happened?"

"A fight. I bumped my head."

"A fight? Who did—"

"Jonesy's dead."

Show covered her mouth. "No . . . how?"

"Shot. Four men came to my girls' school."

"The twins, are they—"

"They're fine. I left them with Alison."

"My, God, Malachi. I'm so sorry." She pulled him into an embrace and nuzzled her face against his chest.

"I needed to make sure you were safe," he said. A wave of vertigo washed over him over him and he teetered.

"I'm worried about you."

"I need to sit down."

"You should see a doctor. I'll head back now."

"I'm not ready to face internal affairs. Let's float out here awhile so I can rest."

Zahra helped him below and into the berth, then she went above to lower the sails. Malachi reached into his pocket for his Gabapentin, but he had left without it. He lay back in bed and pulled the unmade sheets over him.

Could this day get any worse?

.   .   .

Malachi awoke and a moment of panic seized him before he remembered what had happened. He watched Zahra climb down the companionway into the galley. He lifted himself onto his elbows, and his head spun. He had probably suffered a concussion when the car door struck him, but something else was wrong. His legs tingled and felt leaden, and his hands had grown too numb to make a fist. The combination of the heat, injury, and stress had triggered a severe MS attack.

I need a doctor.

He lay back and rubbed his temples while Zahra pulled a pot of boiling water off the propane stove. She spooned coarsely ground coffee into a French press and poured hot water over it. The water blackened, and a rich, velvety aroma filled the cabin. She let the coffee steep and came into the stateroom.

"You okay?" she asked.

"How long was I out?"

"Two hours. I let you sleep."

Malachi stared at the bulkhead.

"I'm so sorry about Jones," she said, sitting beside him.

A deep, primal loss overwhelmed him, and his throat tightened. Images of the gunfight flashed in his mind, and his memory returned in short, unwelcome bursts. They stayed quiet for a long time.

"I've never met anyone like you," Zahra said, her voice low.

He placed his hand over hers.

"You're different," she said. "You worry about acting morally, and you have a strong sense of right and wrong."

"I try to do the right thing."

"You stood up to evil, without a second thought about your own safety. You remind me of a medieval knight."

Malachi looked away, blushing. "You're more courageous than me."

"I don't know what drives you, Malachi Wolf, but I want to be part of it. I strive to be worthy of your affection."

"I never felt like this with Alison, not with anyone. I—"

"At the cathedral you shielded me with your body."

"Yes."

Zahra sighed.

A metallic clank echoed across the water, somewhere close. Something bumped against the port side of the boat. Malachi sat up.

Zahra's eyes widened, and she grabbed his arm.

Malachi slid off the bed onto numb feet, as if he stood on a cloud. The world seemed to rock back and forth and his nausea returned. He sat back on the bed.

"You need a doctor," Zahra said. "Stay here, I'll check it out."

"No . . . wait."

Footsteps thudded on the deck and the boat heeled to port.

"Someone's onboard," she said.

Malachi dug in his pocket and touched his keys. "Where's my phone?"

"You left it on the cockpit table next to mine."

The boat heeled farther to port, under the weight of another person, then their footsteps moved aft along the gunwale to the cockpit.

"Lock the cabin," Malachi said, and stood.

Zahra tiptoed through the galley and climbed the companionway. She pulled hard on the wooden hatch, but a hairy hand grabbed it and held it open.

Zahra screamed.

Chapter Sixty-Six

Malachi used the bulkhead to steady himself and stumbled into the salon.

"This is private property," Zahra said, her fists balled. "Get off my boat."

A man descended the companionway. His muscles bulged against his shirt, and he wore a beard in the style popular with Islamists.

Zahra backed up and froze.

Malachi moved forward but his energy waned, and it took everything he had to walk. His eyes searched the cabin for a weapon and settled on a butter knife laying on the counter. He lunged for it.

The man's shadow fell over him and then something struck his head. Malachi collapsed on the floor, and pain radiated through his body. He wanted to get up but could not move. Fatigue overwhelmed him, and he wanted to sleep more than anything. He vomited.

"We thought you'd be alone, Dr. Mansour," the man said, in a thick Egyptian accent. "You're a hard woman to find. Thank you for mooring in the same area as before. A simple mistake, but a fatal one."

The man's voice came to Malachi as if in a dream, but the word "fatal" confirmed his worst fears. He had to get Zahra out of there, but he could barely feel his legs, and there was nowhere to run.

"How do you know my name?" Zahra asked.

"I know exactly who you are," he said. He flashed a cruel smile.

Another brute with a black beard descended into the cabin and stood beside him. He was shorter, but built like a weightlifter, and together, they took up most of the salon at the beam. He held their cell phones in his meaty hand.

"What do you want?" Zahra asked.

"You know what we want. You're an apostate, and you've sinned in the eyes of Allah."

Zahra's hands shook, and she clutched her stomach.

Malachi knew under Islamic jurisprudence, any Muslim who renounced their faith was guilty of apostasy and a traitor to Islam. The punishment was death.

"I'm a Muslim," she said.

"You're an infidel bitch."

Zahra stepped backward. Her face had gone white, and Malachi understood her nightmare stood before her—in flesh and blood. They had tracked her down. It was over. These men would kill them.

"I never renounced my religion, but I will always condemn fundamentalist monsters, like you," Zahra said. "You allow your weak minds to be ruled by seventh-century morality."

"You slander Islam?" the weightlifter said. His face darkened, and he raised a fist.

"Silence," the first man said. He stepped in front of Zahra and leaned in close.

Malachi smelled the man's cologne—sweet, strong, sickly. Bile rose in his throat, and he thought he would vomit again.

"I only planned to do the Prophet's bidding, but now . . . you know what the Koran allows us to do to infidel whores?" A lascivious smile split his beard.

"Fuck you," she said.

"Bitch."

The man grabbed Zahra's shoulders, but she pulled away and fell on the deck beside Malachi. She looked at him with terror in her eyes. Malachi's mind sharpened, but his body remained torpid.

Zahra crawled backwards into the stateroom. The man reached for her. She tried to kick the berth door closed, but he blocked it with his foot. He grabbed her under her arms and tossed her onto the bed, as if he had thrown a pillow.

Malachi's eyes darted to the second man, who paid him no attention.

"No," Zahra screamed.

The first man reached between her legs and groped her over her bikini bottom.

Get up.

Zahra dragged her nails across the man's face, and he recoiled, grabbing his skin. Ribbons of flesh hung between his fingers, and blood ran down his palm and onto the deck. He growled, with murder in his eyes. He slapped Zahra across her face.

She fell back on the bed and moaned. Her cheek glowed as if sunburned.

The man grabbed her bikini bottom and yanked it off. He towered over her and drank in her nude body.

Stop him.

The man leaned forward and put his hand on her stomach, pinning her to the mattress. He ripped off her bikini top and it dangled from her neck.

"Now I'll show you what we do to apostates."

Malachi could barely feel his feet or hands, but he focused on his aching joints and gathered his strength. Beside him, the weightlifter seemed transfixed by Zahra's naked body.

She appeared groggy from the blow. She tried to sit up, but the goon held her down with one hand. He unbuckled his belt and dropped his pants to the floor. He stared into her eyes as he pulled his underwear down and stroked himself.

A waking nightmare.

Malachi rolled his arms underneath his chest and pushed himself up. The weightlifter turned as Malachi rocked back onto his knees. The man strode across the deck and stomped on Malachi's back, driving the breath from his lungs.

The man tried to enter Zahra, and she slapped him away and covered herself with one hand. She punched him with the other, but it was a weak blow with no weight behind it, and he laughed.

Malachi's breath returned, and he tried to rise, but the weightlifter's foot pinned him to the floor. Malachi's eyes burned, and tears clouded his vision. He ground his teeth, willing his anger to give him strength.

The man grabbed Zahra's wrists with both hands and held her arms over her head. He tried to enter her, but she swiveled her hips and he thrust into her leg.

Malachi's rage filled him, and adrenaline pumped through his veins. The weightlifter's shoe dug into his spine. Malachi glanced at his other leg, a few inches away.

"No, no, no," Zahra screamed. She planted her feet on the mattress and shimmied backward.

The man threw his weight on top of her and thrust, but she twisted her hips again. He released her wrist and reached down to guide himself between her legs.

"Zahra . . . the anchor," Malachi yelled.

Her eyes met his and narrowed.

Do it now!

Malachi swiveled his body and wrapped his arms around the weightlifter's leg. He pulled his face to it and sank his teeth into the flesh around the man's Achilles. The tendon rolled beneath his canines.

The man howled.

Malachi shook his head from side to side like a dog tearing flesh from a bone, Blood filled his mouth.

The man reached for his injured ankle, taking his weight off Malachi's back.

Malachi yanked the foot toward him and the man toppled over, smashing against the countertop. Malachi forced himself to move, as he had on so many runs. He struggled to his feet and reached for the butter knife.

The man pivoted off the counter and punched Malachi in the mouth.

Stars filled Malachi's vision, and he landed on his back. He shook his head, clearing the cobwebs. Both men stared at him.

Zahra used the distraction and bit the thug's wrist.

"*Khara,*" he yelled. *Shit.*

He yanked his wrist out of her mouth and knelt on the mattress holding his hand. Zahra bent her knees and kicked him in the chest, knocking him backward onto the deck. He landed with a crash, then he climbed to his feet at the foot of the bed, squeezing his bloody wrist.

"I'm going to fuck you to death."

"Come on, do it already," she said.

The man grabbed her legs and climbed onto the mattress.

Zahra reached behind her, pulled the anchor off the bulkhead, and swung it at him. He leaned away, and the fluke slashed his groin.

"*Ya Allah,*" he screamed, and grabbed his crotch.

The weightlifter limped toward the stateroom to help.

Zahra struggled into a sitting position, as blood spurted between the man's fingers. She did not hesitate. She twisted her body and swung the anchor again. The fluke pierced his torso an inch below his sternum and sliced through his abdomen. The metal tip poked out between his ribs.

His mouth opened in horror, but nothing came out. Blood bubbled at his lips, and he staggered off the bed. He stood in the doorway gawking at the anchor sticking out of him. His body shuddered.

Zahra grabbed the v-berth above her then swung forward and kicked him through the cabin door. He tumbled backward, clutching the anchor. He collided with the weightlifter, and they collapsed in a heap on the deck, blocking the doorway.

Zahra stood on the bed and unlatched the hatch above her. She pushed it open and grabbed the rim, then squeezed herself through the tiny opening, which was barely large enough to accommodate her shoulders. She fell back, too weak to lift her body weight.

The weightlifter scrambled to his feet. "Bitch!"

Malachi crawled across the floor and grabbed his shin, forcing him to stumble and fall over the first man's writhing body.

Zahra grabbed the hatch again and bent her knees. She jumped off the mattress and sprang through the portal. Her lower body hung out of the hatch as she slithered through the opening.

The weightlifter regained his feet and dove across the bed. He grabbed her legs and tried to drag her into the cabin, but she held on and refused to submit.

Malachi staggered to his feet. He swiped the French press off the counter and lurched into the cabin. He ripped the lid off the press and doused the weightlifter's face with hot coffee.

Zahra swung her knee into the weightlifter's face and connected with a thud.

Malachi swung the French press, shattering the glass over the weightlifter's head.

The man grunted and released his grip, allowing Zahra to wiggle through the hatch. The man shoved Malachi away and lunged through the port. He grabbed Zahra's ankle.

The hatch slammed on his hand, crunching his bones. Zahra stepped onto the hatch, and the man screamed.

Malachi scuffled to his feet again, his muscles cramping. Zahra stepped off the hatch and disappeared, then her footsteps pounded along the gunwale to the stern. The weightlifter pulled his broken hand free, and his eyes locked on Malachi.

Malachi ran to the companionway. Footsteps thudded onto the deck behind him as he climbed. He reached the cockpit and slammed the hatch shut as the weightlifter ascended the companionway. Malachi snatched the lock off the deck and snapped it in place He closed the hasp and held it as the man pounded against the wood.

They were safe . . . for the moment.

"Malachi," Zahra said behind him.

"Are you hurt?" he asked.

She burrowed her face into his chest.

He wrapped his arm around her. She shook, but when he looked into her eyes, he did not see fear—only rage—an emotion he knew far too well.

The man pounded on the hatch, and Malachi hoped the hasp would hold.

Zahra opened a compartment near the backup outboard engine and hoisted a fuel can. She climbed out of the cockpit and walked forward, pouring gasoline on the gunwale behind her.

The weightlifter stopped banging, and his footfalls clomped through the salon toward the stateroom, paralleling her.

Zahra reached the hatch, as the man's hands burst through it, and she sidestepped out of his reach. He struggled to squeeze through the hatch, but the opening was far too small for his massive body. His eyes filled with hate.

Zahra held the gasoline can above the hatch and dumped fuel over him.

The weightlifter coughed and gasped from the fumes as he tried to extricate himself.

Zahra dropped the can, ran back to the cockpit and grabbed her cigarettes off the bench.

"Zahra . . ."

Her eyes met his and radiated determination. She needed to do it. Malachi wanted to stop her, but if the man broke free, they were dead.

Zahra pulled a lighter out of the pack and ran forward.

The weightlifter saw her coming and dropped back into the stateroom.

She sparked a flame and held it under the cigarette package until it ignited. She dropped the burning pack through the open hatch, and flames whooshed out of the stateroom.

The man screamed—an inhuman sound, a dying animal.

She stepped back as smoke poured out of the hatch.

The man raged through the salon. He sprang up the steps and smashed into the companionway door. The wood cracked but held. He banged against the wood over and over as he burned.

The pounding weakened then stopped.

Malachi leaned over the gunwale and looked through a porthole. Flames and smoke consumed the cabin, obscuring his view. The fire raged, engulfing everything below deck. When it reached the fuel tank, the boat would explode.

The men had tied their fiberglass motorboat to a cleat on the port side. Malachi crossed the cockpit and stepped on the gunwale, but the deck scorched his bare feet. He looked across the boat at Zahra standing on the bow. The flames cast her face in an orange, demonic glow.

"We have to swim for it," he yelled.

Zahra nodded. She grabbed the halyard and stepped onto the metal stem protruding off the bow. She glanced over her shoulder at him then dove into the Potomac.

Fatigue and numbness consumed Malachi's body, but he had no choice. He stepped off the transom and splashed into the river. The polluted water irritated his scratched skin as he struggled toward Zahra, thirty feet away. He could not feel where his limbs ended and the river began, as if his hands and feet had melted into the water.

He reached her, where she treaded water without difficulty.

"Are you okay?" he asked.

"You saved me," she said, shivering, despite the warm water.

Malachi turned onto his back and floated. The buoyancy relieved his fatigue, and he took a deep lungful of air. They watched the boat burn. Flames burst through the side portholes and shot high into the night air. The man had stopped screaming.

Both men were dead.

Something flashing in the distance caught his eye. The blue police lights of the Maryland State Police Harbor Patrol bounced across the river toward them.

He floated beside Zahra and waited.

CHAPTER SIXTY-SEVEN

Malachi and Zahra sat on his balcony and watched tethered sailboats sway back and forth in the light wind. Their masts moved rhythmically, like metronomes. He leaned over and topped off her glass from the near-empty bottle of wine. The 2003 Pouilly-Fuisse tasted acidic, with subtle notes of pear and apple. It tingled the back of his tongue.

It felt cool for the first day of July, and the breeze raised gooseflesh on his arms. He retrieved a sweater from the bedroom and draped it over Zahra's shoulders.

She opened her face to him and smiled, her deep brown eyes full of warmth. He stared at the flecks of gold around her irises. Everything looked crisper and more vivid to him after his three-day course of intravenous steroids. The drugs had reduced his inflammation, and he controlled his body again. Colors looked richer, and his breath came without effort. How long it would last?

In the five days since the attack, Zahra had taken to sitting outside for hours at a time, staring at the water, staring at nothing. Dark circles had formed beneath her bloodshot eyes.

The harbor patrol had pulled them from the Potomac, Zahra naked and shivering and Malachi too weak climb aboard without help. Zahra had not stopped shaking until long after the emergency blanket had warmed her. It had taken hours for fire crews to extinguish the blaze and recover both bodies, and Malachi had stayed with Zahra while detectives interviewed them in the Harbor Patrol Office. She had been upset but answered their questions with surprising detail and clarity, displaying a detachment Malachi had seen before. It would take time for her to process the violent incident and recover from her feelings of helplessness. He had asked her to stay with him and to his relief, she had agreed. He wanted her to feel safe.

"Do you want more wine?" he asked.

"Thank you."

He started to rise, but she put her hand on his arm.

"No wine, I'm fine. I meant thank *you* for everything."

"I'll protect you . . . I promise."

Zahra had taken the week off from the Middle East Policy Institute and Malachi remained suspended, so he had been able to watch over her. He had followed the nonstop media coverage of Hamill's murder at the cathedral, careful not to let Zahra see it any of it. Each day she had seemed more like herself. He had offered to stay on the couch, but she insisted they sleep in the same bed, though she said she was not ready for intimacy. He gave her space, happy to be with her.

"I'm going back to work tomorrow," she said.

"You're sure?"

"Yes."

"You've had time to, uh, process everything?"

"That attack was horrible, and I thought I would die. I've always had nightmares about getting raped, a nervousness when I walked to my car late at night or when I entered my dark apartment. On the boat, those nightmares became reality. I felt like a child worrying about the monsters under my bed then seeing them standing in front of me."

She had not spoken about the attack since the police interview.

"You're a survivor," he said.

"I acted out of instinct."

"They tried to kill you, and you stopped them."

"I would have died if you hadn't been there," she said.

"I just wish I'd been stronger, healthier . . . I—"

"You could barely lift your head and yet you found the strength."

"I should have stopped them sooner."

"You saved me." She shook with sobs.

He wrapped his arms around her. "You mean everything to me. You'll be fine."

"As long as I have you."

"I'd die before I let anyone hurt you."

She rested her head on his shoulder and stared at the water. After a while, she bit her lip and spoke. "I need to ask you something."

"Anything."

"Before this, I thought I knew what it meant to be a police officer, but my understanding was conceptual, incomplete. Fighting for my life made me understand the risks, the danger—"

"Most days are monotonous, even boring."

"Sure, but then they're not. What drives you to take chances?"

Malachi gazed at the boats but saw his father's face.

"The marathon bombing incited me to act, but once I became a cop, something changed . . . something inside me. I've always been motivated to have a successful career, but being a cop requires more than that. It's a calling, an internal need to fight evil, an impulse to protect."

"Where does it come from?"

"I don't know, but it's deeper than anything I've felt before and it has changed me. I care more about the community now . . . more about other people."

Zahra nodded and smiled. "That I understand. The attacks at the tower and on the boat put everything into perspective, realigned my priorities. Having this break, being in this safe space with you, made all the difference. I cannot tell you how grateful I am."

"You're feeling like yourself again?" he asked, raising an eyebrow.

Zahra smiled. "I feel better, stronger than before. More determined. I'm ready to return to work, get back to my life."

Malachi ran his fingers through her hair and kissed her. She had the innocence of a young girl and the beauty, intelligence, and sexuality of a woman. She was everything he wanted. He leaned back in his chair so he could see her better and stared into her eyes.

"I love you, Zahra." He said it without thinking and his heart beat hard in his chest. Why did he say that now? She had almost been killed, and he chose this moment to blurt out his feelings. Had he ruined everything?

She ran her tongue over her lips and dropped her eyes down to his chest.

What was she thinking?

"I'm sorry," he said. "I shouldn't have said that. You have been through so much. I . . ."

She looked up at him with wet eyes and placed her fingers on his lips.

"I love you too, Malachi."

His heart swelled like it would explode. He kissed her, and their tongues explored each other.

"Take me to bed," she said.

He reached under her legs, scooped her into his arms, and carried her inside.

.   ▪   ▪

In the morning, Malachi made an omelet with turkey bacon, while Zahra sipped dark-roasted Colombian coffee. She wore a contented smile. She always looked sexy and thoughtful, and when he was with her, he forgot to breathe. Either he was in love or having a heart attack.

Zahra embodied everything he valued—morality, intellectual honesty, reason—but she was also empathetic, caring, and funny. She grabbed life and experienced every moment with passion and curiosity. He never thought he needed someone who shared his commitment to justice, but now that he had it, he could not live without it.

He would defend her with his life.

When Alison had left him and taken his girls, she had ripped a hole in his life and in his soul. He had thought he would never feel whole again, but now he did. Better than before. His bitterness had evaporated, and his emotional barriers were gone. He had been reborn.

"Are you sure you're up for work today?" Malachi asked.

"I'm ready. I'm a little embarrassed I had to take an entire week off. I should have been stronger than that."

"You're the strongest person I know. I'll drive you there and pick you up, and if you have to go out, call me. I don't expect the Brotherhood will attack you again, since there's so much heat on them right now, but I don't want to give them a target of opportunity either."

"The institute hired armed security."

Malachi doubted the Brotherhood would try anything now, but he could not shake his protective instincts. He had been with Zahra since the incident, and she had even accompanied him to Jones' funeral. She had held his hand while bagpipes played "Amazing Grace" and over fifteen hundred police officers stood at attention to watch Jones's body lowered into his grave. It had been the saddest day of his life since his father's funeral, and he vowed he would not lose another loved one to violent crime.

Finding those responsible for the attacks had become self-defense. He picked up his phone and called Collins.

"Have you identified the bodies from the boat?" he asked.

"Good morning to you too," Collins said.

"They have to be Brotherhood."

"The crime lab lifted a print off one of the charred bodies. His name was Ahmed Ebiary, a Qatari national here on a work visa."

"Who sponsored him?" Malachi asked.

"North Star, Baker's firm."

Bingo.

"It's all coming together," Malachi said, adrenaline coursing through him. "Baker financed the Brotherhood's projects, like the al-Azhar Cultural Center, to further fundamental Islam. He also sponsored visas for the Islamists who popped up in FBI cases. We need to identify Ebiary's associates and link him to the Brotherhood."

"We're running that down, but you can't be involved. You're suspended, and if Nuse catches a whiff of you near this, we'll all be in trouble. Stay home and let me handle it."

Malachi hung up. His excitement had vanished. He was on the outside looking in.

Chapter Sixty-Eight

Austin's knuckles whitened on the handle of his buck knife. He stood on the third level of a parking garage in the Metropolitan Building on D Street NW. He leaned against a concrete pillar with a chipped surface, and patched holes. White mineral stains ran from a crack in the ceiling near a dark pipe tethered by rusted brackets. Fluids had saturated the soiled floor until the cement appeared wet.

His dark jeans and commando sweater helped him blend into the shadows. He tried to stand still and stop rocking on his toes, but he could not control his hunger. He had to strike back for what those beasts had done to Dr. Mansour.

When Jane had informed him about the attack on the boat, he had been unable to contain his rage. He hoped Jane had accepted his reaction as a normal response to a violent attack. But his anger came from a deeper well. First the Cathedral then the sailboat. It was too much. Austin needed to hurt them, hit them where it would do the most psychological damage. He had to make them understand their actions had consequences.

"Eye for eye, tooth for tooth, hand for hand, foot for foot, burning for burning, wound for wound, stripe for stripe."

The Council on American Muslim Peace occupied the entire ninth floor of the building and contained the executive office of CAMP President Muhammad Baseem. Baseem acted like a general in the Islamist movement, a public figure directing the war and covering for evil—a spokesperson for the devil.

Austin had downloaded a picture of Baseem and planned to surveil the garage exit to see what he drove, but when he had walked through the facility, he happened upon six spots with "CAMP" stenciled in on them. The closest to the elevators read "BASEEM," and Austin had decided to do it then.

Baseem had backed his Audi S7 into a spot beside a pillar which meant his back would be to Austin when he opened his car door.

Somewhere on the floor below him, a car door thumped shut, and an alarm beeped. His throat tickled with the toxic odor of gasoline and concrete dust, and he suppressed a cough. Anticipation raced through him like an electrical current.

If God had condemned Austin to hell, there was nothing he could do about it. He had murdered those who needed to be killed, and he had enjoyed it, relished it more with each act. Maybe Hegel had been right and deriving pleasure from the act diminished the goodness in it. Either way, what had been done could not be undone.

Footsteps echoed through the garage, and Austin leaned around the pillar. The silhouette of a man moved under the red glow of an exit sign and headed toward him.

Baseem.

Austin disappeared into the shadows behind the column. The footsteps grew louder. He pictured Baseem approaching the front of his car.

Almost.

Austin's rage built, and he let his fury take control of his body like a demonic possession. The car alarm beeped, and the footfalls stopped.

Now.

Austin slipped around the column. He crouched low and skulked toward him. Baseem faced away, offering his back as he opened the car door. Austin came up behind him, the power of God surging through his veins. He clenched the knife handle with all his strength.

Baseem placed his hand on the roof and twisted to lower himself into the front seat.

Austin exploded out of his crouch, throwing his shoulder into Baseem and pinning him against the door frame. Austin grabbed Baseem's forehead and pulled his head back.

He twisted his hips and thrust his knife. The blade struck Baseem between his skull and first cervical vertebra. He drove the knife upward, aiming for the medulla oblongata and a quick kill.

Bassem gasped and wheezed like an animal. His body went rigid, and he opened his mouth in a soundless scream. Austin twisted the double-edged knife, as if he were cutting a pumpkin. Baseem's legs gave out, and Austin rode him to the floor.

Austin's heart drummed and he filled with warmth.

He yanked the knife out, and a fountain of blood poured onto the concrete. Baseem's legs twitched for a moment, then stopped. Austin wiped his blade on Baseem's pants and sheathed it.

An engine revved as a car ascended the ramp on the level below. Its tires squealed as it turned onto his level, and Austin ducked behind the pillar. The car passed and continued up the ramp to the next floor.

Austin took a final look at Baseem. Blood bubbled out of him, as if from a chocolate fountain, and formed a scarlet lake beneath the car. Austin smiled. This murder would send a clear message. They were in his crosshairs. He had declared war.

Time to become a ghost.

CHAPTER SIXTY-NINE

Malachi took a slug of Yuengling Lager as he sat on his balcony and read an article about the Muslim Brotherhood. The chirping of cicada bugs rose from the riverbank, like a thousand music boxes winding. Nuse could suspend him, but Malachi's mind still worked, and his department could not stop him from researching his adversary. Beyond that, he did not know what to do. He wanted to pursue the killer, but he did not possess the authority.

He was lost.

His phone vibrated on the table beside him and the screen read, "Unknown."

He answered.

"Good morning, Detective. This is Jane Evans with the FBI."

"What's up, Jane?"

"I heard about the incident at the cathedral and what happened to your partner. I'm very sorry."

An image of Jones flashed in Malachi's mind, and a lump formed in his throat. "We're all coping with the loss. Jones was one of a kind."

"I only met him once, but whenever a fellow LEO is murdered, it feels personal. An agent I worked with in Tampa was killed during a drug raid, so I have some idea what you're going through."

It was nice of her to call, but her sentiments would not bring Jones back, and every time someone mentioned his death, Malachi slid into a dark place. He had had enough sympathy. He needed to do something, not act like a victim.

"Thanks for calling, Jane. I appreciate it, but—"

"Wait. I—uh—when I heard about your partner and your children being targeted, it pissed me off."

"Join the club."

"No . . . I mean yes, but I'm not calling for that. I think you're right about the Brotherhood, and I want to help."

Malachi sat up straight, hope fluttering in his belly. "How?"

"It's one thing to have my cases sidelined, but coming after family, killing a police officer—that's different. I mean, this is like a war."

"It *is* a war. Fundamental Islam advocates perpetual jihad."

Jane was quiet, and Malachi wondered if she had disconnected.

"I've built several cases against Islamists who supported designated terrorist groups," she said, "but I never considered them as part of a coordinated effort. When HQ closed my cases, I assumed bureaucratic incompetence, but now . . ." her voice trailed off.

"Now, what?"

"This is a life and death struggle. I mean, they killed your partner, and I heard about the attack on you and Dr. Mansour. My partner almost lost his job when our investigation came close to powerful people. I can't sit on the sidelines anymore."

"So how can you help?"

"Let me be clear. I've seen what's happened to other whistleblowers, and I don't want to go public. I'm willing to show you my cases. Maybe you can find some commonality and prove the Brotherhood's involved."

"You know I'm suspended, right?"

"This has to stay between us."

"You mentioned your cases involved powerful people. Who were you talking about?"

"I told you several of our suspects were tied to North Star and Sam Baker, but I didn't tell you Baker supported Senator Dale Hansen."

"I know that. Jones and I interviewed Senator Hansen about the connection."

"Did the senator tell you he was tied to the Brotherhood?"

"The senator? How?"

"My boss told me a staffer in Hansen's office complained to HQ that our cases unfairly targeted the Muslim community. That nonsense pissed me off, so I reached out to my contact on the Hill and learned Senator Hansen has been carrying the flag for the Brotherhood. I'm certain he's the one who pressured the Bureau to close our cases."

Malachi thought about that. Senator Hansen supported Baker's al-Azhar Islamic Cultural Center, and he had received financial contributions from him. Either the Senator had sold his influence, or he had succumbed to identity politics and believed the FBI victimized Muslims.

"Does Senator Hansen know he's endorsing a terrorist group?" Malachi asked.

"I don't know, but his defense of the Brotherhood's projects is undeniable."

"Maybe someone needs to explain it to him."

"Whatever we do, we need to do it soon," she said. "Senator Hansen will win the Democratic nomination for president."

Her words hit Malachi like a punch. If the Brotherhood had Senator Hansen in their pocket, it would not matter if he knew they were the world's most prolific terrorist group. After years of accepting Brotherhood money and patronizing their front groups, he could never abandon them without admitting he had supported terrorism. Disavowing the Brotherhood would be the moral choice, but it would also be political suicide.

Malachi had a moment of clarity.

"I never understood what initiated the murders or why the killer seemed to be in a rush, but he must have known Senator Hansen was a Brotherhood puppet," he said. "The killer's been trying to expose the Brotherhood before they put their man in the White House."

"I asked around, and it wasn't only Senator Hansen who interfered with our cases. My assistant director told me in confidence that White House Deputy Counsel David Burke asked our director to rein us in."

"Don't trust anyone."

"I trust you," she said, "and it's clear the FBI wants to shut you up. You can review my cases, but we can't do it here. If my boss caught me sharing restricted files with a suspended detective, I'd get fired."

"Can you bring them to me?" Malachi asked.

"The files take up an entire Mosler safe, but I can download the reports, memos, and charts onto a thumb drive. I won't bring the classified materials, because that could land me in prison."

"Meet me at my place in an hour," Malachi said. He gave her his address.

He was back in the game.

.   .   .

Jane sat on the couch beside Malachi and guided him through the files on her laptop. In the one case, Jane and her partner, Special Agent Austin Horn, had received a tip about a young Pakistani man planning to set off an improvised explosive device on the National Mall. Jane and Horn had identified the suspect as Iqbal Yousef, a green card holder who emigrated from Karachi, Pakistan. They had compared his telephone number against a National Security Agency database and found contacts between Yousef and numbers associated with the Taliban's Quetta Shura. They had conducted surveillance and spotted Yousef reconnoitering monuments, which corroborated their informant's story.

Once Jane and Horn had gathered enough evidence to obtain a search warrant, they had decided to be proactive and preempt the attack. They had raided Yousef's home and found bomb-making equipment, maps of downtown, and a schedule of upcoming events on the National Mall. They had also recovered dozens of fake driver licenses, passports, and the equipment to make more. They had arrested Yousef and prevented the attack.

Why had he never heard about that case?

Malachi scrolled through the most recent memos and found the reason. Jane and Horn had linked Yousef to the al-Hijrah Cooperative Foundation in Virginia—a radical Islamist stronghold affiliated with the Brotherhood—and FBI Headquarters had stopped them from digging further.

Jane's eyes bore into Malachi as he read.

In another case, they had targeted a group of Yemeni men who planned to travel to Syria and Iraq to fight with Islamic State. Jane and

Horn had arrested them, but when they uncovered the links to North Star, that case had also been closed.

Malachi had never investigated terrorism, but he knew how to put a criminal case together and it seemed clear Jane had uncovered a broader conspiracy beyond the jihadists they arrested. Her cases contained solid evidence, more than enough to warrant further investigation into North Star and the Brotherhood.

"I can see why you're so frustrated," Malachi said. "It's obvious a network existed behind your suspects. It made no sense for the FBI to shut you down unless there's a Brotherhood sympathizer inside the Hoover Building."

"That's what Austin said, only he didn't think it was a single person protecting the Brotherhood. He thought dozens of terrorist operatives had infiltrated the FBI, CIA, and Congress."

"Why didn't he report his suspicions?" Malachi asked.

"He did. He complained about it so much he ruined his career. When FBI management wouldn't listen, he went off-book and reported it to Congress. The next day he received an official warning and knew his senator had reported his meeting to the FBI."

"Do you know which senator he tipped off?" Malachi asked.

"Senator Hansen."

The pieces tumbled together. The Brotherhood had at least one infiltrator high in the FBI, and they had used ideological persuasion, bribes, or blackmail to co-opt support on Capitol Hill. Senator Hansen had supported Baker and Brotherhood front organizations, meaning either Hansen or his chief of staff were complicit—maybe both.

"Is that why they suspended Horn?" Malachi asked.

"Austin said he could no longer work for an agency undermined by a foreign entity, without speaking out. He acted a little crazy. I knew we were getting pushback from above, but he sounded like a conspiracy nut. When he complained to the Special Agent in Charge and got himself suspended, part of me felt relieved. Now, I feel guilty. He was right."

Malachi stopped cold. The ideas that had been running in his subconscious came together like the pieces of a puzzle. It seemed so obvious. Why had he not seen it before?

"I vaguely remember meeting him in your office," he said. "How tall is Austin Horn?"

"God, I don't know. Everyone looks tall to me. Maybe six-three or six-four."

Gooseflesh rose on Malachi's arms. Special Agent Austin Horn fit his profile—a law enforcement officer trained in tactics at the FBI Academy, who had first-hand knowledge about the Brotherhood's infiltration. His cases had been terminated, and he probably felt impotent to protect his country.

"Would Horn ever take matters into his own hands?"

Jane frowned. "This is why I hesitated to come. I can't betray Austin. I'm more than his partner, I'm his friend. I've felt so guilty about not supporting him during his suspension."

"I have to ask. Could he have—"

"You know, you remind me of him, similar in so many ways. You think Austin is part of this?"

"Maybe. Were you and Horn . . . involved?"

"Involved? No." She gave a funny laugh.

"Why are you laughing?"

"I've caught Austin staring at me, and I know he's attracted to me, but he's never asked me out or even flirted. He's handsome and intelligent but he doesn't know how to talk to women."

"Would you have gone out with him?"

Jane bit her lower lip. "Probably . . . yes."

"Has Horn dated anyone else?"

"I know he dated his old partner before he came to our group."

"Who was that?"

"Vanessa Archer. She was killed in Afghanistan."

Jane dug through her file and pulled out a stack of photos from Yousef's arrest. Jane and Horn stood on either side of a man in handcuffs. She looked at the picture but did not give it to Malachi.

"Austin's a decent man and a good partner. He cares more than any of us. He was assigned to the Counterterrorism Fly Team before he came to his squad."

"Fly Team?"

"It's a group of hard-charging agents based in DC. They respond to terrorist attacks overseas and fly around the world on a few hours' notice. They function in dangerous and austere environments, developing intel, collecting evidence . . . all of that. Austin was deployed to Afghanistan with Vanessa when she was killed during a blue-on-blue attack."

"What's that?"

"An Afghan National Army soldier shot up a mess hall in Afghanistan, killing three American soldiers and an FBI agent—Special Agent Vanessa Archer. That ANA soldier was supposed to be on our side, but he played for the other team."

"When was that?" Malachi asked.

"Couple of years ago . . ."

"How did Horn take it?"

"He doesn't talk about it much. He was supposed to travel with Vanessa the day she died, but he stayed back. It tore him up. HQ brought the entire Fly Team back for debriefings and psych tests, and after that, Austin never rejoined them. He couldn't get over her loss. I don't think he ever stopped loving her."

"I know how difficult loss can be," Malachi said.

"Oh, I'm sorry. I know you do."

Jane handed him the photo. Horn was tall, like the man at the cemetery and cathedral. Horn had motivation, and Jane could attest to his irrational mental state before his suspension. Horn's gambling his career had been a rash move—one Malachi understood. Had Horn targeted the Brotherhood out of frustration? He was probably angry, but was that enough to make a federal agent turn against the law? Vigilantism seemed like an enormous leap, unless Horn had other issues.

"You worked with Austin for years. Is he capable of murder? I mean, is he vengeful enough to kill?"

Jane's mouth pinched tight and her knuckles whitened around her coffee mug.

"It's possible."

. . .

Malachi watched Jane walk down the hall. Zahra exited the elevator as Jane entered it, and the women nodded to each other. Zahra saw him standing in his doorway, and he held the door open for her.

She shot him a quizzical look. "Friend of yours?"

"Jane Evans."

"You're entertaining female guests?"

She was teasing, and he did not take the bait. "Jane's an FBI agent. She thinks the Brotherhood interfered with some of her cases, and her partner fits my vigilante profile. An Islamist infiltrator killed his girlfriend in Afghanistan."

They went inside and Malachi related what Jane had told him. He waited while Zahra stared out the window, processing.

"It sounds like someone subverted the FBI's cases from inside," she said, "and the connections to Baker and Hansen are too coincidental. Agent Horn risked his job by speaking out, which was a courageous moral act."

"Or the behavior of someone coming unhinged."

"What now?" she asked. "You're suspended. Can you convince your boss your theory is right?"

"Maybe, but Nuse won't let Collins do anything. This is when I would normally call Jonesy."

Zahra put her hand on his arm and her eyes glistened. "What will you do?"

Malachi thought for a minute, then lifted his phone off the table and dialed Detective Rodriguez. He was young, aggressive, and not yet jaded. Malachi sensed a fire inside him.

Rodriguez answered and Malachi briefed him on his theory.

"Jesus, I don't know, Wolf."

"Come on, Train. It can't hurt to look at Horn. Go ask him what he thinks about the murders and tell him our profile of the killer, which basically describes him. If he's our guy, he may want this to all come out. Makes sense, right?"

Rodriguez expelled a long breath into the phone. "Yeah, it does."

"Don't contact the FBI. I don't trust them. My contact provided Horn's address. I'll text it to you."

Rodriguez sighed.

"Train?"

"I'll talk to Hill and see what we can do."

"Remember, Horn's not your average FBI agent," Malachi said. "He spent time in Afghanistan and knows how to handle himself."

"Right. And if he killed those people, he's a sociopath."

"Maybe . . . it's complicated. Just be careful."

Malachi hung up and looked at Zahra.

"I made a decision," he said.

She looked at him. "Yes?"

"I don't care if I'm suspended. I'm going to stop this killer and expose the Brotherhood."

Zahra beamed.

CHAPTER SEVENTY

The ringing phone woke Malachi at nine-thirty. The stress from the case and his suspension had taken a toll, and without an imposed schedule, he slept later every day. He needed to return to work.

"Hello?" he said, his voice groggy.

"You still in bed?" Rodriguez asked. "You know, here at the MPD we do more before nine o'clock than most people do all day."

"Tell me you have good news."

"I asked Hill about talking to Horn, and he said your theory was bullshit."

"That asshole couldn't find a crook inside a jail. He—"

"Hold on, Mac. I know Hill doesn't like you. You may be a little off the reservation, but you've been right about everything so far, so I visited Horn myself."

Malachi bit his lip. Rodriguez had taken a huge chance, and if Horn complained, Rodriguez would be joining Malachi for afternoon cocktails while he waited out his own suspension.

"And?" Malachi asked, holding his breath.

"I staked out that address you gave me. It's a small apartment complex in Arlington. I didn't see Horn leave for work, so I called the FBI and asked to speak with him."

"Shit, Train. If this gets out—"

"No *problemo*. They connected me to his group and when I identified myself, their assistant told me Horn was on sick leave."

"Hmmm . . ."

"Yeah, the timing sounded strange. I took a chance and contacted the apartment manager, and he told me Horn had paid up his lease until the end of the month and given notice that he would not renew. The manager thought Horn split last night, without leaving a forwarding address. Horn told him he had a terminal disease."

Malachi bolted upright. Rodriguez sounded excited and was leading to something.

"Horn's gone?"

"I told the manager this was an active homicide investigation, and he escorted me into Horn's unit. What a shithole. It looked like Horn had emptied everything out and left."

Malachi closed his eyes. "Please don't tell me you searched without a warrant."

"The manager can access abandoned apartments, and Horn had told him he was leaving. That, coupled with Horn's statements that he was dying gave me exigent circumstances to make sure the manager was safe. I didn't have enough for a warrant . . . yet."

"You're killing me. Spit it out."

"Horn left his furniture and a few belongings, all in plain view. His life looked depressing. I found empty Oxycontin bottles in a drawer."

Jane had said Horn never got over his partner's murder, and he had been frustrated about the infiltration and his suspension. Had he let his anger grow until he snapped?

"I'm guessing you didn't find the murder weapons and a written confession?"

"Uh, no, but I found something. I noticed a loose floorboard in Horn's bedroom, and the manager pulled it up . . . only for maintenance, of course. I stuck my head inside and found torn money bands from HSBC, but no cash."

"He's running," Malachi said.

"I also found an empty box for a prepaid phone, and a receipt for five more phones."

"Tell me the phone contacted one of our victims."

"I had to get a warrant first. I called Hill—boy was he mad—but he briefed the LT and she asked the Arlington Police to get a telephonic search warrant for the apartment."

"She'll have to notify Nuse and the FBI," Malachi said.

"Yep, but we needed to move fast. Hill subpoenaed AT&T, and they said the phone had been activated in Virginia but hadn't called any DC numbers. They promised to send us everything they have by this afternoon. I'll track down the other phone numbers on the receipt."

"So bottom line . . . no smoking gun."

"Not exactly, but the receipt for burners, coupled with the connections you uncovered, make Horn look like a serious suspect. The LT green-lighted us to find him and bring him in for questioning. She's calling the FBI to coordinate."

CHAPTER SEVENTY-ONE

Malachi needed to clear his head, so he slipped on a pair of black compression pants and a tee shirt and headed out the door. Since Zahra had come into his life, he found comfort in running again. He had his temper under control too. Everything with Zahra felt right. She would not abandon him.

He jogged west along the Potomac and down a path behind the Thomas Jefferson Memorial. Through the columns, he caught flashes of Jefferson's bronze statue on the portico. Tourists paddled plastic boats around the Tidal Basin, cutting small wakes through the flat, dark water. Sightseers packed the nation's capital waiting for the Independence Day celebration the following day.

Malachi crossed a small bridge on Ohio Avenue and ran west along the river. Opposite him, green trees on the Virginia shore reflected on the surface of the still river beneath a blanket of motionless clouds. The humidity warmed his skin, and his muscles loosened. Familiar feelings flooded back—not the horror of the marathon—but the comfort and solitude of a thousand previous runs.

He galloped toward the Lincoln Memorial. From there, he would cross the Theodore Roosevelt Bridge into Virginia, then run along the Mount Vernon Trail to the Fourteenth Street Bridge and back home. He focused on his form—the sound of his footsteps, his breathing, his heart beating in his chest. His body relaxed, and his mind sharpened. A body in motion helped synapses connect and provided a cognitive bump, an evolutionary relic from thousands of years of roaming the plains. He did his best thinking alone, away from distractions, sweating the stress out of his body—connected to his old self.

His cell phone vibrated and snatched him out of his thoughts. Zahra's number displayed on the screen.

"Are you okay?" he asked.

"I found something, but it sounds like you're running, should I call you back?"

"I can run and talk at the same time. If I don't chew gum, I'll stay on my feet."

She did not laugh, and Malachi respected her more.

"I've been in a self-imposed news blackout for a week, as you know, so I spent the morning reading what the Brotherhood has been doing. I found something interesting, and it's time sensitive."

"I'm listening." He wished he had brought his headphones. Holding his phone up to his ear altered his gait and his knees ached.

"Several Brotherhood members I follow on social media posted about a high-level meeting tonight. I cyber-stalked the Secret Apparatus members I've identified, and it looks like a few of them will attend."

"You lost me. What's the meeting about?"

"A ranking member of the Brotherhood posted on Facebook saying he was looking forward to seeing his brothers on Friday to discuss the Emerging Challenges to the Muslim Community. I don't know for sure, but I'm guessing this is a leadership meeting to discuss how they should respond to the murders of their key members—especially Muhammad Baseem."

"I read about that. It had to be our killer."

"The Brotherhood may feel pressure because of the story you leaked to the Herald. When we prove those animals who tried to kill us are Brotherhood members, they'll be in a tough position."

"Is it normal for Secret Apparatus members to get together in public?"

"No, but it has happened. They held emergency meetings in Washington after 9/11 and after Osama Bin Laden's death."

"How many people will attend?"

"If it's the leadership, I'd guess around thirty, but they've held meetings with over a hundred members. For something like this, I assume they'll only invite a select few, the real decision makers."

"What are you suggesting?" Malachi asked.

"This is an opportunity for the FBI to wiretap the meeting and collect direct evidence of the Secret Apparatus's conspiracy."

It was a tempting intelligence target, but would the FBI do anything? Hell, they did not even acknowledge the Secret Apparatus existed.

Malachi slowed to a walk and then stopped. Zahra was right, it would be an incredible chance to build a criminal case, but it would also be a target of opportunity for the killer, assuming he knew about it.

"The Brotherhood aren't the only ones feeling the heat right now," he said. "This is a tempting target. The killer could destroy the Secret Apparatus leadership. The Islamist brain trust in America will all be in one place. Where are they holding the meeting?"

"According to one of their posts, they booked a river cruise with Washington Yachts. It departs from the Wharf Marina this evening."

"Why do it on a boat?"

"Who knows? They've used hotel conference rooms in the past, but the FBI has bugged them, and this meeting will be sensitive, because they'll be talking about the murders of undeclared Brotherhood members. Maybe they think the yacht will make it harder for law enforcement to eavesdrop."

"Let me make a call," Malachi said, and hung up.

Malachi had no authority to do anything, and his best advocate in MPD was dead. Despite that, he had to convince them this was their chance to catch the killer. He dialed Collins, and she picked up on the first ring.

"I have to talk to you," Malachi said.

"Sorry, Wolf. I don't have any news about your suspension."

"I'm not calling about that. Brotherhood leadership has scheduled a meeting tonight, and I think our killer may see it as an irresistible opportunity. We need to be there. It may be our chance to—"

"There is no *our* on this case, at least not until I get you back. Nobody here will listen to your conspiracy theories."

Malachi stared at his phone. What additional proof did they need? Was the infiltration so deep that it could stop an investigation? Had the bureaucrats within his department succumbed to pressure from the White House? He tried again.

"The Brotherhood's top leadership, including members of their Secret Apparatus, are meeting on a yacht tonight. The Brotherhood's on alert, even if *you* don't believe they're targeted by a vigilante. Things are hot for the killer too, and he's running out of time. If I were him, that's where I'd strike."

Collins was quiet. "I believe you, but I'm in the minority here, and I can't bring this up without involving you. Even if I could, Nuse will not let me contact the Brotherhood."

"I'm not asking you to warn them. Eavesdrop on the meeting to collect evidence or at least use the cruise as bait. Sit back with a tactical team and watch it. If our killer shows up—he's yours."

"Why would the killer commit a murder on a yacht? There's no way to escape. It's too risky."

"It's called prospect theory in economics. The value of his potential gains far exceeds his perceived loss. The chance to kill top members of the Secret Apparatus outweighs the danger."

"All the murders took place in Georgetown and involved one victim at a time. Targeting the yacht doesn't fit your profile. You have anything more than a hunch?"

"My hunches have been accurate so far. What about Horn?"

"We haven't been able to locate him. Nuse blew a fuse when I told him about the warrant, but he's briefing the chief and making the proper notifications to the FBI. You should have run that by me."

"I'm telling you about the meeting on the yacht. What are you going to do?"

"I can't stick my neck out unless you have something real. I'm sorry, my hands are tied."

"I'm sorry too, Lieutenant," Malachi said, and hung up.

He stared out at the still river. The current flowed through Washington like good and evil flowed through the people of Washington. He would make the river give up its secrets. This was a onetime chance to get ahead of the killer.

Malachi had to get onto that yacht.

CHAPTER SEVENTY-TWO

Duty transcended his job title, morally obligating Malachi to protect both the weak and the United States—the only country on earth founded on individual liberty. He would defend his values with his life, whether or not the police employed him. Faced with an opportunity to stop the killer and expose the Brotherhood, losing his badge and authority seemed like a technicality.

He sought a higher justice.

Washington Yachts owned two boats in DC, the *Diplomat* and the *President*, which they used for dinner cruises, river tours, weddings, and corporate events. It had only taken Malachi one pretext phone call to learn that the American Islamic Shura had reserved the *Diplomat* for a dinner cruise.

The yacht was scheduled to depart from the Wharf Marina, and Malachi had walked down to the pier to inspect it. The luxurious craft exceeded one hundred feet, seated sixty-six guests, and had dark tinted windows. The lower deck housed an eight-table dining room, and the upper deck offered a bar and an open deck above the stern.

Malachi's suspension meant he could not bug the boat or badge his way onboard, but he could still cover it. He rented a thirteen-foot Boston Whaler 130 Super Sport with a forty-horsepower Mercury outboard, more than powerful enough to keep up with a dinner yacht. He planned to follow at a distance and observe by blending in with spectator boats, which had crowded the river to watch the July Fourth fireworks. If the killer showed up, he would notify the Harbor Patrol.

If his hunch turned out to be wrong, he would return the boat and have only wasted a few hours of his time and two hundred dollars. But if he was right, he could save lives and catch the killer. With no official capacity and little time to react, it was all he could think of doing. Besides, simple plans worked best once bullets started flying. If Nuse found out he had conducted surveillance on a covert Brotherhood meeting, Malachi would get fired, but that was likely to happen either way.

That evening, Malachi floated in the Whaler under the Fourteenth Street Bridge. The river smelled like an aquarium. As the sun fell, the still water turned from green to black, hiding what lurked below. Millions of tons of water flowed past, thick, dark, unstoppable.

He patted the butt of the Smith and Wesson revolver tucked into his waistband. Bad people wanted Malachi dead, and Rodriguez had loaned him his personal handgun knowing he violated departmental policy. Adversity separated friends from acquaintances. When things were good, everybody was an ally, but in trying times like these, only friends stuck around. Rodriguez had shown his true character, and Malachi would never forget his loyalty.

He counted thirty-seven guests board the yacht, all men and all probably undeclared members of the Brotherhood's Secret Apparatus. They wore expensive suits, and if he had not already known, he would never have guessed they were members of the most dangerous terrorist organization in the world.

The *Diplomat* sounded its horn, eased away from the pier, and headed south. Malachi gunned his throttle and followed. A few minutes after seven, the sun sank below the tree line, and the sky turned metallic gray. Shadows darkened and merged as clouds blew in from the south and the air cooled. He gripped the wheel and focused on the yacht.

The *Diplomat* motored down the Washington Channel between the National War College and East Potomac Park. The captain seemed to be taking his time, careful to avoid dozens of small craft filled with drunken revelers waiting for the fireworks. Large crowds picnicked on shore, awaiting nightfall. The yacht passed Greenleaf Point and entered the Georgetown Channel on the opposite side of Hains Point, then continued south between Ronald Reagan Washington National Airport and Joint Base Anacostia-Bolling on the Maryland shore.

The yacht made ten knots, slow for a boat that size, but the channel had narrowed, and the waterway grew crowded. Malachi assumed the yacht would speed up once the river widened after Old Town Alexandria. No boats approached the yacht, and everything appeared peaceful on board.

Maybe I'm wrong.

Or the killer could be lurking nearby and waiting to strike. Or he could be stowed away on the boat. Or part of the crew. Or posing as a guest.

Malachi stayed a hundred yards back, and the yacht increased speed after the Old Town waterfront. They motored past a wharf, once used to trade slaves but now surrounded by bars, restaurants, and ice cream parlors. They followed the channel and navigated under the Woodrow Wilson Bridge as nautical twilight fell.

Half an hour later, they traversed Fort Hunt Park and Fort Washington Park, where Piscataway Creek flowed from the Potomac. George Washington's Mount Vernon estate lay to their right. By the time they reached Occoquan Bay, the yacht's interior lights illuminated dark silhouettes inside. The yacht's engines roared, and it turned to port and headed back.

Malachi angled his Whaler toward Chapman State Park and idled offshore to blend in with the wooded backdrop. The yacht passed within fifty yards of him. Passengers sat at tables in the dining room and milling around the bar on the upper deck. A crew member smoked on the second-tier deck over the stern, and his cigarette flared, like a firefly in the night.

The yacht maneuvered up the channel and Malachi restarted his engine and fell in behind. He waited a little too long, and the yacht pulled farther ahead, but remained in sight. The air coming off the water cooled, and Malachi swatted a mosquito on his neck. His plan had not panned out, and he felt foolish. He would tell no one about his field trip, except Zahra. She would not criticize him. Hell, it had been her idea.

After nine, darkness cloaked the river. He pushed the throttle all the way forward and bounced across the yacht's wake back toward the Capital. High above, the sky exploded with red, white, and blue fireworks.

Chapter Seventy-Three

Austin watched the fireworks as he floated in his kayak off Fort Foote Park in Maryland, south of the Woodrow Wilson Bridge. The channel narrowed near the eastern riverbank, and when the *Washington Diplomat* returned, it would have to slow as it approached the National Harbor. If he timed it perfectly, he could reach the yacht unseen.

He wobbled in the kayak from the high dose of narcotics flowing through his system. Had he taken too much to function? Finding the balance between relaxation and stupor had grown difficult, and the line moved every day.

He wore a black baseball cap and a black, long-sleeved Under Armour shirt, which wicked moisture from his skin and protected him from mosquitoes. The sun had disappeared, and his dark clothing and low profile made him almost invisible. He wore a heavy backpack which rested on the stern behind the cockpit, and he shifted in his seat to balance the weight. A long black bag was tied to the deck in front of him.

Austin peered into the river, muddied by soil dislodged in the storm. His life had muddied too. He did the Lord's work, but he lived on the opposite side of the law.

He uncovered the luminous dials of his watch and checked the time— nine o'clock. The yacht would return soon. Most of the small craft floated off the Old Town waterfront or closer to the District, but he focused on the river near Fort Washington. A moment later, the lighted cabin of the *Diplomat* rounded the point and motored toward him. He dragged his paddle through the water and drifted away from shore.

He bobbed at the edge of the channel until the yacht reached him, then he hunched forward and kept still—just another log on the surface of the river. The channel's depth reached twenty feet, but the waterway narrowed here, and the riverbed rose within six feet of the surface on either side. Water taxis and yachts always decelerated and stayed close to the channel markers, their captains' eyes locked on depth finders.

His timing had to be perfect.

The bow of the yacht passed him, and he paddled hard, pushing with one hand and pulling with the other. Years of kayaking made his form powerful and efficient.

The yacht ambled, but its gigantic size displaced water and pushed a thick wave off the hull. Austin's kayak jumped into the air as he hit the edge of the wake, and he paddled hard to cut through the swell. His kayak planed on top, like a surfboard, and his bow came within inches of the yacht's hull. He would capsize if he hit it.

He jammed his paddle into the river off his right hip, and his kayak spun to starboard, parallel with the yacht. He tossed the paddle away and grasped the railing on the yacht's stern deck with both hands. His shoulders strained as his kayak accelerated to the yacht's speed. His kayak bumped against the yacht's hull, and he swiveled his hips to keep his bow pointed forward. The wake pushed his kayak away, but he held on.

This was the hardest part.

He detached the long bag from the deck with his right hand and threw it onto the yacht's deck. With the motion of his throw, the bow of his kayak dipped into the wake and pointed away from the yacht.

He grabbed the railing with both hands and lifted himself out of the kayak. His knees scraped the kayak's cockpit. He lurched forward and his chest landed on the boat's deck. The kayak twisted in the wake and capsized, dumping his legs into the Potomac. He wriggled forward on his elbows to avoid being pulled into the river. He crawled away from the edge and collapsed on the deck.

He rolled onto to his back and gasped from exertion. He was excited—eager to kill.

The door leading into the lower-level dining room remained closed. Two men spoke in Arabic on the upper deck above him. Austin stayed out of the light leaking through the tinted windows. He listened for shouts, the man-overboard siren, or some sign that they had seen him, but only heard water lapping against the hull and muffled conversations inside.

He had to hurry.

He pulled the black bag toward him and unzipped it. He drew a Colt 6920MPS-B carbine from the bag. The weapon had a black finish, rubber foregrip, and sixteen-inch barrel. He removed a harness containing ten thirty-round magazines, all full of .223 ammunition. He dropped his knapsack and slipped the harness over his shoulders, so the magazines hung across his stomach. He inserted a magazine into the well of his carbine and pulled the charging handle back with two fingers. He released it, sending a round into the chamber with a metallic snap.

Pink neon lights from a gigantic Ferris wheel reflected off the water at National Harbor and illuminated the deck. The yacht turned to port and followed the channel toward the Woodrow Wilson Bridge.

Austin stepped forward in a crouch, his muscles coiled. He placed his left hand on the door handle and rotated it clockwise. The door was unlocked, as expected.

He held the carbine in his right hand with his finger above the trigger. He pulled the buttstock into the space between his pectoral muscle and shoulder. He leaned forward on the balls of his feet, and water squished between his toes.

For Vanessa.

He hurled the door open.

CHAPTER SEVENTY-FOUR

Malachi throttled back and kept his distance from the yacht. The Ferris wheel's gleaming lights painted the waterfront restaurants at National Harbor with a pink hue. Dozens of people mingled along the promenade and watched the fireworks. His body had grown sluggish after hours of boating, and his attention lapsed. His hunch had been wrong. His thoughts drifted to a warm shower and cold beer. Maybe he would open the eighteen-year-old Oban scotch he had been saving.

The sky lit up with a purple starburst, followed by a dull boom and Malachi looked up. Yellow, green, and white bursts filled the night sky, and white flashes popped around them. Oohs and aahs rose from spectators on the Maryland shore.

Something clunked against his hull and wrenched his attention back to the water.

A paddle floated past the Whaler's starboard side, and a capsized kayak bobbed in front of him. He yanked the wheel to port, but too late, and the bow of the kayak scraped the length of his hull. He slammed the throttle into neutral.

He turned in his seat as the Whaler slowed. The capsized kayak rocked back and forth in his wake. The hull had been painted black, and he had been lucky to see it.

Did I hit someone?

The thought pushed him toward panic, and he held the windscreen to steady himself. He replayed the scene in his head. The kayak had been upside down before he hit it. Had a kayaker drowned? Was someone floating in the water? Maybe the yacht had struck it.

The yacht.

The *Diplomat* moved through the channel toward the Woodrow Wilson Bridge. Malachi focused on it, but nothing seemed amiss. Should he call Harbor Patrol and give up his surveillance to search for the kayaker? He stood frozen in indecision, pulled between a potential drowning victim and his mission.

A bright light flickered near the yacht's stern and caught his attention. The aft door had opened, and the silhouette of an armed man entered the cabin.

CHAPTER SEVENTY-FIVE

Austin grasped the pistol grip under the barrel with his left hand and stepped through the door. The weight of the loaded carbine comforted him. Eight dining tables filled the room all the way to the bow, and hard, dangerous men occupied every seat. The fireworks had masked the sound of his entry, and the guests faced forward listening to a heavyset gentleman giving a speech in Arabic. Austin stared at the speaker.

Amir al-Kadi.

Al-Kadi saw him and stopped talking. Members of the audience followed al-Kadi's gaze and met Austin with a sea of confused expressions, which quickly morphed into alarm and then fear.

Beside Austin, a guest with a long beard turned in his chair and gawked at the gun. Austin pivoted and shot him in the chest. The retort of the carbine inside the enclosed space deafened him. People flinched and covered their ears, but no one moved.

Austin spun to his right and double tapped two rounds into the closest guest at that table. He swung the barrel counterclockwise, pulling the trigger as fast as he could. Rounds impacted guests seated around the table, and blood spattered the white linen and tinted windows.

Screams erupted around the room, desperate, fearful.

Austin pivoted to the table on his left, where a young guest fumbled with a pistol in a shoulder harness. Austin shot him in the face and half of his head exploded. The man fell backward onto the table and dishes shattered onto the floor. Austin shot three more people at the table as they fled.

Bearded men knocked over chairs and pushed each other in a panic. Austin turned his attention to the next table and fired into the guests attempting to escape. Bodies tumbled into each other. Injured people flailed on the deck.

Al-Kadi stood at the front of the room, gripping the podium with a look of disbelief. Austin met his eyes, raised the carbine and fired. Al-Kadi's head snapped back, and a red hole opened in the center of his forehead before he collapsed behind the podium.

Austin pulled the trigger again, and the carbine's breech locked open on an empty magazine. He dropped to a knee and pushed the release, sending the spent magazine clattering to the floor.

"Cover, reloading," he mumbled to himself—a habit ingrained during training.

With his left hand, he pulled a full magazine out of his harness, turned it upright, and used his forefinger to guide it into the metal well. He slapped the bottom of the magazine with his palm to make sure it seated then hit the bolt release to chamber a round. He never took his eyes of the fleeing crowd in the four seconds it had taken him to reload.

Austin bared his teeth—a predator on the prowl.

A muscular guest near the bow, probably a bodyguard, pointed a handgun in the air as he pushed his way through the fleeing mob toward the bulkhead.

Austin held his breath and dropped his front sight onto the bodyguard's nose. He squeezed the trigger. The first round went wide right and struck another guest between the shoulder blades. Austin exhaled, took another breath, and aimed again. He pulled the trigger three times in succession.

The bodyguard fell to the deck.

Guests scrambled over each other trying to reach an enclosed companionway on the starboard side. It led to the bar and open-air deck above, but they had nowhere to hide. Austin lowered his barrel to waist level and fired into the frantic throng.

Austin dropped another empty magazine, and it clanged against the floor. He inserted a fresh one and walked forward, shooting from the hip. He stopped beside a guest writhing in pain on the floor and shot the wounded man in the forehead. Blood spurted as if it came from a sprinkler.

Austin continued forward behind another injured guest who crawled on his hands and knees. Austin shot him twice in the back and the guest toppled onto another body. The air smelled of gunpowder, blood, and shit. Austin's feet squished in the blood-soaked carpet as he advanced.

A young crew member, wearing white slacks and a polo shirt, huddled in the corner. Austin hesitated before the teenage boy. The kid raised his hands in front of his face, as if he could stop a bullet traveling 2,800 feet per second.

"Can you swim?" Austin asked.

"What?" the boy asked, his hands still blocking his face.

"Can you swim, yes or no?"

"Ye ... yes, I can."

Austin nodded aft toward the stern. "Show me."

"What?"

"Swim to shore."

The boy stood up, his body shaking.

"Now."

The kid ran through the stern door and dove into the river. Austin nodded to himself. God had not sent him to kill innocent civilians.

Austin returned his attention to the companionway and edged around the corner, his muzzle pointed up. A dozen guests clawed, pushed, and pulled each other, all fighting to ascend the stairs. Anger washed over him, warming him, comforting him. He embraced it, letting his rage carry him into the dark deed.

He centered his sights on the first guest's back and squeezed the trigger. The round shattered the man's spine. He crumbled and rolled back down the stairs.

Austin shot the next guest, then the next, until all of them lay in a pile. Groans emanated from the broken bodies, and blood cascaded down the carpeted steps. A hellish waterfall.

"Let death seize upon them and let them go down quick into hell: for wickedness is in their dwellings, and among them."

He felt blissful. He needed to do this for Vanessa, for his country. God had put him on earth for this moment.

He ducked out of the companionway and changed magazines again. Guests on the second deck yelled in a mixture of English and Arabic. Splashes punctuated the screaming as they dove into the river to escape.

Austin gagged on the acrid odor and leaned back into the companionway. He aimed down the barrel of his carbine, but the bodies on the steps had stopped moving. He glanced at his watch.

He had to get moving. Police would arrive soon.

He slipped the backpack off his shoulders, keeping one hand on his carbine. He knelt, unzipped the pack, and lifted a heavy object out and onto the floor. The device resembled the nose cone of a missile. It contained twenty-five pounds of C-4 explosives linked with wires and blasting caps. He had taped a cell phone to the side, and when he called it, the bomb would detonate. A small bag of saline covered the top of the cone and created a shaped charge, which would direct the force of the explosion down through the deck and into the fuel tanks. He set the explosives in the center of the boat. If the schematics he had studied were correct, the main fuel tank lay below him.

He patted his cell phone in his pocket.

The ship accelerated into a starboard turn and listed to port. The Wilson Bridge flashed by the windows as the captain turned back toward National Harbor. Austin assumed the captain had already issued a distress call, and the Maryland State Police were waiting on the dock. The MPD Harbor Patrol and the Coast Guard would be en route too.

Time to finish this.

He ascended the stairs, stepping around the bodies, and peeked over the top step into an ornate barroom. Marble tabletops and chandeliers extended aft toward the open-air deck. Light reflected off gold trim around dark tinted windows, which ran the length of the empty room, Barstools lay overturned on the floor. A dozen guests, probably the non-swimmers, huddled outside on the deck.

He took aim and fired into the crowd. His bullets tore into flesh. Screams filled the air over the retorts of his carbine. People jumped over the railing into the water. Austin emptied his magazine, reloaded, and expended another. He cleared the deck.

He wanted to pick off guests in the river but did not have time. He had to stop the yacht. He climbed out of the stairwell and moved around a faux-oak bar to a closed hatch. A sign above it read "Crew Only." He jerked the handle up and unlatched the metal door. It swung inward, and he leaned around the corner into the bridge. The captain stood behind the wheel, navigating toward a crowd of spectators at National Harbor. Three crew members huddled against the far bulkhead and stared at him in horror. Through the windshield, the lights of the Ferris wheel twinkled on the Maryland shore.

"Stop the ship, Captain," Austin shouted.

The captain did not move, and his hands remained affixed to the wheel and throttle.

Austin fired a round into the control panel. His ears rang from the amplified sound in the small bridge. The noise shocked the captain into action. He pulled the throttle back to neutral and turned to face Austin.

"The ship is rigged to explode. Your guests are in the water. Get your people off the ship. Anyone who stays will die."

He fired another round into the control panel.

The captain pulled a cord hanging from the ceiling and the bridge filled with red flashing lights and the alarm bell rang three times. The captain stared hard at him, then picked up a microphone and raised it to his mouth.

"This is the captain. Abandon ship."

His voice boomed through the ship's speakers as the crew filed out the starboard hatch. They jumped one at a time into the water. The captain went last.

Behind Austin, a small outboard engine rumbled near the ship's stern. He turned toward the sound.

CHAPTER SEVENTY-SIX

The shooting ceased as Malachi maneuvered around people splashing in the water and guided his boat toward the *Diplomat*'s stern. Most guests swam toward shore, but a few thrashed and shouted in Arabic, unable to swim. Malachi wanted to pick them up, but he had to neutralize the shooter first. He tossed flotation devices to them as he motored past.

Lights from police cars flashed behind the dock at National Harbor, but the Harbor Patrol had not arrived. Hundreds of people watched from the promenade. There seemed no point in calling 9-1-1.

His bow bumped against the yacht's fiberglass hull with a hollow thump. Malachi drew his revolver and bounded across the Whaler's deck. He grabbed the railing and leapt onto the yacht's stern. He crouched and listened, then tied his bowline off on a metal cleat. The yacht's engines purred, as it idled eighty yards from shore.

Malachi cupped his hands against the tinted window and squinted to see through the glass. Bodies lay scattered across the dining room, but there was no sign of the gunman. People could still be alive onboard, wounded and in need of help.

How did the killer plan to escape? Would he flee in the yacht? Rendezvous with another boat? Swim to shore? He could have jumped into the river with the other victims, intending to walk away once he reached land. Malachi needed to confirm if he remained onboard.

Malachi stayed in a crouch, opened the door, and quick-peeked right and left. A scarlet tide rolled back and forth across the deck with the yacht's motion.

He crossed the threshold into the dining room and moved left to avoid silhouetting himself in the doorway. Bodies littered the deck. A dozen dead lay in a heap near the companionway. Malachi had seen videos of mass shootings in training, but those two-dimensional images did not convey the unnatural sight of dozens of murdered people. His presence violated this sacred ground—a place reserved for the dead.

If he was careless, he would join them.

His stomach tightened, and he willed away his fear. He aimed his revolver at the companionway and walked forward, alternating his attention between his iron sights and victims on the floor. Blood sloshed over the tops of his shoes onto his pants.

Where is the shooter?

A cylindrical metal object sat on the deck beside a pile of bodies, and Malachi did a double take. The cone-shaped device had bricks of gray clay near the base. He squatted and examined it. Red wires and blasting caps protruded beneath the metal shroud.

Not clay—plastic explosives.

The killer had taped a cell phone to the side to act as a remote detonator. Malachi knew little about explosives other than to call the bomb squad, which sounded like a good plan.

He smelled the charred air on Beacon Street after the bombing.

Something clanked on the upper deck, meaning someone was alive. He glanced back through the stern door at his boat—his means to escape—then he moved forward. Malachi had to get victims off the yacht before the device detonated.

He peeked around the companionway at bodies littering the stairs. Among them was Farouk Abdullah, the professor he had warned at Continental University. He ascended the steps and stumbled over a corpse soaked in blood.

At the top, he peered into the empty bar. Beyond, bodies lay in a jumble on the deck.

On his right, the hatchway to the bridge was ajar. He kept his eyes on the hatch and moved aft along the starboard gunwale. He reached the stern and slipped around the corner. Eight bodies lay motionless on the deck, the tile awash with blood. He glanced over the side at guests swimming for shore. Anyone left alive onboard had to be in the bridge. He stepped back around the bulkhead into the bar and froze.

The killer stood outside the bridge.

He had an AR-15 carbine slung over his shoulder, and a cell phone in his hand. He faced away from Malachi, looking at the companionway.

Malachi raised his revolver and crouched into a shooter's stance. It would be a long shot, but he could hit him.

The killer must have caught his movement out of the corner of his eye because he turned and faced Malachi.

Special Agent Austin Horn.

CHAPTER SEVENTY-SEVEN

Seeing Detective Wolf exhilarated Austin.

No more hiding.

Austin raised the phone, so Wolf could see it, and held his finger above the send button.

"I was wondering if I'd see you tonight, Detective Wolf."

"Get on the ground, asshole," Wolf said. "There's nowhere for you to go. It's over."

"I know that, Detective. I'm not going anywhere. I've accomplished my mission."

"Put your hands behind your head and interlace your fingers."

If he complied, Wolf would get him on his stomach and handcuff him. Austin would spend the rest of his days in a cage. He would never let that happen.

"That's not how this ends, Detective."

A helicopter's rotors thumped nearby, and a searchlight's beam swept across the Woodrow Wilson Bridge in their direction.

"I know who you are, Agent Horn."

"My name is not Horn, Detective. Not anymore. I'm a crusader knight, a defender of the West. I'm King Richard the Lion-Hearted come to fight our enemy."

The sky lit up with vivid color as the fireworks finale began.

"Murder is never justified," Wolf said. "Without the rule of law, we're savages."

"Vengeance belongeth unto me . . ."

"The killing ends now. Put your hands up or I'll shoot. I won't warn you again."

"I wouldn't recommend that. If I press send, an IED will detonate and obliterate both of us."

"You're bluffing. You won't commit suicide."

"And Moses spake unto the people, saying, arm some of yourselves unto the war, and let them go against the Midianites, and avenge the Lord of Midian."

"Drop the phone."

Austin stepped to his right. His finger remained on the screen. Wolf would need to shoot him in the nose and destroy his medulla oblongata to stop him from detonating the bomb—an almost impossible shot with a snub-nosed revolver. Wolf had to know that too.

Austin took another step backward, then dashed through the hatchway onto the bridge.

Chapter Seventy-Eight

Malachi followed Horn with his sights, unwilling to blast him in the back while Horn's finger hovered over the detonator.

Horn disappeared onto the bridge then leaned out from behind the bulkhead. "Here's what will happen, Detective. In ten seconds, I'll press send, and milliseconds later, twenty-five pounds of high explosives will detonate above the fuel tanks."

The matter-of-fact way he said it chilled Malachi. He spoke as if the outcome was settled. Horn had planned this like he had planned all the murders. How did he expect to escape?

What am I missing?

"You won't do that," Malachi said. "Press that button and you'll die too."

"That's the point, Detective. I'll ride the explosion and personally deliver these animals to the gates of hell."

"You're a suicide bomber now? Isn't that how jihadists behave?"

"I'm Michael the Archangel, the Sword of God."

Horn sounded like a lunatic. Would he sacrifice himself?

"You don't want to die."

"And he said unto them, verily I say unto you, that there be some of them that stand here, which shall not taste of death, till they have seen the Kingdom of God come with power."

"Don't waste another life. Don't do this."

"What is one man's life in the eternal battle against evil?"

Is he talking about himself or me?

A helicopter hovered overhead, and its rotors blew mist into the air. Malachi inhaled the organic scent of the muddy water.

"It's time," Horn said.

"Listen to me. I know about the infiltration, and I understand why you think you're saving our country. You don't have to die here."

"If you understand then you'll spread the word, carry on my work. My mission ends in ten seconds."

"Toss your gun out and put the phone on the deck."

"They chose new gods; then was war in the gates. Was there a shield or spear seen among forty thousand in Israel?"

"Let me take you in. There are extenuating circumstances. I'll testify to that at trial."

"Now, you're insulting me. Five seconds."

Malachi was out of time. He took a knee to steady himself and locked his elbows with his revolver extended. He fired at Horn's head.

Horn ducked around the bulkhead as Malachi's rounds ricocheted off the metal hatch.

"Nice try, Detective. Time's up."

Malachi leapt to his feet and sprinted onto the deck. He grabbed the railing and hurled himself over the side. He turned in the air as he fell, and the helicopter's spotlight illuminated him.

Malachi belly flopped into the river, and the impact expelled the air from his lungs. His revolver disappeared into the murky water. He flailed his arms and legs, struggling to reach the surface.

His chest burned as he broke the surface and he gasped for air. He coughed, took shallow breaths, then side-stroked away from the boat. His skin stung where he had struck the water.

The spotlight found him, and a voice came over a megaphone. "You in the water. Don't move. This is the Maryland State Police."

The Harbor Patrol's blue lights flashed near the Woodrow Wilson Bridge and headed toward him. He treaded water and waved at the helicopter, signaling it to get away.

Malachi looked back at the boat. It had been over ten seconds, and nothing had happened. Had the bomb malfunctioned? Had Horn changed his mind? Had he tricked him? Would Horn appear on deck with his rifle and pick him off in the water?

Malachi felt the blast before he heard it.

A shock wave rolled across the water and knocked the breath from him again. A bright light engulfed the interior of the yacht, and he closed his eyes as the sound of the explosion filled his ears.

Pieces of fiberglass splashed in the river, and he covered his head with one hand. His water-logged clothes tugged at him, pulling him down. He kicked hard.

The helicopter's blades whomped through the humid air and cut circles through the sky.

Malachi pulled off his shoes and let them sink to the bottom. He flopped onto his stomach and stroked for shore.

The fuel tanks erupted in a secondary explosion, filling Malachi's ears, and flames shot high into the sky. The boat rose out of the water, then folded in on itself. The center sank amidships, and the bow and stern pointed into the air, forming a V-shape. The two halves of the yacht ground together with a horrific sound, then they broke apart and splashed back into the river.

The yacht vanished into the brown water.

CHAPTER SEVENTY-NINE

Malachi watched the salvage operation from shore as the sun rose behind him. Ambulances, fire engines, and police cars lined the road along the National Harbor. Divers from the Maryland State Police and Metropolitan Police Department had been in the water for hours, combing the murky depths for survivors. Two police boats floated near the wreck to support the dive teams.

Only the tip of yacht's bridge poked above the waterline. The yacht had been an inferno when it sank. Nobody onboard could have survived.

All five crew and thirteen guests had been rescued shortly after the blast, but no one had been found alive in over eight hours, turning the rescue into a recovery operation. The manifest listed thirty-seven guests, so Horn had given his life to murder twenty-four Brotherhood operatives. Would killing two dozen leaders stop the Secret Apparatus or would they reconstitute and continue their plans?

Malachi wrapped an emergency blanket around his damp clothes to ward off the chill. After jumping off the boat, he had swum to shore with the helicopter's searchlight on him, only to be greeted by police officers with drawn guns. The helicopter's spotter had seen Malachi fire his weapon onboard and assumed he was the suspect. After being handcuffed and searched, it took an hour to clear himself from suspicion. Thankfully, the *Diplomat*'s captain confirmed Malachi was not the killer.

Evidence technicians combed through shards of plastic, clothing, and other debris laid out on white sheets along the promenade. Two search teams made their way up and down the shoreline looking for bodies or evidence washed ashore. So far, eight bodies had been recovered, five by divers and the rest delivered by the strong currents. The river still held sixteen bodies—seventeen, including Horn.

Malachi wanted Horn's body to close the case, because without it, doubt would linger. The river bottom was cluttered with branches, logs, and garbage, and would trap water-logged corpses. Powerful currents and tide would spread body parts over a sizable area. The fire had burned like an inferno. How many of the bodies would be identifiable?

"Yo, Wolf," Collins said. "Getting enough rest on your suspension?"

"When did you arrive?"

"The Maryland State Police called MPD when they discovered they had a detective in custody. The Command Center notified Nuse, and he ordered me to get over here. I expect him any minute."

"Lovely."

"You hurt?"

"I knew this yacht was too tempting for the killer."

Collins nodded. "Yes, you did. We should have listened to you. *I* should have listened."

"It was Horn."

"FBI gonna love that."

"He had a detonator. He sounded crazy."

"That's an understatement."

They watched the divers and news helicopters hovering in the distance. A mass shooting within sight of the Capitol would draw national attention for weeks.

"How long do you think it'll take to find Horn's body?" Malachi asked.

"It's a mess down there. Bottom is covered with garbage, bodies trapped in the wreckage, low visibility. It will take days. Mass shootings take on a life of their own."

"We need to establish Horn's pattern of life over the past few months."

"Rodriguez and Hill are writing search warrants now. Any chance Horn got off the yacht alive?"

"Nobody could have survived that blast. Even if he jumped before the device detonated, the police were waiting on shore. Horn's dead."

"Let's stroll over to the Command Center. Maryland State Police need your official statement."

Malachi lowered his eyes. "I had a chance to shoot him, but I didn't."

Collins pulled a pack of Marlboro Lights out of her pocket and lit one. "You said he had a detonator."

"Before he told me he planned to blow up the ship, I could have shot without warning him . . . but I couldn't do it. Maybe I owed him for not shooting me when he had the chance. I don't know, it didn't feel right."

"Killing's hard," she said. "It has to be justified."

"That's the question, isn't it? Horn thought murdering infiltrators to protect our country was justified. The Brotherhood think they're justified in killing for Allah."

"There are differences."

Malachi nodded. "Maybe I don't have what it takes."

"You crazy smart, and you almost had your PhD. Why become a cop?"

"I think I wanted to catch murderers for my father, bring order to things. Now, I understand nothing can fill the hole."

"So why do it?"

Malachi thought for a moment. "Because stopping killers and finding justice for the dead is the ultimate moral act. I'm making the world a safer place for my kids . . . for all of us. I can't bring my father back, but by standing up for justice, I can honor his life . . . and his death. What's right is right."

"That's what makes you a real cop."

Blue and red lights spanned the length of the Wilson Bridge and reflected off the water. They sat in silence, both lost in thought.

Malachi's father had given him the middle name "Rand" to honor his favorite philosopher—Ayn Rand—a woman who championed laissez-faire capitalism. Rand meant "Wolf's shield" and now Malachi had become a cop. He wondered if it had been destiny.

Malachi's right hand tingled and spasmed, and he hid it under his leg. MS was the unseen devil within him, limiting the time he could carry a badge. He would fight it with everything he had and follow his calling for as long as possible.

"What will happen now?" he asked.

"After the state cops interview you, our shoot team will need a statement. Since you're suspended, internal affairs will have questions too. So will the FBI."

"No, I mean what will happen to me, to my job?"

She gazed over the water for a long time before she met his eyes.

"I don't know, but we'll find out soon."

CHAPTER EIGHTY

Two weeks later, Malachi sat at his desk in the Homicide Branch and watched Rodriguez sort through the Baker file. They had a new detective, Jim Simpson, assigned to fill Jones' vacant slot. Collins had asked Hill to train Simpson and had partnered Rodriguez with Malachi. Collins had trusted Malachi enough to pair him with another rookie detective, and Malachi planned to help Rodriguez, the same way Jones had helped him.

A large coffee thumped onto his desk, and he looked up. Hill smiled at him.

"Black, right?" Hill asked.

"Yeah, thanks."

"Good to have you back, College," he said, and walked to his desk.

Rodriguez raised his eyebrows and smiled.

Malachi had been surprised at how fast Chief Ransom had reinstated him, but the media had portrayed him as a hero who saved the lives of eighteen people, so she had little choice. The internal charge of leaking sensitive information had been dropped. Everyone knew Malachi had given the story to the Washington Herald, but he had been right about Horn's motive.

The timing of Horn's disappearance and his statements to the landlord about dying fit the mass shooting, but Malachi still needed sufficient evidence to link Horn to the previous murders. Rodriguez subpoenaed Horn's bank accounts, credit cards, and phone records, but did not find any links to the other victims.

Horn had covered his tracks well.

Horn's frustration must have morphed into an uncontrollable anger. He had damaged his career and had probably decided to act when Senator Hansen seemed destined for the presidency. Horn's life must have felt worthless enough for him to throw it away. Horn had become a mass murderer, and while Malachi could not condone his actions, at least Horn had exposed the Brotherhood. If enough people paid attention, maybe they could stop those terrorists before it was too late. Horn's fiery death, along with twenty-four Brotherhood leaders, had ignited public discussion about Islamism in America.

"Congratulations, Detective," Chief Ransom said.

Malachi spun around. She stood behind him in a pressed uniform, her starched white shirt bedazzled with black epaulets, rows of commendations, and a shiny gold badge. She reminded him of a medieval king. Nuse and Collins stood behind her.

"Thanks, Chief."

"Our nightmare's over, and I won't forget your role in this."

"We haven't found Horn's body yet," Malachi said.

Six bodies, including Horn's, had still not been recovered. Baker and the other murders were not officially linked to the mass shooting, but since the killing stopped after carnage on the yacht, everyone agreed all the murders had been Horn's handiwork.

"Don't worry about that," Ransom said. "The Mayor and White House want this closed. You were right. The killer's dead, and it's time to move on."

"The Brotherhood is still out there. Horn may have killed their top infiltrators, but—"

"That's enough," Nuse said, his cheeks coloring. "You're lucky you have a job. I don't want to hear an—"

"Thank you, Barney," Ransom said. "Go wait for me in the car, and I'll be along in a minute." She smiled, but her eyes took on the intensity of a predator.

Nuse curled his lower lip like a pouting child and walked out.

"Nuse has a point," Ransom said. "Let the FBI worry about why Horn targeted Muslim leaders. Our job was to catch the killer, and you did that. The MPD's moving on, and I don't want to read about the case anymore. We clear?"

"Very."

Collins grinned at Malachi as she walked the chief out of the bullpen.

Malachi had dug deep into Horn's activities in the months before the killings. Outside work, he had been an antisocial loner, a shadow. Rodriguez had discovered a second bank account in Horn's name, which still bothered Malachi. The week before Horn died, he had made three nine-thousand-dollar withdrawals, which all fell under the ten-thousand-dollar reporting limit. What had Horn done with the money?

Chief Ransom had held a press conference announcing the killer was dead, and Collins had ordered Malachi to drop the case. The FBI and MPD had issued a joint statement calling the mass shooting on the yacht a hate-filled act of Islamophobia. The White House branded it terrorism, the act of a white supremacist, and the FBI took over the murder investigations. They promised to continue to investigate, but Malachi knew everyone wanted it to go away.

Pundits floated theories about the Muslim Brotherhood's activities in America, and in response, the Brotherhood spun the mass shooting as an act of Islamophobia and called for including Islam in American culture. Despite their efforts, the genie had escaped the bottle, and for the first time, people publicly debated the Brotherhood's connection to terrorism. The Brotherhood was in trouble and coming after Malachi and Zahra would only hurt them more.

Malachi lifted a framed photograph of Alison, Samantha, and Riley off his desk. He had taken the photo a few months before Alison left him. He examined Alison's eyes for the millionth time since the divorce but still could not see any sign that she had been preparing to abandon him.

Something had changed inside Malachi. He no longer yearned to be with her. He still cared about her, but he did not love her, and his anger had dissipated. He had broken the spell. He opened his briefcase and dropped the photograph inside. He replaced it with a new photograph of Samantha and Riley and made a mental note to take a picture with Zahra.

His telephone rang.

"Congratulations," Jane Evans said. "I heard you're back at work."

"It's Washington. The political winds shifted."

"I wanted you to know that the FBI is finally talking about the Brotherhood. The thugs you offed at the cathedral were Egyptian, all associated with the Brotherhood and the American Islamic Shura. That made the bureau pay attention."

"Is the Brotherhood under criminal investigation?"

"Not yet, but our office is gathering intelligence. The cathedral shooters who escaped can be charged, but that would come from MPD, not us. We would have to call it terrorism to get involved."

"I'm sure the Brotherhood was behind it," Malachi said, "but I had to recuse myself. I won't hold my breath waiting for arrests."

"The Bureau's perception of the Brotherhood has changed, and that's a step in the right direction."

"You think the director will pursue them?"

"Maybe, but AIS is bombarding the public with the Islamophobia narrative. We'll have to wait and see if the Bureau decides to target the infiltration."

"Since the attack, the Middle East Policy Institute has published four lengthy articles detailing the Brotherhood's long-term affiliation with terrorism," Malachi said. "Zahra testified before the House Judiciary Committee yesterday. Do you think that'll have an effect?"

"I watched it on C-SPAN. Dr. Mansour's testimony was damning, but the networks focused on the demonstrations outside the Capitol, which accused her of being an Islamophobe."

"She expected that," Malachi said. "She has received some good feedback from legislators in private messages, but most of them aren't taking sides. I think we're at a crossroads in our counterterrorism policy."

"It'll be hard to dispute the evidence she laid out . . . if Congress was listening."

"Yesterday, President Follet appointed Zahra as his chief advisor on Islamic terrorism, and he's firing staff who defended the Brotherhood. It's a start."

"That's not the only good news," Jane said. "Senator Hansen is ending his candidacy. His connections to the Brotherhood and North Star are not playing well in the media, despite his protestations of innocence. I'm sure he regrets that alliance now."

Malachi inhaled. He had not heard that. If Horn had been trying to stop Senator Hansen from getting into the White House, then his plan had worked. Maybe there was hope. He thanked Jane and hung up.

Simpson carried a large box across the room and dropped it on his desk. "Hey Wolf, Collins asked me to send the Baker file down to closed cases with the others. What should I do with Horn's telephone tolls and bank records?"

"Leave them, and I'll see if there's anything we need to send to the FBI."

"Assuming Horn killed those people," Simpson said.

"He did."

Horn's personal phone had not logged a call or pinged outside Virginia in six months, so he had not carried it during the murders. The same was true for his burner phone.

"Why did he hide a burner phone under his floor?" Simpson asked.

"Maybe he planned more murders before he saw the yacht as a target of opportunity."

"I guess so," Simpson said. He dropped the evidence on Malachi's desk.

Malachi skimmed through all the files. Horn had a telephone registered in his name, so why carry a drop phone?

If Horn had planned to use it for another murder, why had he activated it and carried it around Virginia? He had waited to turn on the other telephones until moments before the murders. Malachi sorted through the folders and found the search warrant return with tracking information and toll records. The phone had been activated months before the killings began and had pinged off relay stations as Horn traveled. The return showed the alpha, beta, and gamma sides of each tower. Rodriguez had scanned them to confirm Horn had not carried the phone into the District, and all the hits had been in Virginia and Maryland.

Malachi scrolled through the cell tower codes again. He opened a law enforcement portal from the telephone carrier's website and entered the codes of each tower the phone had pinged. As he did, red dots popped up on a Google Map. He plotted all of them and froze.

He needed to speak with someone right away.

CHAPTER EIGHTY-ONE

Massive nimbostratus clouds darkened the sky, and drizzle frosted Malachi's windshield as he battled heavy traffic up Seventeenth Street NW. He had texted Zahra asking to see her, and she had agreed to meet him at the White House before her briefing began. He parked and waited on the sidewalk near the West Wing's Pennsylvania Avenue entrance.

Zahra's taxi arrived, the door opened, and her stiletto heels emerged first. She stepped onto the sidewalk wearing a stylish skirt, tight around her knees, and a formal jacket over a white blouse. She smiled and waved.

Malachi's heart skipped a beat. She had allowed him to love again, to move past his divorce—a gift more precious than anything he thought possible.

"My love," she said. She kissed him on the mouth.

Malachi tensed in her arms.

She pulled back and raised her eyebrows. "What is it?"

"I have to ask you something," Malachi said.

Her eyes penetrated his, searching for something.

"Before the mass shooting," he said, "Agent Evans' investigations were closed by someone at FBI headquarters."

"You mentioned that."

"That's what made me suspect Austin Horn. I believed he had uncovered the Islamist infiltration and decided to combat it with vigilantism."

"An excellent theory."

"Several things have bothered me since the beginning, and I need you to help me understand them."

"Okay, but hurry. I'm late for my briefing."

"I couldn't figure out why the murders took place in Georgetown. You gave me a list of dozens of likely infiltrators but Horn only murdered people with links to Georgetown. That seemed too coincidental, and Linda Reynolds didn't even live in DC."

"I can't help you with that."

The clouds darkened above them.

"And another thing, why did Horn take such pains to cover his tracks, yet he used the same gun in four murders?"

"Maybe he didn't own another gun?"

"Getting firearms is easy for someone in law enforcement." Malachi put his hands on his hips. "There's more."

She looked at her watch. "Can't we discuss this tonight?"

"Horn used burner phones to lure Baker, Bellini, and Sharif outside, but why call Reynolds? He must have seen her walk into the bathroom. What purpose did that call serve?"

"I don't know," Zahra said.

A few raindrops spattered the sidewalk.

"Horn spray-painted security cameras near Baker and Bellini's murders, which linked the crimes for me, but he also painted the camera behind La Seine, and it was obviously disconnected. Why paint it?"

Zahra looked down before she answered. "Maybe he didn't see the unattached wires or maybe he wanted to be certain."

The sprinkles turned to a steady drizzle.

"Around the time Horn figured out someone was shutting down his cases from the inside, you published several papers about Islamist infiltration. You even mentioned Sam Baker and other members of North Star. You—"

"I listed Baker and every other infiltrator I could find. I don't mean to cut you off, Malachi, but I'm late for this meeting. What don't you understand?"

"How come Horn never contacted you?"

"What?"

"It's inconceivable that Horn figured out Islamist infiltration had subverted his cases, yet he ignored one of the world's experts on the topic, a respected academic who worked down the street from his office."

"It is odd," Zahra said. Her eyes darted to the White House.

"I thought so too. I rechecked the location information from a burner phone Horn had activated before any of the murders took place. I had ignored it, because he never took it into the District, but when I went back through the data, I found he hit towers in both Maryland and Virginia."

"And?"

"It seemed like he was driving back and forth across the Woodrow Wilson Bridge until I realized he wasn't driving at all. He was in a boat."

"Oh." Something flashed behind Zahra's eyes, and her face paled under the dark sky.

"I followed his cell phone as it went south, down the Potomac. It stayed on one tower for an hour. That tower covered Washington Point. You know the area. It's where you keep your submerged mooring."

Zahra focused on him and straightened her posture. "What are you saying?"

"I'm not done. I went back to Horn's personal cell phone and found a call to the Safe Harbor Marina. That call was two months before the first murder. I called Agent Evans and asked her to look in their file's investigative notes section from the day Horn made that call. His notes had been torn out of the file. Horn had done something, notated it, then removed it, as if he wanted to hide his activity."

"Are you accusing me of something?" Zahra asked. "Do you think Horn and I met before the murders took place?"

"I want to know if Horn contacted you, or if you sought him out."

She pressed her lips tight.

"When did you give him the list of infiltrators?" Malachi asked.

Zahra stayed silent.

"Did you provide the moral justification to kill or had he already decided to become a vigilante?"

"I can't believe you're asking me to admit complicity in murder."

It rained harder now, but Zahra did not move, her face a mask.

Malachi's heart pounded. He did not want to believe it, but he knew it was true. This brilliant woman had manipulated Horn, then she had manipulated him.

"Your involvement answers all of my questions," he said. "Horn used the same gun to link the murders for us and to let the Brotherhood know they had become his prey. He called Reynolds from a drop phone, to make sure we knew her murder was part of it."

"That's quite a theory, Malachi."

"Once I realized Horn wanted to expose the Brotherhood, I checked the dates of your articles. Most were published during the year before the first murder, recent enough so I would find them and uncover the Brotherhood's involvement. You knew I would contact you, the way Horn had. You wrote them for me."

"I've written about Islamists for years."

"When I saw the ping off the cell tower and realized the missing link was you, everything made sense. The murders were committed in Georgetown to connect them for me. Not me specifically, but whichever detective caught the first murder."

"Hmm."

"Georgetown had so few murders, they were likely to get media attention, and what better way to expose the Brotherhood than a sequence of murders in the capital? It almost guaranteed worldwide coverage, with the added benefit of killing some of the most powerful infiltrators. Maybe Horn chose Georgetown, because a tenacious rookie homicide detective caught the first murder—a detective who would understand his motivation, who wouldn't be cowed, and who would never give up. Maybe Horn kept killing in Georgetown because he wanted me."

Zahra stayed still.

"After I accepted that premise, even being in the garden to save Hammond made sense. If I told you I was following him, you would have tipped off Horn, but Hammond was one of the sixty-three potential victims on your list, and you didn't know I'd culled the list to five people."

Zahra had a far-off look in her eyes.

"Horn accelerated his killing to expose the Brotherhood before Senator Hansen announced his bid for the presidency," Malachi said. "If

Hansen had won, the Brotherhood would have had their puppet in the White House. It would have been game over."

"But I'm the one who helped you identify Horn's motivation."

"You gave me just enough information to help me understand the Brotherhood had infiltrated the government."

"I told you about the yacht. If I was working with Horn, why would I tip you off about that?"

"You wanted me to have MPD or the FBI monitor the meeting, not stop it. A recording would have proven what the Security Apparatus was planning. Or maybe you thought Horn was out of control and you wanted the killings to stop."

"That's fantastical," she said, but the corners of her mouth rose.

Was he wrong? Why else would she lead him to the yacht, if not to stop Horn? A chill ran up his spine and he thought he would be sick.

"You told me about the yacht so I could witness Horn's death. You knew the investigation would die with him."

Zahra's eyes gleamed.

"Is Horn alive?" Malachi asked.

"That's another interesting theory."

"If Horn got off that yacht alive, I'll find him. I'll never stop looking."

"Let me ask you a hypothetical question," Zahra said. "Now that you know Horn fought to save his country from the Brotherhood, would you have arrested him if you had the chance?"

"It was my job to arrest him."

"Even though the level of infiltration corrupted the legal system?"

Malachi stared at her. He had asked himself this same question. When was vigilantism justified?

"I would have arrested him."

"Would it have mattered that Horn could have shot you and didn't or that he saved our lives in the cathedral?"

"It's . . . it's not a black and white situation, but my job is to enforce the law."

Zahra stared at her feet. "If Islamists have subverted our government to a point where justice is impossible, and if the media doesn't report the truth, and if the educational system has brainwashed a generation, would violence be justified? Would murder become self-defense?"

"Theoretically, there could come a time when circumstances justify extrajudicial killing."

"This isn't theoretical. They raped and murdered my sister. We have to prevent these monsters from bringing their ideology here. We have to protect Americans from that hell."

"I lost my father too, and I understand your pain, but vigilantism is only morally acceptable if we have no legal recourse, and we aren't there yet."

She moved in close and put her hand on his chest. "Aren't we?"

Malachi's stomach sank, like sand falling through an hourglass, slipping away, leaving him empty.

"We still have hope," he said.

Zahra rested her hands on her hips. "You had a chance to shoot Horn on the boat. Why didn't you?"

"I couldn't. His hands weren't on his carbine. It didn't feel right."

"But you killed those men in the cathedral."

"I killed to preserve life."

"Isn't that what Horn was doing?"

Malachi looked away. Fog shrouded the White House, making it blurry, ill-defined.

"Justice can't be determined subjectively by each person... not when it affects others," he said. "Taking life has to be based on accepted morality. It has to come from the law."

"The Nazis had laws. Stalin had laws."

"Don't give me that moral relativism. There's no equivalence. Our laws are based on the sanctity of the individual, the natural right for people to control their own lives—not statism. Our laws are designed to stop people from hurting others."

"And what if the laws are ineffective? What if they can't stop evil?"

"Then we change the laws."

"Malachi, what the Muslim Brotherhood is doing isn't theoretical. It's real and they're doing it now."

"Murder is real too."

Zahra's face tightened. "I don't think you understand the severity of the problem. You live in a country with rights and laws, and you think things will never change, but you don't understand the United States is unique in history. American exceptionalism is fragile, and it can disappear overnight. It must be protected. The Brotherhood is a foreign power trying to destroy everything you love. They can't allow the American experiment to exist."

Malachi stared through the rain at the White House. "I'll defend my country and its ideals with my life."

"If you're willing to fight, willing to kill something you think is evil, then what's wrong with manipulating it for a greater purpose? Why not use evil men for good?"

"Is that what you did with Horn?"

Zahra flashed a sad smile. She looked at the White House, then back at him. She lifted her chin, putting her face close to his. "If your theory's right and you could prove it, what would you do with me?"

"I guess we'll never know because I don't have proof. The White House wants this thing buried and both the Mayor and Chief want the cases closed. The Brotherhood doesn't want this to go public either."

"So that's it?"

"The case is over for everyone . . . except me. It will never end for me. I have a duty to speak for the dead, an obligation to seek the truth."

"That's what I admire and love about you," she said.

"Do you love me or were you using me the whole time?"

"I love you completely."

Malachi's chest ached, and his throat tightened. She loved him and he loved her. He tried to look tough, but his eyes betrayed him.

"Beyond law and order, beyond what is legal or criminal—I have a duty to justice."

"I know you do," she said.

"When I started this case, I thought success meant capturing the killer. Then I learned about the Brotherhood's infiltration and I knew I had to expose them too. The Brotherhood's running scared, and I may have interfered with their plans, but they're still lurking in the shadows, and people won't listen. At least the killing has stopped. Maybe success means taking a stand against evil and risking everything to do it."

"You were successful, Malachi. You won."

He nodded. "Tell me this, will you use your new position to fight for this country and reveal the truth about the Brotherhood?"

"You know I will."

"And that's what I love about you."

Malachi pulled her against him and kissed her hard on the mouth. He held the kiss for a long time before he released her.

Malachi had identified the killer and stopped the murders. He had also illuminated the Brotherhood's plot and struck a blow against radical Islam—the ideology that murdered his father. His father would be proud. Fighting evil was pure and right, and he believed himself worthy of his gold badge.

"Where does this leave us?" Zahra asked. Tears ran down her checks and mixed with the rain.

In his heart, he knew she had used Horn to stop the Brotherhood—immoral means to achieve a noble goal—but he could never prove it. Maybe figuring it out was enough. Malachi looked into her eyes.

"There's right and wrong, and deep down, we all know it. We're nothing without the rule of law. I can understand what you did and why you did it, but I can't be part of it."

"Malachi—"

"I love you, but I . . ." His lips moved but nothing came out. He clenched his jaw, trying to look strong. His heart threatened to implode inside him, like a black hole.

"Malachi, you're the only man I've ever loved."

"You've been my lifeline. You healed me."

"Then let's fight them together."

A tear broke free and ran down his cheek. "I can't betray my values."

"You understand the stakes," she said. "You know the evil we're fighting."

"We're responsible for our actions. What we do is who we are."

"Malachi, please . . ."

A lump stuck in Malachi's throat. "I'll always love you."

"Malachi . . ."

"Goodbye, Zahra."

He turned and walked away, leaving her standing in the rain.

CHAPTER EIGHTY-TWO

The sun melted as it touched the horizon, and its rays shimmered across the Atlantic turning the sky into a tapestry of color. Palm fronds waved in the breeze and warmth radiated off the sand on Key West. The late September heat dissipated within minutes. For a moment the world became a picture, an image, more memory and emotion than reality.

Austin reclined in a lounge chair and sipped a Guinness Stout. The bottle beaded with moisture as the liquid warmed. It cooled his throat going down—wet and numbing. He twisted the bottle into the sand beside him.

Sophie looked up at him, and he rubbed her ears.

"Good girl," he said.

She nuzzled his leg and went back to sleep.

Austin's fingers moved to the burns on his face and neck, where shedding skin hung off him like old wallpaper. It had only been two months since the explosion, and it would take time for his burns to slough off and for new skin to grow, leaving only scar tissue and regret. His skin tingled beneath his touch, and he cursed himself for waiting too long to jump from the yacht's bridge. Too soon and he would have risked being spotted, but too late and he challenged death. He had hit the water hard, his hair and skin on fire, but he had stayed under water long enough to reach the shadows, away from the burning yacht.

It had taken him ten minutes to swim to his scuba gear affixed to an underwater mooring. Ten long minutes avoiding the helicopter's searchlight and the police on shore. He had donned his regulator and mask and swum upriver to the Virginia shore. He had scampered ashore south of National Airport and climbed into his used Corolla, which bore a stolen license plate taken from another Toyota in the airport's long-term parking lot.

He had made the long drive to Florida, and assumed the identity of Richard de Camville, an identity created from the documents he had stolen during the Iqbal Yousef investigation. The suspect had never noticed the missing documents, or if he did, he had decided not to report it and add another charge onto his long sentence. The new identity would protect him. For now.

Austin smiled at his new name, taken from an English Knight in the Third Crusade. All his aliases had been borrowed from prominent crusaders—King Philip Augustus II, King Richard the Lion-Hearted I, King Henry Curtmantle II, and Emperor Frederick Barbarossa. They had defended the West against Saladin, the Muslim sultan who had waged jihad in the Third Crusade.

Austin had become a crusader too, a modern knight.

He took another swig of stout. He had dealt the Brotherhood a severe blow and avoided capture. He had thought he would feel some modicum of peace after exacting his revenge for Vanessa, but he did not. Killing excited him, but after the exhilaration wore off, it left him empty. He wanted that rush again, the surge of adrenaline when he risked everything to vanquish enemies then watched them die by his hand. He craved it, needed it—like a drug.

The act of killing had become its own reward.

Austin closed his eyes and shook away his growing dread. He had sunken into something from which there was no return. Panic gnawed at the fringes of his consciousness, as it had every night, like an unwanted intruder. His dreams would turn to nightmares, and he would awaken drenched in sweat. His decisions—good or evil—were his own. He had chosen this path and there was no going back.

A door slammed behind him, and he whirled around, his heart pounding. A group of teenagers walked away from a Jeep carrying beer to the beach—just bored adolescents getting ready to party. He inhaled to steady his nerves. He would have to look over his shoulder for the rest of his life. Detective Wolf was out there, and if he ever figured it out, he would come for him.

Austin would never be safe.

The United States was more secure than before the murders. The leadership of the Secret Apparatus had been decimated, and those that remained kept low profiles and hid from the public view. Hid from him.

Dr. Mansour had testified before Congress and alerted the world to the dangers posed by Islamist infiltrators. Now, she briefed President Follet, a man who had purged his core advisors of Brotherhood influence. It was a small step in the right direction. The facts had reached the public domain, but would anyone take notice?

Austin had become a twenty-first-century paladin. He would protect his country the same way he had protected his mother. She had shown him the way. He would hide in the shadows, waiting to see if the world would listen, to see if they needed another reminder—another bloody lesson. He sighed and sipped his Guinness as the last of the day melted into the ocean. He would be there, waiting and watching.

Evil was everywhere.

ABOUT THE AUTHOR

Jeffrey James Higgins is a former reporter and retired supervisory special agent who writes thriller novels, short stories, creative nonfiction, and essays. He has wrestled a suicide bomber, fought the Taliban in combat, and chased terrorists across five continents. He received both the Attorney General's Award for Exceptional Heroism and the DEA Award of Valor. Jeffrey has been interviewed by CNN Newsroom, Investigation Discovery, CNN Declassified, New York Times, and Fox News. He was a finalist in Adelaide's 2018 Best Essay Contest and a quarterfinalist in ScreenCraft's 2019 Most Cinematic Book Competition and 2021 Cinematic Short Story Writing Competition.

https://JeffreyJamesHiggins.com

Note From The Author

Word-of-mouth is crucial for any author to succeed. If you enjoyed *Unseen*, please leave a review online—anywhere you are able. Even if it's just a sentence or two. It would make all the difference and would be very much appreciated.

Thanks!
Jeffrey James Higgins

For fans of **Jeffrey James Higgins**, please check out our recommended title for your next great read!

Furious

"A taut and suspenseful tale on the ocean."
–Kirkus Reviews

CPSIA information can be obtained
at www.ICGtesting.com
Printed in the USA
LVHW092011240921
698682LV00002B/16